Maggie's Shadow

Maggie's Shadow

A Novel

Morrine Depolo

Published by Morrine Depolo 2014

Library of Congress Control Number: 2014911351

ISBN 978-1-312-28275-9

First published in the United States of America 2014

For my daughters
who make my life so very special

ACKNOWLEDGEMENTS

In many ways *Maggie's Shadow* owes its existence to the UCLA Extension Creative Writing Program and the incredible support I received from my instructors and fellow students. They provided encouragement and kept me motivated to continue what had initially started in the 2010 NaNoWriMo annual novel writing event.

I would like to thank my instructors Lisa Cron, Alyx Dellamonica, Valerie Fioravanti, Lynn Hightower, Caroline Leavitt and Victoria Zackheim, all wonderful writers and published authors, who spent focused time with invaluable comments to help me zero in on aspects of my writing.

Another big thank you to Caroline Leavitt who reviewed the complete manuscript and her insight and expertise with detailed notes were very much appreciated. They helped me revise *Maggie's Shadow* and to fine tune the many areas requiring additional work.

I'd also like to acknowledge Jo-Ann Mapson, fabulous author and gracious lady, who generously took the time from her own busy schedule to provide me with more helpful feedback.

To Don Fairservice, a long time and dear English friend, thank you and I truly value your continued encouragement. You also advised me that some aspects of British life had changed since I last lived there and your observations helped generate a more credible environment within which *Maggie* could function.

To my good friend Jody Sullivan, who apparently stayed up late to read my manuscript, thank you again for your support as I questioned whether it was worth continuing. You said it was and made some invaluable suggestions and proofing comments and the book reads better as a result.

To Jhen Fry, Liz Hirata and Linda Miles thank you for taking the time to read the final copy and express your continued interest in how I was progressing. Your friendship over the years has been amazing and very dear to me.

Finally, I would like to thank my daughters, Meggan Raymond and Gemma Depolo. I love you both so very much. It was, and is, your encouragement that keeps me motivated and your efforts that, unknown to me, found my almost final draft whisked off to Lulu Publishing. The surprise was a mind blowing experience to see *Maggie's Shadow* in its first book form. It permitted me to take a deep breath, correct as many typos and formatting errors as I could find, change a few things and get the novel completed as it appears here. That said, and despite multiple revisions, it could perhaps benefit from more, but I'm anxious to send *Maggie* on her way, and to concentrate on a second book that lies in a disordered pile of drafts on my coffee table.

The last four years have been quite an adventure. I never thought it possible to actually finish a novel but somehow managed to do so. *Maggie's Shadow* was often a difficult undertaking but a happy and challenging one and as an avid reader I have to thank so many hundreds of authors, past and present, for inspiring me to join their ranks. There's much work still to be done and I might never achieve what they accomplished, but this is, at the very least, a start.

CHAPTER ONE

Huddled under a thin piece of fabric the airline called a blanket, I was cold and determined not to sleep, convinced the plane would crash if I did. With no control whether the thing stayed up or plunged to the ground, I was just trying to stay awake in the event something untoward happened and made sure I was securely buckled into a seat too small even for me.

Turbulence, physical or emotional, unnerved me so I was an anxious traveler about to confront an irascible mother. I liked to pretend I could remain calm regardless of the situation so continued to visualize myself relatively intact after a successful touchdown with the courage to meet her. I never thought that my suitcase wouldn't arrive with me or that England would be wrapped in a freak heat wave adding more things to worry about.

Hoping for some sympathy as I told the cab driver that my bags were lost, he slammed down the trunk he had opened, shrugged as though their disappearance was an unexpected benefit relieving him of an extra job and said, "Well it's too bloody 'ot to do anyfink anyway."

Resigned, I carefully adjusted myself on the hot leather seat of his taxi and with its open windows tried to keep the wind from blowing dust in my eyes. I had assumed I'd arrive with a semblance of, if not composure, at least some confidence when I saw Norma for the first time in years although knew I was already a mess from being curled up in the plane and feeling like a wet rag from the humidity. I was getting that much closer to seeing her again and could only trust my self-control would take effect when I did. My mother was a formidable woman who had never loved me and my hope was that dur-during the visit to my childhood home I might learn why, although wasn't convinced it would or ever could happen.

My father was very different. He was mild mannered and affectionate but two weeks earlier I learned he was dead and I never got chance to say good-bye. Caring and reserved—the very antithesis of Norma—he read to me when I was a child, discussed music and books and took me out of the house away from her to the library or to his mother's place in London and a necessary break for us both. Always interested in what I did, he was gentle where Norma was rough and sensitive where she wasn't.

But then he was gone and my mother had never said he was sick. When she told me I was so distraught and unable to think or speak clearly I ended the call without learning more of the details.

I used to call Daddy every two or three weeks to say hello and only spoke to Norma briefly during those times. It was a superficial contact and we rarely ventured beyond what restaurant she'd been to, the weather or something new she'd purchased. Always assertive and stressing her independence she ignored my questions when I called back for more information on my father, and complained about herself instead. She said she had since fallen and broken her ankle and was unable to walk.

I wondered how she was dealing with that now she was alone and it made me nervous to ask if I could be of any help. Hoping to be refused, I waited through a momentary silence where I visualized her shrugging me off and surprised when she agreed. What she said was, "Well, he's not here to help so I suppose you should. You *are* my daughter after all." When I wanted to know more about her fall she snapped that it was none of my business.

Norma had always been guarded and I'd learned to expect her hanging up on me with the dial tone humming in my ears if she decided to end the conversation. It only emphasized what I already knew about her, so I decided whether she wanted me there or not I still owed it to my father to go back to see that he would be at rest wherever that happened to be. It would also be an opportunity to spend time with my mother to confront the unhappy memories that had plagued me for years and demanded closure. They required putting to rest too.

Norma still maintained her power to affect me despite a fifteen year absence and living six thousand miles apart. She was an indelible aspect of my psyche like a dark shadow waiting to catch me off guard when I did or said something—anything—that reminded me of her. As a result, I made it a point to be her antithesis. But that hadn't worked either.

I'd once sworn I'd never return from the States yet there I was and without a change of clothing, my toiletries or my books; especially my books so I could escape. I barely registered the green fields and hedgerows the taxi sped past that under different circumstances would've made me happy to see again. I bit my lip as I thought of the woman waiting for me and could feel my underarms get stickier than they were.

Shelly, my best friend, advised me against going. "Maggie, if Norma's still a bitch, then expect problems even if she does need your help. Why spend your time and money to be miserable?"

I generally took her advice. Not only was she my best friend, she was my ex sister-in-law who eventually convinced me to divorce Richard, her brother. She called him a misguided jerk and was right. He was, and probably still is, although I stayed with him for six mis-

3

erable years until she convinced me to get the hell out and stop being a wuss. I kept hoping things would change but even the kind of love I wanted eluded me. I wanted what she had—a great guy and perhaps a little kid. But she was more outgoing than I who followed a less explored, more cautious path, so nothing of any real consequence ever happened.

I was described as quiet and unassuming although that's not how I saw myself. I knew I was stronger than that and could be stubborn and irritable at times but those characteristics reminded me of Norma so I kept that part of me hidden. After Richard I preferred to live alone with Mewfus, my cat, my books and music and perhaps more vegetation than should grow in any one bedroom condo. They were the safe things to love and didn't cause trouble.

I had decided to stay with Norma no longer than two or three weeks until her foot healed so there was I moving into the very heart of trouble and wishing I were back home again. If I'd hoped for a sign of welcome she was as implacable as ever when I called from the airport to say I'd been delayed because of the luggage. "Late?" she said. "I just dropped a glass and there are broken bits all over the floor. Cheryl's not here to help clean up so tell the driver to hurry because I can't go in the kitchen or I'll cut my feet."

I wondered if Cheryl was her housekeeper. I doubted she was a friend since my mother never spoke of having any so I said, "Then wear shoes."

Her voice rose with irritation, "You *know* I can't get shoes on with my ankle."

The tone was intended to demolish and I felt myself yield as I always did when she put me down. "Oh, right. Sorry, I forgot. But I thought you said you broke your foot and couldn't walk."

"My ankle and a sprain but I've had to. I don't have anyone else to depend on, do I?"

Shelly was right, the visit was already seeming like a bad idea but I was committed and if it got too bad then perhaps I could leave earlier than planned. There wasn't much I could do to change the immediate situation so I decided to try and relax and enjoy the trees and fields and small stone villages we drove through and soak up the quiet before the inevitable storm. I did wonder if the broken glass would be there to clean up when I arrived.

The front door was unlocked when I got there. The bell seemed not to work, or at least I didn't hear it ring, and getting no response to my hesitant knock, walked into the carpeted entryway. I wondered if Norma always left the door open and decided it was because I would be arriving but it was a relief to know we wouldn't be in the awkward position of how to greet each other. I'd debated if I should hug her when I arrived but she'd saved me from that.

I set my purse and laptop down next to a plastic ivy plant resting on a spindly wood table. "Hello," I called. There was no answer and I hesitated before walking to the living room where I heard the sound of a television.

I stood by the doorway and looked toward the window where my mother was sitting and was shocked to see how much older she was. In my mind she had remained an attractive woman with carefully applied make-up and neatly styled brown hair but now she was considerably aged and gray with wrinkled skin. Perhaps, I thought, the death of my father had been too much of a blow for her although I knew they were never close so that seemed unlikely but it would've been nice to believe that even she was capable of mourning him.

My mother was reclining in a large green, overstuffed chair with her feet on a hassock of the same color. A tapestry pillow with woolly tassels sprouting from the corners was on that and elevated her cushioned and bandaged ankle. The foot was visibly swollen and her crooked toes that poked out of the dressing had overgrown nails and I wondered who helped her with things like that. I'd never really considered her personal care before but knew I would never ask. She wouldn't have told me anyway.

The place smelled awful. My first reaction was to step back outside again but I stood where I was, raising my chin and tilting my head as I cautiously sniffed to identify the source of the odor. It was difficult to inhale something unpleasant, and reminded me of the same smell I'd once had of a homeless guy squatting outside the market asking for change with his shopping cart filled with rags and junk.

My mother's living room was a mess and I was surprised to see her underwear thrown over the top of the radiator to dry. I wondered what Cheryl did to keep the place clean and felt a rush of sympathy for anyone living in such a state. How had my mother been reduced to this I wondered, then realized that for a while at least, it was where I had to live too.

I cleared my throat and tried to ignore my sense of overwhelm. "Hello," I said again without moving, "I'm here."

"Who is it?" Norma called out although I was standing right there. She was watching a game show and turned her head slightly. She knew who I was. It was just an attempt to maintain control and make me wait. She hadn't mentioned any visitors when I called earlier although I wished I was still in the uncomfortable taxi.

"It's me. Maggie. Sorry I'm late."

"Yes you are, Margaret, and I'm hungry. You can find some bread and ham in the refrigerator. Put the kettle on while you're making the sandwich, I'd like some tea."

So, she'd reestablished the rules of what to expect and still called me Margaret. It always sounded like a reprimand. But that was okay. I'd done nothing wrong and was Maggie to everyone else.

I hesitated and turned toward the kitchen and was as if I'd never left. Although she had aged her attitude hadn't and still seemed the same, and so was the small, round kitchen table covered with a rose print cloth. It created a little floral island in the middle of the room surrounded by four straight back wooden chairs, their mismatched seat cushions secured to the backrest by fabric ties. My mother claimed she had good taste in decorating but these and the floral wallpaper I'd seen since my arrival repudiated that and I thought of my own blue mosaic tiled and stainless steel kitchen that then seemed so far away.

Ceramic pots of trailing Philodendron sat atop my refrigerator and the small tub of Ficus, its branches leaning next to the round, oak claw foot table that held my orchids, stood next to it. What I had were real and alive, not flattened cotton images. I decided at the first opportunity I'd pick up a plant for Norma's kitchen. It would remind me of home. It still wouldn't include Mewfus, alone in my condo, but Shelly had promised she would stop by and take care of him while I was gone and I already missed him.

I lifted the lid of the electric kettle and peered inside and saw there was enough water for Norma's tea, turned it on then opened the refrigerator door. Uneaten parts of an old stale sandwich curled its dried crust away from a plate that had been thrust inside while another dish held the remains of an uneaten meal. The shelf looked stained and needing a good clean and I wondered why Norma hadn't succumbed to some awful stomach problem and decided I'd starve before I ate any of the food from there.

Not seeing the ham I pulled at a plastic drawer that felt sticky, so jiggled it open and found an unsealed package of the sliced meat that I held under my nose and sniffed, unsure of what to expect. There was no evidence of mold or spoilage so decided it was probably okay although I wasn't prepared to taste it to be sure.

As I wondered if I should give it to Norma I decided I had to go shopping not only for fresh food, but also for some sturdy rubber gloves to clean everything. The place discouraged any appetite and I wondered if I would be able to eat there at all. My mother might be difficult but no one should live in such awful conditions. It wasn't my place to have a word with Cheryl but I wondered how much, or even if, Norma was aware of her surroundings.

My sandals crunched on a piece of broken glass. I stepped carefully, not wanting to get the slivers kicked into my feet as I saw little pieces glistening across the floor with the remains of the stem of the wine glass angled against one of the lower cabinet doors.

I set down the ham and looked for the broom and dustpan in the laundry room adjacent to the kitchen, reminding myself not to go barefoot, although I was beginning to wonder if I wanted to even undress while I was there. I wondered what Shelly would do under the same circumstances. She'd probably get a hotel somewhere and just visit and take care of business from a distance. But then Shelly probably wouldn't have gone at all.

"What are you doing in there," Norma called out. "You're taking too long and I've changed my mind. I want wine instead of the tea."

I sighed and unplugged the kettle that was beginning to boil. "I'm sweeping up the glass," I said. "Do you want the wine before the sandwich or with?" I had to strain my ears to hear above the TV and figured that perhaps her hearing was shot.

"Now," she said, "and there's another glass in the cupboard. I can sip it while you're out there." She paused, "Do you want any?"

I was surprised she asked but decided she was being sociable and it meant nothing. I remembered Norma offered everyone a glass of wine and considered it a refined gesture on her part, regardless of who it was, including contractors like electricians and plumbers.

I looked around. I preferred red wine but saw only the sweet white that Norma drank. It was better than nothing although I wondered if there was anything stronger that she had and preferable to that. I generally didn't drink hard liquor but decided that being there was probably an exception. I hadn't been there half an hour and already thinking of how to make things easier on myself.

"Think I will. Thanks," I said as I continued sweeping the tiny shards together. Norma had continued to talk but I tuned her out until her voice became louder.

"Are you listening to me Margaret? I said that the bottle already opened is *mine*. You're not to drink that. You'll find another unopened one in the fridge. It's the cheaper one for visitors. Have that instead."

If I had expected any form of welcome after so many years it didn't appear it was going to happen, so one question I'd had as to what it would be like to see my mother again was pretty much answered. I was a visitor and probably an unwelcome one. I felt the familiar tightening in my stomach and hunching of my shoulders along with the sense of protecting myself against her ability to reduce me to feelings of inadequacy. But I wasn't going to let that happen again and consciously straightened my back but decided to give her the benefit of doubt. Perhaps she was feeling awkward and vulnerable too, and this was her way to compensate. I didn't have much hope for that but it was something to hang on to.

I tossed the broken glass into the waste bin then rested the broom back in the cupboard before I opened a cabinet and drew out two wine glasses that had an opaque film and water spots. They felt sticky so I ran them under the hot water, washing them thoroughly before ripping off a sheet of paper towel to dry them.

The glasses were warm but I didn't care. At least they were now clean and I figured Norma had developed enough antibodies against all the little bacteria the place was probably harboring. I hoped my suitcase would be found and delivered very soon as the airline had promised because I wanted to take some of the vitamin C I'd packed. I needed all the help I could get.

I poured some of her Riesling and tasted it; sweet and fruity I spat it into the sink without swallowing. I wouldn't have wanted it anyway—it would have been like drinking perfume. I filled the other glass and took it to Norma who reached for it without comment before I returned to the kitchen.

The stale food smell hit me again as I opened the fridge. The visitor's bottle was on its side among two more of Norma's. I wondered how much she drank and who came to see her. As I twisted the bottle opener into the cork I got pleasure from the little familiar ritual even though the wine was white and probably cheap.

I angled and twisted the metal deeper and pulled the cork with a pop, sniffed the contents then poured some into my glass and took a careful sip. It wasn't great but it was cold and dry, not as sweet as the Riesling but figured it would help me relax. I might not want to be there but I could make it interesting to learn what made my mother tick and she couldn't hang up on me if I was right there.

As I prepared her sandwich I made a mental note to get some better wine and decided I should start a list. Then I realized I would need transportation. Norma hadn't driven since she was denied a license because of poor eyesight but I'd seen her old Mercedes in the driveway and wondered if it still ran. It wouldn't be unlike her to keep it there to impress everyone, but inconvenient if it didn't work.

"Does your car still work?" I asked as I handed her the plate. I became more aware of the homeless person smell and hesitated to put the sandwich down but she reached out and grabbed it.

"Cheryl uses it to take me places. Why do you ask?" She leaned away to look around me at the television that blasted away in the corner of the room. I stepped back and wondered just how much of it she could actually see.

"Because I'll have to go shopping fairly soon," I said. "Do you mind if I turn that thing down?" I reached for the remote but Norma drew it away quickly and tucked it between her and the arm of the chair.

"No! I want it on." Then, taking a gulp of her wine and with a slight cough after she swallowed said, "You're leaving? You just got here."

"Not immediately, but there's no food."

"What's wrong with the ham, then?" She paused and held the sandwich to her nose, sniffing it. "Seems okay to me," she said, and took a large bite.

"You probably don't remember that I don't eat meat. I'm a vegetarian." I knew I had told her once or twice during one of our boring conversations on what she'd had for dinner.

"There's some frozen fish in the freezer. Defrost it and you can have that."

"No fish, either."

Norma stopped chewing and peered over her glasses. "What *do* you eat then? You look as skinny as you always did."

I decided to ignore her. I'm five foot five and weigh about a hundred and twenty pounds but not skinny. Obviously she could still see well enough to notice that I was fairly slim. Her hearing might not be so great though. With the television kept so loud I remembered she often yelled at me on the phone to speak up, irritated if I was silent or spoke softly.

"Will Cheryl still help you while I'm here?"

"She's wonderful! Couldn't do without her. Why?"

I knew Norma's helpers were generally gone after a few months. They were either fired or they walked out, so I figured the woman must be new since she was 'wonderful' although perhaps not enough to keep the place clean. I wondered how long that would last. "Just curious. I'd like to meet her."

"You will. Since my fall …" Norma raised her foot in the air for emphasis, "… she now comes every day because I can't get around and tomorrow morning she'll be here to get the laundry together. You can help her since you won't have anything else to do."

"I've plenty to do but came to help you." I didn't add that with or without Cheryl's help, once I'd cleaned the place I would extend my shopping trips and look for an internet café, perhaps even eat there. It wasn't something Norma needed to know.

"Does she do your wash then?" I wondered if it was she who had draped the panties to dry and if so why. Perhaps Cheryl was kept busy doing other things that prevented her from actually cleaning the place or had to drive Norma to the mall.

I knew Norma liked to shop for clothes. That had once been a favorite activity of hers to find new things for a party or a vacation. Before Daddy died, she had planned a cruise and said she'd purchased the dresses she needed. I wondered if it was cancelled. I didn't know if my mother had any friends but from the look of things in the house I figured who would want to accompany her and share her cabin? I decided I was being mean but how quickly she was beginning to rub off.

"I have a service for that," she said. "Cheryl just puts everything into the laundry bag. Sometimes I rinse out a few things and put them over the radiator to dry although they're off in this heat but with so many visitors coming to see me, it doesn't look respectable." She shrugged her shoulders as though dismissing the image.

Obviously I didn't count and I wondered who could have been there. I looked around and saw a bra and nightdress flung over a chair by the French doors to the garden, "So are those clothes on the chairs drying too?"

"Really Margaret, why else would they be there? How stupid. I wonder about your thinking sometimes."

I ignored the comment and wondered what kind of damage they would do to the wood. "Why don't you hang them outside or toss them in the dryer?"

"I don't want the neighbors to see my underwear and the dryer doesn't work."

"Why?"

"Don't be ridiculous. How should I know?" She took a large bite and I wondered how her teeth were or if she ever went to the dentist. Perhaps she had false teeth but if she did she'd never say. I really knew very little about my mother's health other than that she was prone to bad colds and caught the flu if it was going around.

"Why don't you get someone to repair it, then?"

"I did," she mumbled, her mouth full, "but the electrician said it wasn't worth fixing and I should get a new one."

I wondered if the electrician was considered a visitor and offered cheap wine. "Perhaps we should go and find you a new one." I didn't add that it would contribute to keeping the place tidy and even if it didn't bother her it bothered me.

"I was thinking the same thing but I don't want to spend time with you while you do your own shopping. You can do that alone. Without me. Here take this, I'm finished." She handed me the empty plate except for a few uneaten crusts. "You can throw these out for the birds."

I took it from her, pleased to think she liked birds and that we had established a valid excuse to get out of the house. I remembered I'd seen a folded wheel chair on the porch when I arrived although from a quick glance at the shabby leather and chipped chrome it looked well used. I hadn't paid much attention to the wheels and now I wondered what kind of shape they were in and if the thing would support Norma on any kind of a trip.

"Do you use that wheelchair outside?"

"Of course. Who else would use it? Cheryl takes me to the doctor's office and now you can do that." She jerked her chin towards me as though to emphasize an order.

I recognized and remembered that habit she had and it brought back memories of how, as a child, I hated the look. It was so dismissive and I realized that nothing had improved over the years. Well, I decided, I'll just have to sharpen my wits and not let her get to me. I was seriously out of practice though. Under different circumstances I might've excused her hostility as symptomatic of frustrated old age and wished I could feel sorry for what must be an annoying lack of mobility and failing sight, although Norma had been antagonistic long before her decline when she could see and get around.

"Yes, well, you didn't tell me you had one. From our phone conversations I thought you never went out."

"I don't have to tell you everything."

"Fine." I decided to ignore her and remind myself I was an adult and not a sensitive kid any more although she still had the ability to hurt. The more control I maintained the less power Norma had and if we were going to get out of the house, she was going to need a working chair. "When did you last use it?"

"Last week." Norma reached behind her and straightened the pillow, digging into the side of the chair to locate the remote control and change the channel.

"Where did you get it?"

"Questions. Questions. Does it matter? Are you going to be this way while you're here? If you are then I'd rather be alone."

I thought I'd rather be alone too and could feel the tightness in my chest give way to a defensive irritation. "No you wouldn't. You'd have no one to make you a sandwich or clean up your mess. Did somebody give it to you? How nice of them." I rattled on not waiting for an answer. I was getting into the swing of what it took to have a conversation with my mother although wondered how long I would be able to keep it up before my brain totally fused.

"Reverend McLean brought it by for me. It was a gift. He saw how I struggled and struggled so with my walker ..." She glared at me as though it was my fault.

"But you can walk though? Excellent. And a vicar? Where did he see you struggling?" I was curious since I didn't recall Norma ever going to church except for Christmas and Easter and she only went then because she could dress up for the occasion. She'd also change churches, regardless of denomination, when she found another minister she preferred more.

"When I was in the hospital. After the fall he saw me there and said I was amazing for a woman of my age to walk the way I did with this." She used the remote to point to her foot then added, "I probably looked a bit older, though, because I was in so much pain."

"You must have done marvelously well. You don't give up. Ever." I was using my complimentary voice. She seemed not to detect its insincerity and I hated myself for doing that, it seemed so superficial but it always worked with her.

In many ways that was true. Norma was resolute. Indomitable, although the same energy better focused would have made her a formidable woman of a different kind. She was inclined to believe all and any amount of flattery. Complimenting her was like applying butter to hot toast—she melted and became almost civil but I grew tired of feigning admiration just to have a few minutes of conversation. It made me feel tired and depleted as though Norma had tapped into one of my veins and drawn blood.

"So you go to church now?"

"I don't have to. Reverend McLean comes to see me here because I'm one of his parishioners. He's such a sweet man and seems to care for me. But I think he's a bit too weak and rather effeminate if you ask me. Not a manly man. No backbone but he's got a job to do and sees to it that I'm taken care of."

There she goes again, I thought. The woman still views males in terms of their spine. Norma had always considered men as either weak or strong; strong if they were charismatic and flirted and made her feel beautiful and weak if quiet and thoughtful like my father.

Norma considered Daddy spineless despite him being a successful CPA with his own business. He was a dear, sweet man and I missed him even though he was unable to stand up to my mother for me when she called me worthless. He'd say very quietly, "Now, Norma dear. That's a bit unkind don't you think?" Then she would become angry and he would withdraw with an apologetic glance at me and shrug his shoulders. He simply wanted to diffuse what could escalate into a major battle.

Over the years and after hours of therapy attempting to resolve the conflicts of a miserable childhood and unhappy marriage I'd come to the unpleasant conclusion that some of Norma's combative blood ran in my veins too. My father never left her but I rebelled and ran away from home and, eventually, from Richard. It was justifiable rage although rarely expressed. I kept it hidden and under control.

On the surface I was quiet like Daddy but knew I was stronger than he was, but since I could never figure out why Norma was so mean and what made her that way, I was always afraid that whatever it was could happen to me. It had been one of my fears of being like her that had maintained its grip on my mind and another reason to return. I wanted to face the woman who still maintained an influence on my life. I hoped there was a good chance I would learn more about myself and to develop some understanding for the mother who had rejected me and her dislike that haunted me.

The smell penetrated my thoughts and brought my attention back to where I was. "Will I have my old bedroom upstairs?" I said realizing I could close the door and throw open the windows and breathe in some fresh air.

I wondered if anyone had used the room since I'd left and was curious as to what it looked like now. When I had it, the place was filled with my books and was my means of escape. Reading kept me sane, and although I could retreat to my room Norma would find ways to get me out of it; there were dishes and laundry or cleaning to do or making her tea and going on my bicycle to the local shops for groceries.

I used to think I was her Cinderella and relieved there were no stepsisters to make things worse. I was realistic enough to recognize there probably wouldn't be a prince in my future but Grandma Clare was definitely my fairy godmother. She never buckled around Norma like most people and could silence her with a look or a frosty word that put her in her place but it didn't happen often because they rarely met.

"Yes, but it's not your old room," Norma said. "It was your father's although there's no more of his stuff in there either. There are sheets in the cupboard but keep the windows closed. I don't like to feel a draft." Norma hunched her shoulders and gave a mock shiver. "Ugh. I hate the cold."

The odor was evidence that despite the outside heat, everything had been closed. I wondered what it would take to disinfect the place and decided a good strong blaze would work. I visualized the place engulfed in flames and smiled at the thought of everything blackened and charred, nothing left, burned to the ground. Then I felt horrified at the image I'd generated. Now then Maggie, I thought, enough of that. Be nice. Make conversation.

"You used to work in the garden. You liked doing that even if it was cold."

"Not with my lungs I can't."

"Who does the garden then?"

"Malcolm, but I fired him."

"Why?"

"Why? Because I did. That's why."

"I thought you said the gardener was doing a good job." She'd told me over the phone that everyone started by doing a good job but later had to be fired for some trivial offense. People she hired probably thought she was nice at first, too. She could fool anyone by being charming until she decided to make unreasonable demands on their time.

"He did but then made excuses he couldn't come."

"Was he sick?"

"Not as sick as me. Such a baby." Norma seemed restless and fidgeted with her empty glass. "Here take this and pour me another."

I took it and went into the kitchen and could hear her begin to move off the chair. I glanced through the door then quickly moved back when I saw her struggle. "Do you need my help? Here let me …"

"No!" Norma interrupted me as she eased herself off the cushion with small jerky motions of her hip. Blue veins bulged under the translucent skin of her hands as she gripped the chrome leg of her walker and held the arm of the chair with the other for support. She placed the weight of her left foot on the floor holding the injured one up from a bent knee. Her back was hunched as she leaned into the metal frame that wobbled precariously and tipped slightly as she took her first unsteady hop. I felt rooted to where I stood unable to help although my inclination was to rush forward and do so.

Norma stopped and looked up and stared at me, her watery blue eyes were almost white in their intensity. I took an involuntary step backwards, the gaze transporting me back to my early childhood. Stronger then, my mother would glare at me in the same way and for no reason that I could fathom. It was a look to wither and still was. How could anyone glower with such calculated rage, I thought but said, "Are you sure I can't help you?" surprised to hear myself ask although the words felt automatic and disingenuous.

"If I want help I'll ask for it," Norma said as she headed for the downstairs bathroom then entered and closed the door behind her. I saw a light stain on the back of her robe and the armchair pillow looked damp so moved closer to check. There was the cause of the smell. Norma was incontinent and I wondered if it was symptomatic of her age or the result of the injury. It was something else to be concerned about and I felt momentarily overwhelmed. I wondered if I would get used to trying to help Norma who obviously needed it but who rejected it with such force. But then, I thought, Norma wasn't just anyone.

I grabbed my things from the hall and ran upstairs to the bedroom and closed the door behind me, throwing my bag and laptop on the bed before hurrying to the windows. They were closed tight and the casement crank was stuck. I jiggled the handled ineffectively and it became the recipient of my frustration.

Seizing the end of the bedspread I pulled and wrapped it around the handle for leverage, "Come on, move damn it," I muttered as I leaned into the turn. It gave slightly then with a creak, its resistance broken, the window jerked open and the humid air poured into the room. Thank god, I thought, rubbing my hand that was red from the effort and felt I would've broken the darn thing if it had stayed shut. I leaned against the sill and took a deep breath, filling my lungs and holding it in as if to cleanse my insides before breathing out in one gasp that sounded less like an exhalation and more like the beginnings of a sob.

A different quilt was on the bed from what I remembered and ugly in comparison to the earth tone Indian cover I had on my bed back home. This one was purple with green wavy stripes stretched across the fabric and matched the heavy green brocade drapes that blocked half the light from the window. I hated drapes and even worse, the white lace curtains that many English homes seemed to use. They hung like a netted portcullis keeping anyone from peering in but letting the observer see outside. I remembered Norma would stand back a little, unseen behind them, to spy on the neighbors. Even as a kid I disliked them.

There was no reminder of me ever being there. Nothing of Daddy either. Everything was gone and as though we had both been erased. I wondered what had happened to the books and toys I never took to Grandma's. Probably long since tossed, I thought, and wished I had some memento of when I was there as a child.

But back then neither I nor Norma experienced any sentimental feelings about my room. It didn't even smell the same as I stood there and couldn't immediately place what it was. Different from the one downstairs it was almost pleasant. I sniffed deeper, searching my memory for what it reminded me of. It smelled woodsy and then I remembered it was from my father's old pipe.

I felt my eyes fill with tears as I realized I would never get to see him smoke it again. Just two months ago I'd been attending a Gardeners' Fair in San Francisco, and by the time I returned and called him to say hi, Norma answered and said he was gone.

"Gone? Where?" I said.

"Dead is where."

Stunned, I let this information filter through my brain. My father had seemed fine the last time I spoke to him and although his voice sounded a little different and slightly indistinct I attributed it to the long distance and said I'd call when I got back from my trip.

"Have fun, Maggie love," he said.

So those were his last words. Speaking with Norma my heart pounded as I clenched the phone, "Why didn't you tell me? Why didn't you call me when it happened?" Knowing she had never voluntarily told me I was speechless as she refused to discuss the details of his death.

"Well," she said, "it was fast and he was already dead so there wasn't much you could do about it was there?"

I was angry and confused that her insensitivity extended that far. "How did he die? Was he cremated?"

"A stroke and yes. That was what he wanted but when *I* go, when I *do* eventually go, I'm to be buried not burned. But I plan to make all the arrangements before then so I'll know it's done right."

"What did you do with his ashes?"

She hesitated, "They're in one of the cupboards somewhere."

"Which cupboard?" I had asked and was crying.

Norma ignored me and continued, "Your father was so weak, such a wimp. I should've had a better husband."

Having arrived I planned to take care of his remains and wondered where I would scatter them or if they should be buried. I still felt a mixture of anger and heartache for the man who had been unable to protect me from Norma. Even he was a victim. But he was gone and I was in his room that looked sterile and uninviting but it would be mine for the duration of my stay.

I felt my spine and scalp tingle as I wondered for just how long that would be. Already it felt too long and wished I was in my own place at home, surrounded by my books and prints and seeing Mewfus purring on the bed. Dear old cat he would cheer me up. I took a deep breath and sighed, shaking my head. Get a grip, Maggie, I thought, it's not the end of the world and you've got an open ticket back. You can go any time.

I felt hungry and wished I'd remembered to bring up the wine but didn't want to go back down to get it. I searched in my purse for the peanuts they'd given me on the flight and pulled open the cellophane top. Salt sprinkled onto my hand as I crunched down. I'd already eaten the energy bar Shelly had given me as I left for the plane. We'd had a farewell dinner together the evening before and she told me again she thought my trip was a waste of time.

"I still don't understand why you're going through with this," she said.

"I have to take care of Daddy's ashes and although I'm still pissed with Norma she *is* my mother needing help and I haven't seen her in years. I'm curious what she's like now and maybe I can learn what makes her tick and why she dislikes me. Maybe I'll learn something more about myself."

Shelly looked surprised and paused, holding her fork before taking the food balanced on the end of it, "Like what?"

"I've always thought I'm more like her than I want to be. I'm quick to become defensive although I don't express it and stay quiet. I find fault with people and wonder why, so have to backtrack and think of what it is about them I dislike." I swirled my fettuccini, mixing the noodles with the pesto sauce and glanced up at Shelly who was looking like she was about to argue. "Okay, so Norma just blurts out what's on her mind but I still don't like feeling I'm like her. Perhaps being around her will prove me wrong."

"There you go again," she said. "Lighten up on yourself, Sweetie, we've all got stuff we'd rather not admit to. Hey, we can blame it on our genes or our parents or environment or all of it and all heaped together in one shit load of issues. You worry too much, besides which I like you so what else matters?" She nodded toward my plate, "And stop playing with your food. You remind me of Brian."

I laughed. "Thanks. I like you too and I'm not your little kid. But there's more. If it makes you feel any better, there's one other thing that I really want to find."

"What's that?" She tilted her head and looked over at me, curious.

"My grandmother left me her jewelry with some gorgeous old gold and opal earrings she always wore. They had belonged to her mother and now Daddy's dead Norma has them and I want to get them back."

"I remember you telling me about them. You think your mother will let you have them? Probably likes them for herself."

"Doubt it although they are valuable. She never wanted her ears pierced and wears the screw on kind and I can't tell you the number of times we went hunting for the missing one that had fallen off. Actually, I'm pleased she never wore them because I still remember Grandma's sweet old face with the earrings dangling behind her hair. They're an heirloom; a connection to her and the past. My past."

"Okay, then you can go. Those are *much* better reasons for going." She laid her fork down on an empty plate. "You've still not finished. Eat up and then we can split a chocolate mousse."

I wished that Shelly was with me as I felt the humid air breathe into the room as I ate the last of the peanuts, the salt lingering on my tongue. I looked around at the yellow wallpaper and cringed. This house will be mine someday, I thought. Not that I'd want it and Norma could still decide to leave it to the plumber or to some godforsaken guy she'd taken a fancy to. My mother viewed herself as thirty years younger than she was and still attractive. "I have no wrinkles," she'd told me. "It's amazing how good my skin is." I figured with Daddy gone she might consider herself an eligible candidate for re-marriage. If anyone would have her, I thought.

I drew a final breath and decided to leave the windows open and if I kept the door closed my mother would never know. I'd lie if she asked me and besides which Norma was unable to climb the stairs to investigate. Even if she screamed bloody murder that she felt a draft I'd pretend not to hear. I'd walk away. Go for a drive. Do something.

I heard the toilet flush and waited for the sound to stop and of my mother returning to the living room before I returned downstairs. When I did, Norma was fiddling with the remote and the television trembled between a picture and static. She clicked it until a game show appeared and left it on with the sound of canned laughter filling the room. She seemed disinterested and readjusted the pillow under her foot and I said, "Does it really need to be so loud?"

Norma held the remote in the air, her finger poised above the mute button. "Do you have something more important to say?"

"I suppose not although I should know what you want for dinner so I can get it ready."

"I've just eaten and want to watch this. Go unpack or something."

She doesn't remember what I told her, I thought. I wish I did have something to unpack, and hoped my suitcase would be found and sent to me as the airline had explained. There were more books I'd brought but they were packed too and unless I went to the library or bookshop, I'd go crazy with nothing to read. I wandered into the kitchen and opened the back door to the garden.

If nothing else my mother had once loved to garden and it was one of the few things we had in common that I didn't mind sharing and perhaps the reason I now teach horticulture. I owe her that at least. I remembered watching her quietly involved with her trowel, gently transferring the brightly colored blooms from their packs into the soil, wishing I received the same care and attention but it reflected who she was. Annuals are flashy and only last a season; she'd be bored with perennials and something longer lasting.

But even that color was missing and a tangle of weeds confronted me as I walked past the patio and apple tree onto the lawn, or what was once the lawn. Without Malcolm nobody had watered and the recent heat had scorched much of it brown and dry compared to the oases of green I saw on either side of the neighbors' fences. I bet they hate looking out of the windows and seeing this, I thought. The English love their lawns.

I could see the small hothouse in the back and wandered towards it, wondering what was in it. The glass was grimy from disuse and pots once filled lay upturned on the benches. I picked one up and dry soil fell onto my fingers as I rubbed them together, rolling the grit into little granules before dusting it off my hands. I wasn't permitted to go in there when I was a kid, at least not alone. "You're too clumsy," Norma told me. "You're bound to tip something over and break it." Well there was nothing to tip over now. Despite its condition the place was recoverable and offered some solitude and Norma would never come this far to check on what I was doing.

I looked around for the hose and saw it kinked and abandoned where it lay by the side of the wall and imagined the gardener throwing it down, perhaps in disgust, without winding and putting it away before he left for good. I decided I'd pick up some seedlings when I went to the store. The garden would be my escape, my sanctuary and refuge—and quite possibly, my sanity. Then I stopped, shocked as I realized I was thinking long-term. "Are you kidding?" I asked the silence that surrounded me. "I don't intend to stay long enough for *anything* to grow here. Remember? Two or three weeks max," and felt relieved that I had decided on a cut-off date.

I headed back for the house and decided to go find a market. The thought of fresh food after so many hours of travel was something to look forward to. At home I would normally be asleep but here it was late morning and eight hours later. I wanted to lie down and pretend this was all a bad dream, but decided to ignore the weariness that seemed to penetrate my whole being and take my first drive in the left lane instead of the right and in an old Mercedes with the wheel on the wrong side. In fact I felt I was on the wrong side of everything.

CHAPTER TWO

"Hallo dear, haven't seen you in here before. I can tell by your accent you're an American. You on holiday?" The woman at the cash register had passed the items I'd purchased over the sensor and slid them towards the end of the checkout.

Her own pronunciation was poor, dropping her aitches as she spoke and I knew I had more of a drawl than the clipped and measured speech I once had when I left for the States nine years ago, but in the U.S. I was still recognized as being English. I was caught between worlds. I smiled. "Yes and no. I grew up in England although now live over there and came back to see my mother."

"Who's that then? I know most of the people who come in here."

"Norma Resnick."

The cashier paused, holding a plastic bag of carrots midair as she peered at me. Her eyes widened in recognition as she leaned forward and grinned, displaying a missing lower tooth.

"No! It can't be. You wouldn't be *Margaret* Resnick, would you? My goodness, I can still see the resemblance of what you used to look like as a little kid. I'm Daphne. We was in school together years ago before you left. Remember me?"

I stared. I didn't. I was thirteen when I ran away and the woman in front of me looked nothing like any of the students I could remember in this small town. The rest of my education was in London and she would never know me from there.

Nobody had known that I planned to leave home but I'd dream about it when I could. Daddy used to take me up to London to see Grandma in her flower shop and she'd always hug me and say I looked beautiful. By the time I was twelve I began to learn train schedules and although I was scared, ran away from home with a small suitcase a year later. That was the only time I took money from my father's wallet but I promised myself I would repay him some-time. I took a taxi getting from King's Cross to Grandma's place because I didn't know the bus routes from there.

By the time I arrived my parents had found the note I'd left and called so she knew I was coming. Her little apartment was over her florist shop and when she saw me she hung the closed sign in the window and took me upstairs and made me some tea and a sandwich. She smiled but looked concerned. "Maggie, darling," she said, "I knew you were unhappy but not enough to run away."

She sat me at her kitchen table and moved some books and a vase of flowers to one side before handing me the plate. "This is all rather serious but if you want to stay and your parents agree then I'd love you to be here." She looked down to her two cats, Bluebell and Tinker that were purring and winding themselves against her jeans, and said, "Wouldn't we love Maggie to stay? And you'll have another person to curl up in bed with."

I never knew the conversations she'd had later with my par-ents although could hear her soft murmur over the phone and occasionally her voice would rise slightly and become cool and clipped and I recognized it as the one she used for Norma. About a week later Daddy arrived with the rest of my clothes and I never went back home to live. Grandma would suggest I call Norma as a courte-sy, which I did although the conversation was always strained, and we never knew what to say to each other.

My mother never expressed much interest in what I was doing and when I told her about my new school she said, "Uh-huh," and when I said I was learning floristry she said that at least I was making myself useful.

Now I was being recognized by a heavyset woman with graying hair pulled back in a ponytail, who could have been anyone. Anyone. Anywhere. I hadn't a clue who she was.

"I'm not sure. It's been a while …"

"Yeah. You must remember. We was on the school swim team together."

I had a sudden recollection of freezing water and my horror of jumping in. I had shivered in the changing room and would look down at my long, thin legs with knees that seemed to bulge from bone. I wasn't a good swimmer and never pretended to be. I could do a slow, easy breaststroke if I wasn't browbeaten by the coach and then it became a wild thrashing for speed. I struggled to take in a breath when I did the crawl and was never sufficiently coordinated to lift my arm and turn my head to take that necessary breath without inhaling water. I would arrive at the end of the pool, out of breath, grateful to see the blue green wall loom in front of me aware that on either side of my lane the other swimmers had already arrived and I was last. My involvement lasted a season before I was replaced. No, I didn't want to remember the swim team and I'm still not a strong swimmer.

I felt my usual reticence and an unwillingness to participate in superficial conversation. I didn't want to admit anything further. I fiddled with my purse so that I didn't have to look at her. "No, I'm not sure that I do."

The cashier's lips tightened and her eyes closed momentarily as though willing her own memory to take shape for me. She opened them again and took a breath. "Yep, yer Norma's daughter alright and now I looks at you would recognize you anywhere. You even look a bit like her you know."

Oh my god! I thought. Did I? Did I really? I hope not. I always considered I resembled my father and even though Norma was attractive when she was younger if I did look like her I had my own hazel eyes and a fuller mouth and not lips that were drawn into a tight line.

Daphne continued adding the items and pushing them together with the others. "Of course you're still thin but I suppose it's because you eat all of this stuff." She indicated the fruit and vegetables and other items I'd purchased, "Although I hate eating nuts, myself. They get in me teeth."

I wondered how the nuts could lodge in absent teeth and decided I was being mean again and tried to recall the woman before me and with teeth. There was a harsh and brittle tone to her voice and then my memory was jolted into recognition and I remembered that voice when it was cruelly vehement. "Get movin', skin n'bones. Ain't no hope for you to even float. Why don't you give it up? Sink and save yerself the misery." Daphne was the loud bully, the early developer who emphasized her breasts with tight sweaters and mocked girls like me who were flat chested. I experienced a quick feeling of smug satisfaction in seeing the blowsy frump she had become and hoping to keep my thoughts hidden felt compelled to admit remembering her.

"Why yes! Daphne, now I remember. How are you? How lovely to see you." I decided her body looked like a couch that needed to be reupholstered and I could see the cheap brown looking diamond and gold band on her ring finger. I figured she was probably married and had sunk into complacent early middle age as a result. It bothered me to have such ungenerous thoughts about someone I didn't know.

"Yeah. Likewise. Never see your mum here now but I suppose that's not a surprise with that foot of hers. Marvelous how she's still hanging on though, isn't it? But I know she has help. Cheryl comes in here to do her shopping." She carefully placed a carton of eggs into the bottom of a plastic bag. "So how long will you be staying then?"

More questions I didn't want to commit to. "Not sure really. Perhaps until her health improves and if not that," I paused and moved a bag of vegetables toward the scanner to speed the process, "then who knows, maybe I'll stay and settle down here." It was a complete lie but I was involved in the idle chitchat role I hated.

"Really? Thought you was already married."

I wondered how she knew. Perhaps Norma had mentioned it. Small town gossip gets around and is not forgotten. I wanted to leave and get out of there. "Divorced."

"Wouldn't have thought this old town would be big enough for you—London maybe, and wasn't that where you went when you took off like you did?"

She said it with a smile and quick laugh but I felt I was being taunted all over again as though I was a schoolgirl.

"Actually I love small towns and villages. Love the quiet and it's so peaceful here. I can read and garden and paint a bit." I smiled. It was the truth but not if it had to be with Norma. "And if the library and the little bookshops I love don't have what I need I'll try to get them online." I wondered if they would even arrive on time but establishing a connection was a vital next step.

"I've heard about that computer shopping stuff but don't do it meself. Like to touch what I buy first." Her pronunciation became more exaggerated as though emphasizing her disapproval.

I slid one of the bags into my cart. "Yes. Well I can understand that but it's very convenient." Then smiling with what I hoped was my friendliest expression decided there was a use in continuing to chat. "Daphne," I said, "you don't happen to know of an Internet café do you?"

"Hmm," she said, "You might try *The Golden Crumpet*. I heard people can do that there. It's a café closer to town. You can't miss it. Big green tree growing outside. Oh, and maybe the pub might have a place you can sit. It's called *The Rose 'n Plough*. That's where I go with my hubby." She laughed. "Yep, that would definitely be my choice although not in front of a computer. So, will that be all for you today then?"

"Thanks Daphne, yes, and I appreciate your help."

So, a big green tree outside the café and possibly a pub although knowing she might be there didn't lend itself to finding out, but getting online and having access to the rest of the world suddenly seemed the next most important thing on my growing list of things to do.

CHAPTER THREE

hey shelly ... yay! at last a connection and writing this from the golden crumpet café with good coffee and a helpful waitress called dina who leaves me alone to type or read ... place not far from dear mama and i m doing this as she naps and snores with throat clearing gasps spiked with whistles so i have to get out of there ~ hope to god i don't sound like that when im asleep ... flight over nerve wracking tho uneventful but they lost my suitcase and i was really worried about that but it was delivered this morning covered in tags and none the worse for wear ~ love to know where it ended up and rather wish i had been wherever that was instead of here but it felt great to have clean shirts and undies again ... norma still a royal pain and the reality worse than i thought but oh well ... the national health service provides her with a nurse caregiver or carer as they're called here to help with the more personal stuff and she came this morning and looked relieved when she left and so was i because it removed the guilt of not helping norma bathe herself although doubt she would let me anyway ... still not used to the time change so was awake last night and now wanting to crawl back into bed but cant because we'll be seeing

*her doctor this afternoon and im hoping for a real sta-
tus update instead of the one she wants me to hear ~
maybe it ll mean i get to go home sooner and wouldnt
that be luverly ... but now i gotta go and get her
dressed ~ she's already thinking of what she'll wear so
more later and thanks again for taking care of everything ... give mewfus a smooch for me ~ so miss that
dear old cat ... luv maggie*

Getting Norma dressed for the appointment wasn't easy. The removal of the pink flannel bathrobe she always wore and into something else should've been a simple procedure but turned into a major production. It was the something else that proved difficult. The robe had lulled me into forgetting that Norma's appearance beyond the overstuffed chair and four walls would require a complete metamorphosis.

"No, that won't work," Norma said when I brought down some clothes from her closet, "and if you were with me this morning where you should've been all this could've been decided by now. Since I won't be able to walk with elegance, I need to look even more refined in the wheelchair."

This isn't a damn fashion show, I thought, as I retraced my steps back to the upstairs closet for the third time with an armload of clothes. But Norma thrived on attention and compliments and that required dressing the part even if it was just a doctor who was going to have her remove some again.

I stared into the closet, looking for the beige skirt she'd asked for, shifting the plastic hangers that clunked together as I pushed aside various pieces of clothing. I'd thrown the rejected outfits I'd brought back onto the bed with the intent of hanging them later knowing Norma would have a fit to see the multi colored pile of her things flung one atop the other with empty sleeves entwined and wrapped among various tops and skirts, all in a muddled heap.

I hated what I had to do. The smell of stale perfume and old makeup, released from her closed closet emanated from the clothes left hanging and those in the pile. It overpowered everything and I could feel my nose twitch and start to run before I sneezed and a little explosion of droplets sprayed forth onto her clothes.

I sneezed again and looked around for a tissue shaking one loose from a blue box disguised in a stiff crocheted lace cover, no longer white but slightly yellowed from age. It sat on the dresser next to Norma's antique rosewood jewelry box, a miniature chest with several sets of drawers, each with their own gold plated lock. I was tempted to open it and see if Grandmother's jewelry was there and about to pull on one of the tiny ivory knobs when she called from downstairs. "Margaret? Margaret, what are you doing? How long does it take to find a skirt?"

I'd found it hanging next to a long black loose fitting one and took that instead, remembering the stain I had seen on the robe and beige was not something my mother should wear. I ran down the stairs into the living room. "No," I lied, "I didn't see it and we're running out of time."

I could see the irritation begin to flush her face and before she could say anything I continued, "But you've got some really nice stuff." It was true, and although nothing I would ever wear, I figured the compliment would soften her and make the rest of the preparation easier.

"Of course I do."

I held the black skirt up for her inspection then swung it across the front of my own body, the hanger jutting out like frail yellow plastic bones. "How about this? You could wear it with one of your silk blouses."

She hesitated and leaned forward. "Come here."

I stepped closer and Norma peered over her glasses and rubbed the fabric between her fingers and I wondered if she was determining which skirt it was by touch. "This one goes with my red blazer," she said. "Why didn't you bring that down, too?"

Shit. How the hell should I know what goes with what but I'd seen it in the closet. "That may be too warm to wear now. It's still quite muggy outside."

She ignored me. "Yes, that'll go nicely with my polka dot shirt and besides, the doctor's office is always cold. Now help me to the bathroom. You'll be faster than using the walker."

I was surprised she asked but looked at the clock and placed the skirt across the back of an elaborately carved wooden chair never designed or intended for comfort. "Okay. Here, take my arm to get you off that chair. I'll help you get dressed when you come back."

"I'm quite capable of doing it myself." She fussed with her robe.

"No you're not," I said surprising myself, "and I don't want to have you fall again. For once listen to me otherwise we'll not make it on time. I still have to figure how to get there." Cheryl had given me directions but driving on the left side of the road was still a challenge and made me nervous.

Norma stopped, her mouth open in surprise. She looked as though she was about to argue but shut it instead and remained quiet.

Well, what d'ya know? I thought. Maybe I do have some say around here after all.

Leaning heavily on me and using her cane for leverage, Norma hopped slowly and laboriously to the bathroom. I had an arm around her waist and took small shuffling steps next to her, supporting her weight as she moved forward while endeavoring to maintain my balance for both of us. I felt uncomfortable with the close proximity as Norma's fingers gripped my arm like talons.

No one, including my father, had been permitted to use her bathroom and I hadn't seen the inside again until now. I pushed open the door and the smell of ammonia that had pervaded the house intensified. I'd already started work cleaning the refrigerator and kitchen wearing the thick rubber gloves I'd purchased, but this was worse.

I held my breath, my mouth scrunched tight as I turned my head away from the odor. Norma released my arm and leaned into the room, reaching for one of the handgrips on the wall. I could see more of them with others in the shower and was surprised to see a geriatric seat perched over the toilet. It had a sturdy chrome rail and I wondered if they were all recent acquisitions or if Norma, aware she was becoming weaker, had them installed before the fall. They spoke of a concern for a safety that I took for granted.

I wasn't used to dealing with the infirm and it was an unanticipated reality check that unnerved me and wondered if that would eventually happen to me. I closed the door behind Norma for her privacy who yelled, "And just *how* am I supposed to dress without the clothes?"

"You're not dressing in there. Do what you have to do and I'll come get you again." My voice had risen and with the change it resembled hers. "Oh. My. God," I whispered. "Oh dear god I sound just like her."

I drew in my breath and felt the blood pound my temples. It was something I had dreaded and decided that when I was alone again and felt more composed I would replay my response, examine the words and trace their root to where they had lain hidden in my subconscious—hopefully to shed more light on that other me. The one I'd been hiding.

I waited outside the door prepared for another outburst. Instead there was only the muted sound of a body on the bolstered invalid seat, the thin splash of pee hitting the water followed by the toilet flushing and Norma calling out to say she was ready.

Back on her chair she said, "You didn't get the polka dot blouse while I was in there. Go and get it."

I ran upstairs again to the closet and shuffled through the blouses and wondered which one. Norma had so many and mostly silk; red ones with white polka dots and white with red; black shirts with white and white on black. She had dark green, navy, light blue and pinks. All colors festooned together like the colors of the rainbow and I hadn't a clue which one she wanted. I pushed them apart and finally grabbed the black dotted one on white that would go with the skirt and as an afterthought, pulled out the white on black. Norma could decide and I'd return the others later. It was getting late and the woman wasn't dressed and everything was still on hangers.

Norma took the shirts and held them close to her face before thrusting one back at me. "Why on earth did you bring two? Isn't it obvious that the black dot was the one I wanted? Really Margaret, you have no fashion sense."

She was perched on the edge of her chair, her robe hung slightly open from around her stooped shoulders and I could see how the skin above her thin pink cotton undershirt hung in tiny furrows that disappeared beneath it to become small and saggy breasts.

"Close your eyes," Norma ordered, "and help me with this skirt."

"How can I see what I'm doing if I close my eyes?"

"Just do it then." She clutched the robe to her with one hand and raised the other in the air.

"Okay. Ready?" I felt like I was dressing a little kid and wanted to add "peek-a-boo" as I pulled the skirt over her head. I felt sad that I couldn't play and laugh with my mother like Shelly did with Brian and felt a momentary sense of loss that I'd never had that experience.

"Now pull out the robe," she said.

I tugged and struggled to raise it from under the skirt. "You're still sitting on it. Here shift up and move your butt." I pulled harder as Norma eased off the chair.

"You don't have to be so rough. Now give me the blouse and you can leave."

I recalled how roughly she had dressed me as a little kid and wondered if I was unconsciously doing the same thing but hoped not. As I handed her the blouse I was reminded of her reserve in being seen undressed. It obviously hadn't changed over the years and memories I'd forgotten leapt unbidden into my mind. "You gonna put that on over the robe too?"

"Don't be ridiculous."

She was already easing one arm out of the robe as I walked to the kitchen but I continued to watch from the doorway as she slipped out of the other tucking both sleeves around her waist. With the robe bunched under the skirt like a bulky midriff, she carefully picked up the shirt next to her and slid one arm into the sleeve then groped behind her for the other. The static of the fabric clung to the silk as Norma twisted and turned to her left and right as she tried to pull it to her. I wanted to laugh.

"Margaret? I need you in here."

"Problems?"

"No! Just give me the other sleeve."

I reached behind her releasing the sleeve that crackled with the electric charge created. "Here," I said, "give me your arm and put this on and I'll help you with all the buttons."

Norma tried to close them with me, her hands getting in the way.

"Leave them alone," I said. "We can't both do it and I can see what I'm doing. Now stand up and lean on me and let me get the robe out." Again the proximity felt too close.

Norma was breathing heavily as she stood, the skirt following gravity slipped down as the robe was released, and she sat down again and began tucking in the shirt. I realized that at some time later in the day I would have to help undress her again, but figured it would be an easier process than the one we had just gone through. I wondered how she was with Cheryl when she had helped her.

Norma fiddled with the long ties of the collar, forming it into a soft bow. "What are you going to wear?"

"Me? Just what I'm wearing."

"Those blue jean things? We're going to the doctor's office. You have to change."

Under my breath I said, "Yeah right! Screw that." Then louder so Norma could hear, "He's not interested in me. He's going to be seeing you. I'm just the unpaid help around here."

"And as it should be."

I felt the heat of my anger rising and felt flushed. Norma still hadn't thanked me for being there. Not that I really expected it and I wondered what she would've done without me. She needed full time care and since Cheryl couldn't be there she would've had to go into a nursing facility. I knew that would be totally unacceptable to her and probably the reason why she tolerated me; I was the lesser of the two evils. But there were things I could've done at home.

I'd been thinking of changing jobs and moving to Oregon as a fresh start after my divorce although I tend to make such major decisions slowly. Prior to learning about Daddy's death and then her fall I'd planned to spend this time driving north to Ashland since I'd heard it was lovely and everything would be so much greener up there. I was still very much an English female at heart and missed the seasons that never occurred in Southern California. I still wouldn't know anyone of course and had even thought of adopting a dog to keep me company although I knew Mewfus could be an issue. All that was now on hold while I took care of Norma and it would be too late once school resumed.

I considered where I had wanted to be instead of where I now was and again wondered what had possessed me. I still hadn't found Daddy's ashes and when I asked Norma she said that they were probably behind a box or something before saying she needed to nap and not bother her.

My irritation with the whole situation was reaching the tipping point and even going outside to read wasn't helping. I wondered if I would snap, go back home and leave her to her own devices. Her NHS carer would probably report the situation and Norma would have to submit to doctor's orders. I shrugged and decided not to get into an argument and ignore her comment that so trivialized me.

"I have to go get your wheelchair," I said, "so just wait and try to be patient."

I stood on the porch looking at the pancaked apparatus of cracked worn leather, wheels and chrome and shook my head. Under my breath I muttered, "Now how in hell's name does this damn thing unfold?"

The device was a reminder of me—all folded up and unfathomable but with sufficient recognizable attributes that I knew, once correctly aligned, would make sense and eventually provide the support I needed. At least that was what I hoped.

CHAPTER FOUR

Doctor Sutton's office was in the medical building adjoining the hospital although I didn't know what room it was in. As I searched the wall directory for the suite number, I ran down the S's looking for his name. It wasn't there and felt a rush of heat as my adrenaline began to surge. Damn, I thought, please don't tell me I'm in the wrong building, it took long enough finding a parking spot as the handicapped area was full. I looked again at the slip of paper Cheryl had left me and then back up to the building number I could see reflected backwards over the main door. It was the right one. I looked again at the names. Sutton wasn't listed.

I decided to do it by the process of elimination. Ruby Salinger, MD was female. Not her. Bruce Schultz, MD, Cardiology. No, not him—not yet at least. Richard Stanford-Ford, MD, Dermatology. Nope. Him neither. Brian Suffolk, MD, Orthopedics. Probably bingo but Norma had been referring to him as Doctor Sutton. I'd take a chance. We were already late and the worse that could happen we'd have to reschedule.

I had locked the brakes and set the wheelchair by the elevator and looked at Norma as I walked back toward her. She sat perched on the chair, her wrapped foot dangling over the footplate, her hands clutching an old alligator purse that had been worn smooth by the clasp. She tilted forward and away from the backrest and looked too warm in the red jacket but birdlike and regal with the black skirt draped around her ankles and the polka dotted shirt tied in a jaunty bow. She really looks like a dear little old lady, I thought with grudging admiration. How looks can deceive. Now hopefully, she won't open her mouth and spoil everything.

Doctor Suffolk was encouraged. He said that Norma's heart was strong and her blood pressure normal. She was eating and sleeping well and the swelling was going down. I felt like adding, "Yep, but what do we do with the rest of her?"

He finished writing a note in the file, closed it and jabbed at the pocket of his jacket to insert his pen, nudging aside the stethoscope dangling around his neck. I watched as he kept missing the opening until he glanced down then shoved it in. I noticed he bit his nails and decided that with patients like Norma it wasn't so surprising but he seemed nice and I decided I liked him.

He gave a quick smile at us. "Nasty little fall that. Could've been worse. Nothing broken. Slight ligament tear but bad enough. A bit confused when she got here. Fortunate thing that it wasn't worse." He spoke in short quick sentences and peered over his glasses. He addressed his comments to me as I stood behind the wheel chair and felt it move as Norma squirmed.

"So then she didn't have concussion as well?" I said. "I thought she might have. Well, that's good to …"

Norma suddenly interrupted me. "I wasn't confused, Doctor. Don't tell me what I was or wasn't. I'm never confused. Are we finished? I'd like to leave now. Margaret?"

The doctor stared down at her, his face seemed impassive, unaffected by Norma's sudden outburst and I gave him an apologetic smile although I figured it looked more like a grimace.

"… know," I said, completing my sentence. "So how long do you think she'll continue to need around the clock care?"

I knew my mother might start arguing again although suspected she'd wait until she was outside. She generally kept her temper under control around other people to maintain the image of being a lady. I didn't care either way and wanted to make my stay official in the doctor's own words.

He looked down at Norma. "What do you think, Mrs. Resnick?"

I was surprised. Damn. Of course Norma would prefer I stayed. Who else would she have to make things comfortable? I didn't want to be involved with her personal hygiene even though I felt guilty thinking it. But then she wouldn't have wanted it either. The carer handled that and from the noises that emanated from the bathroom, it sounded like the bathing of a reluctant kid having an adult tirade.

Norma's voice broke my thought. "Of course I need her. She's my daughter. She should be home and caring for *me*. It's not time for her to go back to America. Not yet, anyway. When I'm ready will be soon enough."

"Hmmm." The doctor said and stared at me over his glasses. "America huh? Really! Interesting that. D'you have a job? Do anything? Need to go back soon? What?"

I didn't have chance to answer as Nora interrupted, "She doesn't do a thing as far as I can tell. It's me you worry about, Doctor Sutton. Not her."

I cringed over the name as Norma pushed against the wheel but they were both locked and I had a firm hold of the handle. "I teach gardening but school's out for the summer and I'm an herbalist so yes I have some time. Not forever though." I didn't add that prior to coming I had even considered I might be of some help to Norma by using readily available herbs like lavender for relaxation and even packing her foot in comfrey if I could locate any. That was before I realized those skills were not an option with her.

"Interesting. Herbs? Wouldn't mix any of that stuff with her meds though. Huh?"

I remembered when I was about twelve and felt I was more like my mother's servant than a daughter and had wanted to grind up Oleander and serve it in her pudding. Wishing Norma dead was extreme, though, and besides which chopped green leaves in custard would have been obvious—and I couldn't spike her tea because everyone drank from the same pot. I might have wanted her to be gone but not to die in agony but perhaps the doctor wanted to be sure. I knew it to be an order.

"Of *course* not," I smiled, "and thank you, Doctor. When do you want to see her again?" I unlocked the brake and angled the wheelchair toward the door."

"Next week. Same time. Make an appointment for then. Sooner if you think otherwise. Give me a call if so." He patted Norma's shoulder, "Well, take care, now," and with a flurry of white jacket and glint of stainless steel from his stethoscope, he turned and held the door open for us to pass through.

So now it's up to me, I thought, irritated he had not provided the excuse to leave that I wanted. "Well let's get going then." The old brake hadn't fully released and I jerked the wheel chair causing Norma to slip slightly forward and grab hold of the armrests as her purse dropped to the floor. I stooped and bent to pick it up and placed it in her hand. "Oops, sorry Norma. You okay?"

I wondered if my frustration was the cause and it bothered me to realize that in that moment I once again resembled the mother I so disliked. She was my Shadow materializing not only inside where I could keep it hidden but also before me where it could be observed by everyone.

I jabbed at the elevator button and waited and looked up expectantly then poked it again although it was lit and I could feel the vibration of the elevator moving somewhere above us. Helping Norma wasn't getting easier and my own foul mood was getting in the way. I felt lopsided and missed my sense of balance and an equanimity I had taken for granted. What was happening to me? I wanted to find out how much of her I had in me but not this much and I didn't like who I was becoming.

The elevator stopped with a bump on the other side of the door and I leaned into the handle of the chair ready to push it through the doors as they opened. I hoped it would be empty so I could turn the wheelchair around once inside and ready to exit. Pushing, I found, was easier than pulling and already my back was starting to bother me.

The enclosure was occupied by half a dozen people who all drew closer to the wall when they saw Norma's chair. I felt irritated but said, "Thanks. It's okay, we can wait for the next one."

"There's enough room. Push me in, Margaret," she said.

I hesitated then moved the wheelchair into the clearing that had been provided. It was tight and I hoped the wheels wouldn't poke anyone. A vicar standing in the right far corner leaned toward the chair.

"Well, hel-*lo*. Why if it isn't our *dear* Mrs. Resnick. How lovely to see you. But here," he said to me, "let me help with that."

He tried to squeeze between the wheelchair and the wall and there was an awkward maneuvering to get around Norma. He reached over to take the handle from me as I was between the doors as they started to close so I thrust my hand against one side of the rubberized edge and it swept open again. I knew the doors were sensitive to touch but it always unnerved me that one day I would be slammed between them. "Really, it's okay," I said, "I've got it. Thanks anyway but if you don't mind being squashed in the corner over there I can just make it." I smiled apologetically at him and the others who had made room for us.

I pressed myself further into the back of the chair, my purse slipping down from my shoulder. As the elevator closed tight behind me, I could feel the knuckles of my right hand bunched as it gripped the handle that dug into my hip.

"Well, well, well ladies. This *is* a lovely surprise." The vicar beamed, his lips not quite open and head tilted. "I was just doing my rounds, visiting a few of my parishioners in the hospital and on my way out." He leaned closer to Norma while glancing up at me then back again.

"Why, it's our vicar," Norma said. "How nice to see you again Reverend McLean." I couldn't see her face but could tell it was Norma speaking through a smile and it sounded more like a chirp. I recognized it as her phony voice, the one where she enunciated each word as though she was practicing elocution. It was the voice she thought gave her class and always embarrassed me. My bloody Fair Lady, I thought. So who are we trying to impress now? A minister?

He was leaning toward her. "So *how* are we doing today? And how's that poor old foot of yours? Hmmm?" he said.

"Much better and we're *very* well, thank you. Aren't we Margaret?" She reached out her hand to him and he took it, transferring the Bible he was holding to his left hand as the elevator stopped with a thump on the ground floor.

I felt the doors ease open behind me and backed out into the lobby, dragging the chair with me. I didn't want to make small talk with anyone nor stand waiting while Norma did. I hoped we could make a polite getaway into the parking lot and swiveled Norma around and started to move toward the main exit to the outside.

"I'm going to my car," he said to me. "Perhaps I can accompany you to yours on the way and have a few quick words with this dear lady?"

Norma answered quickly and without hesitation, "Of course you can, Vicar. Of *course*. That would be lovely. Wouldn't it Margaret?"

It was a rhetorical question and part of the act. I nodded.

"I said wouldn't it, Margaret?"

"Yes. Very nice."

The large glass doors swung open and I pushed the chair through. Large scudding gray clouds had appeared since we had first arrived earlier and the outside felt humid and sticky. Maybe it's going to rain at last, I thought. Good, that'll clear the air a bit then realized I'd left the bedroom window open although knew there wasn't much I could do about it. The vicar was trotting in front of me next to Norma, making quick little side steps to avoid being caught by the wheels.

"Now where on earth is the car?" I kept forgetting it was Norma's Mercedes I was looking for and not my own truck. I stopped and peered around and Reverend McLean paused and looked at me directly without averting his eyes as he had been doing.

"And so," he said, "just who do I have the pleasure of meeting, here?"

Norma fluttered her hand toward him. "Ah yes, I'm sorry I should have introduced you already. How very rude of me. This is my daughter. Margaret. From America you know." Norma turned slightly and tilted her shoulder up toward me with a little smile intended for him then quickly resumed her position, ignoring me again.

"How do you do, Margaret? But of course I did hear your dear mother refer to you as that. I'm Reverend McLean. John McLean." He reached out his hand and I took it.

As it rested limply in mine I looked at him more closely, paying attention to the person I'd tried to ignore. Black, all in black; black suit, black shirt with the traditional white circular dog collar although it had another black one raised outside it. I thought that all priests wore the whole thing showing. What do I know? I thought. It doesn't matter—but what a fawner. He goes overboard on polite. He seems just like the weather, all clingy.

I decided not to ask him to call me Maggie but felt I had to say something to the poor guy. He hasn't done anything wrong, I realized, in fact he was trying to do everything right. "I believe you were responsible for providing this chair for Norma?" I said.

"Norma? Your mother? Oh yes, yes, indeed. I hope it has been of some help. But dearie me, I suppose it has because you're using it now. Ha ha. You're most welcome. It once belonged to a sweet old man, a parishioner of ..."

I wasn't really listening and still looking for the car then saw it parked on the other side of the lot which meant turning around and retracing my steps.

"Oh excuse me," I said, "I don't mean to be rude but our car is over there."

"Well, now, that's where mine is too and I was just keeping you company. What a coincidence. Ha ha. So then, let's walk back there together. Excellent."

I nodded and Norma sat quietly holding her purse as we moved in silence. He was a little shorter than me and thin. I'd noticed that his hands were white with long, elegantly tapered fingers and his pale face was small and oval with a tiny cleft chin, and when it wasn't pulled into a smirk, he had a little rosebud mouth. With his drooping eyelids he reminded me of a female in a Pre-Raphaelite painting. Way too pretty to be a guy, I thought. Not my type though but pity he crops his hair so short, he'd be rather cute if he left it long. Then I wondered if there were vicars who wore their hair long and if not they should.

"Margaret. Margaret," my mother's voice interrupted my thoughts and her voice had resumed its brittle edge. "Hurry up, I think it's going to rain. I don't want this red jacket to get wet." She ignored the Reverend who trotted by our side like a little dog.

"We're almost there," I said, then hoped he would stick around long enough to help Norma from the car or lift the chair into the boot. I'm starting to think like a bloody Englishman, I thought. Boot. Trunk. Same thing.

I stopped before the Mercedes and searched in my purse for the keys that had slipped to the bottom. I could hear them clink but couldn't see or feel them. Reverend McLean hovered anxiously beside us. "Did you lose your keys? Oh dear, dearie me. I hope not. I hope not indeed."

"Nope. Okay. Got them." I set the brake on the chair and unlocked the passenger side door. I still felt weird that the steering wheel wasn't where I was used to it being. "Alright, Norma, now ease off there and lean on me and ..."

"No, no, ladies. Allow me. Please. Let me help you. It would be my pleasure to assist. Perhaps you would hold this for a moment, though?" He handed me the Bible and I noticed the edges were worn and slightly frayed. Small scraps of paper that bore neat, tiny script slipped from the bound covers and I hastily pushed them back.

I stood back a moment and watched as he struggled to help Norma from the chair and was surprised to see her go suddenly limp as he placed his arm around her back. I almost laughed out loud. What a ham. She was perfectly capable of moving herself with a little help even if it did take her longer.

Reverend McLean seemed startled too and I saw his features draw together in a slight frown. Bet he doesn't offer to do *that* again, I thought as I walked around to the driver's side. I unlocked it tossing my purse and the Bible onto the seat, careful to push back his papers again.

Large drops of rain were starting to splash on the pavement and car and I hurried around to the other side to get the chair. He was still easing Norma onto her seat and looked disheveled, making little clucking noises under his breath.

I released the handbrake then moved the footrests before lifting the seat that brought the armrests together then dragged it over the lip of the trunk. The wheels made small skid tire marks on the ground and the chair was awkward and bulky. It seemed to me that it personified all the disagreeable things involving Norma as I heaved it up, slamming it inside. I pushed it further in and closed the back down with a thud.

As I turned, I was startled to see the vicar next to me. "Oh. Sorry," I said. "Didn't know you were right there. Thanks for helping with Norma. Appreciate it."

He was slightly out of breath. "Not at all. Not at all. Anything to help the poor dear lady."

Dear lady my ass, I thought. "Well, thanks. Don't get wet." I began to walk around the car again while he followed. What on earth does he want? I wondered. It's going to pour any minute and he'll be soaked.

"Um ..."

"Yes?"

"May I please have my Bible?"

Right. Of course. His Bible! "I'm sorry," I said and I meant it. "I totally forgot."

I reached next to my purse and handed it to him. I could feel the rain stick to my head and saw his hair begin to flatten. Poor guy would get soaked. "Can we give you a lift to your car?" I didn't wait for him to answer but leaned over the back of the seat behind me and unlocked the door. "Here, get in."

He tumbled through the door and closed it behind him. "Thank you. Why thank you Margaret. Splendid. Splendid. Brilliant thought and most awfully kind of you."

"Not at all. Now where are you parked?"

I looked at him through my rear view mirror and it reminded me of the cab driver who had looked at me like that when I had first arrived just yesterday and already it seemed like I'd been there years.

"Not far. Just a little ways from here. It's the little blue Vauxhall over there."

"I don't know what a Vauxhall looks like. There are several blue ones. Which one? That one?" I was feeling even more irritable and making no attempt to be polite.

"Not that. It's the one with a squarish back. There. Yes that's it," he said as I slowed down and stopped then waited for him to open the door and get out.

He continued to sit where he was. "Thank you, Margaret. It was a pleasure meeting you and how nice of you to be so considerate. Now I'm not as wet as I would have been. Ha ha, no hardly wet at all."

"Mmmm. No problem and yes, nice meeting you too." I wanted him to get out so I could leave.

Norma started to squirm. She was being ignored. "So lovely seeing you, Vicar, and thank you for all your help."

She had her smiley voice again only this time I could see that her mouth was pursed into her rouged cheeks and formed deep, tiny pink furrows. With her head slightly tilted she peered around her seat. He leaned forward toward her.

"Not at all and I do hope that poor foot of yours heals quickly."

"It will. It will."

"Yes, God willing."

It was beginning to rain in earnest as large drops splattered against the windshield. His presence in the car was annoying. Helpful perhaps, but his manner was ingratiating, and I was beginning to worry about driving back in the rain, "Where's the switch for the wipers?"

Norma raised her hand toward the steering wheel. "Turn that lever. Don't you know where it is?"

I fumbled with it and the right turn indicator began to click, the light blinking green. I just wanted to get home and escape to my room. Reverend McLean leaned between the seats and pointed, "Twist it," he said, "that should work." He leaned back again with his hand on the door handle, seemingly reluctant to leave. "So will we er ..." he hesitated, "... will we see you both again? Soon? Perhaps this coming Sunday for our family service?"

So that was it. Church. He wanted us to go to church. No way! I never went to church and didn't think Norma would want to go either.

"Perhaps we should leave that up to my mo ..."

"Of *course*. We'd love to come," Norma interrupted and jerked her head dismissively towards me. "Don't listen to her. Can we sing *Joy to the World*? I just so *love* that hymn." She started humming the melody.

"Well, dear Lady, I'd be *delighted* to but the service has already been programmed—along with the hymns and music. It *is* an Easter song though," he added, "and we just had that one a few months ago. But ha ha, yes indeed a lovely hymn. A lovely one indeed but hopefully you'll find the others just as pleasant."

I looked at him again and I could see he was smirking at Norma perhaps to convey his regrets. I couldn't tell. I didn't care. I was now committed. Damn it.

"Well then, yes I suppose so. What a disappointment. But we wouldn't dream of missing it no matter what you play—would we dear?" She looked at me.

Dear? Who was she trying the kid? The woman is impossible, I thought and switched the wipers up to the next level and watched them swish back and forth more quickly as the engine idled.

"Marvelous. Brilliant. Just perfectly marvelous." He didn't wait for me to respond and rested his hand on Norma's arm. "Then I will expect to see you both then. Ten o'clock sharp? Excellent. Splendid. Now a quick dash to the car and I'll be off."

He started to leave, one leg outside, his black pants already becoming wet then pulled it back in again and said to me, "And Margaret, when you arrive you can wheel your dear mother down to the front. We have a place for the poor handicapped souls there. So goodbye then. Goodbye." With a quick, determined flourish he jumped from the car and pulled his neck and head into his hunched shoulders. He waved to us as we drove away, the wheels already splashing in the wet asphalt.

I was peering through the windshield ignoring Norma when she said, "Handicapped? I'm *not* handicapped. Why would he call me handicapped?"

I bit my lip. No way could I laugh. We had more than half an hour in the car together and I didn't want to listen to tirades the rest of the way home. What happened to the smiley voice?

"I'm sure he didn't mean you. Don't worry about it. He knows you're not handicapped, just slightly injured and besides which you'll be right down there in the front."

"Oh yes, I didn't think of that. Well perhaps you're right." She hesitated. "But it was so nice of him to lift me into the car though."

"Mmmm, yes it was." I remembered Norma's limp body, one arm dangled lightly over his, "Indeed it was."

Norma was silent for a moment then added, "But did you notice how he smiles and coos? I think he likes me but he's a bit too young—even though I do still look good for my age."

I didn't answer. I couldn't. It was difficult to believe that such comments came from my own mother. Glancing into my rearview mirror to the rain drenched back window I could see the wavering blue of the vicar's car behind us. I was thinking ahead to Sunday and felt my world was beginning to close in. I hoped it wouldn't be raining and what, among the armloads of clothes I had brought down for Norma, would she want to wear for church?

Then I wondered what I could wear from the limited selection of things I'd brought with me. Oh well, I decided, I'll wash my hair and put on a clean shirt and since I'll be pushing a handicapped person perhaps no one will notice. It bothered me that I was concerned.

CHAPTER FIVE

hey shelly ... weather suddenly turned cold and drizzly and became what i remember of real english summer so now bundled up in sweats and having a hot chocolate instead of coffee – oh for california sunshine ... some interesting developments ~ the local vicar invited us to attend sunday family service and since norma accepted i had to go too but it turned out better than i thought ... getting her dressed for the occasion was a test of patience just like the doctor's visit only this time she insisted on wearing a hat and said i should too although i said none of hers would go with jeans ... she quit bugging me when i said that she looked jaunty and regal and even if i didn't she knew how to dress for the occasion ... almost got lost on the drive there with all the little narrow country roads with their glorious green hedges and wildflowers and the open fields and woods beyond ~ quite beautiful but several wrong turns later stopped at a little house that had a TEAS & SCONES sign and a sweet woman in a gingham apron pointed down the road and gave me directions ... found the most wonderful little stone church that apparently dates back to the sixteenth century surrounded by tumbled headstones in various

*stages of collapse ... had to take norma over the gravel
driveway that crunched under the wheels and a bumpy
ride for her and hard on my back but once inside ~
omg shelly it was so lovely and quite small with a
carved vaulted stone ceiling and ancient stained glass
windows that threw shafts of colored light everywhere
and like stepping into another and very peaceful world
... the air was permeated with incense and the smoke
from candles that were burning and have burned over
the centuries and i felt i was breathing in something
hallowed and very ancient ... some of the pillars and
arches had some really old paintings virtually worn
away and almost obscured with faded colors that de-
picted the last supper and some others i couldn't see
too well but i plan to check them out later when i can
go back alone ... wheeled norma down to the front
which wasn't too far away from where i sat on one of
the long heavy church wood pews ~ incredible pieces
of high back oak benches all pockmarked and pitted
as they were they shone and seemed polished to a deep
rich brown ~ probably from the countless parishioners
who had slid and seated themselves there over the
years and who knows ~ perhaps now in some of the
graves outside ... the pews had delicate woodwork
carvings at each end of the benches of flowers and
plants and little animals ... although i tuned out the
vicar for the most part the music and hymns were lovely and the sound in those acoustics gave me goose
bumps ... the organist was exceptional and i was surprised to think that such a musician was tucked away
in this little country parish ... his touch was ethereal*

but from where i was sitting he looked like a big bear of a man with a beard who wore dark glasses and long hair taken back in a pony tail ~ on the floor by his side was a gorgeous german shepherd that periodically raised its head and looked around but otherwise seemed quite content to just lie there so i wondered if the guy was blind ... at the end of the service reverend mclean dressed in his black cassock and white surplice with long black scarf around his neck chatted with everyone at the door on the way out including norma and me ... he looked good in the ritual getup and beamed and nodded and folded and unfolded his hands like he didn't know what to do with them but shook mine and chatted then suggested i might be interested in attending some of the ladies groups ~ hah can you imagine me in a ladies group? wasn't sure how to politely refuse but said i didn't think id be around long enough to participate ... he looked surprised and raised his eyebrows and looked back down at norma and said that god would guide me to make the right decision ~ i wondered what kind of guidance i got in coming here in the first place ... he asked how i d enjoyed the service and looked pleased when i said the music was great and the church was lovely so he grasped my hand again and thanked me profusely ~ he tends to an overabundance of nice that becomes annoying ... i d noticed some rather threadbare tapestry rugs along the center nave and by the massive stone font i think they might cover some old brasses and would love to do some rubbings if i had the paper and wax and he agreed ... sooooo that said im gonna finish this hot

choc close up and get going back to the house ~ yuck
... chat more later ... so miss mewfus cos I can't send
him emails ...luv maggie

I got back from the café and was thinking of escaping outside
to read when Norma stopped me. "I just called Reverend McLean and
he said we should be there by three this afternoon."

I nodded. It wasn't a surprise. I'd heard Norma say at church
that she wanted to see him although didn't know what for. It would be
a good break to get away from the house. Although I had scrubbed
and cleaned the kitchen the house still felt oppressive and there remained a faint odor.

As I had guessed, Norma wore diapers although had hidden
the soiled ones and my nose eventually led me to a swollen plastic
bag in the hall closet where they'd been stuffed away. I burned sticks
of sandalwood and the smoke drifted down and helped disguise some
of the lingering smell I had been unable to get rid of. Norma had
sniffed the air, her chin high and mouth scrunched and asked if it was
my perfume. I didn't feel like explaining. "No," I lied, "it's my soap."

"Then use mine or something else. That stuff stinks. Make's
you smell like an Indian market."

I thought it interesting that she had found the original smell I
was trying to disguise acceptable. Perhaps she had grown use to it. "I
didn't know you'd been in an Indian market."

"Of course not *in* one—never inside. When I used to go into
the city with your father I passed them all the time. Ugh!" She gave
one of her exaggerated shivers, "Too many foreigners that's what I
think. Not like the old days but not much I can do about it." She
shook her head as though dismissing the thought and settled further
into her chair.

After I'd discovered the bag, I put on thick rubber gloves and a mask and tossed everything into the outside garbage and Norma never mentioned that the bag was gone. I knew my mother was probably embarrassed and wondered how best to approach the subject without making her feel uncomfortable. For Norma to be incontinent must be the worst of all possible humiliations and I felt sorry for her.

"By the way," I had said, "I left a box of small plastic bags inside your bathroom. When one is used just set it outside the door and I'll get rid of it." I then quickly changed the subject, "Would you like anything right now? A cup of tea with some biscuits, perhaps?"

Norma nodded and said nothing. Neither of us mentioned her incontinence although I wondered where she got her pads and later discovered that Cheryl brought them in and deposited them discreetly in her bathroom. Obviously she hadn't removed those that were soiled and I wondered how long my mother had had the problem or if the doctor knew of the situation.

There were medications that perhaps could help if not cure it and I'd seen Norma sit up and lean toward the television when an ad recommended medications for an overactive bladder. Then she would relax and sit back and say nothing. Norma rarely engaged me in conversation unless it was a request for something and having told me what she wanted to wear for the appointment with the vicar that afternoon said, "So. Who's looking after your pussy?"

"My *what?*"

"Your pussy. Who's looking after it? I thought you said you had a cat."

"Oh! A *cat*. Yeah. I do. Mewfus. My friend, Shelly."

"You don't say much you know. You're closed mouth like your father. What do you think about other than those books you've got your nose buried into all the time?"

Norma was not a reader and had hidden my books when I was a child. Even those given to me by my father. It had been one of her milder forms of punishment to deprive me of something I enjoyed doing. I recalled a time I returned from the library with an armload of books among the groceries she had wanted and found her angry at the door. "You didn't come right back and I've been waiting," she said. "Now you can just go and return everything you checked out."

I was unhappy not to read them but more concerned and embarrassed that the librarian might scold me for returning the books the same day. She seemed not to care but for a shy, introverted kid like I was then, the reactions of most grown-ups, except for my father and Grandmother Clare were a mysterious unknown and something to avoid.

I'd often thought that the same reticence had affected my lack of adult communication with Richard but not totally. He was unfaithful and was and probably still is, a womanizer and the primary reason for the divorce and no amount of counseling to help me overcome my reluctance to defend myself could change that.

I'd gotten better but still knew enough not to be trapped into an unwary yielding of information with Norma though. On the rare occasion I had opened up about myself I had grown to understand that disclosing anything personal was filed away in her brain and later used against me. I remembered how my father had sat quietly reading or watching television or wandering outside to smoke his pipe in the garden. He too had learned to say nothing.

I hesitated. "What do you want to talk about?"

"Anything rather than listen to the TV." She muted the sound and stared at me. "It gets pretty lonely sitting here by myself saying nothing—especially when there's someone else in the room." Her watery eyes stared at me as though they registered everything.

My mother's comment lowered my defenses and I felt a wave of sympathy for her. Perhaps being immobilized was having an effect and probably she did feel lonely. On the rare occasions when the television was off and she was trying to nap I was conscious of the thick silence that usually enveloped us like a fog that could settle and muffle every sound. I never wanted to break it if it seemed Norma was content watching television although the atmosphere felt strained and uncomfortable as though something unpleasant was about to occur.

I paused, choosing my words carefully. "Well right now, I think about you and your health."

"What about it? I have a sprained ankle. You already know that."

"Yes I know but have you er … have you mentioned your incontinence to Dr. Suffolk? You could have an infection or something and maybe there's some medication you could take."

The room that had seemed to be warmer, froze. Norma's mouth tightened and her chin jutted out, her lips pursed. I knew the signs.

"It's Dr. Sutton and don't talk of what you know nothing about. It's none of your business what I discuss with him."

"Okay. I'm sorry. I thought I could be of some help but forget I said anything." I got up, "D'you want another biscuit or glass of wine or anything? I'm going to go outside in the garden for a while."

I didn't wait for the answer but knew she was still speaking as I moved to open the French door then hesitated as she snapped, "Are you listening to me Margaret? I said we were going to see Reverend McLean this afternoon. Are you deaf or something? You never answer me."

I nodded my head. "Yes I heard and of course I'll take you."

I started to slide the door open but Norma continued, "It's a matter of great importance. I want to discuss my funeral arrangements."

I stopped and turned back into the room. "Your funeral? When?"

"Not when. I'm not planning on going yet even though you might be hoping I will."

"Of course I don't hope that. I didn't know you had made arrangements, that's all."

"Not yet but I've thought about it. I've decided what I want and must make sure that everything will be exactly the way it should be and not messed up."

"Are you suggesting I would screw up your funeral?" I thought of Daddy and that I had still been unable to find his ashes but here she was concerned about her own passing.

She tapped the remote on the arm of the chair as though to emphasize what she was about to say. "You might. I want the best and I want to pick out my own coffin and where it will be put. I don't want it stuck in a corner lot somewhere. Reverend McLean needs to know all that along with the hymns and other music to be played."

"That's a good idea to pick out a plot but I doubt you're going to need it soon. You could stipulate all that in your will and I would handle it and make sure it was done. But what kind of music besides hymns, do you want played?" I had never known Norma to be appreciative of anything other than popular songs.

"I want Frank Sinatra. I want a recording of him singing '*My Way*' but softly you understand, as people are arriving at the church."

"Frank Sinatra? Well okay. A little unusual perhaps, but for you, appropriate." I wondered who else would be at the funeral.

"Yes. Of course it is. Now leave me alone and go do something I want to take a nap so that I'm quite refreshed when I talk to the Reverend."

I was sufficiently aware not to interrupt her when she settled into the chair and annoyed that I had let a golden opportunity slip by without learning where she had put Daddy's ashes. Knowing her, he was probably in the greenhouse next to the potting soil and she didn't want to tell me. Despite that ungenerous thought I still wanted to believe that on some level Norma was capable of feeling ashamed, no matter how little, for behavior most others would consider reprehensible.

I brought the car to a crunchy stop in the gravel driveway then opened the door and paused before I got out. Someone was playing Bach and the music filtered through the heavy, closed church doors. I walked back to the trunk, taking my time to listen before removing the wheelchair then angled it by the passenger door for Norma before helping her into it. I leaned into the handles, trundling it over the bumpy stone to the rectory. Father McLean stood on the path, beaming, clasping and unclasping his hands before trotting down to take the wheelchair and push Norma himself. The guy might be obsequious, I thought, but savvy enough not to get trapped into helping Norma again.

I had planned to leave them and go into town and email Shelly, but the music held my attention. I paused then turned to them both, indicating the church doors. "Think I'm going to wait inside while you two chat."

The vicar's smile grew wider than I had seen before and he looked genuinely pleased. He nodded. "The doors are open to you any time, Margaret, any time. Yes, any time. Go in and pray."

I'm not going to pray anything, I thought, but listening will be good for the soul.

I pushed against the heavy brass handles, polished to a high shine, and then let the door close quietly. Massive oak as they were they were hinged not to make a sound. The relative dark inside seemed to move and position itself around me. I stepped in further on the old cracked tile besides the font and stopped. Absentmindedly, I moved my hand over the trailing ivy and birds carved into the stone. I remembered it from the last visit and thought it was beautiful and wanted to touch it then. But now I was staring ahead and not at the font.

I could see that the person playing was the longhaired guy I had seen at the Family Service. Hunched over the keys, he appeared oblivious to anything or anyone except his music. He was wearing jeans and an old blue sweater instead of the suit he had worn before and his feet were sandaled and this time he wasn't wearing the dark glasses.

It was cool inside and I shivered a little, but it felt like a combination of air and the chill his playing produced. I wondered if I should remain standing where I was but then decided to move closer to the front. His large German Shepherd raised its head and watched me until I sat down, then settled its muzzle again on her paws.

When the organist finished playing and the last notes echoed into the vaulted ceiling and quietly faded, he seemed unaware of me sitting in the pew.

"That was lovely. Thank you." I said and felt like clapping. It was the best thing that had happened to me since I'd arrived. My voice seemed too loud and there was an echo that interrupted the mood that had been generated but I didn't want to surprise him.

He spun around and started to stand, then corrected his position and sat down again. He was wearing a patch over his right eye. "Oh. Hello. I didn't know anyone was here."

"Are you going to play some more? I hope so. Do you mind if I stay and listen?" I realized I was speaking too quickly and wished I hadn't said so much. Thank you would've been enough.

"I can. I wasn't planning to. Is there anything in particular you'd like to hear?" His voice was deep as I had imagined for such a big man. The dog was resting its head on his thigh, shifting her eyes between us both as we spoke, while he gently moved his fingers up and down along her ears.

The question was unexpected. I was totally unprepared and I felt a bit flustered. "Er ... Bach. Haydn. More of the same. You choose."

He nodded, hesitated, and then swung around on his seat, his fingers on the keys and his feet moving against the pedals.

As he began to play, I recalled my last trip to Paris after separating from Richard. It had been an impetuous decision to escape and to get away and put distance between us and a time for me to think. I had gone to Notre Dame and there had been a service in progress. At first I had hesitated and felt that as a tourist I was invading the privacy of the congregation but as other people quietly slipped in beside me and moved further inside, I followed and felt myself become an immediate and vital part of the ceremony. It became mine, too. I felt uplifted and spiritually moved in a way that had never happened before. Until this time.

Sitting in the front row of the little church, before this unknown man and his music, I experienced a sense of wonder that no sermon had ever generated. I wasn't religious and held negative opinions about the church, but it redeems itself through its art, I thought. Although not completely.

The door opened and a shaft of light blazed in from the outside then was gone. I turned my head slightly and saw Reverend McLean tiptoeing down the aisle towards me his head bobbing with a little smile on his face. I didn't smile in return and looked back toward the organist as I remained seated.

"Lovely, isn't it?" the vicar whispered next to my ear.

I slid away slightly and nodded.

"Your dear mother's ready. She's in the car," he said. He paused and stepped back as though I would go with him. When I nodded again but remained where I was, he coughed slightly then murmured, "Well then, hmmm, I'll just go and keep her company for a few more minutes." He seemed to melt away from where I sat and light flooded in and disappeared as he left through the massive doors.

I wondered if Norma had played the helpless female again when she was assisted into the car and was torn whether to go or not, then decided that they could both wait. He's not going to leave her sitting there by herself, I thought. At least I hope he doesn't and if he does then I'll deal with it later.

It was almost ten minutes later the organist stopped playing. He turned toward me and this time his smile seemed more confident. "So you're still here? I didn't drive you away?"

"No. It was lovely. Thank you."

"You're welcome. Nice to be appreciated. Do you want me to continue?"

"I'd love that but I should go. My mother's waiting outside. Do you play often? Perhaps I can come the next time you play. I'm Maggie, by the way." I moved out of the pew and extended my hand.

"Alex and this is Kay," he said patting his dog. He smiled then turned, reaching for a cane by his seat.

I lowered my hand. "I'm sorry," I said. "At first I assumed you might be blind but then you chatted with me so I thought not. How well can you see?" I wondered if that was polite to ask but somehow it seemed okay.

He laughed. "I'm not completely blind, just the one eye, although the left one's not as good as I would like. Need the cane for walking sometimes but not all the time. Only when I go more than a mile or two or I've been sitting for too long." He leaned heavily on it as he eased down the three red-carpeted steps from the organ to the front pew where I had been sitting, the dog close to his side. "And of course when I go down steps." He grinned, his teeth white and slightly uneven behind his graying beard. "Now I think you were offering to shake my hand."

His accent was American and I wanted to ask but decided not. I took his hand and felt mine lost inside his gentle grip. "I shouldn't keep them waiting," I said, "but you play so beautifully."

"A gift from the universe I suppose. I'm lucky. It keeps me sane."

His body moved lower on his right side as he limped toward the door. In the darkened interior he seemed to be measuring his steps, careful as he placed his feet on the slightly irregular and uneven tile of the nave then hesitated.

I instinctively reached my arm toward him, "Do you need any help?" I thought it ironic that within the space of a few days I was asking two very different people if they needed my help to walk. Unlike Norma I wouldn't have minded sharing his space.

"No thanks. I'm used to this but have to watch it right here there are some uneven slabs. And beside which you're just a little thing and I'd probably squash you if I fell." He laughed down at me and Kay wagged her tail, her tongue hanging from her mouth as though appreciating his humor.

I laughed with him. "Not so little but I appreciate the concern. The vicar told me you were a vet. Are you a musician who also cares for animals?"

He laughed louder and the sound reverberated into the arches above us. "Not that kind of vet although a nice idea. No, Persian Gulf and I was among the few injured during the war. I lost the eye and screwed up my leg."

I wanted to remain there with him, listen to him, look at him but the doors opened and this time, were held wide open. Father McLean, propped himself against the wood, his whole body appeared tense, his hips extended back into the door and his upper body twisted toward us. "Ah. Good. There you both are." His smile was polite.

I realized I'd left him too long with Norma and turned to Alex, "I'd better go." Then genuinely apologetic said to the vicar, "I'm really sorry. I didn't mean to keep you waiting for so long."

"No problem. No problem. Dear me, no. Nothing to apologize for." He seemed relieved as he closed the door behind us as we all moved outside then added, "But I've left your dear mother waiting in the car, though." He hesitated, visibly unsure of whether to stay with Alex or walk back with me. His head began to bob, "But I really must get back to my office. Lots to do. Lots to do. Thank you for coming, Margaret, and I do hope you'll be back soon," he said, then quickly trotted away and back toward the rectory.

I stared after him, thinking that he looked liked a little pony as he picked up his feet and hurried away. I could see the back of Norma's head as she sat in the car. Held motionless, I knew it was how she stiffened when she was pissed.

I turned back to Alex, "I'm sorry to rush off but ..."

"I totally understand and I'll be here tomorrow afternoon if you want to come back and listen."

69

I nodded. "Perfect! Yes I'll be here." Come hell or high water, I thought, I'll be here. Then I wondered how he was going to get home. He'd mentioned walking. "Can I give you a lift?"

"No thanks. Kay and I will walk. It's not far and the exercise is good for us. Perhaps some other time."

I watched him and the dog as they moved away; Alex more confident in the daylight and Kay bounding beside him. I opened the car door and, as I had expected, Norma was rigid as she sat staring ahead.

"Didn't mean to keep you waiting but did you hear that music? So wonderful." I continued to fill the icy silence, "Did you get all your arrangements completed with the Reverend?"

"No, not all of them but it's as well I'm starting the process myself because quite obviously you would be distracted if it were in your hands." She shook her head, her lips tightly clenched and turned to look out of her window.

Well, she's too angry to talk, I thought. But that's actually a good thing because now she won't break the spell of my chat with Alex, although I wondered what she was seeing outside. It's a pity she can't relax and enjoy this gorgeous countryside, I thought, because it might put her in a better mood but I felt great.

Thinking about my meeting with Alex I wondered what would have happened if he had taken me up on the offer. I thought it would have been interesting to have had him and the dog climb in the back seat and seen how Norma reacted and just as well he had refused although I decided to ask him again some other time. When Norma wasn't there.

CHAPTER SIX

hey shelly ~ sorry ive not written in a few days but things are looking up for a change ... took norma to discuss her funeral arrangements with the vicar ~ although the real event isn't likely to occur anytime soon ~ and i met the organist the one i mentioned before ~ alex and his dog is called kay ... the guy plays like an angel and looks like a scruffy giant ... went back again the following day to listen instead of coming here and writing to you but figured you'd forgive me under the circumstances ~ he's amazing and gives me goose bumps ... said he teaches music part time at the local school ... he can still see well enough to drive in the daytime but not at night .. he's got a going gray beard and i think that's to hide some of the scars on his face ~ they're not bad but you can see he has them ... he wanted to know about norma but i didn't feel like going into detail ~ why spoil a nice thing by bringing her into the picture so i just said that she was rather strong minded ... he reached over and put his hand on mine and said "difficult to be around, huh?" ... probably heard the strain in my voice and here i thought i was being neutral so guess he's sensitive to tone ... won't see him again until the end of the week on sunday and cant wait ... who would believe id be anxious to attend church? ok hon gotta go ~ more later ... big hug for mewfus ... luv maggie

As I was finishing I looked up and wondered why Dina was hurrying to my booth.

"Excuse me, Maggie." Her voice was breathless and seemed higher than I was used to hearing. I wondered why she was so anxious and figured I'd spent too long at the table although there were other empty ones around.

"It's okay, Dina," I said. "No more coffee, thanks. I'm just about to leave and you can have this table." I smiled hoping she'd take that as an apology.

"No it's not that. Your mum just had another fall and is on her way to the hospital. You better go now and can pay me later."

I stiffened. It wasn't what I had expected and was momentarily stunned. "How do you know that? Are you sure?"

When Dina first starting serving me and learned I was Norma's daughter, she told me that she was Cheryl's sister. Deciding it was good diplomacy to establish a gossipy familiarity I left her a generous tip for taking up one of the back tables. After that Dina became friendlier and wanted to chat, so I let her and discovered that she knew about Norma and the house.

"It's fortunate your mother has that downstairs bathroom now she can't make the stairs," she'd said. "But she's a feisty old thing and will probably live to be a hundred."

I had been surprised that Dina knew about the extra bathroom. Then I figured Cheryl must have described it to her although she might not have known that once it had been a study next to a small guest toilet and both converted when I was a kid.

Norma wanted her own dressing room with a shower separate from the master and guest bedrooms because when my father was alive they played bridge at their club and ate out at expensive hotels so she, seeking admiration, dressed for attention. She wanted no interruptions while in the process of getting ready and when the door was closed it was an indication for everyone else to stay out.

Now Dina was telling me she was in hospital. "When? How do you know?" I repeated.

I realized I was stalling for time but I needed to calm down. My heart was beating and my hands were shaking. Having Norma back in hospital wasn't something I had ever anticipated. I'd been thinking it wouldn't be much longer before I could return home and relax before school started again.

"Cheryl just called and told me to tell you. She thought you'd be here since you left the house with your computer." Dina was wiping her hand down her apron, "Apparently your mum tried walking without Cheryl's help and lost her balance." Dina removed her receipt pad, and handed me the check. "Like I said, take this and get moving and you can pay me later. Oh, I do hope she's going to be alright."

As I unplugged my laptop and put it in the case, I was in shock and not sure what I hoped.

After I parked and hurried across the parking lot toward the glass doors to the hospital, it started to rain. "Shit," I said. It was sunny when I left earlier. At home in California, I generally checked the weather daily even though it was usually the same—sunny—although I always hoped for the freak shower that when it happened invariably made the local evening news. Here the weather could change at a moment's notice and nobody seemed to care. I remembered Grandmother Clare would rub her hips and say it was going to rain, she could feel it in her bones and I'd wonder why my own bones didn't convey the same information.

As I caught myself thinking of the past it annoyed me that my attention wasn't on the present and Norma. She could be dead or in a coma or in worse shape than she had been before. I stopped by the Information Desk. "Where will I find Mrs. Resnick?"

"First name?"

How many other Resnick's were in there? I felt impatient and wondered why she didn't type that into the computer instead of waiting until she had the full name. Then I realized that not having my thoughts under control disturbed me more than she did and hoped it wasn't obvious so I consciously focused on making my face appear calm by relaxing my brow and mouth.

"Norma."

The receptionist tapped her keys and stared into the computer screen. "Emergency. Lower level. You'll have to take a left here and go down the hall halfway then take the lift down."

I nodded and moved away without saying thanks. I heard my sandals slapping the ground faster than a walk so slowed down and tried to focus. I wasn't happy about the prospect of seeing Norma and hoped she'd be asleep or drugged or both. If she was awake and not dead or in a coma, I was sure she'd have something to say about me being away from the house when she had fallen and it would all be my fault. I was in no mood for an argument, but then I never am.

I felt guilty. Perhaps I should have paid more attention and not taken off to listen to Alex or gone to the café. I had suspected my mother might fall again simply because she was too stubborn to ask for help although I chose to believe that the first time was a fluke and wouldn't happen again. Obviously it had, though, and I felt relieved it was Cheryl who found her and not me. Right Maggie, I thought, some great daughter you are.

I paused before the heavy gray doors to the elevator and pushed the button, looking up as I felt the vibration of it moving down the shaft. It stopped with a soft thud and I poised, ready to leap in but as it opened an orderly backed out, pulling a gurney towards him. His head bulged softly with a blue cap that billowed around his hair and clasped his eyebrows so that just his brown eyes peered over a white mask. His eyes stared at me and crinkled so I wasn't sure he smiled. It didn't seem like a smiling situation and I watched as he pushed the wheeled stretcher away from the doors toward the opposite hallway.

But it was the still body on it that caused me to stare. I couldn't tell if it was a male or female lying there. The head was covered in gauze and a bottle of clear fluid dripped down a tube connected to the taped hand resting on the cover. I wondered if it was Norma and whether I should follow to find out or descend to the lower level as I'd been told. I hesitated. "Think," I said. "Get a grip lady," and watched him move away before looking back at the elevator.

The doors were beginning to close again so I slammed my hand against the rubber edge and they reopened at my touch as I moved inside, waiting for them to close. A voice called out from the hallway. "Wait. Wait please. Hold it for me." It was Reverend McLean.

I put out my arm and the doors opened again and a distant bell began to ring as they remained open. The vicar jumped inside, breathing heavily and visibly out of breath.

"Why Margaret, my dear. It's you." He looked distraught, his brow furrowed. "Oh your poor, poor dear mother." He blinked and shook his head, clutching the worn Bible to his chest.

So we were going in to see her together. Damn, I thought, then because of his nervous fluttering wondered if perhaps he knew more than I did. Perhaps Norma was already dead. My heart skipped a little. If that was the case then I would have preferred to find out alone and not have him hovering with condolences regardless of how appropriate they might be.

"She's dead?"

The elevator landed with a thump on the lower level and the doors eased open. I could see a red arrow sign that flashed 'Emergency' to my right. I hesitated and Reverend McLean took my arm in a surprising display of strength, pushing me firmly out the door. "Dear me no. At least I hope not. That wasn't what I was told."

"Who told you what?"

"Cheryl. Poor dear lady was quite terrified when she called me."

I'd stepped away from his hand and began hurrying after him as he trotted down the hallway, following the signs and the painted arrow along the floor. He walked as though he could have done it blindfolded and obviously knew the way and had been there before. I hated the fact that I tried to keep up. Left to my own methods, I would have walked slower to maintain control. I wanted to appear as though I was in charge of whatever it was I was going to find.

It occurred to me that even though I had thought of Norma being dead it hadn't produced any tears. Would I cry if I were to find she was gone? I found that hard to believe and considered it much more likely I'd remain dry eyed. I figured it would be expected I should cry though and viewed as cold hearted if I didn't but I didn't want to be found lacking in emotion either.

How can I appear solicitous when I'm feeling so numb? I thought. Under different circumstances, with somebody else, I knew I could become upset. I cried when I heard that Grandmother and Daddy had passed and just thinking of Mewfus dead made me want to cry. I even got upset when a plant died. I thought it interesting that a plant meant more to me than Norma.

I had never ventured so close to what my emotions would be when eventually faced with the reality of Norma's death. I'd always thought I would receive the information from her solicitor by phone six thousand miles away and it would allow me to be less emotional or not be emotional at all.

I was still behind Reverend McLean when he stopped at the Emergency desk. Okay, I decided, I'll follow him and he'll be the first to see Norma when we get to her room. Perhaps she wasn't dead otherwise the receptionist would have said so. Maybe protocol forbade her to say but even if that wasn't so I figured the vicar was used to seeing not only the living, but the almost living and of course the dead too. It was his job to bury them.

My mind still felt scattered and I wondered about the thoughts I was having and wasn't sure I liked what they were. I remembered what Anne, my therapist, had suggested many times as I struggled to understand so many mixed and uncomfortable thoughts. "Get in touch with your Shadow, Maggie, there's a lot to learn from your dark side and what it has to say." Maybe this was my Shadow causing problems again.

After my divorce, even though I was pleased the marriage was over, it left painful memories and I thought I knew how bitter I could feel when hurt. Obviously it was still there with Norma and just that much darker than I had realized. But at least I knew about it and could work on it later and even though I was concerned it still felt like my Shadow really didn't give a damn one way or another.

CHAPTER SEVEN

Dr. Suffolk was standing by Norma's bed when we opened the door and a nurse was adjusting the leads that came from under my mother's gown to the heart monitor. Norma's eyes were closed and across her right brow a large gauze pad was attached to her skin with white tape. I could see a small brown stain that I realized was blood. Her hands rested on the cover, the blue veins of one was punctured by an intravenous needle and taped tight. She looked pale and her lips were slightly open and relaxed, her mouth softened.

That's probably about as close to looking angelic as I'll get to see her, I thought. I couldn't get any nearer to the bed to see if she was really awake or pretending to be asleep. Ever the drama queen Norma knew when she had an audience so I didn't put it past her to milk even a situation such as the awful one she was in.

The doctor stepped aside as the vicar moved beside him and laid his hand lightly over Norma's fingers. She didn't move. Perhaps, I thought, she really was out although obviously not dead.

"How is she doctor?" I said from the foot of the bed. My voice sounded concerned and that pleased me.

Dr. Suffolk peered at me over his glasses. "Your mother is okay. In shock. Nasty bump. Cat scan normal. May have a little concussion though. Gave her a sedative. Help her relax. She was hyperventilating and not happy to be here." He was writing something on her chart while he was speaking. "Not happy at all. Said she was fine. Wanted to go home. Hmmm, determined lady."

I suddenly wondered if this would prolong my visit then realized I was thinking about me again. Another Norma characteristic. "How long do you want to keep her here?"

"Best to keep her under observation. Won't know until she's fully awake tomorrow. Don't worry. Elderly are prone to falls. Fortunate it wasn't worse. Call if you have questions." His white coat flapped open as he brushed past me and out of the door.

The nurse followed him and Reverend McLean pulled up a chair next to the bed and sat down.

"Ah, your poor mother, your poor, poor mother. I'm so sorry. So very sorry." He was gently tapping her hand lightly and it was beginning to irritate me. On some level, I thought, it was probably annoying the hell out of Norma, too.

"She's not *dead* you know. She just fell and the Doctor said there was nothing seriously wrong, although she could have concussion ... but you probably heard that too."

I realized I had been expecting the worst and was experiencing a sense of relief tinged with disappointment. I didn't want to think of why, it seemed too unsympathetic. Maybe the vicar was expecting me to react the way he considered a loving daughter would; to be distraught or demonstrative in some way. Dealing with this unexpected emergency added a new element of wondering how to behave or what to think. Well I had no desire to lean and kiss Norma's quiet face and tears weren't necessary. But I didn't want him hovering there either. "She'll live," I said, "and if you have something else to do, there's no reason for you to stay. Why don't you go?" I sounded clipped and efficient and cold and very different from the sensitive person I preferred to think I was.

He seemed surprised and started to stand then sat down with a thump, and his Bible fell off his lap and onto the floor. He leaned forward and scooped up the slips of paper that had fallen out. I had noticed similar pieces the day in the parking lot and wondered what he jotted down; perhaps it was thoughts of a sermon and I wondered what kind of focus that took to think of the spiritual well-being of others when I couldn't manage that for myself.

I felt bad though. I knew I was being unfriendly and it was totally unnecessary. I reminded me of Norma and realized it was an effort to remain in control when I felt I was losing it. Perhaps that was her problem too. She had to stay in control because otherwise it permitted someone else to step in and take over and for that trust was involved.

I couldn't think of anyone I fully trusted since Grandmother. Not even Daddy because he hadn't been able to help me with Norma. I wondered who could trust me. Mewfus? My cat? That didn't say much about who I was but browbeating the vicar wasn't the solution although I wasn't sure how to change the direction of the conversation. Poor guy, he probably meant well, and annoying as he was, his concern was most likely genuine and more heartfelt than mine. I waited for him to get up but he remained where he was and stared at me before lowering his gaze.

"You don't like me very much, do you?" he said.

I blinked and jerked my head back in surprise. I certainly never expected that to come from him and glanced at my mother. Her face was still unmoving. She was asleep and lightly snoring. I looked back at the vicar unsure of what to say. I felt suddenly exposed as though he had seen directly into my head. Could priests do that? He had caught me off guard and I was surprised to hear my answer. "Er …" I hesitated. "Well to be honest, no I don't actually. I'm sorry if it was that obvious." I meant it but the confusion that had disturbed me returned and I wasn't sure what I thought.

"Why? What have I done to make you think that way?" His expression was calm, but he tilted his head, his pale face slightly flushed and waiting for an answer.

"Nothing really. No. Nothing at all." Now I was feeling uncomfortable. It was like a confession that was being extracted against my will. Why should I tell him what I thought? I needed to understand that myself before voicing it to someone I hardly knew.

"It would help me if you could provide more ... more details on why." His voice quavered and dropped so that it was more difficult to hear over the sound of the monitor and Norma's breathing. "My work isn't the easiest one but it's what I've chosen to do." He looked at me, his eyes fixed on my face. "If you don't like me I must ... I must know so that I can do a better job."

I felt terrible. I wished I'd said nothing or lied. I couldn't remember anyone who had asked me for something so personal although I knew the feeling. It was something I had wanted to ask Norma so many times during her life but never had the courage. I didn't want to be rejected either.

I took a breath, and decided to be more gentle. I ran the answer through my mind before I did and wished Norma would wake up so the conversation would end right there but I owed him a careful response. "It's probably me. In fact I think it is. My problem. Not yours." I fiddled with the cotton blanket on the bed. How did you tell a vicar, or anyone, what you thought of them? Goddam Shadow, I thought. This was just the thing I didn't want to get involved in. The room was so quiet and I felt the need to communicate more fully. Maybe, I decided, I can tell him and be honest for a change no matter how difficult it was. I'm going to have to deal with him later so better to do it now. Nobody said I had to like him but even that felt as if it was changing. My Shadow was becoming a chameleon. "Are you sure you want to know?"

He sat with his thin knees together like a little black bird perched on the chair. "Yes. Yes please."

I hesitated. By contrast, the room was so white and sterile. So unfriendly it wasn't the place to be mean. But then nowhere was.

"It's your manner ..."

"My manners?" He looked up quickly. "How strange. I thought I was polite. At least I try to be." A frown creased his brow and he looked puzzled. "Oh, maybe you should be sitting here." He started to rise.

"No. Don't get up. I'd prefer to stand. It's not your *manners*, it's your *manner*. The way you express yourself."

"I don't understand. What's wrong with it?"

Okay, I thought, this is getting nowhere and making things worse. I took a deep breath and slowly exhaled. "I think you're disingenuous. You overdo the good reverend bit. It comes across as fawning and insincere. Maybe it works for some but it's annoying to me and that's probably what you're sensing." There, I thought, I've said it.

I felt my armpits dampen and started to sweat, my shirt clinging to my skin. Confrontations tended to do that. I felt uncomfortable and wanted to leave. But telling him hadn't made me feel any better either. In fact I felt worse although pleased I was being honest. It was confusing.

"Disingenuous. Fawning." He mumbled. It wasn't a question but a flat repetition of what I'd said. Then his voice rose slightly, "Insincere? Really? You find me insincere?"

I decided I had transferred my dislike to where it belonged but he looked devastated. He looked the way I often felt. It was the first expression I had seen that I could relate to.

"Well yes. Actually I do— or did. Like I said, it's probably just me although you tend to overdo solicitous, then it becomes obsequious and reminds me of Uriah Heep and becomes unctuous." Maybe I had gone too far, obsequious would've been enough and Uriah Heep was a lot worse. Well he asked. I was feeling defensive and didn't like that either.

"Dear God. Is that how I appear to you? Perhaps to everyone?" His face turned pale and he slumped further into the chair.

If ever I had seen a forlorn expression, his was one. So the guy underneath that man of God exterior was real after all. I noticed his hands again and they were shaking. Then I remembered how he had placed one on Norma's when we first came in and was something I had yet to do.

"Not sure I can speak for everyone and now I think I was definitely too harsh on you." I said. "I'm sorry. I shouldn't have spoken so frankly."

"No, I asked you to." His voice seemed stronger.

"You may have a difficult job, but you did choose to do it." Then annoyed with myself thought, who am I to tell him what to decide.

"Yes. You're right and you know I do … I do find it a bit of a challenge. He started to look around him and squirmed, clutching the Bible so that the knuckles of his already white hand seemed to gleam. "Can I be honest with you, Margaret?"

I wondered what he was about to say and said, "Of course. god knows I've been honest with you, and please, call me Maggie." I rather hoped he wasn't about to tell me I reminded him of my mother although felt I deserved it.

He seemed to struggle with his words. He looked over at Norma as if to confirm she was asleep and not listening to what he wanted to say. He seemed undecided whether to tell me and hesitated.

He coughed slightly, then reached over Norma's table and removed a tissue, shook it and blew his nose.

Now what? I thought, I've made the poor guy cry. I stood irresolute. Why was it that when someone was sad I didn't know what to do. Had Norma made me resistant to sympathy? I didn't like to think so but reaching over and putting my hand on his shoulder didn't seem appropriate either. I waited while he took control of his voice.

"This is such a small village ..."

"Is that what you want to tell me?" I tilted my head and looked at him, puzzled.

"No. You were honest and yes, forthright, and perhaps that's why I asked because I believe Americans are that way and you're from California."

"Not everyone, although in L.A. you're probably right about that." I still wasn't sure where he was going with this and remained quiet.

He paused then continued. "There are not a lot of people I can talk to here. In fact none on a personal level. I feel you might be the only person I can be open with."

"Me? A stranger and after I've been so rude to you?"

"Not rude. I sense something deeper in you than that."

He was able to sense depth in me yet I had dismissed looking beyond what I saw as superficial in him? I felt apologetic but curious and wanted to make amends. "So how can I help? What do you want to say?"

"I'm gay."

I stared at him. I wasn't sure what to expect but not that. "You're what?"

"Yes, yes. I thought that would be your reaction." He shook his head back and forth and bit his lip, "But yes I'm gay."

"So?"

He stared at me and his mouth quivered. "So I took the vow of chastity not to sin."

How do I deal with this? I thought. What am I supposed to say now? But I wanted to reassure him. "Being gay isn't a sin. At least not in my book. It's a state of mind. It's a sexual preference. It's who you are."

"Yes but I try to compensate. Obviously I overdo it." He smiled bleakly.

I wondered how to be supportive. "You shouldn't have to. So you think being especially nice and caring to the point of being ... " I didn't want to repeat the words I had used earlier. They had totally lost their meaning with respect to him.

"Fawning?" He smiled up at me and tears made his eyes glisten. I remembered thinking he looked liked a Botticelli painting of a beautiful woman the first time I saw him. He certainly looked beatific now.

"I was wrong to say that although perhaps it needed to be said otherwise we wouldn't be talking like this now. I get the impression, though, that you wish you were straight. Do you?"

"Yes, of course, Mar ... Maggie." He sniffed and reached for another tissue.

"Why of course?"

"Because then I could do my job with a clear conscious. Being straight would remove some of my struggle."

"Could you be?"

"What? Straight? No, otherwise I would be so I assume this is my cross to bear." He crumpled the tissue and put it in his pocket. The action seemed determined and without the fluttery motions he generally had.

I felt I was flailing in a swamp with nothing to hold on to. Damn, I thought, I'm not a psychologist to be of any help, but I was careful in choosing my words.

"One's sexuality shouldn't be such a painful issue. It's who you are." I thought of my sessions with Anne where I wondered if my dislike of having sex with Richard was a fault of mine until I saw it was an incompatibility between us. It seemed like a similar situation here between him and the church and society. "Have you spoken with anyone about this? Talked to a professional?"

"I'm a priest. Remember?"

"Does that make it impossible?"

"It's not something I could discuss. Especially with strangers and I was afraid people—my parishioners—would find out and perhaps reject me and the work I have to do."

"Why? You think you're the only gay guy in the church?"

"I know I'm not but in a small village such as this the thinking isn't quite as accommodating as in a larger city. And even the church itself has very mixed views on homosexuality."

"But you're a guy first and a gay guy who's in denial and sharing your problem will help." I realized what he must have gone through to keep his secret and the torment it must have caused him. I wanted to hug him he seemed so dejected. "I'm beginning to realize I was totally wrong and owe you a huge apology."

"No, no apology," he said. He shook his head as though regretting having told me, "Perhaps I shouldn't have burdened you with my problem, though."

We had forgotten about Norma and she stirred, her arm moving across the cover. Reverend McLean and I paused and looked down. She sighed and then released a loud belch, her mouth remaining slightly open and her eyes closed, still asleep. The vicar looked startled and glanced at me. We both smiled and then laughed. She would have been mortified if awake but I thought, it's okay Norma, even refined ladies have to burp occasionally, but the laughter had eased some of the tension in the room.

I turned back to him. "I'm glad you did tell me," I said, "and church or no church and even with narrow minded parishioners— although they may not be as prevalent as you think—you need to be more lenient on yourself." It occurred to me that perhaps the same thought could apply to me but I pushed that from my mind. "I can't believe you've struggled to handle this alone all these years."

"I have God."

"Has that helped?"

"Sometimes but not enough and I question my faith because of that."

"Well I don't want to seem insensitive, but perhaps you need to find help elsewhere in addition to God. If there is a God ..." I stopped as his expression changed so ameliorated what I was about to say "...perhaps He or She has already helped provide a solution since you reached out to me. We've got options and one can either sit and stew or try and do something to change a difficult situation." I had the thought I was also referring to myself again, but added, "You really do need to discuss this with someone who fully understands these issues."

He shook his head. "It was difficult to tell even you."

"Is the Church so opposed to gay clergy?"

"Yes and no although it's considered a sin if homosexuality is practiced." He glanced over at me, obviously deciding whether to divulge something more. "I don't but I would ... I would like to have a partner with whom to share my life and still remain an integral part of the church. I love what I do."

It seemed we had similar thoughts of spending life alone. "The Church only blesses heterosexual unions?"

"Yes."

"Is that the final thinking on the matter?"

"It's become a subject of much discussion. That and female priests. Now if I was to live in America or Canada I could." He smiled, " But I'm not there and must deal with my situation here."

I wished I could wave a magic wand and make things right for him. "I'm sure there are gay doctors and therapists if you don't want to confide in someone straight. Perhaps I can help you search for a professional on line who is fairly close by. Surely there must be." I wished I had a computer to start and check right there. I felt so much closer to him than I would've believed earlier but decided we should probably save more of the conversation for another time. "I think my mother's going to be out for a while but if not I wouldn't want her to be a part of this if she wakes. If you'd like to chat some more call me," then added, "about anything. I'd really like that." I looked in my purse and handed him my card. "Here's my cell phone number and you won't have to call the house and have Norma answer if she gets home. She'll want to know more than she should."

Reverend McLean stood up and patted Norma's sleeping hand. "Well, I had intended to stay but there's not much point now. I'll stop by again later." He smiled at me. "So. Obsequious, huh?"

"Yes, well, I don't think so now but you're the antithesis of my mother. You both go to extremes but she means it and knows exactly what she's doing. I think you just overdid nice, Reverend."

"Bless you, Maggie. And please call me John. I feel as though God sent you."

"I'll never know that for sure but pleased I could be of some help, John. And you've helped me too. But we all have problems and worrying about being gay shouldn't be one of yours. At least that's how it seems to me." Then I laughed.

"What's funny?" he said.

I hesitated but decided to tell him the thought I'd had. "Norma thinks you're soft on her," and laughed again.

His mouth dropped and his eyes widened. "Oh dear heaven. Now I really must work on that attitude." He shook his head but laughed with me. "This has been such an interesting and fruitful day although I suspect your poor mother wouldn't agree." Norma moaned slightly although her eyes were still closed.

I thought that if she knew what had transpired this last hour she might choose to never wake up. I felt as energetically charged as I did after listening to Alex although not in quite the same way. Perhaps I shouldn't have been so brutally candid with John but I gained additional insight into myself and although it must've been painful for him he seemed happier than I had known him to be. He'd lost the conciliatory expression and seemed more relaxed. In fact I now really liked him and felt I could probably talk to him about anything if things got too intense with Norma. I had no intention of letting my Shadow overwhelm me when I was beginning to trust someone who had trusted me.

CHAPTER EIGHT

I decided to get back to the house while Norma was gone and to throw open the doors and windows to let some air into the place then look for Daddy's ashes and my grandmother's jewelry. I hated the thought that I was a snoop and knew Norma would be incensed if she ever found out. But it was rather exciting to do something she would hate me for and I could feel my adrenaline surge.

Cheryl's car was parked in the driveway when I got there. Since my arrival she generally parked in the street in front of the house so I was surprised it was blocking me from my spot. I wondered if she thought I would be at the hospital with Norma. Now I was annoyed because I knew I couldn't look for the earrings while she was there since she might tell Norma. But what reason did she have for being in the house when we were both gone?

I parked and quickly walked up to the front door. It was locked. Locked? Why if she was inside? I fumbled among my mother's keys for the front door, dropped them and they clinked onto the mat. I picked them up again and about to fit one into the door as Cheryl opened it.

"Hello," she said, "I thought you'd be with your mother." She stepped aside to let me in and closed the door. "How is she? Is she okay?" Then her face creased with concern. "Oh, you're home, does that mean that ..."

"... that she's *dead*? No she's fine, or as fine as she can be with that cut, but the doctor gave her a sedative to relax her a bit. She's sleeping or was."

"Thank goodness. She gave me such a scare this morning when I found her and you weren't here." She glanced at me and frowned slightly, before adopting a more neutral expression that left me no clue as to what she might be thinking.

It bothered me to think I was being judged. I didn't know the woman and we'd had very little communication since I'd arrived. What we did say was based primarily on chores. Perhaps Cheryl was resentful of my few requests, even though I was Norma's daughter.

Cheryl only worked when my mother was there. I felt I could be disapproving too. "Why are you here? I noticed your car was in the driveway. You must've left and come back again. Did you forget something?"

She had started to turn away as though ending the conversation but stopped and looked at me. "No, but I thought with your mother gone I could get some more work done and get the place in shape for when she returns." She indicated the vacuum that was plugged in the hallway. "After I called the ambulance and they took her away, I called Dina to tell you then went back home. It shook me up a bit and I needed to get away for a while."

"How did you get back in if you don't have a key?"

Cheryl looked uncomfortable and fiddled with the cord. "I thought it would be okay to leave the back door unlocked. I came in through there. Oh, I'm sorry. Perhaps I should've asked first."

That was reasonable. I felt I was being unfair to her like I had been to John. I'm just like Norma, I thought, distrusting everyone and being paranoid. I suddenly felt more charitable and wanted to make amends; not that I had done anything to cause Cheryl to feel upset but my thoughts softened. I didn't want any more tension although Cheryl had shown little inclination to talk when I first arrived and I had tried to be friendly. Screw it, I thought, enough of this. "Are you feeling okay yourself?" I said. "I'm sorry I wasn't here. Finding Norma must've been a shock. I think I would've been stunned too—and thank you for acting so quickly and getting her to the hospital."

Cheryl's face relaxed into a small smile and she looked pleased. "I was just relieved to think I was here. If today wasn't my day for coming, she might still be lying there until you got back."

Again that slight accusatory tone to her voice but I decided to ignore it. I had known it was her day to work and figured Norma would have help if she needed any while I was gone. I didn't really care if Cheryl thought it was wrong of me to go. If history was any indication, Norma would find some reason to fire her when she got home anyway and then her disapproval would be better placed. But I was curious. "How did you find her?" I said.

"Right here." She pointed to the floor in front of the bathroom door. "I suppose she must've tripped and banged her head against the corner of the door. Poor old thing. Nasty cut over the eye and it scared me with all that blood."

"There was a lot of blood? Was she conscious?"

"Oh yes, it was running down her face, but she couldn't pull herself up and just lay there."

"Why didn't she use the walker?"

"She did. Took it to the bathroom. She must've lost her balance somehow and it tipped over."

I knew the thing was a little shaky and could go over if it took her unbalanced weight. I visualized Norma lying on the floor and felt a rush of sympathy at how helpless she must have felt.

"When she fell the first time, did you find her then too?"

"Yes. I used to tell her to be careful of the stairs but she would say she could manage. Shake me off. You know how she is?" She looked at me out of the corner of her eye then looked away again. "She can be a stubborn lady sometimes. I heard a clunk, clunk, clunk when I was in the kitchen, and there she was splayed out on the floor only it was at the bottom of the stairs. When I rushed to her she was unconscious. No blood but her foot was all twisted beneath her. She was all crumpled up and for sure I thought she was dead then." She added in a sudden rush of confidence, "It's mean of me, I know, but I'd rather have unconscious anytime than blood and awake. She made a real fuss about going to the hospital today and yelled at the paramedics as though they were killing her. You wouldn't have thought it possible for an old lady with a cut head to be so angry."

I remembered an earlier telephone conversation with Norma after the first fall. She wanted to be home and out of the hospital even then.

"No wonder you were shaken up." Then I said, "Did she ask for me?"

Cheryl pursed her mouth and shrugged. She looked uncomfortable. "In a way."

"What do you mean, 'In a way'?"

"Well, she said that ..." she stopped and began twirling the cord of the vacuum unwilling to go on.

I nodded for her to continue.

"She said, 'Why isn't that Margaret here? She's never been of any use.' I thought that was an odd thing to say about your daughter."

"Never of any use? Are you sure?" I had never heard Norma express her dislike in quite that way before.

"Yes. Perhaps I shouldn't have said anything." She moved the vacuum in front of her. "Do you mind if I run this a bit while you're here?" She leaned over to plug it into the wall socket.

I didn't want to hear the vacuum. I wanted quiet and to be alone. "You know, Cheryl, my mother's going to be in hospital for a few more days. They want to keep her there for observation. Why don't you take the day off and go home and rest. I can clean up a bit. It will give me something to do when I'm not with her."

Cheryl looked surprised. "I couldn't possibly let you do that."

"Why not? I *have* been doing some cleaning around here already." I glanced toward the hall closet. I figured Cheryl knew about me removing the soiled pads. The place smelled better as a result.

"That's very nice of you, Margaret." That was the first time she had called me by name. I figured we were making progress.

"Maggie. Call me Maggie. Only Norma calls me Margaret and I hate that name. It reminds me of all the times she used it when she was annoyed—which seemed like most of the time."

"I'll do that then, Maggie. And I know you cleaned out there." She nodded toward the closet. "I really appreciated that. It made me gag when I found them, so I left them there." She looked down and away and from me, her face flushing slightly.

"The place smelled anyway," I said, "and they only made it worse. Do you have any idea why she put them there?"

"I think at first she might have been embarrassed and not wanted me to know but then they piled up and it just got worse especially since she was unable to walk far. She wouldn't have mentioned it. It was too personal and she's a proud lady."

I nodded. "That makes sense. Do you know how long she's been incontinent?"

"I think it was before she fell and not really incontinent, she just seemed to go more frequently. She could still go to the bathroom and get up the stairs before that but it was the getting down that was the problem. She was slower, probably with arthritis and couldn't make it to the bathroom in time and started using the towels."

"Oh my god! *Towels*?" I hoped that the clean ones I was using hadn't been put to that use.

94

"Don't worry. I tossed those and that's when I started bringing her the pads. She didn't want to discuss it. I had asked her if she wanted me to get her some when I went shopping but she got angry and said it was none of my business."

"I can imagine her saying that. But you got them anyway and she still refused to talk about the problem." I was feeling friendlier toward Cheryl and relieved that I could discuss this with her.

"Yes but I didn't know what she was doing with the used ones. I didn't want to ask. When I figured it out, I opened the door and closed it shut again." Her arm went through the motion of opening a door and pulling back. "It was too much and I was so happy when they were gone. I thought I was going to have to quit because of it. I felt it should've been my job and you had to do it for me. I'm sorry."

So that was it. The poor woman felt guilty. Small wonder she was as uncommunicative as she had been. There was a subtle irony about the whole thing and I smiled—brought together by Norma's soiled pads. Between her and John, Norma was inadvertently creating new friends for me with quite unexpected people.

"Not a problem and absolutely nothing you should feel sorry about. Thank you for everything you do. Now go home and rest. Call me tomorrow if you like and we can discuss when you'll come back. Consider it a holiday." I fumbled in my bag for my wallet. "Here's some money for your time. I don't want you to be out of pocket because of it." I handed Cheryl fifteen pounds.

At first she hesitated and took a step back, holding up her hands. "Maggie, you don't have to do that. Mrs. Resnick generally gives me a check for the week. It's really okay and very nice of you."

I persisted. "I'm very grateful and I'd like you to have it. You've had to put up with Norma's outbursts and her …. her personal stuff so I'd like you to have it."

95

"Yes, well then, thank you. I could certainly use it and I appreciate it." Cheryl took the money. Then she smiled and said, "It was my birthday this week and I'll consider this another lovely gift and my husband's taking me out to dinner tonight to celebrate." Then she added, "Should I put the vacuum away before I leave?"

"Well, happy belated birthday and no, it's not necessary to do anything more here, thanks. But I have to call the hospital to see if Norma's awake and how she's doing."

"If you get chance to speak to her say hello for me. Tell her I'll pop by to see her later."

"I will and oh, Cheryl, while you've been here have you seen where Norma put my father's ashes? She said they were in a cupboard."

"Ashes? Mr. *Resnick's* ashes?"

"Yes. Have you seen them?"

Cheryl looked stricken. Her mouth opened then closed as she stared at me before she said slowly, "Mrs. Resnick didn't say?"

"No she was rather vague about them." I looked more closely at her face and could see she was struggling whether to tell me. "What is it Cheryl?"

"There are no ashes. Mr. Resnick had a stroke but he's not dead although maybe the poor man should be."

I stepped back. I felt as though I had been delivered a blow. "Not dead? Where is he then if not here?"

"He was quite paralyzed and in a nursing home somewhere closer to the city. Oh Maggie, you look so shocked. Are you alright?" She reached out an arm to steady me as I grasped the handle of the vacuum. "I thought you knew—that your mother would've told you." She shook her head. "I only went there once to take Mrs. Resnick and she never asked me to go again and I don't think she has either. I don't remember the name of the place but can find out for you if you like."

I nodded. Speechless. My father wasn't dead and Norma had led me to believe he was. It was almost diabolical. I'd been there a week and hadn't been told and if not for the fall and talk with Cheryl might never have known. I wondered if John knew. "Thank you Cheryl. I think I need to be alone with this information by myself for a while. If I'm not here when you remember the name of the place, leave me a message although hopefully I can find it among my mother's papers."

As Cheryl left and got in her car and started the engine, I wondered why I had thought ill of her. The news of my father filled me with fury toward Norma but excitement at seeing him alive again along with dread over what I would find. As I headed upstairs towards what used to be his little home office, not much larger than a walk in closet with a tiny window, thoughts of finding the jewelry were unimportant compared to locating his whereabouts even though it meant delving through Norma's files. But screw it, I thought, now I want to know where everything is and certainly felt justified in knowing.

My heart was pounding as I pushed open the door. Suddenly I was a kid again and prying into my mother's things. Norma kept her life hidden, both inside her head and her possessions outside and knew where everything was. If the contents of a drawer were disturbed Norma would know and there would be hell to pay if she thought someone other than she who had touched them.

My mother rarely left me alone in the house when I was a kid, but I took advantage of her absence when she did. I'd carefully go through her closets and drawers and carefully snoop through her things. I don't think I would have thought of doing that if Norma hadn't always accused me of being nosy. I was about eleven when it occurred to me that if I was being accused of something that I didn't do perhaps there was something Norma didn't want me to find. So I was curious and looked with a deliberation and care to keep things the way I found them.

I'd looked in the desk and carefully replaced the bills and papers that were there, but it was mostly my father's stuff and I found it all boring. I preferred to look in my mother's dressing room and examine her makeup. There were always new lipsticks and perfumes and I had to be careful of the scent. If she knew they'd been meddled with and could smell them on me she'd be furious.

But it was her underwear drawer that fascinated me most. Until then, I didn't know what my mother wore beneath her clothes and without too much analyzing figured she wore the same cotton underwear as I did. Because her dressing was a private matter looking at Norma's bras and panties was intriguing. I was seeing my mother undressed when I wasn't supposed to and my own developing body and mind made me even more curious. I'd hold the lacy bras to my chest then become terrified that Norma would know and so would carefully fold and replace them, my heart beating while I listened for her unexpected return and dreaded her confronting me if she found out.

When it seemed my investigations went unnoticed, I became more confident and looked further and became adept at replacing everything the way I found it. Once, tucked away in the back of one of her drawers I discovered a letter that had been torn and taped back together. It wasn't Daddy's writing and I had trouble reading it. It became a challenge to understand and because of the mystery was the first thing I looked for when Norma left me alone.

When I eventually deciphered the words I was puzzled and it preoccupied me. I re read them over again as I carefully scanned the lines, looking beyond the ragged tears under the tape and crease of the paper. I began to realize that it referred to a relationship Norma had when I was small. It was her secret that became mine and I never told anyone what I had discovered.

As I got older and understood what was involved it angered me to think that she had betrayed my father, and what I committed to memory of the letter I still recalled.

Norma darling, this thing between us must end be-fore it gets more complicated than it already is. I'm sorry if this letter comes as a shock but I didn't have the courage to tell you personally. I've given it a lot of thought but I never did like kids and having one that doesn't belong to me isn't in my plans, even if she is yours - but then neither was having the wife of some-one else. You could always get a divorce but a child changes everything. It's been fun and I do care for you and want to remember it that way. By the time you re-ceive this I will have moved and left for Canada. It will make the ending easier on both of us where we won't be tempted to resume what can no longer be because of all the dynamics we chose to ignore. Love, Bob

I was about four when Norma forbade me to pick up the mail that dropped through the letter box to the mat below and put it on the hall stand as I used to do; instead she would race for the mail herself when the letterbox rattled. The postman was usually prompt regard-less of the weather and sometimes she would wait at the gate for him and sort through the mail there.

I was hurt and puzzled why this little job was taken from me. I liked to arrange the envelopes in size; big ones to the back and the exciting ones, like postcards in front and so I asked why I could no longer do that. Norma had scowled and told me to shush, so I asked my father, who was at work when the mail was delivered, "Daddy, why won't Mummy let me pick up the post anymore?"

He'd lowered his newspaper slightly and said, "Don't know, Sweetheart. Norma, why can't she?"

"She's careless and drops it. I found some bills that had slipped behind the hallstand and into the umbrella holder. They were a mess. The water from the umbrellas had made them soggy."

I knew I hadn't dropped anything. Later, Norma had taken me roughly by the arm and said, "Don't disobey me, young lady, and don't bother your father with stupid questions. He's too busy to have to think about your little outbursts." It was about that time Norma had become more unreasonable. What had once been signs of irritability became angry attacks on me and my father that became progressively worse.

Years later, after I had found and finally understood the letter, folding it carefully and replacing it again in the back of the drawer it had disappeared when I looked for it again. I realized it wasn't something Norma would accuse me of reading, because then she would have to admit it existed. Perhaps she had waited for another letter and one that never came.

I sometimes wondered if my mother had suspected I'd discovered the one I read and had destroyed it or hidden it somewhere else. I figured it was probably under her mattress or maybe she threw it on the fire when nothing else was forthcoming. She'd already tried to rip it once and changed her mind to repair the damage. Just like I used to change my mind about Richard, hoping to somehow repair the damage he caused and was a topic discussed during my many sessions with Anne. Unlike my father, my husband was charismatic and exciting, and perhaps Bob had seemed the same way to Norma.

Richard was, and still is, a commercial airline pilot and on a layover from the States when we first met. He'd come into Grandmother's shop for flowers and flirted with me, a then naïve and shy girl of nineteen. The flowers were for someone else and except that he was handsome and charming, I didn't give it more thought until I received a little card from him saying that the next bouquet would be for me. I was intoxicated by the attention. A few weeks later he called the shop and invited me out to dinner.

Grandmother Clare wasn't happy about me going and said she hoped she was wrong but didn't trust him but that I had to make my own decisions and learn from them. Three months later Richard proposed and wanted to take me back to the West Coast. I was afraid and excited and in love—or so I thought.

Daddy gave his reluctant permission and Grandmother her blessing although never warmed to my new husband. Norma claimed she was too busy to attend the wedding that was a small civil ceremony in London and, I later realized, a paperwork convenience by Richard for me to get a green card. Of course I had always dreamed of a formal white wedding but the excitement involved lessened the disappointment. Grandmother, though, had insisted on a long gown and made the bouquet of mixed wildflowers herself. She wanted it to be a simple comment on what she considered to be a complex situation. She was right.

Richard's schedule led me to expect hours and days and nights away from home because of his job. What I came to understand was that he also considered it his job to make as many conquests outside of the marriage during that time as well. I wanted to believe he loved me and perhaps he did but not enough to be faithful. Rather like Norma I suppose. Capricious and self-serving.

But I wasn't interested in my mother's disloyalty and her old love letter now though; I needed her files and the jewelry box I'd initially wanted to check was unimportant compared to finding out where my father was. I quickly rifled through the paperwork and there

Morrine Depolo

it was—a statement from Aidenscroft Manor Nursing Home, a good forty-five minute drive from the house. I looked carefully at the telephone number and picked up the receiver to call but as I did so it rang loudly and the unexpected noise startled me.

I still felt guilty for going through Norma's stuff although I was furious and my hands shook as I gripped the receiver. How dare Norma claim Daddy was dead and if it wasn't for Cheryl I might never have known. There was a time I expected Norma to suddenly appear behind me, and if not the actual presence then my own imagination created powerful images of an enraged mother. It was as though part of me never grew up. I was still a little kid; afraid of getting into trouble. When I learned the facts though, then it would be her to feel guilty—if she was even capable of such an emotion.

The phone continued to peal and I hesitated. I wanted to have everything straight in my mind before I confronted Norma but perhaps it was the hospital to say that she had taken a turn for the worse. Nah, I thought, doubt it, not if Dr. Suffolk was right so held the receiver to my ear. "Hello!" My voice was shaking.

"Where *are* you?" Norma yelled. "I'm here in the hospital and could've been killed and my head's all wrapped in bandages and this may be very serious—not that you'd care."

I wanted to blast the woman and say I didn't give a shit, she could die for all I cared, instead I decided to act as normally as possible. "I *was* there, Norma, and so was Jo … Reverend McLean." I decided it would be best not to call him John. "You were asleep and Doctor Suffolk said you'd be okay."

I could hear her breathing heavily with little catches in her breath as though in pain. She's laying it on a bit thick, I thought and said, "There's nothing broken. You're just unhappy you're there."

"Really? No. This place is like the Hilton. It's wonderful!"

"Well that's great! Then you won't want to leave in that case."
I imagined Norma's face becoming puffy with irritation and waited
for the expected backlash and pleased I had the phone and distance
between us.

"Margaret, I want you to get me out of here. *Today!*" Norma's
voice had risen and she caught her breath and began to cough. "Now
you've made me cough."

"You're in the best place right now."

"Then I'll leave without you."

"So you're just gonna trot out of there, weak as you are and
with a bad ankle?"

That silenced her.

Maybe she forgot about her ankle, I thought, and thank god
she can't walk otherwise she would have released herself already. But
I wasn't ready for that.

"I *want* you to get ..." Norma's voice trailed off and suddenly
became soft and weak sounding. "Why *hel-lo*, Reverend McLean.
How *nice* of you to come. I'm sorry I'm such a mess but ..." then I
heard a click and the phone went dead.

I smiled. Norma had a new and more sympathetic audience,
poor John. But it left me time to call the nursing home about Daddy.

CHAPTER NINE

Mrs. Hargreaves, the nurse administrator of Aidenscroft Manor Retirement Home, had been charming over the phone when I called to ask about my father. At first she was hesitant and inquired politely if I was Mrs. Resnick, his wife, and when I said that no I was his daughter, she seemed immediately friendlier and asked how she could be of assistance. I wondered if Norma had made things difficult for him there.

"We knew he had a daughter in the States," Mrs. Hargreaves said. "Would that be you?"

I said yes, and she asked if I was calling from there. When I told her I was fairly close by and wanted to see him she became almost animated and reminded me of John when he got excited over something. "How lovely," she said. "We never thought we'd get to see you here. Mrs. Resnick said that you were … you were …" She hesitated.

"I was what?" I asked as gently as I could. What had Norma told them? Quite possibly it was a lie.

"Well, perhaps I shouldn't say, but we rather thought you were alienated from the family and weren't to be contacted. Next of kin is Mrs. Resnick although Mr. Resnick keeps your photograph by his bed." She paused, "We have wondered about that."

"Really? No I'm very concerned about him," I said. My thoughts were zipping through my head. I'd got the impression from

Cheryl that my father was perhaps mentally incapacitated and since Norma wouldn't have provided the photograph perhaps he had taken it himself and was more aware than I thought.

Mrs. Hargreaves seemed rather chatty and considering she didn't know me from Adam had commented on more personal matters. I wondered about the privacy laws, and, hungry for information about what she could tell me, prompted her for more details. "I understand he had a stroke and wondered how bad that was. How's he doing?"

"We can't divulge that information over the phone," she said, "and so sorry but would you like to visit and see him for yourself? Perhaps," she added, "we can provide more details then."

"I was thinking of coming now."

"Excellent, excellent," she said. "Do you know where we are?"

She could be a relative of John's, her profuseness seemed exaggerated but I wasn't about to make the same mistake twice of finding someone obsequious before I knew them. I smiled and hoped it would be transmitted through the phone line. "Only the name and the address I got from the invoice I found among my mother's papers. Can you tell me how to get there?" I knew that the route would probably involve some new challenges with freeways or motorways as they were called and hesitated and she picked up on that immediately.

"Are you used to the trunk roads?" she asked.

I had visions of me trying to deal with the English traffic although never had problems on the L.A. freeways. "No," I said.

"Well if you don't mind a slightly longer drive then I can give you directions for that although even some of those roads can be intimidating for someone not used to driving. But," she added, "I'm sure you'll do just fine."

I wasn't as confident as Mrs. Hargreaves credited me with being, but I wrote down the directions and wished I had a connection to the Internet for a visual map. She explained that I was to look for the name Aidenscroft Lane after many described twists and turns to get there. "Named after the Manor you know," she said. "The sign's tucked between a tall hedgerow but can still be seen from the road. It has a beautiful picture of a Peregrine Falcon although that really needs to be repainted," then added "and although it's a teeny bit hidden we think it adds privacy." I could hear her smile as she said that. "If you have problems finding us pull over and call and we'll direct you from there. I think your father will be happy to see you. He doesn't get any visitors."

Her directions had been clear and I found the place easily although not without some anxious moments. She was correct about the traffic and I was pleased I'd not taken the motorway. I'd grown almost complacent with the quiet countryside driving I'd been doing until then, but discovered the speed of traffic, along with the big trucks or lorries as they're called, were intimidating. I infuriated several drivers who found me too slow as they honked and zoomed around me and I felt like giving them the finger but gripped the wheel instead and simply muttered for them to fuck off. "Not friendly, Maggie," I said. "Not friendly at all."

My Shadow tended to be more confrontational while driving and given the chance could escalate itself into road rage where I sounded like a fishwife. Shelly had warned me that if that continued I could get shot by someone crazier than me. She was probably right although it didn't prevent me from expressing anger that way and was sort of a release and very satisfying to swear and not care because nobody heard me.

When I first read the name of the nursing home, I thought it was an oxymoron of sorts since a croft is a small farm and a manor is a large country estate, so I wasn't sure what to expect. When I finally saw the house as a mansion it took my breath away it was so lovely and looked nothing like the austere medical building I was expecting.

Aidenscroft Manor was beautiful—an enormous red brick and stone building with a steep gabled roof and square paned bay windows with thick ivy tendrils clustered around the frames, which had probably been growing that way for years. The wide driveway circled a large, manicured lawn with its carefully cut grass clearly reflecting the light and dark paths where it had been mown. Set within the center of that, a stone fountain surrounded by a lily pond, splashed water from the statue of a mermaid holding a conch shell. Flowers and shrubbery were everywhere in a heady landscape mix of formal and cottage gardens rampant with color.

Closer to the side of the building mature shrubs surrounded wrought iron garden furniture with furled, dark green sun umbrellas. I figured they were probably closed because of the rain, but how lovely, I thought, to sit in their shade when it's sunny. Daddy had certainly picked a great place to live although I hoped he was well enough to appreciate it. The stroke might have rendered him incapacitated but Mrs. Hargreaves' comment about my photograph encouraged me. Obviously his memory was still fairly good although by how much remained to be seen. I also wondered who had selected the place for him. Surely not my mother and wondered who had owned the house before it was remodeled into a nursing facility.

The hallway inside was spectacular with dark hardwood floors and wall paneling. A large staircase swept upwards and I thought of Norma who would've loved to have made a grand entrance down them, but then figured if she could fall down hers at home, a tumble from this would be more dramatic. Then I decided I was being mean again and the image was simply my Shadow reminding me to watch *my* step.

I stopped by the highly polished oak table to the right of the entrance, admiring the vase of mixed flowers that filled one end and since no one was sitting in the large, leather chair next to it, rang the bell placed there for attention. I could see carers pushing wheelchairs and others slowly walking and supporting elderly patients across the hall and into various rooms that branched off of it. I wanted to explore and see everything.

"Ah, you got here. Welcome, welcome. I'm Laurie Hargreaves."

If I'd imagined someone small and pale like John I couldn't have been more wrong. I looked up to the woman who emerged and who seemed to fill the door behind the desk. She was almost six foot tall and big and resembled a glorious Amazon. Her scoop neck blue dress exposed an expansive chest upon which lay a heavy gold chain with a carved dragon stone pendant that looked tribal. Her wiry grey hair was drawn up in a twist and held in place by a bone clasp that only seemed to emphasize her height. As she smiled down at me her dark eyes sparkled and white teeth dazzled from her beautiful black face. She radiated energy of strength and kindliness and I liked her immediately, spontaneously clasping her offered hand with both of mine.

"Your directions made it easy," I said, "and I *love* this place already. What a wonderful house this must've been in its time."

"I feel blessed to work here and it certainly lends itself to making our residents very comfortable and happy. I'll tell you a little more about it as we walk." She nodded as though it were a given and continued, "Yes, well let's do just that. Splendid." Then pausing, she leaned over the vase of flowers and sniffed among the petals. "Ooh," she breathed, "take a good whiff of these. So lovely. From the garden you know."

She waved her hand toward the door through which I'd come and I nodded, having seen at least a section of the grounds as I arrived. She continued, "The house belonged to Sir Peregrine Aiden who was a politician and great benefactor of his time," she said. "He had a fine eye for beautiful landscapes and architecture like our Prince Charles who also loves gardens and conservation. You can see his tomb in the little ancient church close by that he fully restored." She stopped and laughed, correcting herself before she trotted off again, "Oh, not Charles' effigy, dear me no, but Sir Aiden, recumbent in all his marble glory, poor soul."

I wondered if the little church was anything like John's and if it had an organ and if so who played it, but I was too preoccupied with the tour of the downstairs section and keeping up with her to ask and becoming more anxious and excited to see my father.

Mrs. Hargreaves was indicating with her strong arms as she was giving the tour. "Over there is our main dining room, we have another smaller one for snacks, and we have an excellent chef who's very careful to provide nutritious meals that our residents find appealing. Over here is the library, one of my very favorite spots to be. We can take a very quick peek if you like before I take you to the conservatory where Mr. Resnick is waiting. Perhaps you might like to sit with him here instead. It's more private but I'll let him make that decision." She was speaking about Daddy making the decision. My heart leaped and I wondered just how many decisions he could still make.

The double oak doors were wide open and I stared in fascination at the walls of books that reached to the beamed ceiling above as deep comfortable leather armchairs were set before an enormous carved fireplace. More flowers were arranged on side tables and the sound of the Vivaldi I'd heard in the lobby was also playing in here so figured it must be piped throughout the house. I felt I could spend hours in there myself and how very different it was to Norma's place. Daddy must feel like he's in heaven.

"This is so lovely," I said. "What it must've been like original-ly and to have lived here and claim it as one's own home."

"Well, Sir Aiden had an enormous staff. All the wealthy, in-fluential men did at the time, along with large families. They were certainly lords of their manors while the majority of their poor wives spent their time producing children and directing the staff in addition to being the gracious hostess." She touched my arm and smiled, "Think I would've rebelled if I was one despite the perks."

"Now," she said, "we're almost there. It's on the west side of the house that captures most of the sunlight. During the First World War, the manor and its magnificent grounds were made available to care for the wounded soldiers brought back from France, so it's al-ready got quite a varied history. Ah, there he is."

After walking through the dark paneling I was taken aback by the flood of light that poured in through the large French windows of a conservatory that opened onto a tile patio. The ceiling was high and instead of the oak and leather chairs I had observed in the rest of the house, this room was furnished with blond wicker chairs and settees with pillows and cushions in earth tones. More flowers topped side tables and it felt like an enclosed extension of the garden.

There were more people gathered in here than I had seen through some of the open doorways we had passed. Several elderly individuals sat together at a glass table, laughing and playing cards while others sat relaxed, watching the TV or reading. The wicker chairs looked comfortable and several had a cane leaning by the arm-rest, much like the one Norma used. But the place then wiped her from my mind as I looked around for my father and saw no one I rec-ognized. "I thought you said he was in here, Mrs. Hargreaves?"

"But he is," she said, "and do call me Laurie, everyone does." While she was talking she pointed to a corner of the room close by the windows. An elderly man sat quietly in his wheelchair, focused on where we stood, but I didn't recognize him. Frail and slightly balding, his stiff gray hair sprung from the side of his head and rested against his collar. His left side was obviously paralyzed because his hand lay bent and motionless in his lap and his leg jutted over the footrest. He had what looked like a small laptop in his right hand resting on a flat pillow against the arm of the chair. As I last remembered him my father was not only bigger but had dark hair slightly graying at the temples and cut short. Nothing like the man Laurie indicated.

"But," I hesitated, unwilling to go toward this stranger, "he doesn't look like my father."

"Mr. Resnick? Yes it's him and such a lovely man we all adore him even though he can't speak—at least not well. He uses his laptop to communicate with us."

"Laurie," I said, "before we go any further can you give me some more information." I placed my hand on her arm and drew her back into the hall. "Tell me what happened to him. My mother has told me nothing. Actually," I hesitated, "she said he was dead so all this is a complete unknown to me."

She looked at me surprised. Her head jerked to one side and she peered down into my eyes, "What an unkind thing to tell you. No wonder you didn't show up before now." She gazed toward where my father was sitting. "He had a stroke—an ischemic stroke—that has left him paralyzed down the left side of his body and although weak he can use his right side. The physical therapy is helping that get stronger. He's already so much better than he was a few months ago."

"Ischemic?" I said. "Are there different kinds of stroke?"

"Yes," she said. "The majority of strokes are ischemic and among those the effects can vary dramatically depending on the brain damage. Your father's stroke also caused aphasia that affected his speech so he's unable to talk."

That must've been why he never called me, I thought. "Anything else?"

"Among other things strokes can cause depression along with uncontrolled emotional laughter and or crying both. His vision is somewhat impaired but he can see and thank god for that because he's a reader and loves the library. That said, his glasses are a strong prescription and often he'll use a magnifying glass in addition to those."

I thought of my father and his love of books and suddenly realized that they were what was absent from the house. I'd forgotten. Norma must've cleaned them all out. "Daddy loved to read, yes. I imagine the library reminds him of his own collection. Pity he doesn't have his books now."

"Yes I think he does. We encourage personal items and furniture for our residents to make their stay remind them of what they loved at home. Later we can go to his room and you'll get to see for yourself. Are you ready for your visit now? I told him you were coming and he did smile and nod. Come," she said, indicating the chair. "Come say hello to your dad."

As I walked across the carpet toward him I was aware of the chatter around the card table stop momentarily. Perhaps they were interested in whom I was, but my eyes were blurry and I felt the tears roll down my cheeks. "Daddy?" I said, my voice quivering. I saw the right side of his mouth raise upward and while the left hung down the smile was his. "Oh Daddy, I missed you and so happy to have found you here." I leaned down and put my arms around his thin shoulders and kissed the top of his head then stood back and stared at him. Through his glasses, his eyes were the warm, hazel brown I remembered and they shone with the love I'd never seen in Norma's.

Laurie had hovered by our side as I reached and hugged him. "Do you want to stay here and chat, or go to your room or the library?" She asked him and waited while she looked down, I saw him carefully pick the letters from the keyboard and read. *room*

"Great then that's where we'll go." She unlocked the brake on the wheelchair and I saw how much newer and more efficient his was compared to Norma's. "Can he work this himself?" I asked although felt uncomfortable speaking about him in the third person as he sat there."

"Not really well since he's still weak but hopefully when he's had more physical therapy he will go further but I'll take you both there. He's on the ground floor although we have other rooms upstairs for those more ambulant."

I thought of the great hall staircase, "They can manage the staircase?"

Laurie laughed and I heard my father's familiar dry chuckle. The sound was like a gift from the gods. "Well some do but most don't. You probably didn't see the small elevators that we have to make it easier."

"My father ... Daddy you laughed."

"He can do that and does. He can make sounds but the words don't always come out as something comprehensible, do they Mr. Resnick? It's easier to chat with his laptop. Thank heaven for electronics, huh?"

We had left the beautiful sunroom and walked down a long carpeted hall that seemed more modern. It led past several doorways, some open and others closed. Each one that was open showed a different room, all with a bed but decorated with personal items of paintings and photographs and with different pillows and quilts. I wondered what my father's room would be like, and trotted to keep up with them. I realized that even though this was a retirement care facility it didn't have the familiar sanitized smell and atmosphere of a hospital when I visited Norma.

"Here we are," Laurie said. "When you're through just wheel him back to the conservatory. You may stay as long as you want but Mr. Resnick gets tired easily and we don't want to overtax him. Hopefully you'll be back again and very soon, now that you know where we are. You might want to stay for lunch too. I'd suggest dinner later, but perhaps the drive at night might be more difficult."

I nodded and thought of Norma and of having to visit her later. I knew what my druthers would be.

Laurie walked quickly from the room leaving Daddy and me alone as I looked around. A photograph that had been taken by Grandmother Clare of me as a teenager smiled out from a silver frame by his bed. What I remembered of his study was as though it had been transported through time and space, because a large bookcase against his wall looked like his old office. I reached out and clasped his hand and he held onto mine, the blue veins showing through the back of his skin and, unlike Norma's, I stroked it gently.

"So what's with the long hair," I said. "You look different and except that you're obviously restricted in so many ways, you're alive."

He slid his hand from mine and picked at the keys. *now im the boss* he wrote.

I laughed. He obviously meant Norma and I remembered her telling me he was dead. "Did you … did you know Norma said you had died?"

thot you were busy

I ached to think that he might have wondered why I hadn't been in contact with him. "Never and would've been here long before now. I'm so sorry."

He tapped again. *norma*

Obviously he didn't know. "She fell again and is in hospital. Concussion and ..." I hesitated, "but still feisty."

I heard him chuckle again. *not here tho - good*

"You're in the best place."

He was writing more and I waited. *had 2 have stroke 2 escape*

I laughed as he chuckled again. "That's really so sad, though, Daddy. I so wish it hadn't happened. Is there anything you need or that I can get for you?"

He shook his head and indicated the room and then the gardens one could see from his window.

"Yes beautiful and very peaceful." I wondered what else we could talk about and noticed his pipe resting on his small table. "Daddy, you're not still smoking that are you? It's probably what contributed to the stroke."

He shook his head and I watched him write. *just a reminder* His lopsided smile beamed out at me and then he pointed to his desk drawer, nodding his head and looking directly at me.

"You want me to open the drawer?"

He nodded again so I stood up and drew it from the desk. Among some pens and paper was a sealed envelope with my name written shakily on the outside. "This? For me?" He nodded again so I opened it, curious what it contained. It was his will. "Daddy, no. You're not going to die. Not now that I've found you."

He stooped over the pad and I watched him write. *u must have not norma*

"Thank you, though. I'm pleased to have this. It might make things easier when you do go. But you're not going anytime soon."

He was writing again. *u back now*

I felt awful. How could I tell him that I'd come for Norma and intent on returning to California. Then I thought of Alex and John and now him and somehow that decision wasn't so clearly a given in my head.

"I have to return home eventually ... soon but now I know you're here I can come visit and perhaps we can email when I go home."

He nodded then inexplicably began to cry. Tears poured beneath his glasses and ran down his grizzled cheeks. "Oh," I said searching for a tissue, "I didn't mean to upset you. I'm sorry." He shook his head as he wiped his eyes and began writing again. *not u it happens im happy*

I remembered what Laurie had told me about the sudden and often inappropriate tendency to cry or laugh or both and I leaned over and hugged him again, holding his frozen left hand, wondering if he had sensation and could feel it. "Happy is good," I said, "and if you have to cry at the same time then don't mind me."

I decided to learn as much as I could about strokes and what one could do to help those who had had one. Then I thought of Norma and it flashed that if anyone in the family was to have one then the wrong person had had it. I knew it was wrong to think that but whether prompted by my Shadow or not it could still hold some truth. It was for me to untangle what that was.

I looked up as Laurie knocked on the door. "How're you both doing?" she said. "Mr. Resnick are you getting tired?" He shook his head and looked up at me then back to her again. "Well," she said, "it occurred to me that since the rain is holding off and the sun's out you might want to take a stroll around some of the gardens." She looked directly at me and smiled, "He likes to do that, don't you Mr. Resnick?"

"Great idea, that would be lovely," I said and stood, releasing the brake as I had seen her do earlier. "Lead on."

As I was pushing him with his back to me I decided to tell him more about my life in California, about Mewfus and my job. I wondered if I should tell him about Alex and John and decided that if it seemed appropriate then I would. I figured he didn't want to know about Norma, nor did I want to discuss her or the earrings.

The garden was exquisite and as we wheeled along the path designed for wheelchairs and slower walkers my father raised his arm for me to stop. I leaned over his shoulder and watched him write *left*. I could see a smaller path that led off the one we were on and did as he requested. Within minutes we were beyond the manor with only its tall roof visible behind the distant trees. I walked slower and wondered where we were going.

He was obviously familiar with the place and I began to slow down as he moved his arm up and forward for me to continue. With just the imperceptible scrape of the wheels on the path the sound of the birds became more distinct in the silence. It was beautiful and calming and I wondered if Sir Peregrine Aiden had wandered this little trail himself a hundred years ago to think and be alone.

The shrubbery opened up and a large pond came into view. Tall bulrushes and Iris grew around the edge and I could see various mallards swimming and quacking toward us. Then I saw the swans gliding in our direction. "Do they come say hello?" I asked.

He nodded and dug into the side of his chair bringing up a napkin that he slowly peeled away to unfold the cloth and remove crusts of bread. I wanted to reach down and do it for him but decided it was more important he accomplished it by himself. By now the birds had waddled from the water and pushing toward us as he threw the pieces down for them.

It was all so serene and surreal at the same time. I saw he was crying again although surely it wasn't from being unhappy. I decided not to say anything about it. He would let me know by the rest of his behavior if he was sad.

"Do you come here often?" I asked, then laughed. "Obviously you do because they know you." I looked around and saw a carer walking towards us and pushing another wheelchair on the same path. She smiled and waved and the swathed and blanketed individual curled into the chair seemed oblivious to us being there. "Lovely day," the nurse called out before she disappeared again.

We watched in silence as the ducks and swans waddled back to the pond when they realized no more bread was forthcoming. I stood and breathed in the quiet and serenity that surrounded us. Definitely I would prefer being here with my father than being with Norma, although I was beginning to feel her nag at my mind. I had to get back fairly soon and also to avoid the afternoon traffic.

My father had been quiet and, I thought, reflecting too but as I leaned down saw he had fallen asleep. "Time to go back," I said quietly, "but just know that I'll come see you as often as I can."

As I wheeled him back into the Manor I wondered where I would find Laurie but she found us. The woman was a dynamo of quiet energy. "Ah," she said, "thought he'd fall asleep. Why don't you let me take him and you can either sit in the library or …"

I interrupted her. "Laurie you've been so kind and I appreciate your help but I must get back. Can I call you when I plan to visit again? Soon?"

"We have an open visiting policy so feel welcome anytime, and because of the constraints on your time, we'll try and make it easy for you. If you don't get me on the phone when you call then leave a message and I'll get right back." Then she smiled, her lovely face shone with pleasure, "And I'm so pleased you came to see your dad. You seem to fit in as though you belonged here." Her smile disappeared but then she grinned again, "Not as a patient of course, but as someone who genuinely loves the place. I could tell that about you right away."

Except for Alex and John and now my father, I hadn't felt as wanted and appreciated as I was here. I had the quick thought of what it would be like and without knowing where the words were coming from said, "Maybe I should apply for a job as a gardener. Looks like there's lot to maintain."

She became immediately serious. "You may be joking—or perhaps you're not—but are you qualified to do that?"

"I teach horticulture in California."

"Then you are and yes, excellent, we would love to have you with us. We often employ individuals who have family here. Why," she added, "we could be friends and if you like old churches I can take you to see Sir Aiden. There are some sketches he left of his beautiful restorations—you might enjoy seeing those, too."

"How interesting. I'd love that."

"Then if you ever decide to live here, I'll endeavor to find you a job in our garden. There are more than ten acres, you know, and that includes a large greenhouse, a smaller hothouse and a rather enormous vegetable garden not to mention a small orchard."

My eyes must have widened as she spoke because she laughed. "Don't let me overwhelm you with all that. We do have a team of gardeners but I was thinking that if you teach we could have you conduct small classes for our residents and the outside public who like to stroll and take in the scenery. We're always looking to increase the activities here."

I was astounded and just a little overwhelmed. Suddenly my life was opening up in ways I had never dreamed of or thought possible. And I had made another friend.

CHAPTER TEN

It was already mid afternoon by the time I left the nursing home and though I didn't want to go to the hospital or even care if I saw Norma again, I still had to drive past the church. As I passed the old grey stone façade surrounded by its wonderful large Oaks and Sycamores, I wondered if Alex was there. It was becoming my favorite place and I let up on the gas and began to slow down, unsure if I should stop or continue on but decided in a second and made a quick turn and pulled onto the gravel. There was no other car parked, but I knew he had walked with Kay the last time, so it was possible he had done so again.

I turned off the ignition and rolled down the windows and heard the strains of the organ. It reminded me of a Bach CD I had and knew if I went inside I'd stay there to chat when he was through playing and then I'd be really late for Norma. Hey, Maggie, I thought, it's a no brainer, Lady. She's gonna be pissed regardless of when I get there but still not as pissed as I am with her.

I opened the car door and clicked it closed. I didn't want to impose the slamming of a car door over the music before I walked up to the massive oak doors, pushed against them and went inside.

Alex was there with Kay. I walked quietly down the stone aisle and sat again in the first pew and smiled. This is becoming my seat, I thought. Kay saw me and her ears pricked forward as she lifted her nose and wagged her tail. Unaware I was there, Alex continued playing. This time he had the music, although he didn't appear to be reading it, his head and body moving in time to the music.

He stopped suddenly, and I began to rise thinking he would turn and see me but instead he leaned forward again, his face close to the paper and his hand against the score, running his finger along the page to check the notation, before commencing where he had left off.

I should've left then but settled back on the bench and watched his hands fly over the keys, his feet pressing against the pedals. I was beginning to feel guilty that I wasn't en route to the hospital and hoped John was there but that wouldn't be fair to expect even him to go twice in one day. I didn't know who else would visit Norma or who her friends were if she had any. No one had come to the house, although people at church seemed to know her but apparently not really well and with just a polite nod of recognition.

I decided to stay and listen to the end. I'd make some excuse about being late. I wasn't going to mention seeing Daddy and would leave that information until Norma came home. I was angry and she didn't deserve my sympathy but I wanted to pace myself and think carefully of what I would say. I didn't want her to know yet. Maybe I'd pick up some flowers or chocolates as a peace offering although it bothered me that I was being devious.

Angry as I was about my father I decided that I'd learn nothing if I antagonized Norma even more. I wanted to know why she had lied. I relaxed against the hard back of the wood seat and decided I'd leave after saying hello to Alex then wondered if I could do that. I wanted to stay and feel him close as he smiled down at me.

It wasn't just the music I'd gone for. Alex was beginning to creep into my thoughts more than I wanted or expected. After six years of marriage to Richard and our less than friendly divorce, I had sworn off any intimate relationship, resolved to keep my injured emotions from becoming bruised again. I didn't want to think about Richard or his betrayals. Not here, and especially not now.

Until I met Alex I'd been largely successful in my decision to remain detached from other men. There had been several opportunities to get involved, but the males that had expressed an interest failed to interest me. I shook my head to clear my thoughts, irritated with myself for thinking of them at that moment.

Alex stopped playing and rested his hands on his lap as the last notes echoed up into the rafters. I stood up and seeing me Kay did too and moved from her space on the floor. He looked down and then around toward me. "Ah, so it's you. My Maggie audience of one." He smiled and used the seat to ease himself up and off. "Kay doesn't usually respond to visitors like that. She must think you're special." He gathered up the music, and then patted the Shepherd who gazed up at him. She obviously adored him and I could understand why.

I experienced a sense of panic. I wasn't sure what to say. Telling him that the Bach was beautiful was true but a bit lame and I was afraid my voice would be unsteady. I'm acting like an awkward tongue-tied girl, I thought, but I have to say something and get out of here. I glanced at my watch. I would be more than an hour late and picking up flowers would take more time. "The Bach was beautiful," I said even though I had decided not to say that. Then I wondered if I was correct. "It was Bach wasn't it?"

He smiled. "Even though it seems obvious to me, not everyone would know that. Do you play?"

"I wasn't sure if I was right and yes and no; don't play although grueling piano lessons as a kid." I was pleased the interior was dimly lit because I began to feel myself flush. "Hated to practice. The piano was off in a spare room and it was freezing in the winter and my hands got cold then my mother said I had no talent and sold the piano but I was happy she did. That's my excuse, anyway." I was babbling on and felt my tongue was running away with me. I should've left while he was playing instead of making idiotic comments.

"That'll do it. But apparently you grew to like music."

"When I hear it played well and can be more selective."

"I was born loving it." He and Kay had moved closer and were standing next to me. I could smell his warmth from the denim shirt he was wearing and the musky, doggie smell of the Shepherd pressed against his leg. I wanted to inhale all of it and draw it deep inside me. Then I remembered Norma waiting. Trust her to creep in and spoil everything.

"I hate to be rude, but I must go. Norma's in hospital and I should be there." It occurred to me that he might think it strange that I'd stopped to listen and wasn't with my mother instead. To have him think less of me made me squirm. I wanted him to like me but then he could be married although I'd not noticed a ring while he was playing. Perhaps he didn't wear one. I felt myself blushing again and wished I wasn't so self-conscious.

"How is she? John said he'd seen you earlier and you'd both chatted." He smiled. God, he's so gorgeous, I thought. I found his beard and long hair tied back in a band attractive. He seemed totally unaware that my heart was dancing the quickstep and that I wanted to escape before I made a fool of myself. He continued. "Apparently she was knocked out with a sedative or something and you were planning to go back later. He left here earlier to see if she was awake."

I felt relieved. He was still smiling. "Yes I hoped he was there and decided to make a quick detour and see if you were playing; to sweeten my journey." I felt flustered and looked down at my sandals and bare feet and wished my toenails were painted. Get a grip, Maggie, I thought and looked back up at him, conscious of his size. He seemed gentle yet maintained a quiet energy of strength.

"Yep. You need all the sweeteners you can get before going to hospital."

I wondered if he meant going to hospital or seeing Norma or both. Didn't matter.

"Thank you for another wonderful recital. I loved it." I rubbed Kay's head reluctant to leave as the dog nuzzled my knee, "But I do have to get going."

We moved toward the font and the closed doors. I didn't want to go through them and into the full light of the day. I wanted to continue to wrap myself in the peace and seclusion of that wonderful old church with Alex and Kay. We were silent and I was aware of the sound we each made on the old stone: the uneven step of Alex, the light tread of my own feet and the click of Kay's paws. I wondered who would speak first and hoped he would because I was at a loss for what to say.

Alex cleared his throat and hesitated. "I'm thinking that with your mother hospitalized you'll probably eat alone. Although that's a bit presumptuous you could have lots of friends here." He shrugged and took a small step back as though uncomfortable with what he'd said.

"Actually, I don't." I wanted to reassure him and continue.

"Great. Well not great that you have no friends but great you will be free." He laughed. "I'm going to get myself in trouble if I continue so will just ask if you'd like to have dinner one evening? I had planned on inviting you for coffee or something but dinner seems even better. I'd enjoy your company."

I felt as though my heart stopped and did a somersault in my chest. I was sure he could hear it pounding. "Really? I'd enjoy that." I needed to think clearly. "Maybe we can arrange a time. I'm not sure how long Norma will be there, though."

"Do you have plans for tonight?"

I thought of what I had to eat at the house. I'd probably have stopped at the café and written to Shelly then gone back to read. "No."

"Do you have any favorite restaurants?"

"I don't know of any. Not here. Norma and I eat in. She's an elitist and prefers expensive hotels when she does go out." I saw his smile fade and an expression of horror cross his face so quickly continued, "But I prefer small and quiet and like most traditional foods although not wild about Chinese. I'm a vegetarian other than that I'm not picky." I watched his face relax again. "Are there any little Italian places around here?" I spoke too quickly trying to erase the image of fancy restaurants. I would prefer a little hole in the wall with good food.

He looked relieved and nodded. "There is, actually, Gino's, and Kay really likes the bread there." He grinned, "and anything else that drops on the floor."

It never occurred to me that he would take Kay. She would be considered a service dog and it would be a treat to have a warm, furry body under the table against my legs.

We had stopped while we were talking and began to move toward the door again. "So how d'you feel about other people eating meat?"

"No problem, although it would be great if they didn't to save more animals. Fish and chicken okay although I feel strongly about pork and red meats."Right! I thought. Now is *not* the time to get into any of that. I felt a bit unnerved at the prospect of sitting with him at a table. If I was going to garble my thoughts now then sitting opposite him could be a nightmare. I was acting like an idiot.

"Rarely eat red, never pork and mostly fish or chicken. Guess we're almost compatible there." He reached forward and opened the door and Kay bounded outside. "You better get going. John's due back soon. He said he had a meeting to attend to so your mother will be chomping at the bit."

So he did know a little about Norma. Well, I decided, that made it a lot easier to discuss whatever it was that was going on. I didn't want to edit or watch what I had to say to him; not Alex. I felt excited about having chatted with him and seen my father. It would give me something to think about while Norma was complaining.

I'd seen a small flower shop when I went to the market and decided to make a quick stop and parked. I ran in but the florist was on the phone. I knew it would add to the wait if I handpicked the arrangement instead of grabbing a bunch already made, but they were all in shades of orange and reds and I had never liked those intense colors together. The scent of the place, though, was heavenly and helped soothe my growing anxiety, although the florist seemed in no hurry to serve me and was laughing. From the conversation it could've been her boyfriend.

I stood at the counter and quietly began to strum my fingers across the glass thinking of the beautiful freshly picked flowers at Aidenscroft. She nodded to me and smiled as she raised her index finger in a silent request for me to wait. When she got off the phone she continued to wind a blue ribbon she'd been playing with while talking.

"I'm in a bit of a hurry," I said. "My mother's in hospital. Can you get an arrangement together?"

She stopped and let the ribbon dangle from her fingers. "Why don't you take a bunch of those that are ready to go?"

I shook my head and peered into the tall containers of single blooms. "I'm not wild about the colors. I rather like these blue Iris and purple ..."

"Delphiniums," she said.

"Yes, I know." I sounded too officious so moderated my voice somewhat. "So perhaps these Delphiniums and a few white roses. Can you put in some green fern or spray of something, too?"

"Will your mother have a vase?"

Darn. Why hadn't I thought of that? "Good thinking. No. So let's have something in a basket then." I felt the minutes ticking by. The florist indicated more containers of the flashy reds and pinks. I shook my head, "Don't you have anything in blue or lavender?"

"Well, I can still arrange the flowers you want and put them in a vase for you, but it will cost a bit more." She smiled slightly as though apologizing.

She's going to think I'm a cheapskate if I say no, I thought, and I was really running out of time. I spotted a basket of mixed blue African violets with a tiny bear peeking out of the green leaves. Norma is definitely not a peeking bear person, so said, "Can you take out the bear and replace it with more violets?"

"You don't like it?" Her smiled disappeared and she frowned as though it was a rejection of her.

"Cute, yes, but take it out. I'll pay for it separately if it's a problem but I want more violets." I was speaking quickly and sounded unfriendly and it bothered me.

I remembered Grandmother Clare's floristry. She had said she wanted to create a little oasis of beauty for people who stepped inside, a momentary departure from the frenzy of the outside world, where one could take a deep and marvelous breath of mixed scents and have one's eyes absorb the colors of nature. She taught me that and now, as a customer, perhaps I was destroying a similar atmosphere that this poor woman wanted to generate. I shouldn't have stopped for flowers and was blaming Norma for my decisions.

The woman's lips had tightened and she mumbled something that I couldn't hear and I decided I didn't want to. I was being obnoxious but she removed the bear and held two small pots of violets, one white and the other white with purple flecks. "Which one?" I indicated the one with flecks and the she went behind the counter to cover the basket with clear plastic. "Do you want a card to go with it?"

"Thanks, no. That's fine. It's lovely," I added by way of trying to absolve myself of more offense.

"Then that will be four pounds plus tax. That comes to ..." she was adding on a little calculator

I knew that if I charged it, it would take even longer to process so opened my wallet and handed her six pounds. "Here. Keep the change and don't bother to wrap it." I picked up the basket. "Thanks for your help."

The door jangled behind me but I stopped and opened it again and the woman looked up, surprised. "Just wanted to apologize if I seemed rude. You have a lovely little shop here and when I'm not in such a hurry I'd like to come back and we can spend some time and talk about flowers."

Her expression was my reward. She radiated back a smile that caused her face to glow. It took only a second to change unpleasant energy to good. Who was it who said, "Take time to smell the flowers?" or was that "roses?" Didn't matter; they were right. It was a little more time away from Norma who would probably be furious I wasn't there, but the flowers were pretty and I wondered if they would be appreciated. It'll take more than a basket of flowers to please her, I decided, and took a deep breath and wished I was still with Alex or visiting Daddy.

Just as I thought, the flowers that signaled my presence as I walked in the door were dismissed with the wave of a hand. "I've been *waiting*, Margaret. Reverend McLean came and left already. He thought you'd get here before he had to go. Where've you been?"

Right. So I say that I was in church listening to Bach and admiring a guy and his dog and before that I was visiting my poor father and your supposedly dead husband. I don't think so. I thrust the basket of flowers on the bedside table and decided to ignore the question rather than concoct a lie. "Has the doctor been back?"

"No but some little nurse that doesn't look old enough to be out of high school keeps coming in and fidgeting with this monitor. I told her to take it out it makes too much noise but she said it had to stay."

"Now I wonder why she would say that?"

Norma either ignored or failed to register my sarcasm. "I went through this the last time I was here. Ugh, so stupid to be back and if Cheryl hadn't called emergency, I'd have been just fine and got back on the chair. *You* weren't anywhere around, of course." Then added, "Take those things away. Having flowers indoors make me sneeze and besides which I don't think flowers are allowed in hospitals. Did you ask first?"

I controlled my voice. I wasn't going to snap and give her the satisfaction of seeing me riled. "Fine, I'll take them when I leave. I guess you find these white walls and stainless steel pleasant enough."

"No need to be snippy, young lady. My head hurts quite enough as it is." She groaned slightly and let her shoulders slump against the pillows as she closed her eyes.

"It probably will for a bit. Doctor Suffolk said you might have a concussion. Maybe you should try and get some more sleep and I'll come back later." I couldn't wait to leave again.

Norma's weak blue eyes flashed with unmistakable hostility. Someday, I thought, I'm going to ask what I've done wrong. I knew it had to be the right moment and it wasn't now. But how much courage or time did it take to ask and would I ever get an answer from a woman who was so self-serving? Did life's disappointment and frustration cause her to take that as a personal affront and become embittered instead of recognizing we are all, more or less, in the same boat? Norma seemed to operate within her own toxic bubble of assuming she was always right and never appeared to question that it might be affecting everything and everyone with whom she came in contact.

"Stay. Leave. I don't care." Her voice became whiney as she mollified the tone and became devious, "Just get me out of here, Margaret."

She was, after all, totally dependent on me or someone else to get her removed from there and I hoped she wasn't strong enough to call a taxi and get home by herself. "I'll have the nurse give you a sedative so you can rest," I said.

"No sedative!" The whine was gone and the brittle rasp was back.

I felt pity for the staff that would have to tend to her. Norma groped for the buzzer and pressed her finger hard into the button. I could hear a bell ring outside the door and down the hallway.

"Why d'you do that?"

"I want someone to remove these flowers."

I reached over and picked up the basket. "Fine. I'll get them out of here and be back after dinner this evening."

"If I'm asleep don't wake me."

"I can assure you of that."

"And make sure those flowers are gone by the time I get home. I don't want them there, either."

I was about to open the door when the nurse pushed it from the other side. "Did you want something, Mrs. Resnick?"

"No," I said, "and sorry to bother you. These were making her uncomfortable and she wants them gone, so I'm taking them with me."

"What a pity," the young woman smiled, "but it's true, they can be problematic for some patients and not permitted in other wards although they would have brightened up the room."

"That's what I thought," I said, "but it would take more than a basket of flowers to do that." I indicated with my head for the nurse to follow me. Outside I said, "My mother can be a difficult patient. Try not let that upset you. I'm apologizing for her. She won't do it herself."

"I know. We remember her from the last time she was here. Sometimes it gets really busy and we can't always answer her buzzer as quickly as she wants." She smiled and I decided it was almost conspiratorial.

"Yes, I totally understand." Then with an impetuous gesture I thrust the basket into the nurse's hands. "Here, take these and put them on your lobby desk or give them to someone else. They'll get more appreciation than if I take them home."

"Are you sure?" she said sniffing into the basket. "I love the scent of violets, thank you."

"Absolutely." I thought it would perhaps make up for some of the grief that Norma would be generating but for that a full floristry wouldn't suffice. "I'm Maggie, her daughter. What's your name?"

The nurse patted her name tag, "Bryony."

"I see that now. A lovely name for a lovely flower," I said. "Well Bryony, she may reject these violets, but you're one flower she'll need to have around."

CHAPTER ELEVEN

I could hear my cell phone ringing as I got to the car. I'd left it there to charge and didn't want any calls while I was in the hospital. Shelly had told me she would call periodically and I didn't want to miss her, although I didn't want it to ring around Norma. I'd given John my number, perhaps it was him.

By the time I unlocked the door and got inside, it had stopped. I checked to see if there were any messages. There were two. I entered my code and listened to the first. It was from John.

"Hi Mar … Maggie. It's me. John. Saw your mother and wanted to wait for you but had to leave. Another appointment. Busy, busy!" He giggled slightly. "Sorry I missed you. Maybe we can meet for a cup of coffee or lunch tomorrow. I'd enjoy that and we can chat some more. Perhaps I can be of help with Norma. She's not happy but I think she needs to stay there and rest. Give me a call. Bye."

I felt a twinge of guilt at how I had treated him and pleased I could now move on and decided to call him later and pressed the key to listen to the second message.

"Hey Maggie. Alex. Got your number from John. Hope that was okay. We still on for dinner this evening? Kay's looking forward to some Gino's chicken and bruschetta."

I clicked on his number and he picked up immediately. Maybe he was waiting for me to call, I thought, and hoped so. "Alex. It's me. Maggie."

"Glad you got my message. Wasn't sure what was happening with your mother. Can you still meet for dinner?"

"I'm looking forward to it. What time?"

"Is six thirty or seven okay?" Then as though an afterthought he said, "So how is she?"

"Unhappy with being there." I glanced at the clock in the car. It was almost four. "Can we make it earlier though? I said I would go back this evening to see her." I didn't add that I would prefer to spend more time with him.

"Five-thirty then? Think Gino's would let us in earlier since they know me. Do you want me to go back with you when we're through?"

"To the hospital?" I was astounded. He would do actually do that? But no. Never. Never would I have Norma in a position to spoil everything. "Alex. That's sweet of you, but I really need to do this alone although think I have John for support."

"That's John. He'll help anyone."

"I'm beginning to realize that."

I wanted to get home and change. When I'd packed before leaving, I hadn't anticipated going out on a date while I was with Norma and now wondered what I could wear. I needed to get myself ready or as ready as I was ever going to be.

"I better get home and change first. Oh," I remembered, "where's the restaurant?"

"Not far from the Church and on the way to the hospital. It's on the left hand side of the street by a small strip of shops that has a florist and a pub, *The Rose 'n Plough*. Gino's is opposite there and hidden by some big Hydrangea bushes but you'll see their sign. It's not far. I'd give directions from the church but it would be more confusing even though it's closer."

I remembered the florist and tried to visualize what the opposite side of the street looked like. "Yes, I know where that is. Would you like me to pick you up?"

"Kay and I will walk it's not far and she loves the exercise. Maybe you can drive us back. Yes?"

"Perfect. Five thirty then." I knew it was early for dinner and wasn't happy about leaving to see Norma, but decided that if dinner was in any way uncomfortable and the conversation died, my mother would be a good excuse. Somehow I didn't think it would happen though and using my mother as an excuse for anything made me smile.

I drove faster than I should've but I wanted to make the most of getting myself ready. It had been a long time since I had gone on a date and the last time I'd had my full closet to choose from. Not that I wore anything fancy. Somehow, though, it didn't seem a problem. Alex appeared to approve of me the way I was and he had a comfortable, rumpled appearance and I hoped his suit was kept for Sunday service and dinner would be casual.

I decided to take a quick shower to wash my hair, that always helped, and to replace my jeans with a skirt and blouse and take a sweater. Restaurants could have the air conditioning turned up too high and I invariably froze. Another thing that I shared with Norma but that was physiological and nothing I could change.

I knew that any plan to look for the earrings would be delayed at least until later that evening or even the following day. They seemed unimportant after finding Daddy but I still wanted them. What I did do when I got back to the house was open all the windows to let in the fresh air although the place was already reflecting the lack of Norma's presence and no longer had her stale, unpleasant odor. That had been my plan earlier before I was focused on the more important thing of finding the nursing home.

God, I hope my clothes don't smell of this place, I thought, as I pulled my skirt from the closet. I sniffed but couldn't really tell, so lit some patchouli for the smoke to curl gently around it and out into the room while I undressed for the shower.

I let the hot water pour over my head as I moved the soap over my body. Sliding the bar down my legs I realized they felt rough and needed to be waxed. Even if I had the time to shave, I didn't have a razor. Darn. Couldn't wear the skirt. Now what? Screw it, I decided, it's a clean pair of jeans and another shirt. Well, I'm more comfortable in those anyway.

I wondered if there was a local spa for later although figured if there was it would be closer to town. At least I could pick up a razor and some blades at the chemist. I missed being able to check the Internet for information. Getting ahead of yourself, Maggie, I thought, as I rubbed the shampoo through my hair. What makes you think there'll be a next time where having smooth legs will be important? The thought made my heart skip a little faster and I was glad I still had the remains of my California tan.

By the time I had bathed and changed it was almost five. I didn't want to be late. My hair was still damp and felt cool around my neck. I fluffed it and decided it needed to be dried some more. I wanted to wear it loose and not pulled back. It would look softer and I knew I'd appear more attractive and besides which, a wet head in air conditioning was an invitation to becoming cold and becoming cold was miserable. I shiver like a little kid when I feel chilled, and although others found it funny, I didn't. After a few minutes of waving the hair dryer over my head, I unplugged it, then picked up my bag and sweater. I'd prefer not to be cold with Alex.

I found the restaurant with time to spare and pulled into the tiny parking area and sat for a few minutes. I didn't want to be the first to arrive but neither did I want Alex to get there before me and have to wait.

I hated first dates. They made me feel edgy. If we knew each other better, would either one of us really care if we weren't exactly on time. I realized I was already thinking in terms of more dates with him where a comfortable communication had been established.

I disliked pretending to be someone I wasn't or what the other person thought I was. I'd decided long ago I'd be as honest as possible and not play games. I'd not had many dates after Richard and I divorced but had been lonely and curious about other guys since he was the first one I'd been with.

Not that I hadn't been lonely with Richard. Even though I knew his job kept him away from home, when he was there he was always off doing something else like playing tennis or partying; no good at the first and disinterested in the second I was left to my books and eventually to studying and getting a degree. That was the plus side of our marriage but one didn't need to be married to do that although Richard's financial support made it possible. He liked that I was studying and think it relieved him of the guilt of leaving me alone.

When it was over I learned that other men could be more attentive and on their best behavior to begin with but then after sex, they'd often relax into a comfortable nonchalance and what had begun with interest collapsed into indifference. Norma had done a good job in my childhood by telling me I was too thin to be pretty and too shy to make an impression so it came as a surprise when I discovered that males found me desirable. I tried to downplay it, which gave the impression I was quiet. But it was usually I who ended the relationship because I was bored.

I was in no rush to remarry and not sure if I ever would although I thought I eventually wanted to have a child so that narrowed the field a bit. Many guys didn't want to be a father and I didn't know what I wanted in a mate but it wasn't parties and it wasn't athletics. Shelly would say I was more in love with books and plants and I'd say yes, and of course Mewfus.

I was more than curious about Alex. He already seemed different than anyone else I'd met. It was hard to believe I discovered him hidden away in a church playing Bach and keeping company with a great dog. But supposing this thing does take off? What then? I wondered. What do we do with the six thousand miles between us? That's a chunk of distance to consider. I shook my head to clear the thoughts, "Just go inside, Lady," I said, "and quit speculating."

The restaurant appeared empty, although from where I stood inside the door, I could hear the sound of kitchen clatter; of pots being shuffled on a stove and the sizzle of cooking. A tiny Venus de Milo water fountain gurgled beneath a sign that requested one wait to be seated.

I peered into the dimly lit interior. I didn't see Alex and hesitated, wondering if I should go back outside again but then a big woman, her black hair knotted in a thick braid, pushed through a swing door and hurried towards me. She beamed, her mouth closed and drawn up in a smile, her cheeks shining. "Hi, I'm Judy—waitress, maître d' and occasional cook and bottle washer. You must be Maggie. Alex is waiting for you towards the back. He likes to sit there with Kay. This way." She turned and surprised by her familiar greeting I followed as she guided me past empty, red checkered tables set for dinner, toward a small alcove off the main area.

Set under dark oak beams, long wood shelves filled with dusty wine bottles lined one of the red brick walls, next to oil paintings of Greek ruins and grapevined arches. The lights were dimmed and candles flickered next to a tiny vase of flowers on the tables; the place had a comfortable, intimate atmosphere and the air was heavy with the smell of garlic. I realized that apart from the church and Aidenscroft, this was the nicest place I'd been in since I left California; I also realized I'd not eaten all day and was really hungry.

I saw Alex at a corner table and he rose as Judy and I approached, while Kay's head peered from under the table, lifting the cloth with her muzzle so that it draped her eyes. She looked like she was wearing a babushka and I laughed. Alex looked down and told her to stay, but I could hear her tail thumping against the underneath of the table in greeting and the silverware clinking together from the motion.

Alex pulled out the chair opposite his, "Terrific! You're here," he said.

I nodded, then wondered how much he could see of me through his dark glasses. Guess we're destined to meet in filtered light, I thought. "Great place. Hope you didn't wait long," I said as I sat down and placed my purse on the chair next to me.

Judy interrupted me, "Excuse me, but I'll be back in a jiffy with the menus. Would you like anything to drink?"

I wanted some red wine but not if I had to drink alone and glanced over at Alex who was looking at me. So much for being myself, I thought, if I can't even decide to order a glass of wine.

"Don't know about you," he said, as though picking up on my thoughts, "but I'd like some wine. Sound good?"

"Sounds perfect."

"A carafe of the house okay?"

"I need to walk, not fall into the hospital. Better just a glass."

"Kay will lead me home if necessary. Just two, for now, thanks Judy. So you approve of the place! Wait 'til you taste the food." He bent down and petted Kay and I could feel her warmth pressed again my leg and resting on my sandaled foot. I wriggled my toes into her fur and felt her lick my skin.

"You come here often?" It seemed like such a cliché or a line out of a movie and I felt awkward, aware of Alex so close to me across the table. This was different than being in church and I hoped my fork wouldn't wobble and betray how nervous I felt.

"Not really. Occasionally when John and I decide to take an evening off or when I don't feel like cooking."

"You cook?"

"I'm a fairly decent one, although," he added, "I've not focused on vegetarian so probably not as good as I thought. I suppose you're an expert." He grinned.

"An expert what?"

"Meatless meals."

"I open a recipe book, look at the colored photographs, like what I see and follow directions. Back home I was getting really creative with Indian food with all the spices involved. I love cumin." I reached over the table and opened the red napkin that covered a small basket. "Warm French bread. I could live on the stuff; lots of butter though." I tilted it toward him and he took a piece.

"Red wine, French bread with butter. Excellent. Do you eat cheese?"

"Cheddar to Chevre and everything in between." I suddenly felt I was being a bit too lively before I'd even had the first sip of wine. Slow down, I thought, take a breath and relax.

"Goat cheese. Great! Although I have to watch eating it before I go out in public and play. Next time we have dinner, I'll cook and you can bring the cheese and if our breaths smell so what!"

He was talking about the next time already. I laughed. "So where does one find the Bries and special cheeses around this small town? I've looked already."

"There's a small deli about twenty miles from here but worth the drive." He looked up as Judy arrived with the wine and menus and placed them on the table.

"Take your time," she said as she left toward the door to greet some new diners who had arrived.

Alex was feeding Kay some bread. "I already know what I want."

I was scanning the entrees. "Maybe the gnocchi with pesto." I folded the menu and put it on the table over Alex's. "So what are you having?" I wondered if I'd been too hasty. Pesto managed to stick in my teeth and I visualized myself smiling like a lawn with bits of green tucked between them.

"Aubergines and a side of chicken for Kay."

"Eggplant?"

He hesitated. "You don't want me to have the eggplant?"

"No," I shook my head, "that's great. Most people I know hate it." I felt pleased and took a sip of wine. "I *love* it!" I bent down and lifted the edge of the tablecloth. "Here Kay, French bread with butter."

"She'll get fat."

"This is okay, though, isn't it? How often does she get taken out to dinner?"

"Not often. You'll be one of her favorite people if this continues. And," he added, "I hope this continues." I nodded and had been thinking the same thing. "So, John's helping with your mother?"

"He's very attentive. I didn't fully appreciate that at first."

"At first?"

I decided to be frank. "At first I thought he was a bit ... a bit ingratiating."

Alex paused. "John's a nice guy but tries too hard to be nicer than he already is so it comes across as a bit much."

"That's more or less what I said." I broke off a piece of bread and buttered it.

"He's relaxed with me," Alex said. "When he's being the vicar he gets nervous. Wants to be a man of God but still a regular guy. But he likes your honesty."

"He told you that?" I wondered what else he'd said.

"Not the details. So what did you tell him?"

I felt myself squirm. I didn't want Alex to see the Norma side of my personality and paused. "John sensed I didn't like him because I er ... well I was rather brusque. He asked why, so I told him." I kept my eyes lowered and felt the heat rise to my cheeks and begin to flush. "He was understandably upset and I felt bad, really awful that I'd said I found him obsequious, but it seemed to clear the air and he became more natural, whatever that means." I took a sip of the wine and set down my glass. "I even told him that Norma likes him and thinks he's soft on her."

I had been looking down conscious of how much I was blabbering and was startled at the burst of laughter that came from Alex. It boomed across the tables and seemed to reverberate off the ceiling. "That's great. Your mother and John! Hah! Poor guy being hit on by an old lady especially since he's gay."

"So he said."

"He doesn't speak about it but I think he's got issues with that and being a vicar and a conflict of interest."

I was surprised that Alex was so intuitive and nodded. "He needs to talk about himself. I get the impression that he holds it all in. We'll probably get together tomorrow for coffee."

"Maggie to the rescue for a noble cause."

"Noble cause. Huh! Although if John qualifies as one then okay." I decided I was being teased and felt the heat rising to my cheeks again. I broke off another piece of bread. I wouldn't have to say anything if I was chewing.

"No other causes? How come? You look like you've got a heart of gold."

I definitely felt he was teasing me. "Nope. Too selfish!"

"So where does attending church fit in?" Then he chuckled, "Or do you just go for the music?"

I felt definitely unsettled. This man was capable of reading my mind. "Only music played really well in really old churches."

"That's it?"

I wondered if he was attempting to get me to mention him too and felt I was on shaky ground. "It's not enough?"

"Then you're not one of the religious faithful?"

"Nope!"

"John won't be happy about that although just seeing you in church is a good thing. So ... atheist? Agnostic?"

"I'm spiritual with a reverent respect for the Universe and a higher power not in the conventional God image. He's too much like man and we're woefully deficient."

I knew I had to stop. When I came back from a date Shelly would ask me if I had gotten into any heavy stuff, meaning just what I'd embarked on with Alex. Often the guy never called me back and Shelly had mumbled, "Told you so." I felt that if I couldn't talk about the things that interested me and had value and that frightened guys away then I'd prefer not to have them around.

I glanced up and realized Alex was looking at me and could feel his gaze through the dark glasses. I wondered what it would be like to see him without them.

"Me too," he said.

That was a surprise. "Really? But you're always there."

"Church? I know but I love playing in them and the energy it generates and it's something others sense very strongly. I'm a huge believer in feeling strongly—about anything!" He took a bite of the bread and continued, "And I love to think my playing continues to reside in those old stones somehow."

I found it hard to believe I was hearing what I did and how close he came to expressing what I felt. I was silent.

"So tell me about your mother."

"You had to bring her into the conversation."

"She *is* a major part of why you're here. We wouldn't be having dinner if not for her."

"You're right. If it wasn't for her ... although perhaps I'd better call soon." I trailed off without completing my thought. I knew that by the time we'd eaten I would have to rush to the hospital.

We both looked up as Judy came to the table. "Ready to order?"

"Maggie wants the gnocchi with lots of pesto and I'd like aubergines and a side of chicken for Kay. Maggie has to get back to the hospital, so we're a bit pressed for time. Next time we'll spend all evening."

I had never met anyone so comfortable and self assured. I'd initially thought him shy. I couldn't have been more wrong, but he was talking about a next time. I felt my heart begin to race again.

He turned back to me as Judy picked up the menus and left. "Okay. No mother talk. How do you know so much about music?"

"I really don't."

"Okay so you like Bach. What else?"

"Renaissance and classical but not keen on the romantics. Too much syrup with my sound. But you're brilliant."

"Brilliant no, but gifted in a way that gives me pleasure. My father forked out money he couldn't afford to get me lessons. My in-

143

structor recognized some ability and spent more time with me than the meager amount he paid her. She was an angel and took me to the church when it wasn't occupied, and provided the basics for playing the organ."

"And you took it from there!"

"Discovered I could weasel my way into the hearts of various vicars to play for their sermons and the hymns they wanted, and in return I could stay and play what I wanted. John too. It keeps me sane."

"You said that once before."

"It's true. Music keeps me focused. It seems to nullify everything that runs amok in my head and quiets the unwanted demons." He wasn't smiling and leaning forward, his arm beneath the table stroking Kay.

"Demons?"

"Of course. Demons and unwelcome Shadows we have in our thoughts whether we're conscious of them or not. Jung said some interesting things about them."

I felt that a door had opened into my head and Alex had walked in like a brilliant light. "Well I'm getting to know mine and they tend to resemble Norma. I'm only just learning to deal with them. It's a struggle." I wiped my mouth with my napkin and hoped I'd not said too much.

Alex nodded and raised his glass towards me and I picked up mine and did the same. "Cheers," he said, "with more time to understand Shadows that are really quite interesting along with other mysterious things that can go bump in the dark of night."

I laughed. Relieved my Shadow wasn't just something I had to deal with, I said, "Do you mean ghoulies and ghosties and long legged beasties, or humans getting it on?" Not eating and a few sips of wine and already I felt lightheaded.

He laughed and set his glass down. Kay thumped her tail as though sharing in the joke. "Ghoulies and ghosties, huh? Yes that's part of it. I forgot and just remembered the 'bump' part. D'you know the rest?"

"It's a Cornish prayer. 'From ghoulies and ghosties and long-legged beasties, and things that go bump in the night, good Lord deliver us.' It pleases the pagan side of me and I have it as a refrigerator magnet at home."

"My refrigerator could do with some brightening up. Mine has just one that says, 'I love to cook with wine ... sometimes I even put it in the food.' But bumping sounds like fun." He was wiping his mouth with his napkin but grinning as he did so.

If he continues like this, I thought, I'm in big trouble. I took another piece of bread and slid it under the table to Kay, unsure of what to say or how to answer. Alex was still smiling and I realized he could see more with one eye than most people could with two, and pleased Judy was coming toward our table to distract us from the subject.

Her hands were wrapped in cloths with hot plates in both. "Here you go. I'm a pesto person myself and asked the chef for extra." She grinned at me. "He puts in lots of garlic so don't breathe too hard when you're around company." She winked and nodded toward Alex.

"It's okay," he said, "garlic among friends keeps the devil at bay."

"Then perhaps we should all consume more garlic," I said wishing I didn't have to leave early and decided to call the hospital to find out how Norma was doing. "Alex, before we start, will you excuse me while I call the hospital?"

"D'you have your cell phone?" He was reaching into his pocket for his.

"It's okay thanks I have it."

I pressed the contact number for the hospital and waited while it rang. A nurse answered and I asked to be put through to Norma. She said, "We transferred her from emergency to room seventeen on the first floor but she's sleeping right now. She had dinner and then made a fuss about wanting to leave so Doctor Suffolk gave her another sedative so she can get some sleep. She'll probably be out for the night. Do you want to leave a message?"

"No. No thanks." Then I changed my mind, "Okay, yes, say Magg … Margaret called and I'll be there first thing in the morning. Are you sure she'll be sleeping through the night?"

"We thought she'd be more comfortable."

"But if she wakes do you permit late visiting hours?"

"Within reason but I wouldn't be too concerned about her waking. If she does she'll be groggy and probably fall back asleep. Don't worry."

I thanked her and slipped the phone into my purse while Alex looked at me, his head angled slightly. "Well?"

"Seems like I can enjoy you and my dinner without further interruption. The evening is mine." I felt my heart kick into high gear.

"It's *ours*! Excellent. Do you like zabaglione?"

I laughed. "We haven't finished the entrée and you're thinking about dessert? You're gonna make me fat and happy like Kay."

"I have an appalling sweet tooth as you might have suspected from my girth but you? Fat? Never. Happy? Yes. Hope so." He leaned down towards his plate and breathed in. "Mmmm, this is good. Want some eggplant?"

I had been wondering if I should ask him for some. It looked and smelled delicious. "Absolutely. Maybe we can trade. Here." I pushed my plate toward him and he jabbed a piece of the gnocchi.

"You can give Kay some of this chicken."

146

I picked up a piece and held it between my fingers under the table. I could feel Kay's wet nose sniffing it, then felt her lips curl over my fingers and gently remove it. "Good girl." I loved having a dog under the table and patted her head.

"Just don't share any of the zabaglione. It's bad for her teeth."

"It's okay for ours though!"

"That's what toothbrushes are for. Getting rid of the evidence. So now we can relax and you don't have to leave early. Good." Alex was cutting into the eggplant. "Here, put some of this on yours and I'll take some gnocchi. Then we won't have forks being passed across the table all the time although not that anyone would care. And by the way, I don't mean to be too personal ..."

I wondered what he was going to say. Already getting personal with John had revealed some interesting things so I said, "Go ahead."

"I'm happy you wore jeans. I was afraid you'd show up in heels and hose and wearing lots of makeup."

I was stunned. "Really? You saw me at the church and I was wearing more or less the same thing."

"I know and liked the casual look, but in the past I've been surprised when another female appeared other than the one I asked out. An invitation to dinner can sometimes do that to a woman; she thinks she has to overdress for the occasion." Then he added, "Not that I've invited that many out."

I remembered my earlier concern and wondering what to wear. The wine was having an effect and making me feel relaxed; he was so comfortable to be with.

"To be truthful, I didn't bring anything to dress up in and I don't wear much makeup if at all. I thought of wearing a skirt but changed my mind." I stopped short of telling him that my legs needed shaving. "Last time I wore anything really fancy was probably my wedding dress and even that was a simple long dress."

"You're married?" The fork he was about to put in his mouth was held poised in front of him. "Married? Really?"

"Was. Divorced and have been for about two years now. Don't worry. I'm not cheating on anyone. What about you?"

His face was serious. "I was too—or am. My wife left me for another guy and I was a bit crazy at the time and the reason I signed up. Within six months I found myself serving in the Gulf and I'm not sure which of the two surprised me more. Even if she had come back she probably would've left again if she'd seen me looking like this with one eye and a limp." He indicated his scarred face. "I've no idea where she is now although think she's still in California where we lived."

I felt my stomach muscles tighten, "You're still married, then?"

"Technically, yes. Actually, no. I could probably get an annulment or divorce if I wanted to, but why bother? She's been gone for years. Probably committing bigamy somewhere for all I know."

I noticed his hand grip the fork and stab a piece of the eggplant. From the change in his voice and deliberate action I realized it was still an issue for him and said gently, "There's nothing wrong with your face. I like it, and the beard looks great."

He relaxed. "Thanks. Kay likes me, and now you make two females who find me attractive. But it's not about looks, is it?" He pushed away his plate. "Enough. Think I'll take the rest home."

"No dessert?"

"That's why I'm leaving the rest." He peered at my plate." You've not left much though. I love a woman who doesn't pick at her food. But your glass is almost empty, and since you're not going to see Norma, how about another?"

"I'll be fuzzy headed for driving. Better not."

"I'm going to order another one and if you want a sip of mine then you can go ahead. Okay?"

"Okay." I wondered what it would be like to have dinner if he cooked and decided I'd try and keep a clear head when I did. Yeah! Right, Maggie! I thought. You really think *that's* gonna happen? and wondered when he would ask me.

I looked up as Judy took our plates and said to us, "So will it be zabaglione, Alex?"

"You know me too well," he glanced at me, "and this stuff is too good to share. Shall we make it two?"

I nodded. The last great meal I'd had was with Shelly before I left. Before that I couldn't remember a date that came with good food and interesting conversation. Shelly and I could talk about anything although restaurants were an occasional treat we both enjoyed. A girls' night out. But never would I have believed then I'd be where I was now even though I might have fantasized about one like this.

"Cappuccinos?" Judy asked.

"Yes. Lovely. It'll clear my head a bit."

"Not for me," Alex said. "Another glass of wine, thanks."

Judy nodded and walked toward the kitchen. The restaurant was beginning to fill and the noise level was increasing. I became aware of a throaty gulp and stared at Alex. "What's that noise? Where is it coming from?" I looked around and as I did so felt a little tremor against my leg.

Alex laughed. "Kay has the hiccups."

"That's funny! I didn't know dogs could get hiccups."

I reached under the table to pet Kay simultaneously with Alex as he did the same thing and our hands met over her back. We stared at each other, our chins almost resting against the top of the table.

"There's probably a more comfortable way of doing this," he said and his laugh boomed across the room again. Momentarily it stopped the chatter around us and I was delighted that here was a man who had no reservations with laughing loudly. We sat up and he reached across and took my hand. "There! That's much better," he said.

I looked down and gazed at his strong fingers wrapped around mine and thought of their sensitivity when they played. Such a giant paw, I thought; strong hands are such a turn on. Then I remembered Norma's views for what characteristics signified a strong male; hers were ones that consisted of empty compliments and flattery that validated her own opinions. But I'm still thinking like her, I thought, and what constitutes manly men, annoyed that she had crept in as a comparison but I don't ridicule them like she does and a charming male is still attractive. Richard had been charming and I had definitely fallen for him but his were superficially generated based on his good looks and didn't run deeper than that.

Judy brought the zabaglione, cappuccino and his wine, "Let me know when you're ready and I'll bring the check."

Alex nodded and unclasped my hand. "We can pick up where we left off later although getting the check hints that the dinner is almost over. Pity! I rather like holding your hand."

I nodded. I'd been thinking that I wanted to hold even more of him then flushed as I realized he was staring at me rather intently and wondered if he had been thinking the same thing. "Me, too. An Alex in hand and a Kay on foot and what more could a woman ask for? Mmmm, this zabaglione is fantastic."

I was babbling on again, relieved to change the subject although bothered I was unable to express my pleasure and not feel self-conscious. I didn't behave this way with a guy in whom I had no interest, so why did my heart have to race and cause my words to tremble? I was pleased the place was dimly lit and could compose myself again.

"You know, when we're through, I can't be the gentleman and drive you home neither can I ask you to walk home with me. So can I take you up on that earlier offer to drive us back to my place?" He grinned, "And with no strings."

I wondered why he would have said that. I would've been happy with strings or even a rope and very firmly attached. "Of course. I was going to ask you that anyway," I said. I wanted to extend the evening further and have him sitting next to me in the car.

"Great. You hear that Kay? Maggie's going to give us a lift home." At the sound of her name, Kay thumped her tail and stretched out from under the cloth, looking up at him.

I smiled, "Where do you live?"

"About a mile from here and not that much further from the church. It's out of the village a little way and surrounded by more countryside. Doesn't take long before that happens and I feel fortunate to live where I do."

I had been wondering how he lived hidden away in this small village. "How did you come to move here."

"My father emigrated to the States and became a citizen. Both my parents are dead but the cottage belonged to my grandparents who left it to me. I figured it was a great place to recover from all kinds of wounds—physical and emotional." He lifted the tablecloth and peered beneath changing the subject. "But Kay probably needs to stretch her legs so although I hate to say this we should perhaps get going."

I nodded. I hoped I'd learn more about this gentle giant but where had the time gone? At least the evening wasn't yet completely over.

Kay jumped into the back seat and Alex slid in and filled the seat next to me. His shoulder pressed against mine and I could feel his body's heat as I turned the ignition. "Where to?" I asked.

Alex directed me and within minutes pointed out a small cottage surrounded by trees and shrubs from what I could see in the dark. He'd left the porch light on and it was very different from Norma's plain brick terrace house and I smiled. This was the kind of place I loved. A red slate roof hung over tiny square blue paned windows and rustic oak door within a porch covered in roses. It radiated old English charm that I missed in California and certainly wasn't present in my mother's. I pulled up in front of the path and little picket fence.

Kay sat up and whined. "She knows she's home and probably wants to pee," Alex said. "D'you want to stretch your legs a bit and come with us?"

I turned off the engine. Of course I did. As we got out of the car, I felt the cool air and pulled my sweater around me as we followed Kay, who was sniffing around and squatting. I shivered slightly and Alex who had taken my hand felt my shudder. He stopped and folded his arms around me. I breathed in the smell of his shirt as the buttons pressed against my face. I began to shake more but from him and not the cold. It had been a long break between men and being held. I could feel his beard and chin in my hair and raised my head.

Alex took off his dark glasses and put them in his pocket and looked down at me. I could see from the light reflected from the cottage that his right eye had been severely damaged and it looked like scar tissue had pretty much closed it, the wrinkled and folded skin pulled against his temple and brow.

He brought his face down to mine and kissed me. At first hesitant, we stood there cheek touching cheek and I rose on my toes and kissed him again, mouths and lips together, tongue seeking tongue, breaths intermingled. I could feel him hardening against me and I shivered again but with pleasure.

"You sure you don't want to come in?" he said softly.

I shook my head. I would never leave if I did. I folded my arms around his neck and pulled his head down to mine, sliding my hands down his cheek, feeling the texture of his face and beard. "I would love to ... but can't."

"Then when?"

"Soon. Let me see how Norma's doing and then we can ... I can come back another time." I hated speaking Norma's name in the same breath. I felt it spoiled the mood that had been generated.

"Tonight?"

"Wish yes, but I must stop by the hospital even if she's asleep." I wanted to do both, but was using Norma as an excuse to give me more time to collect my wits and gather my emotions that were ready to explode and deprive me of thinking straight.

I knew that if I went inside with Alex my control would dissipate. I had thought I would never be emotionally involved again and here I was embarked on something that was already more intense than anything I had previously experienced.

I sighed and gently pulled away. A thin mist was settling moist air onto my shoulders. I hoped it wasn't about to rain and felt cold, already missing his warmth.

"If you must, then you must." He put his arm around me and opened the car door, "I'll call you tomorrow and depending upon what's happening with your mother, I think we should take advantage of the time." He grinned and kissed the top of my head. "I'll be playing again tomorrow, we could have lunch together if you'd like?"

I shook my head. "I may be meeting John and if not then I'll probably grab some toast and coffee and spend that time with Norma. Not my first choice though."

"Then," Alex said, "that leaves dinner and the big question where?"

I liked that he took it for granted that I would say yes. I settled myself behind the wheel and placed the key in the ignition. "Yes. Let's chat and decide tomorrow and Alex …"

"Hmmm?"

"It's been lovely!"

CHAPTER TWELVE

I could see him watching me as I drove off, Kay leaning against his leg as he petted her. Happier than I'd felt in years, I decided I was well prepared to go to the hospital although would've preferred to go back to Norma's house—empty of her—and to continue to think of all that had occurred. I wanted to replay everything and savor the memories.

Instead, I turned on the windshield wipers to clear the rivulets of water that were starting to form. Yes, I decided, better go check the hospital and confirm Norma was sleeping, and then I'd head back and dream sweet dreams of the next time with Alex.

I knew where I wanted the next time to be but still felt reluctant going to his place so soon. With the kiss, the bedroom would undoubtedly be where we would head next. The idea excited but terrified me. Anyone would think I'd never been to bed with a guy before.

After Richard, I'd had a few one night stands as well as a couple of longer, disappointing relationships and I didn't want the first and was scared to have more of the second. Neither had been particularly successful.

Now I wanted to prolong the promise of something better and wondered how I could slow things down without it creating an uncomfortable separation between us. Perhaps Alex would sense this too and ease into the transition. The transition to what though? I was perfectly happy with my single state. Alex raised more questions than I was ready for. No, I thought, as I entered the hospital, not now Maggie. Think about that later.

The hospital was quiet and the lobby was virtually empty except for me and a woman behind the reception desk who looked up as I passed. She nodded then continued with what she was doing. I found Norma's new room but this time she was sharing it with another female and they were both asleep when I opened the door. Flowers spilled over the other patient's table and get-well cards were pinned to the wall. By contrast Norma's bedside looked sterile and empty.

I stepped closer and could see that Norma's hand was bruised under the tape that held the catheter in place. She was snoring; her mouth open and saliva glistened at the corner of her lips. The gauze over her temple was still in place and her hair was messy and unkempt as though she had tossed and rubbed her head against the pillow. I'll have to remember to bring her brush when I come back tomorrow morning, I thought.

Norma suddenly snorted and closed her mouth and stopped snoring although she was still breathing heavily. Surprised, I took a step back and knocked the chair beside the bed. I froze. That's all I need is to have both women wake up, I thought, and when Norma finds herself in a shared room there'll be hell to pay. She'd insist on a private one.

Neither woman stirred so I breathed easier. There was a strong odor of disinfectant coming from the attached bathroom and the hum of the bedside equipment from the next bed seemed invasive. At least Norma wasn't on oxygen. She didn't have that to deal with.

Not much I can do here, I thought, it's time to leave. Then Norma coughed and I hesitated, and stepped closer to the bed. Her eyes were open but looked watery and unfocused as though she was trying to determine where she was.

Her gaze fixed on me. "What are you looking at?" Her voice was weak and raspy.

"I ..."

"Don't just stand there. Get me something to drink. My mouth's dry."

"Here's some by your table." I lifted the carafe and poured some water into the glass.

"What table?" Norma turned her head and appeared puzzled. "Where am I, then?"

She doesn't know where she is, I thought. Great! "Here, drink this." I supported her head while I held the water to her lips.

Norma took a few sips then pushed it away. "Turn off that TV," she said as her eyes closed again. "It's keeping me awake."

I realized Norma was still groggy and had no idea where she was. There was no TV that was playing and she probably mistook the noise of the equipment for one. I waited a few minutes, expecting her eyes to flash open again but they remained closed and soft grunts came from her throat. She was asleep and would probably have no recollection the following day that I had even been there. I was off the hook until then.

As I passed by the desk on my way out I stopped and spoke to a nurse there. "My mother in room seventeen is sleeping, but I think you should know that when she wakes and is coherent enough to fig- ure she's sharing a room, she'll probably want a private one."

"Really? Not sure we have any of those available right now, but I'll leave a note for the change of nursing staff tomorrow morning. I won't be here then."

"Thanks and fortunate for you," I said, "because I don't envy anyone having to deal with her tirades."

The hallways were quiet as I rang for the elevator. I realized how tired I was and just wanted to get back and go to bed. I wished it

157

was my own bed, in my own house instead of Norma's that would probably be a cold because I'd left all the windows open. Cold or not it would be refreshing, though. Then I remembered Alex's arms again and wanted him there to warm the bed with me.

The loud peal of a telephone jolted me awake the following morning and in quick succession the vibration of my cell phone next to my pillow. Still sleepy, I could hear the house recording pick up. It was Norma, awake, loud and furious. I groaned and slid under the covers with my cell phone and hoped it was Alex. It was John and he sounded distressed.

"Mar … aggie," he said, "I just left the hospital and your mother is extremely upset. She apparently expects you to be there. Are you okay?"

I was surprised. "Yes. Fine. She's awake already? I stopped by to see her late last night but she was rather out of it. I planned to go first thing this morning. What time is it?"

"Almost ten …"

"Ten? Oh my god! I must've overslept. Thanks John. Listen, I'll call you later when I've seen her but now I must get ready and dash."

"Well thank heaven you're okay. I was worried. Would you like to have lunch a bit later? I'd enjoy that and perhaps we can get to know each other a little better."

I threw back the covers and sat up, "Thanks, John, I'd like that too but let me see Norma first and I'll get back to you. Okay?"

"Yes, but I should warn you she was making quite a fuss."

"I can believe it. Does she want another room?"

"Very much and they're doing their best to give her one. The woman in the next bed was becoming rather upset and perhaps it's more for that poor lady your mother will get her way." He clicked his tongue and made a small tsk sound, "and I really thought she was a most charming old lady, but I'm beginning to see that perhaps there's another side to her. Oh dear, dear ..."

"Yes, John. Definitely another side but I gotta go."

I threw the cell phone on the bed and grabbed my jeans, pulling them on. Norma had been the caller on the other phone and although I had missed much of what was said, heard her yell that I, Margaret, was an ungrateful wretch to leave her there alone. I pushed the erase button. That was one message not to replay. I didn't need or want to know what else was said.

There was no time for coffee. Maybe, I thought, I'll grab something from the hospital lobby. I'd seen the machine earlier although the coffee would probably be foul. I could see that the day was grey and overcast and pulled on my sweater. Probably more rain, I thought. Better close the windows and take my lightweight less than adequate California raincoat but it was better than nothing.

As the front door shut behind me, I remembered Norma's hairbrush and hesitated, unwilling to go back for it since I was already late. Norma was pissed but Norma would be pissed regardless of when I got there. Why rush when the response would be the same? I placed the key in the lock and went back in again. At least I wouldn't arrive empty handed and perhaps she would appreciate that I had thought to bring it.

I opened the door to Norma's bathroom and again, the smell of ammonia and stale air took over my nostrils. I held my breath and pushed aside the curtain to the small window above the toilet. Rain or no rain, this place gets some fresh air, I decided as I struggled with the catch before it eased open and the wind blew the scent of the *Lonicera* vine outside. I stuck my face closer to the opening to breathe in the sweet scent before looking for the brush.

It was on the counter where Norma had left it last. I picked it up, about to toss it in my bag, when several of my mother's gray hairs brushed against my hand. I flinched and set it down. I didn't want it next to my things and went into the kitchen and removed a large plastic bag from the container drawer and took that into the bathroom, pulling apart the opening as I went.

My action was more revealing than I liked to consider. I hated handling anything personal of hers. It made Norma too close for a woman who had spent her life remaining distant. I tossed the brush in the baggie, closed it and threw it in my purse. I realized that I could've made some coffee while I was getting ready and the hospital vending machine was looming as a grim prospect. Later than I wanted to be, I decided to stop by the café and get a coffee to go, and maybe something to eat to go with it. I'd be fortified for confrontation, I thought, and the idea made me feel better.

With my hot coffee and bagel I was pleased I'd reconsidered. It made my drive to the hospital more relaxed and I was able to recall the prior evening with Alex. Kay's doggie smell was peppery and still in the car. I smiled and half turned my head expecting to see the German Shepherd gazing at me expectantly from the back seat. I realized I had to air out the car and take it to be vacuumed before Norma's release, but wasn't about to do that until I knew when that would be.

In the daylight I could see doggie hair adhering to the dark brown upholstery and liked what I saw. It's interesting you don't mind doggie hair yet cringe over your mother's, I thought. But I liked having a beautiful and well behaved animal keeping me company not to mention its lovable owner and Norma was very different than well behaved and far from lovable.

I took a bite of the bagel. By the time I got to the hospital it would almost be lunchtime and I didn't want to get in the nurses' way and I didn't want to watch Norma eat, either. She'd complain about the food, push it aside, grumble that she didn't deserve to be treated so badly and would expect to leave and have me help her do it.

I saw Cheryl leaving and walking to her car as I drove into the parking lot. She was slightly hunched against the drizzle and hadn't seen me. Hmmm, I thought, Norma's had at least two visitors including John and so perhaps she's been too preoccupied to think about me being late. I'll have to thank her for taking the time to go the next time I see her.

Pulling on my raincoat, I grabbed the half finished coffee and bit into the rest of the bagel before hurrying into the hospital. I could smell the industrialized cafeteria food as I pushed open the doors. It smelled overcooked and the clank of the carts as they jostled the dishes didn't invite an appetite. I was relieved I'd stopped and wasn't getting the coffee there and took a quick sip from my plastic cup. Already lukewarm it was still better than the scalding dishwater tasting liquid I would've had from the machines.

I passed the nurses' station headed for my mother's room when I heard a voice call out, "Oh, Miss. Just a moment, er … Maggie." I turned—it was the nurse I had spoken to yesterday.

"Hi Bryony. How are you? What is it?"

"Your mother got moved to another room. It's down the corridor that way, not the way you're going. Room twenty-three." She indicated the hallway behind me.

"So you found another room for her. Great! Didn't think you had one available."

She pursed her lips and shrugged. "We had to move another patient to do it but it was for everyone's peace of mind. Your mother can be a determined old lady, can't she?"

"Yes. Now imagine what she's like when she not sedated and nursing a concussion."

Bryony smiled. "Well sometimes we have to make allowances for the elderly."

"We do? Well if that's the case I think my mother has allocated herself more than her fair share of it."

I tossed the rest of the coffee in a waste bin and counted the numbers on the doors. Most were open and I could see patients in their robes or printed floral gowns. They were getting ready for lunch and the smell of food was stronger, with no avoiding the institutional canteen aroma.

Norma's door was closed. I rapped softly and waited. There was no response so I knocked a little harder and opened the door a crack. My mother was sitting up in bed, facing the door. The gauze on her head had been replaced with a large flesh toned adhesive bandage strip and didn't look as serious as it had earlier. I still wondered what the gash looked like underneath.

"Hi," I said. "How you doing?"

Norma sat stiffly upright, staring ahead as though I hadn't entered the room and coughed slightly.

"Are you okay?" I said, walking further into the room. "What's wrong?"

Norma reached for a tissue and coughed again. It sounded genuine and not something she was doing to elicit sympathy. I asked again, "Seems like you've got a cough. What's that all about?"

"This place is freezing and I probably caught a cold while they were moving me from that last room. I didn't have enough blankets. Still don't." She wriggled under the thin white cotton blanket that covered her waist and the catheter in her hand caught against the sheet. "I want you to get me out of here." Her voice was weak and even hoarser than I'd heard earlier. I wondered if screaming at everyone had caused her voice to crack or whether she really might have a cold in addition to everything else.

"Has the doctor seen you this morning?"

"I have to stay for at least a few more days." She ran a trembling hand through her hair and I could see it was slightly matted from lying on the pillow.

"Here," I said, rummaging into my purse and pulling out the baggie. "I brought your hairbrush. Thought you might like to have it."

Norma took it and removed the brush, pulling it through her hair. She really does have lovely hair for an old lady, I thought. It's still thick and the gray is turning into silver. I hoped that when I got older, and if I had to resemble Norma in any way, then I'd settle for hair like hers. The rest she could keep.

I knew that in many ways I resembled Norma although not enough to be a striking similarity. I had my father's eyes; hazel and large and warmer than the icy blue of my mother's but from photographs taken years ago, they had once been one of her most attractive features. Pity, I thought, that the laughter went out of them then wondered if it had ever been there. Not that I could recall.

"Did you bring my toothbrush?"

I was surprised then apologetic. "No. Sorry. Now why didn't I think of that?" Then I remembered that toothbrushes and toothpaste were routinely provided to all patients. "Didn't they give you one when you checked in here?"

"I didn't want theirs. I prefer natural bristle."

"I'll bring it next time …" My cell phone vibrated in my purse and it sounded distant and muffled. I was irritated with myself for not leaving it in the car and decided to ignore it.

"What's that sound?" Norma said.

"My cell phone."

"Aren't you going to answer it?"

I decided I could always make an excuse I was visiting my mother and would call back later. I fished it out of the corner pocket

163

of my bag, its lights flashing and pulsing louder as I removed it. I looked at the dial and answered. "Hi John. Yes, just got here and with her now. Can I call you back in awhile? Okay. Yes I'll tell her that. Thanks. Bye." I clicked it to off. I didn't want Alex to be heard if he called.

"Who's John?"

"John?" The woman didn't miss a thing. "Um, Reverend McLean and he sends his best wishes."

Norma lifted her shoulders back, ramrod straight, her head cocked to one side. "Reverend John McLean? No!"

She emphasized the no as though spitting it out as something distasteful. Then repeated, "Reverend McLean? You call him John?"

"Why not?"

"When did that happen?"

"Yesterday when you were first brought in and I met him here."

"And now you call him John? What are you two doing being my back?" Norma's voice rose.

"We're not doing anything behind your back." Now why did I answer the damn thing? My mother's invasion of my privacy was a reminder of so many other similar occasions when she'd demanded information from me but I said as evenly as I could, "He's very concerned about you and we chatted. That's all."

"About me?"

"Of course about you." I wasn't about to tell her what else we had shared. "He was sorry you'd fallen."

"We have chats all the time but I don't call him John. Not yet," Norma added. "I think it's disrespectful to call him by his first name, Margaret. He's a vicar and a man of God."

What's she going to say next I wondered? "True. But a man first with a name and he asked me to use it."

"He never asked me." Norma was becoming petulant.

She's behaving like a jilted schoolgirl, I thought. Stupid old woman. "Perhaps you didn't have the kind of conversation that invited a first name basis."

Norma voice rose again and she looked flushed. She cleared her throat and reached for another tissue, her hand fluttering over the box unable to reach it. I stepped closer and pushed it toward her. Norma shook one loose from the opening and held it to her mouth. She coughed and gagged slightly, the rasp coming deep from her throat, then spat into the Kleenex and handed it to me. "Here throw this away."

I hesitated and grabbed a clean one to hold the one Norma was handing to me and looked around for a waste container. Not seeing one I opened the door to the bathroom and threw it into the toilet then rinsed my hands in the washbasin. That was even worse than the hairbrush.

Norma was watching me from the bed and I could see she was struggling to appear composed. Her mouth was pursed and her eyelids closed as she shook her head. "I think I gave Reverend McLean the perfect opportunity for me to call him John. Why, I've already donated a great deal to the church and we've spent a long time discussing my funeral arrangements." She blinked open her eyes again, "Why didn't he tell me to call him John?"

"Perhaps it was out of respect for you." I wanted to change the subject but Norma was holding on like a dog with a rag.

"Respect? What would you know of respect?" She started coughing again and I became more concerned. Norma was subject to bad colds. She'd had bronchitis twice in the past and each time it had been progressively worse but she'd pulled through with antibiotics. She spat some more then opened the tissue to observe what had been ejected. "Look at that," she said. "Look at it, Margaret. It's green. You know what *that* means."

I grabbed two more tissues to take the one Norma was shoving towards me and despite my reluctance looked into the slimy mass my mother was holding. "It's not green. It's more or less clear and that yellow stuff is natural."

I wondered just how natural it was but at least it was a change of subject from John. I carried it to the bathroom and flushed the toilet, then ran the hot water to wash my hands more thoroughly with soap, pulling on the paper towels to dry them.

"You know he's not your type."

"Who's not my type?" What on earth was she babbling on about now? There was no way she knew about Alex.

"Reverend McLe … John." Her chin was raised and her mouth tightened. "John's not your type. You're too placid, like your father. John wants, needs, someone strong who has a mind of her own."

"Like you?" I was smiling and trying to keep from laughing. "John and you?"

"Yes."

"He could be your son."

"He's older than you think. And it's the connection between two people that's important."

"You're absolutely right about that."

I was thinking of Alex first then back to John and of his anguish when he admitted being gay. I felt a sudden warmth and surge of sympathy for his unhappy rejection of something he was unable to change. I would have to be more supportive. Maybe help him consider dating. I wished I was back in California where I knew some guys at the school who would love to take him out. He was really sweet and rather cute in a pale, delicate sort of way.

"I'm always right!"

"Perhaps. But I don't think you're his type, either."

I was relieved to hear a rap at the door and the sound of lunch cart stopping outside. Thank heaven, I thought. Someone's here to change the subject. An elderly woman poked her head around the door. "S'cuse me, ladies. Lunch time."

She pushed the door open wider to allow for herself and a large tray to enter. "You didn't order from the menu yesterday, Dearie, so you get the chicken and mashed potatoes. It's really good you'll see," and began to arrange the dishes on Norma's bedside table that she swung around and over the covers.

Norma coughed again. "I'm not hungry."

"Come now, Lovey. You must eat. Just try a little bit and you'll feel much better. I'll be back in about an hour to take the tray from you, although you can push the table away from the bed when you're finished. But you already know that." She seemed oblivious to Norma's hostile glare intended to send her scurrying.

I looked more closely at my mother. She was definitely flushed and without the pallor she had exhibited earlier. Against my better judgment I laid my hand against Norma's brow and she flipped my hand away from her. "Don't do that," she said.

Ignoring her I said, "You know I think you're running a slight fever. Are you drinking enough fluids? When was the last time they took your temperature?"

Norma pushed against the table of food and I caught it before it spilled onto the covers. I spun the trolley away from the bed and set it against the window. The bread roll and butter looked good and I realized I was still hungry but resisted the impulse to take it. I decided to wait until later.

"Let me go find a nurse. I think you might be running a slight fever," I said again and left the room in search of Bryony who was on the phone in the nurse's station. I waited for her to finish talking, and then asked if she would mind checking on Norma.

"She had a slightly elevated temperature this morning when we moved her," she said, "but it was just under a hundred so the doctor wasn't too concerned. Let's go take it again."

Bryony moved efficiently, her pretty soft blue uniform brushing against her legs as she walked while I trotted to keep up. We passed open doors where patients were eating lunch and I thought that Norma's closed door was so symbolic of everything my mother represented. The nurse turned the handle and pushed against the door with her hip, holding the thermometer while she slipped it from its sterile case. "Open up," she said, and I was surprised to see Norma obediently widen her mouth.

She inserted the thermometer, holding her pulse as my mother clamped down, her eyes closed. She started to cough again and it was removed then reinserted, and we waited for the tiny buzz to indicate the results. She actually looks sick, I thought. Now what?

The nurse peered at the dial. "You're right," she said. "Must've gone up some more since this morning. I'll call Doctor Suffolk and let him know." She looked over at the uneaten food. "Hmmm, she didn't want her lunch, then?" She poured some water from the covered container by the bedside. "Here, Mrs. Resnick, drink this. We need to keep you hydrated." She scooped Norma's head where it had flopped against the pillow, all signs of her previous protests gone, and held the glass to her lips. Norma took a few sips then weakly pushed it away.

"That's good," Bryony said, "I think you should try and get some sleep now." She nodded toward me, "If you haven't already eaten and want to go get something to eat this might be a good time to leave."

I loved her for saying that. I was starving."Is it okay with you, Norma, if I come back later?" I said, "and I think you do need to rest."

My mother didn't answer and I wondered if she was pretending. It was difficult to know although I could tell from the way her limp hands rested on the covers that she wasn't feeling well. I hoped the doctor would visit her soon to figure out if something else was wrong.

The concussion was probably causing her to feel lousy. After her little outburst she probably had more of a headache but that didn't produce colds and it seemed like she'd caught one. Despite myself I was more apprehensive than I would've believed. If it went to her lungs it could be more serious than the concussion but she was in hospital and the right place to be if that was the case.

With a final glance toward the bed, I followed the nurse. "Thanks, Bryony. How long will you be on duty?"

"Until seven tonight. Don't worry I'll take care of her and let the other nurses know about it. I'm going to get her doctor now. If you want to call me, I'll be in station three and you can ask for me if I don't pick up myself."

"You're a love and I appreciate all your help." I was relieved to be leaving the hospital and know Norma was being taken care of. I could relax thinking she was in good hands and, for a few hours at least, I could think of something else.

As I reached the car and got in, I took the phone out of my bag and started to punch in Alex's number but changed my mind and called John, instead. I wanted to see them both but I was hoping for dinner with Alex. At his place.

John picked up at the first ring and I said, "That was quick. It almost didn't ring. How are you?"

"I'm at my desk. The phone's right here. Fine, thanks to you."

"To me?"

"I feel as though a weight has been lifted off my shoulders. I needed to speak to someone and not just to God. He sent you to me— an angel in disguise," and laughed as he said that.

"Not sure about that, but pleased I was around to listen." I wanted to change the subject and get off the phone. It was almost one thirty and needed to eat something. "I have to get back to the hospital again, but thought you might want to join me for lunch. I'm sorry I'm so late in getting back to you. Have you eaten yet?"

"I did but can I still join you and you can tell me about your dear ... er, your mother. Maybe I'll have a piece of pie or something and some coffee. Where shall we meet?"

"Golden Crumpet? It's where I plug in for the Internet and they have fairly decent food. Basic but good. It's late but I still want breakfast."

"Of course and I go there too. Dina works there."

"You know Dina?"

"Maggie. I'm the local minister and it's a small town. It's my job to know everyone. Even if not that well for some people it seems." He laughed again and it sounded stronger than anything I'd heard from him before.

"Right. Of course you are. Okay see you in a bit."

CHAPTER THIRTEEN

I tossed the phone in my bag then rethought, pulling it out and pressing the number for Alex. I knew there was no time to chat so clicked on the text button, wondering if he used that too. "alex ~ sorry will call later ~ 2 much going on 2 chat now ~ maggie."

Starting the car, I pulled out of the hospital parking lot, the wheels splashing through the wet pavement. I could feel my blood sugar plummeting and realized if I didn't eat soon I'd get too light-headed. I should've taken that roll from Norma's tray, I thought.

John was already waiting for me when I got there. "Hey, that was fast," I said.

"I'm closer than the hospital. It's past lunch hour and the place is almost empty. Good. We'll get a table right away."

"Perfect. I'm famished."

Dina waved to us as we came in although I thought she looked a little startled to see us both together. Her eyes widened and she stopped on her way to the kitchen carrying the plates she'd removed from the table. "Sit anywhere," she said. "Be right with you."

"Booth or table?" John asked as we surveyed the almost empty café.

"Booth. Over there, perhaps." I pointed to a place midway across the floor. "Let's sit there. But first I have to go to the ladies room." I suddenly realized I had to pee and wanted to wash my hands from being in the hospital and around Norma. "Be right back." Then added, "If Dina comes over while I'm gone, can you ask her for some coffee and toast, I'll order the rest when I get back."

The ladies was a small room in the back of the café down a little hallway. As I passed the kitchen, the smell of food was overwhelming. I was so hungry I didn't care that I was even appreciating the smell of greasy hamburger.

The toilet was dark with no window, so using the light that came from the hallway, I peered inside and felt along the wall next to the door for the switch, flipped it on, and the area was illuminated, exposing an overflowing basket of crumpled paper towels and a dripping faucet with rust stains along the porcelain. The walls were in serious need of some paint but it was clean. I never sat on a public toilet even when there were paper seat covers. It was a habit I'd acquired from the time I was a kid and Norma made me use the toilet before we left the house.

"But I don't want to go," I'd whine, although knew it was inevitable.

"I won't have you sitting on any strange toilets," she'd say. "You don't know who's been using them and I'm not having a kid of mine catching some strange disease and it be something else I have to take care of." When I really had to go Norma would grumble and carefully tear off long strips of toilet paper laying them in a crisscross pattern over the seat before jerking me onto it.

I wondered why I would remember that. Perhaps it was because I had been around her continuously without a chance to separate myself and hoped it wouldn't generate more unpleasant memories to slip back into my mind causing me to question myself and my actions. It's taken too many years to figure out who I am, I thought, and even then there are still times when I continue to wonder.

As I was washing my hands my cell phone rang and wondered if it were Alex, although wished I wasn't in the toilet. Without looking at the dial I hit the incoming call button, "Hello."

"Hey Sweetie, how's it going?"

"Shelly, it's you!"

"Who did you think it would be?"

"Alex."

"Ah hah, Alex? So you've gotten him out of the church already? So tell me how."

"Yep but Shelly, I really can't right now although there's a ton of things I want to talk about but I'm in the ladies room and I'm starving and John's waiting for me in the restaurant. It's so lovely hearing your voice but I really gotta go. How's Mewfus?"

"Cat's fine. Misses you I can tell. And John? You double dating or what? What are you up to Lady?"

"No and not a date. John McLean, the vicar and I'll tell you later. Really sorry Shelly, because I'd love to chat. Will you be in this evening?" As I said that I wondered if I would have time even then.

"Whose evening? Yours or mine?"

"Oh, right. So what time is it there?"

"Five thirty in the morning. Brian woke up from a bad dream so thought I'd call before I hopped back in bed."

"Darn. Keep forgetting about the time difference. I'll email and we can set up a time but I don't know if I'll be at the hospital or seeing Alex later. Hospital more likely though."

"Alex rates a ten. Norma zero. How is the old biddy?"

"Not great. Not good but I've really got to go. God I'd so like to chat, I have so much to tell you."

"Then go. Later then."

"I'll email with some possible times when we can relax with no interruptions. Love you."

I hung up and put the phone on alarm. As I was doing that it started to vibrate in my hands. It was a text from Alex. *"no prob alex."*

Tucking the phone in my bag I hurried back to the booth. I sat down in front of John, and poured cream into my waiting coffee. Dina followed me to the table. "Do you know what you want?"

I wanted something that could be prepared quickly. "Yes. A late breakfast of two fried eggs and hash browns." Then I remembered Dina called them potato cakes and those came swimming next to baked beans. "That's potato cakes," I said, "and no baked beans, and if you have any marmalade for the toast that would be great."

"Bacon? Oh no, right. You don't eat that either." She shook her head as though failing to understand why I would want to leave off such an important part of the meal. "What's for you, Vicar?"

"Just the apple pie and if you can fill up my coffee, thanks."

Dina flipped her notepad and stuck it and the pencil in the pocket of her apron. As she turned, she stopped and looked down at me. "How's your poor mum doing?"

I remembered I'd not paid for the coffee and fished in my purse for some money and handed it to her. "Think I owe you this, Dina, thanks." Then although I wanted her to go and get my food said, "She seems to be doing okay but now developing a cold or something. Her temperature was elevated a bit when I left an hour ago."

With few patrons left after the lunch hour rush Dina seemed to be in no hurry so I added, "But, I do have to get back there fairly soon, though." I bit into the toast.

"Yours shouldn't take long then." She turned to John, "I'll be right back with the pie and did you want that with custard or whipped cream?"

"Thanks. Neither. Have to watch my waistline." He patted his stomach hidden below the table.

Dina laughed and trotted off to the kitchen and I could see her give the order to the chefs behind the counter.

"So you're going right back again?" John said.

"Yes. I should call to find out what's happening. She wasn't her usual self when I left."

"Is that a good thing or bad?" He smiled.

So he had a sense of humor beneath his more serious and professional role. I tore open a second packet of sugar pouring it into my coffee and stirring. "Both actually. Bad in that she obviously wasn't feeling so well and was running a slight fever and good in that she wasn't still screaming to be let out of there."

"She's a determined old lady."

"Yes but I wouldn't let her hear you call her old if I were you. She thinks she still looks younger than her age and when she's not piss ... angry, is still attractive. Beautiful twenty years ago but time has caught up with her."

He fiddled with his napkin, then shook his head as he looked at me, "She certainly does make me nervous though."

I laughed. "She makes everyone nervous, John. Is that why you tiptoe around her like she was going to explode?"

"Dear me, yes, I'm afraid so. Yes certainly it's that." He smiled apologetically as though it was an indication of some failing of his. "I often wonder how people develop into functioning adults with all our prejudices and fears, or indeed how much better we'd all be if we were more honest. Even trying to be nice would be a good thing, although ..." he smiled, "... without overdoing it, huh?"

He wasn't going to let me forget my comment but I knew he was more concerned with Norma. "Don't take her personally, she explodes at everything and everyone."

"That's what you've said but I'm not sure how I would react if she did that with me."

175

"If she does just tell her you have to go. My guess is she's going to be on her best behavior with you." Then I wondered how Norma would react toward him because I called him John. I decided not to mention it and let any possible situation happen in its own time.

"Well it'll be good practice to remain professional but firm and I'll have you to thank for the change." He glanced up as Dina set the pie in front of him. "Thanks, Dina." He looked over at me. "I'll wait until you get yours and then tackle this. It's a big piece. I think she's spoiling me." He was poking a large, syrupy chunk of apple with his fork.

He's like a little kid, I thought, and so sweet. I preferred my new opinion of him. "Eat. Don't wait for me."

"This really looks very good. Really good indeed. Would you like a piece?"

I shook my head. "Mine'll be here any minute." I was wondering what to talk about next. My mother and the apple pie wouldn't make much conversation. I was curious what he did when not traipsing around hospitals or delivering sermons. "So what else do you do, John?"

"Besides visiting the sick and elderly and delivering sermons?"

He'd read my mind. "Yes. Besides those."

"There's still a demand for weddings and funerals and the rather nerve-wracking experience of baptisms."

"Nerve-wracking?"

"Have you ever held someone's squirming baby that has no sense of the seriousness of the procedure?" He glanced up at me as though apologetic for his views, then continued, "But I rather like children and I'm on a few committees to help with food and clothing distribution for the needy. We have a homeless shelter here you know. Terribly underfunded but we have to make do with donations and our charity shop. Doesn't bring in much but every little helps. Ah! Here's your food."

"Great. I'm famished. Thanks Dina. Can you pour me a little more coffee when you have a moment?"

"How's the pie?" but she scurried away without waiting for a reply.

"So you keep pretty busy. What do you do to relax? You do relax don't you, John?"

"Relax? Hmm yes, that. Well I do garden and like to read. I like my solitude when I can find the time to be alone. Most of my days, and often nights, involve the church." He looked over at me. "Does lotto count?"

I laughed. "Well does it?" I was already beginning to feel the effects of putting food into my empty stomach. "Are you a serious gardener? I teach horticulture."

"Do you? Do you really? That's marvelous! I wondered what you did. Yes, I suppose I can consider myself a serious gardener and perhaps you've seen some of the flowers and plants I have around the church. But the weeds are so very invasive." He shook his head as though recalling the problem but then remembered our conversation. "That's wonderful. Wonderful! Now we have lots to chat about. I already consider you a friend, you know that?"

"Me too and I'm glad you had the courage to confront my rudeness."

"Not rude, not rude at all and perhaps it'll help me become more accessible to my parishioners. I always felt they kept their distance. Now I can understand why." He hesitated and began to toy with a piece of the piecrust, moving it back and forth across the plate with his fork. "Can I ask you … er … discuss something more personal again?"

Now what, I wondered. "Of course but do you want to talk about whatever it is here?" I looked around but the place was virtually empty. Dina was standing, wiping the counter and she started to walk toward us then stopped as I called to her, "It's okay Dina. We're fine." I turned back to John. He was looking rather solemn and chewing carefully on the remainder of his pie as though trying to make it last a little longer before speaking. I waited for him to swallow and wondered if he was reconsidering what he was about to say.

John lowered his voice. "Since our conversation, I've been wondering if I should, er ... if it would be appropriate if ..."

"If what?" I said, biting into the toast.

"If I should socialize more?"

I chewed slowly and wondered how to respond. I wanted to be careful with what I said. "What do you mean, socialize? Don't you do that with everything you're already involved in?"

"Yes. No. What I mean is, become friendlier with individuals like me and on a more personal level."

I hated that he felt he had to differentiate himself from people. Did other gays do this I wondered? Men and women or was it that the straight community did it to them. Probably the latter. I'd never given it much thought or even asked that of someone I knew to be gay. I had heard of teachers being fired when they came out or it was learned they were homosexual. How painful that must be and how insensitive I was to take my heterosexuality as the norm and never think beyond that. Another Shadow check. "You mean date?"

I didn't say it loudly and certainly not loudly enough that Dina or anyone would hear.

"Shhhh."

"I'm sorry." I dropped my voice, "I don't think anyone heard or is even listening. Is that what you mean?"

"Yes."

"Obviously dating shouldn't be an issue inside or outside of the clergy. Is that permitted in the Church of England?" I knew nothing about the rules or regulations that would apply to an Anglican priest. I didn't really want to get into the history of the church at the coffee table. Later perhaps but not here and not now but asked, "Is it anything like Catholicism?"

"Yes and no. Not quite the same although there are similarities in the services." He was on more solid ground. He paused. "The topic is controversial, you know, very controversial but same sex partners are becoming more accepted or at least considered although not for religious leaders."

"Well, what do *you* think?" I didn't want to add that I thought it should never be an issue although curious to hear what else he had to say. I thought of Norma in the hospital and decided that going back could wait a little longer. John seemed to be in need of speaking with me and that was more important.

He was still looking down at his plate and mumbled slightly so I had to lean forward to hear him more clearly. "I used to think my own homosexuality was a sin, although intellectually I knew it to be otherwise and truly think God understands. Somehow I could accept it with others but not me. You helped me confront that about myself."

"Perhaps you were already close to acknowledging that and I was just the catalyst. I'm pleased I was but did you think any more about finding a professional to help you figure it out, to understand it more?"

"Yes and I've been looking into that. And praying, too. Quite a bit."

"I still think you also need to find people you can trust until you feel more comfortable about this." I wanted to get the check but knew that he wasn't finished. "Can you talk to Alex? He seems like a caring and understanding guy."

"I never thought of Alex." Then added, "I don't think he's gay."

I laughed and John looked startled. "No he's not," I said. "We went on a date last night. It was very pleasant."

"You did? Really?" His face lit up in a smile. "Alex is such a wonderful person but he tends to keep to himself although I consider him a friend. Yes, perhaps I should engage him in more conversation. We British tend to be too polite and reserved I think."

"Alex is a great guy and I think he would be sensitive and understanding."

"I think you're right about that," he looked past my shoulder, "Oh, there's Cheryl. She's Dina's sister you know."

I turned around and saw Cheryl walking between the tables toward the kitchen.

"Yes. She helps Norma."

"Me too, and comes to church every Sunday. Such a nice woman. I like her."

"She seems kind hearted although I really don't know her that well."

I watched as they hugged and then Dina leaned back and seemed to touch Cheryl's hair as though in a gesture of affection. They chatted for a few minutes then both strolled toward the door.

Cheryl had waved towards our table as she came in but hesitated and walked over to John and me as she was leaving. "Hello, Vicar. Hi Maggie. I stopped by to see your mother this morning for a quick visit. Seems like she has a bit of a cold starting."

"I thought so too. And thanks for going in. I saw you in the parking lot earlier and I'm going back again as soon as I leave here."

"Say hello again for me and tell her I hope she's feeling better."

Cheryl was moving her hair back from her face and as she spoke I saw the quick glint of gold. I stared in disbelief at the opal earring that hung from her ear. It was my grandmother's earring. One of the pair and I would have recognized it anywhere and thought they had been in my mother's jewelry box. What was she doing with them? They were mine. I could feel the blood rush from my head and felt dizzy as my heart began to pound. I sat and stared at her, too shocked to speak.

She seemed oblivious to what was happening to me and said, "Well I'll be going then. See you in church, Vicar. Maggie, give me a call when you want me to come over and tidy up." She turned toward Dina and they both walked to the door with Cheryl leaving.

"I'll bring you your check," Dina called out as she passed.

I heard John's voice that seemed as though it came from a great distance instead of across the table. "Maggie, are you okay? You look like you've seen a ghost." He reached his hand towards me. "Maggie? Is anything wrong?"

I shook my head. So Cheryl was a thief. My grandmother's earrings. The ones promised to me. Unable to speak I began to cry and rummaged in my bag for a tissue. Finding none, I grabbed a napkin.

"Maggie. Oh dear, whatever can be wrong? Was it something I said?"

"No, not you, John. Cheryl. She was wearing my grandmother's earrings. They originally belonged to my great grandmother then passed down. An heirloom intended to be mine. She must have stolen them." The words tumbled from my mouth as though I had no control over what I said.

Dina placed the check between us, stared at me, hesitated, then obviously decided not to interfere and left us alone again.

"Stolen them? Surely not. There must be another explanation." John shook his head his brow furrowed as he handed me another napkin.

I was crying in earnest now, and didn't care if anyone saw or heard. I was confused and upset at the loss and felt violated as my mind replayed the image of seeing the jewelry on Cheryl's ear. "What other explanation is there?"

"Perhaps Norma gave them to her."

I stared at him. "Why on earth would she do that? Norma's not known for her generosity. She knew they were valuable. Yes, of course monetarily, but in the real sense of value as an heirloom. They belonged to my father's grandmother." I started to cry again as the extent of the loss became more real.

"Maggie, please don't cry. Dear me, but do so if you must. This is a very serious problem." John leaned over to an empty table and picked up another napkin, handing it to me. "Would you mind very much if I became involved and tried to discover what this is all about. It is the kind of situation in which I might have some expertise."

Through my tears I could see him looking down at me, anxious and concerned. He was nodding. "Yes, let me handle this, although I think you should ask your mother if she knows anything about it." He reached for the check and pulled out his wallet. "Lunch is on me. I feel like I've not only found a new friend but one that needs me too."

CHAPTER FOURTEEN

Unable to think clearly, I unlocked the car and slumped inside without turning on the ignition. Cheryl had stolen Grandmother's earrings; an integral part of my heritage and a reminder of someone I had loved. They were beautiful and were gone. I wanted to confront Cheryl and rip them from her but knew I never would, or could, do that. Be angry perhaps, and probably cry and then get even angrier because I would become inarticulate and unable to express what I wanted to say.

Then I thought of Norma lying in the hospital bed—Norma who had no trouble expressing her anger with anyone or anything. I wasn't like her though; slow to infuriate like my father, but when confronted with an injustice could become incensed and let it simmer inside my head although I was trying to change that.

I'd often wondered if my ability to rage had been deeply buried as a result of living with my mother. Anger and defiance as a child brought swift and painful repercussions—painful spanking or being frightened when my father was absent and locked in a darkened closet with no one to respond to my cries. I'd learned to suppress my emotions until I was able to move away from her and even then they were difficult to express.

Any anger I might experience was usually safely under my control because of my early years. But no longer. Thinking of the earrings, and the injustice of having something precious taken from me, my body and hands shook as I cried some more. I became aware of someone standing by the window of the car, knocking on the glass and I looked up. It was Dina.

"Are you okay?" She mouthed the words as though the window prevented me from hearing.

I stared through swollen eyes. Dina was Cheryl's sister and perhaps that was what Cheryl had come into the café for. To show them to her but surely Dina must've asked where she got them although if stolen would Cheryl have been so overt in displaying them? That didn't make sense, but what other explanation was there? That Norma had given them was too impossible to consider.

I partially rolled down the window and nodded. "Yes. Thanks. Upsetting news that's all." And turned the key in the ignition and the engine hummed.

"Not your mother is it? She okay?"

"Not Norma, no. I have to go, Dina, thanks for asking."

Dina nodded, her face scrunched in concern as she stepped away from the car. "Then you take care and I hope everything turns out all right."

I dried my eyes although the tears continued to fall. Fuck it, I thought, I'm angry and a mess and I have to see Norma. She'll ask me what's wrong and I'm not sure I want to deal with all this until I know more. Besides, I realized, if she learned that Cheryl had stolen the earrings then I would have to deal with her rage in addition to my own. No, I didn't want to go back to the hospital.

Then I thought of Alex. I didn't want to see him either; not in this state. Having him be sympathetic and holding me about a loss wasn't the way I wanted to see him. I wanted to go home, my own home but that was almost six thousand miles away. Instead I had to go back to a house I hated and gather my wits. But first, I decided, I would call the hospital and start to put some order into my thinking.

I pushed the menu key for the hospital and waited while it rang. I hoped Bryony might answer but it was a male who said hello.

"Hi," I said. "I'm calling to find out about my mother Norma Resnick in room twenty-three When I left this morning she was running a slight fever and I wanted …"

"Please hold for a moment and I'll transfer you to the nurse in charge." The phone switched to piped music while I waited. I wondered how I had the wrong number and reminded myself to get the correct one. Maybe if Norma didn't demand room changes all the time I could keep things organized.

I waited and the music stopped and a voice said, "Hello, can I help you?"

I repeated my request.

"Hold on a moment. Let me check."

Well at least I had the right location. "Is this Bryony?"

"No, this is Monica and yes, Mrs. Resnick well she's …. er, may I ask who's calling about her? We're not supposed to give that information over the phone."

"This is her daughter, Maggie. I was there this morning and she wasn't doing so well. Bryony took her temperature and it was slightly elevated."

"Yes, Doctor Suffolk saw her and just left. She has concussion."

"Yes, I know she has concussion. What about the fever?" I was becoming impatient. My anger was still throbbing inside my head and I was taking it out on the poor woman at the other end of the phone.

"She has a slight cold. Nothing to worry about. Do you want the telephone number to her room?"

"That's a good idea. Why don't you give it to me and I can call her now. What time do they serve dinner and I'll try and get there after that."

"Usually between five and five thirty. If you come around six we should be putting stuff away by then and her extension is her room number. Just call the main hospital number and the operator will put you through."

"Thank you very much. I'll come by then."

Monica put the phone down with a click and the line went quiet. Then I realized I didn't have the main hospital number and would have to call back. I looked at my watch. It was already almost four. I had less time than I had realized and decided to go back to the house and pour myself a glass of wine. Late breakfast, early aperitif. I sighed. I had a lot to think about.

The phone was ringing when I opened the door and I hurried to answer before I heard the machine pick up. If it was Norma I was prepared with an excuse. I'd say the car had stalled and I had to call the AA to come help me. Norma was clueless about cars and wouldn't question other than to perhaps rant on about it preventing me from being with her. Then I would say I'd called, which would be true, and I planned to visit after the dinner, also true. I was pleased I'd thought of that. It made the lie more convincing.

"Hello?"

"Margaret? Where are you?"

Her voice sounded husky but with the familiar disapproval. I walked into the kitchen and slipped the receiver between my chin and shoulder reaching for a wineglass and the Merlot. I poured a little, hesitating with my response as I took a sip, "I'm back at the house," I said, wishing I had let the phone continue to ring.

"What are you doing there? Why aren't you here? With me?" She coughed into the mouthpiece. "The doctor said I have bronchitis."

"I thought it was just a cold. How do you suppose you got bronchitis?"

"I have weak lungs. This place isn't good for me. Have you spoken to anyone to get me out?"

I didn't tell her I hadn't. "They said you had to be under observation and since you're now running a temperature you'll probably be there a bit longer. I'm planning to stop by after your dinner."

"I'm not hungry."

"Did you eat anything at all?"

"Jelly and ice cream."

I paused for a moment, I thought she'd eaten jam and visualized a sandwich then realized it was jello. "That's not enough. Do you want me to pick something up for you?"

"No! Why weren't you here this afternoon?"

I thought she'd forgotten when she didn't get an answer the first time she asked, so I lied and told her about the car stalling.

"It's my car. Are they going to send me the bill? You were the one driving it. It worked fine when Cheryl drove it." She was losing her voice although still held the customary vehemence.

"The Automobile Association. There's no charge. They fixed it."

She ignored what I said as though disinterested. "Well I'm going now. My throat's sore and I have a headache."

I felt genuinely sympathetic. Nobody should have a throbbing head and raw throat.

"See you later then," I said. "Try and get some sleep."

She always had the last word. "It's too noisy to sleep and don't bring flowers."

CHAPTER FIFTEEN

It was almost four-thirty. I poured myself another glass and realized that with two I shouldn't be driving. I wasn't hungry but figured I should eat something and checked the refrigerator for some cheese. I pulled out the cheddar and some crackers and nibbled on those and thought of my mother's jewelry box but decided against checking. What would that prove? I'd already seen Cheryl with the earrings. I wanted more time to collect my thoughts to see if anything remained of Grandmother Clare's things. What if they too were gone? If I found nothing I'd completely lose it and wasn't sure I had the courage to look and find out.

I decided to take a quick shower before leaving again then heard the faint sound of my cell phone ring in my purse and went back into the living room where I'd dropped it. I didn't feel like talking, though. My head throbbed and my eyes felt puffy and the dial looked blurry. Alex. I let it ring and turned off the sound. Later, I thought. Later.

The hot water poured over my head and body and I turned, slowly, feeling the pressure as it beat down on my back and shoulders. I soaped my arms and ran my hands across my breasts and over my stomach and down my thighs. I poured some shampoo into my hand and rubbed it into my hair, massaging deep into my scalp. The image of my grandmother's earrings on Cheryl was etched into my memory and my anger still pounded my mind and seemed to obliterate all else.

I still believed they had to be stolen. Perhaps Cheryl lied to Dina and said they were a gift if she had asked. I shook my head and let the water rinse away the suds. I had to think clearly but being the effect of the theft, if it was that, and being a victim regardless of how she got them, wouldn't give me the space to do that and I had to act. There was to be no more crying when I confronted Cheryl, no outburst of anger that would reduce effective communication or ability to think.

I wondered if I should report it to the police. That's what I wanted to do. Have the woman arrested and the earrings returned and returned to me and not to Norma. If my mother hadn't known they were missing then obviously she wasn't the right person to care for them and besides which they were mine, not hers. But I still didn't know if she knew they were gone. She might not have wanted me to know. If she hadn't told me about Daddy then for sure the reason behind the missing earrings would be kept hidden. I have an old sepia picture, brown with age, of my great grandmother wearing them although their color is missing from the picture. Now they were completely missing from me.

Stepping out of the shower I grabbed a towel and began drying myself, rubbing it across my skin so the blood flowed to the surface in blotches. I wanted to pass the earrings on as they had been passed down to me. Then I stopped. Pass them on to whom, though? I had no children, no siblings with offspring of their own.

I had once thought of having a child but that was no longer an option after my divorce from Richard. I'd even considered being a single mother but had then dismissed that idea as being not only impractical but too much of an emotional challenge without a partner.

So who would I leave the earrings to? Perhaps Cheryl had daughters who would wear them after her.

The thought drove another wave of anger through me. I dried off my legs and wrapped the towel around my head and rubbed moisturizer onto my body. I pulled on a pair of panties and hooked my bra before trotting into the bedroom for my jeans and a shirt. It was getting on for five o'clock and I'd be late again.

I grabbed the hairdryer and turned it on high, blowing the hot air across my head then switched it to a lower setting. I knew that my hair would never be completely dry, it was too long and thick, and I'd have to leave with it still damp. I glanced in the mirror. Great, I thought, just great. Puffy eyes and wet hair. Well the hospital isn't the Ritz, not that I'd want to go there either, and I'd just be seeing Norma who wouldn't give a shit anyway. Perhaps if I stood far enough away from her she'd never notice and John, if he were there, probably wouldn't care either if he saw me, in fact he would be solicitous and caring.

I remembered what he'd said to me in the restaurant while I was crying—that he would help me resolve the problem. A wave of relief escaped as an exhalation of breath, of reassurance that he would do that and that I wasn't entirely alone in trying to solve the problem. He meant it when he said he considered me a friend and god knows I needed one.

Then I thought of Alex—of his deep laugh and his bear like size and his arms and mouth. Alex was becoming a good friend too, only of a different kind. Then I remembered he'd called and I hadn't spoken or texted since that morning. I had to do it before I saw Norma otherwise it would be too late and with excuses I didn't want to make.

I ran down stairs, my hair flopping across my shoulders and making my shirt damp. As I picked up the cell phone it rang. "Hello?" I said. It was him.

"Maggie? I was worried about you. I didn't hear back so thought I'd try calling again. Hope you don't mind." His voice was deep and warm and sounded genuinely concerned.

"Alex. I'm sorry. I'm okay but it's been a bit of a trying day with more than I wanted to think about."

"Your mother?"

I didn't want to go into any further explanation. "I'm on my way there now—at least in a few minutes I will be. I was just going to call you and the phone rang as I picked it up."

He chuckled. "Great minds, huh? So can ... do you want to talk about whatever it is that's bothering you?"

Richard had never been that way when we were married. He always seemed oblivious to my emotions until I either got mad or cried or both. It was nice to know I now had three very different males, my father, Alex, and John, who seemed to care what I thought.

"That's so sweet of you. But not now. Can I call you after I've been to the hospital? It might be late. I don't know what's going on with my mother." I glanced at the clock. "Damn, I said I'd be there by now."

"Go. Kay and I will go for a long walk and I'll wait to hear back from you."

"Thanks. Yes. Alex ... I really appreciate your calling and ..."

"Yes?"

"I had a lovely evening last night."

"Me too."

I experienced a sense of relief that I hadn't felt all day. Alex, the hot shower and remembering John's offer of help all combined to help relax me. I felt back in control.

"Good. Gotta go. I'll call you later." Then, "How late is later?"

"Anytime. But if you don't leave your mother will be chomping at the bit."

I laughed. "Bye," I said and hung up.

I tossed the phone into my purse and grabbed my keys, locking the front door behind me. I wondered how many other people had keys to the door besides Cheryl. I'd have to ask Norma and find out.

I drove faster than I should've and got to the hospital a little after five thirty, parked and as I leaned to get my purse caught sight of my face in the mirror. Limp, damp hair hanging around red eyes stared back at me. I looked like a drowned rat.

Opening my purse I groped around for my sunglasses and snapped open the case, sliding the dark glasses onto my nose and tucking the earpieces behind my ears. This must look stupid, I thought, wearing these this time of the evening but better than having fish eyes. I didn't care and hurried into the lobby and saw Dr. Suffolk waiting by the elevator.

He glanced at me and nodded and held back to let me in first as the doors opened.

"Thank you, Doctor Suffolk. Have you seen my mother? How is she?" I said as I stepped through the door.

He looked puzzled and his forehead creased as though trying to remember where he'd seen me.

"Your mother? Who is …?"

I realized with dark glasses and wet hair the poor guy wouldn't have recognized me after only two meetings. I whisked off the glasses.

"I'm sorry. Norma Resnick. I'm her daughter. We met earlier."

"Yes. Resnick. PCS. Bronchitis. Prescribed some antibiotic."

"PCS?" I was startled. Was that something new and was the antibiotic for bronchitis?

192

"Post concussion syndrome. Not dangerous. Uncomfortable. Headaches and dizziness."

The elevator had come to a halt and the doors were opening. He stared at me. "And you? Don't worry. Your mother will be fine. The antibiotic should help."

I was startled. His voice was solicitous, a caring bedside manner in shorthand speech. Then I realized he'd noticed my eyes and must've figured I'd been crying perhaps because of Norma. That was almost funny—I wouldn't know how to cry for her. I nodded.

"Well, thank you Doctor. That's nice to know." But he was already hurrying down the hall in the opposite direction. I sighed and walked past the nurses' station towards Norma's room.

The basket of flowers I had given Bryony was still on the counter and looking fresh. I was pleased I'd left them there and not taken them home with me. They provided more pleasure where they were. I wished that Norma had been of a mind to enjoy them herself.

Orderlies were beginning to haul carts of trays loaded with finished dinners. I could smell the remains of uneaten food and decided that if Norma still had hers and had left her bread roll I was going to grab it this time. The crackers and cheese had worn off and the earlier breakfast was digested and the sense of being satisfied was gone. I was hungry again and as I pushed open my mother's door wished I had a glass of wine in hand, too.

Norma was reclining against her pillow. She still looked a little flushed and as I walked through the door she squinted, then recognizing who it was, slumped down and started coughing. Drama queen, I thought, another guilt trip. "How you doing? I saw Doctor Suffolk in the elevator and he said you had bronchitis."

"I knew that before he told me." Her voice sounded gravelly and unlike her usual assertive self.

"Let's hope the antibiotic works and your lungs don't become too congested," I continued, "but you're in the best place to see that it doesn't."

I noticed the unfinished dinner pushed aside like the lunch tray earlier, although it looked as though she had picked at the mashed potatoes and bread and her dessert was eaten. Good, at least she's eating something, I thought, but I was disappointed that she had chewed into the dinner roll. I wasn't about to finish the rest of it and wished I'd brought her some chocolates as I had thought to do when I purchased the flowers. I could've had some of those. I reminded myself to pick some up the next time or bring some crackers.

Norma was peering at me. She had leaned forward and closer to where I was standing. I'd forgotten about my hair. Trust her to notice my appearance. I hoped she couldn't see my eyes.

"You look a mess. Is that the way you come here to visit your mother? What will people think?" She started coughing again and reaching for a tissue. I hoped she wasn't going to gag up any phlegm again and handed her the box. She pushed it away. "I've already got some here," she said and patted another box by her pillow. "I don't need those. So it's raining?"

"Raining? Oh, no. I took a shower before I came and my hair's still wet." I ran my fingers through the damp hair.

"You'll catch pneumonia if you run around with a wet head."

I never knew if that type of comment was prompted by caring, although didn't think so. It was more a platitude. I remembered her telling me things like that when I'd lived at home. She also told me that it was dangerous to take a bath when I had my period. I wasn't dead yet.

"Yes, well, I wanted to get here as quickly as I could. I called earlier but was told you were napping and I didn't want to disturb you."

"It's boring here."

I thought that if I were in her place the bed would be surrounded by books, but Norma didn't read and her eyesight now would've made it more difficult. "What about TV?"

"There's nothing on and I don't know where the remote is."

"If you don't have the remote how do you know what's on?" I knew she liked to watch the news and sitcoms. I didn't know what else she watched. There had to be something that would entertain her. I looked on her table for the remote and couldn't see it. "Let me ask the nurse if there's one for this room." I left before she could say anything.

I walked back to the nurses' station and on one of the carts noticed a container of bread rolls so reached out and grabbed one, biting into it. It was crunchy and yet doughy. Better with some butter, I thought, but better than nothing. I was still chewing as I reached the desk and swallowed. A young woman looked up at me expectantly, "Can I help you?"

"Yes, actually. There doesn't seem to be a remote in room twenty-three. My mother would like to watch television."

"That's strange," she said. "Every room has a remote. Perhaps she dropped it and it's on the floor."

She rose and walked around the desk towards Norma's room and I trailed behind her, chewing into the rest of the roll. "Thanks. What's your name?"

"I'm Monica. I spoke with you a earlier. I recognize your accent." She turned and smiled at me, then pushed open the door and we saw Norma coughing into a tissue. Taking it from her, Monica glanced under the side table to check the floor then pulled so that it moved smoothly on its rollers away from the wall. "There it is. It must've fallen. Sorry about that." She bent down and picked it up. "Here you go," she said. "If it drops again, just let us know and someone will get it for you." She handed it to Norma and tossed the tissue into a wastebasket that was close by.

"I suppose I could've done that," I said, "thank you. You're very sweet."

"You're welcome and if you're still hungry I can bring you some more rolls if you like, although the cafeteria upstairs might have something better."

I hesitated, not realizing there was a cafeteria, but said, "That would be lovely."

I had the thought that remaining cheerful and tending to others on a daily basis, especially with patients like Norma, took a certain, generous person and realized I was too selfish to do that and wondered just how much more like my mother I was. It wasn't very reassuring. I thought about the earrings and wanted to ask Norma about them but now didn't seem to be the right time. I didn't want to get into whatever might be involved. Norma had already raised and pointed the remote toward the television. Noisy canned laughter filled the room. It was intrusive but better than the silence of us not speaking.

The door opened again and Monica entered with a plate of rolls and butter. "If you'd like anything to drink, there's a vending machine down the hall. The coffee's lousy but if you want some tea, there's hot water and we keep some tea bags at the desk." She hurried out before I could say anything to thank her. What a love she was. I looked at Norma who seemed oblivious to anything other than the screen so set the plate down on my chair and moved to the door.

"Where are you off to now?"

"To get some tea. Would you like some? You probably should be drinking more fluids," I added.

She continued staring at the TV, then said, "Yes. I would."

I left and walked down to the desk and smiled at Monica who held a small basket of tea bags up to me. "Take what you want," she said. "We've got a good selection there."

I picked through the various bags and located a Chamomile and I wondered what Norma might like so selected an Earl Gray. I was grateful to have something better than what could have passed for beverage machine dishwater and decided to pick up some tea bags next time I was in the market and donate them to the pile in the basket. "Thanks Monica." Then I realized I needed cash for the machine and returned to Norma's room for my purse. She continued to ignore me but coughed dryly, her breath ragged.

At the vending machine two white styrofoam cups dropped down from inside and filled with the hot water and I hoped it wouldn't spill and burn me. It was awkward holding my wallet and the two cups and trying to open Norma's door at the same time and I experienced a sense of irritation. Why couldn't she keep it open like other people? Unfriendly old biddy.

It crossed my mind that I had been more upset and in more foul moods within the last week than I had in years. I wondered if this was the effect of being around Norma or whether she simply triggered something deeper within me that I kept hidden; perhaps avoiding situations that would bring it to the surface and fooling myself I was someone different. I was that certainly, and losing my equilibrium as a result.

I hesitated, wishing I had a little tray, then leaned down, about to set one of the cups on the floor in order to turn the door handle when I heard a familiar voice say, "Here let me help you." Half bent over, I looked up past the green polyester pants and jacket, into the smiling face of Cheryl.

Hot water spilled out of the cups I was holding and onto the floor. My heart pounded and the anger I thought was under control surged back into my mind, mixed with the surprise of seeing her there. What was this woman doing here and why now? How should I react? What should I say? Should I still pretend I knew nothing of the theft or confront her now? I stared through and into the blond hair that curled past her ears and hid the ears although could see she was no longer wearing my earrings but a pair of silver hoops that dangled into her neck.

"Sorry. Didn't mean to surprise you," she said. "Here let me get some paper towels from the ladies room and wipe some of this up. We don't want anyone to slip." She hurried back down the hall.

Shit, shit, shit, I thought. I hated my mother and Cheryl and the hospital and being placed in a position of feeling helpless. I set one of the cups down and turned the handle and in a display of the anger that was taking hold of me, kicked the door with my foot and slammed down the door prop to keep it open. To hell with Norma. To hell with everyone. I picked up the remaining cup and slapped them both down on the bedside table, spilling more of the hot water that dribbled across the top, wetting the bottom of the tissue box. Cheryl was already back at the open door mopping what had spilled with the paper towels.

She glanced over at me and smiled. "Be right there, just getting the last of this taken care of. Hi Mrs. Resnick. How're you doing?" she called and without waiting for a reply said, "Was driving by and had a few minutes so thought I'd pop in to see you, again. Now where can I throw these things away?" She looked around the room and tossed them into the wastebasket that someone had placed there since I had last looked and now half filled with Norma's used tissues.

Norma had sat up in bed and was straightening the coverlets on the bed, coughing slightly. She glared at me and turned to Cheryl, "Would you mind closing the door that Margaret left open?" Her voice was as sweet as she could manage but it emerged as a hoarse whisper.

"Oh, you poor thing. You don't need a cold, too."

"Bronchitis. More serious than a cold." She coughed some more and slid down against the pillow. "So nice of you to come, Cheryl, I don't get many visitors so a friendly face is welcome."

Well to hell with you, I thought. I'm not a visitor, not even a daughter to her and I'm breaking my neck to get here whenever I can and for thanks she's piling on abuse. I was staring at Cheryl who was standing close to Norma's bed, patting her hand.

"No you don't look well. That's too bad." Cheryl glanced over at me and smiled, "Can you shut that door for your Mum. It's probably a bit draughty with it open."

I hesitated. I would've preferred a gale force wind tear into the room and give Norma pneumonia. I kicked the doorstop again to the up position and the door swung closed. I decided not to discuss the earrings but would wait until I was under better control. I also wanted to know what John had discovered and perhaps talking it over with him would give me some solid ground on which to take a stand.

I debated whether to leave both of the women and call Alex. What I really wanted to do was go and get drunk but a bar was out of the question. Going back to the house and getting drunk there was just as bad. I suddenly felt very alone and vulnerable. Not for the last time did I wish I had never come to the UK in a fit of compassion for an unsympathetic mother then having to discover she was as strong and as objectionable as ever.

As I considered whether to go, I heard Norma saying to Cheryl, "... and you've been such a help to me. I don't know what I would have done without you."

"It's nothing Mrs. Resnick. Really. I was paid to do a job and just did my best. That's all. You're an old lady and need all the help you can get, what with Margaret living so far away and all." Cheryl turned her head toward me and smiled.

I couldn't decide if it was genuine or simply gloating that she had my mother's favor. My anger made me decide it was catty triumph and that she had the upper hand. Well, wait until Norma learned the woman had stolen the earrings. I hesitated. The hospital room would not be a good place to have a scene and Norma was looking flushed again.

As I watched the two women together it was as if the action suddenly became one of slow motion. I saw Norma reach up towards Cheryl's face that leaned over her and moved her hair away from her ear, exposing the giant hoop that I had seen at the door.

"Where are the earrings I gave you? You're not wearing them?" she said. "They're prettier than these."

I stared in disbelief, unable to grasp the full impact of what Norma had just said. Perhaps I'd heard incorrectly. Perhaps I was dreaming all this. Cheryl *hadn't* stolen the earrings after all? Perhaps, then, she'd coerced them out of Norma. I shook my head. Norma couldn't be coerced out of a kind word if her life depended on it.

"Yes, thank you again, Mrs. Resnick. It was a lovely birthday present and I wore them last night when I went out to dinner with my family. Everyone thought they were beautiful and you were so kind and generous. I took them off for these because I wanted to keep them in a safe place."

I couldn't believe what I was hearing. I felt frozen to the spot and my voice was raised and sounded like a shriek. "You gave her my earrings? My earrings?"

Cheryl straightened and looked at me and Norma waved her hand in dismissal, turning her head toward me. Her eyes were like stone and although it seemed an effort to speak rasped, "They were mine to give. It was a gift for Cheryl who has helped me so much.

Perhaps you should've been a more considerate daughter." She turned her head back towards Cheryl. "They're yours and I want you to have them. Ignore her. But you both better leave because I'm not feeling so well." She reached for Cheryl's hand, "Can you please ring for the nurse I need to be changed."

It was the first time I'd heard her admit to using pads. It was the first time I was unable to fully comprehend that the woman lying in the bed in front of me was my mother. How could anyone so dislike her daughter who had done nothing to cause such hatred? I picked up my purse and walked to the door. I didn't care if I never saw her again. I was leaving.

As I stormed along the hallway to the elevator I realized I was crying and speaking aloud repeating, "How could she? How could she?" I felt some nurses hesitate as though to stop and perhaps help me as I ran. I didn't care.

I slammed my fist against the elevator button and waited, unsure of what I was going to do or even where. Cheryl suddenly stood beside me. "Maggie, I'm so sorry about your mother's gift. I had no idea …"

Shrugging off the hand she had placed on my arm I said, "Don't. Don't do that." Even if it wasn't Cheryl's fault, she was involved.

I turned away as the doors opened and instead moved away toward the exit and stairwell. I would walk down. I didn't want to continue any form of conversation, sympathetic or otherwise with Cheryl until I was in a condition to do so. I didn't know if I ever would.

As I stumbled down the concrete stairs my steps echoed through the open space and the walls around it. I was in a grey, cold alien world and no longer trusted myself to behave in a way I considered normal. Was I worth so little that my mother intentionally hurt me? Was she so divorced from feeling that she hurt my father too?

I stopped at the bottom and stared at the heavy stairwell door, then thrust my shoulder against it, turned the handle and walked into the lobby. Through the glass doors to the entrance I could see Cheryl in her green suit in the parking lot and hesitated as I watched her stop and open her car door. I was still breathless from the confrontation and walk down the stairs and my heart pounded and temples throbbed.

Seeing Cheryl drive away, I almost ran to my car then fumbled for my keys. I groped for them in the side pocket of my purse and felt their hard, cold metal in my still shaking hands.

Clutching the automatic door opener I pressed the wrong side and heard only the inside click as it tried to relock what was already locked. My temper ready to explode I looked down and pushed hard against the correct button to release.

It was a sudden quick mechanical action that seemed to symbolize me—a recognition of something I was reluctant to fully acknowledge. I was endeavoring to unlock something closed to me and I didn't have the proper key.

Frail to the sight with an indomitable will behind that façade, Norma was filled with rancor. I might never learn what generated such animosity feeding from that vein of spite within her, but heaven forbid I shared any part of that. She lived in her own egocentric world and one I never could or wanted to be a part of so why attempt to enter and understand what that was? But it left unanswered questions of where I fit in.

CHAPTER SIXTEEN

I threw my bag on the passenger seat, slammed myself behind the wheel then switched on the ignition, continuing to sit there as the engine turned over. I didn't know where to go. I felt dislocated, a disruption of a normal awareness of who I was and my location in space and time. I realized it was similar to how I felt as a kid when Norma would berate me and call me names when no one else was around or could hear. I had nowhere to go then and no one to turn to and had learned that my father wasn't the strength I could depend upon. I was on my own and had learned to handle my mother's hostility by creating a wall inside my mind—a wall that neither she nor anyone else could penetrate.

After I left home it took years for me to develop a sense of trust with others; years to eventually let down my guard and feel safe and even then I was wary. Now I was back I'd forgotten to defend myself with my inner protection and could feel the impact of that now. I continued to sit staring through the windshield. I had to go somewhere. I thought that perhaps I would get a motel room for the night, somewhere neutral and plastic. Somewhere that didn't have the slightest connection to Norma.

I thought about my earlier intention of looking for the rest of the jewelry but now I didn't want to be part of anything that was Norma's even if it did mean locating Grandmother's things. I felt the very act of handling my mother's belongings—her paperwork and files, her jewelry—would be toxic in some way. Mentally I wanted to wash my hands to remove the images.

I didn't want to go to a motel either. I'd done that when I was in the final stages of my marriage with Richard and wanted to get out of the house but not descend on my friends. I'd done that too and there was just so much goodwill that could be extended without my unhappy presence becoming an imposition.

Shelly is Richard's sister and my friend and although she supported and encouraged my decision to leave him I couldn't abuse that support and have it become a crutch. But it was Shelly who had told me Richard had been married before and divorced. He'd never mentioned that. It was she who told me that Richard was like their father who was unfaithful and caused their mother to slip silently into a world of feigning ignorance that affected everyone as she acted the happy housewife and mother. It was Shelly who first recognized that I was pretending Richard's infidelity didn't exist until my unhappiness became obvious and I broke down when she confronted me with the obvious. "When," she had demanded, "are you going to acknowledge that Richard's a jerk and you must leave otherwise you'll become a Stepford wife like mom."

I knew Richard's mother and her chirpy denial that all was wrong in her world. I even knew of Richard's father who openly flirted with me while I attempted to deflect his unwanted attention. But where was I supposed to go I wondered? Certainly not back home. It seemed that I was forever running away.

Motels were a deadly place to go when one felt alone and miserable. The beds with their folded down comforters over stretched cold, white sheets were no place to relax and hide. I always wondered how many others had lain on them in who knew what states of dress or undress or what transpired on the covers. I hated the plastic covered glasses in the bathroom that I used for my wine. I always took a bottle with me although there were times I opened the tiny miniature bottles of alcohol that sat in the fridge. How many times had I turned on the television and then searched for the yellow pages or sheaf of flyers advertising pizza delivery, waited for it to arrive and then sat eating it and watching something on the television that was an annoying distraction. I hated the sounds that came from the thin walls next to mine and another TV or voice, laughter or the quickening thump of a bed and privy to the unwanted sounds of sex. No. I didn't want to go to a motel.

I thought of Alex, of him and Kay. I thought of his little cottage surrounded by a flower garden. I wanted to go there and have Kay push her wet nose into my hand but I didn't want to go to Alex in a state of need, feeling vulnerable and wanting. If I was going to have a relationship with him I wanted it to be balanced. Equal. But isn't that what relationships are supposed to be? I thought—a balance where both people contribute to the whole. That's what I'd hoped for with Richard but it didn't turn out that way and it was too soon, way too soon, to know with Alex.

I remembered Richard's inability to recognize anything deeper than what was obvious. Emotional commitment and communication were a threat to his equilibrium. He felt uneasy when he had to confront anything that required getting in touch with his feelings. My determination to examine and dig deeper into my psyche was disturbing to him. "Do we really have to discuss that now?" he would say. "You're too intense, Maggie," and avoid further discussion when my feeling of disconnect became such that I would demand he talk with me to help understand my unhappiness and his lack of connection.

I often wondered if he was unhappy too but recognized it was unlikely if we were having sex, I knew he wasn't then. For him sex was having fun. Sex wasn't making love and my body felt like it could've belonged to any female he was fucking at the time. Richard never made love, he screwed and I always experienced a sense of distance when we did. Having an orgasm was a physical thing that never touched upon a psychic connection between us. Yes, I was unhappy but that was then and why I was reluctant to make any attempt for an emotional commitment now. I was afraid to be hurt again.

My phone rang and startled me. I wondered whether to answer but picked it up and looked at the blinking display. It was Alex but I pressed the connect key and said, "Hello, Alex." My mind reached past my reluctance to talk and was a basic instinct to make contact with a sympathetic soul. "Hello, Alex," I said again.

"Hi. I was getting concerned. Hope you don't mind me calling although maybe I should've texted instead." His voice seemed hesitant.

"No. No. It's okay. Really I don't mind." I wished my voice sounded more normal. I was surprised by the unsteadiness of the words as I heard them and closed my mouth.

"Maggie? Are you sure you're okay? You don't sound very happy."

I've only known the guy a short while, I thought, and he can already tell there's something wrong. I experienced a sense of relief as though I had discovered a path that suggested a way through the chaos I was feeling. I started to cry again. I didn't want to do that, though, not over the phone, not with Alex.

"What's happening? Hey Maggie, where are you? Let me come get you wherever you are."

"No. I'm already in the car. Can I drive over there?"

"Of course. You sure you don't want me to get you?"

"I'll be fine." I reached over to my purse and removed a tissue and wiped my eyes. "I'm a mess though," I added.

"Aren't we all at some time or another. Kay's not though and we'll both be here waiting for you. Drive carefully there's a heavy mist starting to form."

I had to think carefully of where I was going. The last time I'd gone to his house he was directing me from the restaurant but now I was alone and finding my way from the hospital. Damn, I thought, I don't want to get lost. The reality of where I was headed gradually dawned on me. I wasn't sure if I had made the right decision and thought to turn back but it was fate that was directing me now. I was just the passenger; unwilling to get off, reluctant to move into the unknown, but curious to see what was ahead.

I passed Gino's and then knew where I was. I felt less hesitant and gripped the wheel more securely, stepping on the gas and driving faster than the thirty mile speed I'd been going. I was hungry and wanted a glass of wine and wanted to be held and I knew I would find all of that with Alex. For the first time in what seemed like forever I smiled. I knew without a doubt that he would be waiting and Kay would be there with him. It was a given.

I spotted Kay first, running along the pavement with Alex standing by the gate waiting for me. When he saw my car, he waved and indicated the small driveway for me to pull into. He must've called the shepherd because she ran to him and sat down by his side. I eased up next to them and turned off the ignition. I leaned over and pulled my purse toward me as Alex opened the door. The interior light flipped on and I glanced in the mirror and saw my still puffy face and swollen eyes. This was not how I wanted to appear but it was already too late to change my mind. The door was open and Kay, tail wagging, pushed her nose into my leg so that I paused and ruffled her ears.

"Hey, Kay," Alex told her, "let Maggie get out and then you can say hi." He chuckled and reached for my hand, easing me up next to him. He was warm and I could smell his wonderful smell that I remembered from the last time I'd stood close to him. I thought he might kiss me but he simply hugged and released me while Kay bounded round us both. Holding my shoulders, Alex steered me toward the house and in the light from the door stopped and stared down into my face before looking away. "Welcome," he said, and held the door wide for me to step inside. "You could probably do with a drink. Wine? That's all I've got, although, hmm, I may still have some brandy."

I thought brandy would be heaven and visualized its sting warming my throat and insides. I nodded and leaned down to tousle Kay's head again and felt her wet tongue on my cheek. Probably can taste the salt, I thought. I looked around. Oak beams crossed the knotty pine ceiling and a large cast iron wood stove sat in a brick alcove. Paintings and photographs covered the white walls and another of books held my attention. It filled one side of the room from floor to ceiling, spilling some of them to the floor and reminded me of a much smaller version of Aidenscroft library. It had the same feeling of peaceful relaxation.

A deeply cushioned dark blue sofa, its soft pillows squashed down where obviously Alex stretched out, sat by a large, paned window outside of which a vine of some sort was tapping the glass as it moved in the night breeze. An open doorway at the far end of the room led to what I figured was the kitchen from which wafted more wonderful smells of garlic and basil. Along with the male smell of Alex and the doggie one of Kay, it was almost a sensory overload. I could become addicted to this, I thought.

"Uh-oh," Alex said as he hurried through the door, "I forgot I had something on the stove. Make yourself comfortable." He indicated the sofa and I stepped around the coffee table in front of it, carefully moving an open book from the pillows as I sank into them. I relaxed back and breathed a sigh as Kay squeezed by my leg. "She really likes you," said Alex as his big body framed the doorway. He was holding a wooden spoon in one hand, stirring something in the cast iron fry pan he held in the other. "Garlic," he grinned. "Garlic, olive oil, pesto and Asiago cheese. Simple fare and no meat. Thought you might be hungry. Are you?"

I nodded. As though he read my mind, he said, "I found the brandy and the wine's red although it should probably be white with the pasta but hey ..."

"Can I have the brandy first? I think I need to kick-start myself into some semblance of life again. Maybe the red with the dinner. Alex," I said, pulling myself off the deep cushions, "is there anything I can do to help out there?"

"If you don't want to sit in there with Kay then you can join me here. Actually I'd rather like that."

The kitchen was almost too small for him but it was obviously one in which he loved to cook. The walls were paneled and appeared to be the original wood of the cottage. The place was probably quite old but someone had made some wonderful renovations. The stove looked modern and was stainless steel as was the double sink. The countertop around it was a brown and dark green stone that had been broken then arranged and set in a dark grout. I saw a large butcher-block counter at the far end on which was French bread and some Brie along with an open bottle of Merlot. I ran my palm over the stone. "This is lovely. I've never seen anything like this before."

He seemed pleased. "When my grandparents owned it, it was old tile that had seen better days. After they died and they left the place to me I ripped it all out and got this granite from the stone yard in large chunks then broke it into smaller pieces and arranged it in this mosaic pattern. I don't get many visitors to admire it."

He opened the brandy, a half filled bottle of Courvoisier. "Don't drink much of this unless I have a cold and that doesn't happen very often. He sniffed, "Umm good," he said, "think I'll join you though I don't have a cold." He laughed suddenly, "Well, it'll prevent one if there's one on the way." He poured enough to cover the bottom of two brandy snifters and handed one to me. "Cheers," he said and we touched glasses.

I swirled mine gently and watched its golden movement, breathing in the fumes. This was already wonderful. Better than an empty motel room, better than Norma's house by far and, I was surprised to realize, better at that moment than my own home would've been with Mewfus.

"There's some French bread and Brie, if you like. I wasn't planning on making a full dinner, just snacking until I spoke to you. I was hoping we were going to get together for dinner although not quite under these circumstances. But," he added, "I prefer it here and no doubt you do too considering what you seem to have been going through."

It was the first reference to my state and I nodded, remembering what had happened earlier. I still didn't want to talk about it and wanted to fill that unhappy void with the wonderful energy I was experiencing with him.

He was putting the pasta into a pot of boiling water, stirring it as he did so. I felt he understood because he glanced at me quickly then back again to the stove. "Don't let me pry but I know you've been—and probably still are—upset over something. Perhaps your mother, huh?" He looked at me again and then away, "But Kay and I want you to be happy and if you feel like talking I'm here to listen. If you don't then I understand." He turned down the gas so that the boiling water simmered around the softening noodles and stirred it some more. Then he said, "Speaking of listening, the CD is finished." The quiet became more obvious as I realized that a violin concerto had been playing when I had first entered the house.

I followed him as he moved back to the living room to the stereo that was above a TV in a small entertainment section. He was replacing the CD into its case. "That was a Haydn violin concerto wasn't it?" I said.

He smiled and nodded. "Anything special you'd like to hear? I probably have it here and these are about the only things that are really organized in my life."

I thought that even though he'd said that I sensed he maintained an easy control of his life and hoped I didn't appear as out of it in mine. "I can sort of recognize a composer although not really well and definitely can't identify the piece." I stared at the hundreds of CD's that filled the case. "You're the expert. You choose. I'm sure I'll like anything you want to play."

"Modern, classical, romantic, baroque...?"

"Not much the modern." I hesitated, unwilling to admit to my lack of knowledge on the subject. "Classical and baroque yes but some of the romantic stuff can get a bit too saccharine." I sipped my brandy and felt it warm my tongue down into my stomach. I was starting to feel better.

"Saccharine. I like that. So no sugar but this is sweet, nevertheless—you'll probably like this." He clicked the CD into place and pushed the close button, waiting for it to start, his huge shoulders gently sloped toward the player.

I recognized the opening bars of that too, and actually something I had in my own limited collection. How coincidental was that? "Don't know which specifically, but isn't that one of Mozart's Flute Concertos? I've got that. I love it."

Alex turned and grinned. "Right. A woman after my own heart."

I laughed and thought I probably was a woman after his heart but not in quite the same way as he had meant it.

As the music filled the house, we went back into the kitchen and Alex cut some of the French bread. "Butter or Brie?"

I loved Brie but hesitated a fraction of a second wondering how it would affect my breath, but he continued, "I'm going to have the Brie and there's a ton of garlic already in the sauce." He seemed to know my mind better than I did. How comfortable I felt with this man. I pointed to the cheese and he handed it to me on the bread. As I bit down a small piece broke off and fell to the floor.

"Oops, sorry," I said but Kay was there and already had it in her mouth, crunching down and chewing.

Alex laughed again. "She's a discerning creature and knows what's good in life but," he took a sip of his drink, "it stops just short of brandy."

He slid a fork into the churning water and eased out a piece of the pasta, blew on it and held it for a moment before popping it into his mouth. "Done!" he said and turned off the flame. He picked up a colander and poured the contents into it, draining off the hot water and capturing the pasta, shaking it as he did so before he poured it back into the pot. He turned and with the wooden spoon folded into it the hot garlic and basil he had been sautéing in olive oil. "We're ready," he said. "D'you mind if we go sit in the living room on the couch and put all this on the coffee table?" At that point I would've happily eaten on the floor with Kay.

As I had guessed from the fantastic smells that had emanated from the stove, the meal was delicious and leaving the brandy snifters for wine glasses, Alex brought the Merlot to the coffee table and poured us both some wine. "Hope you don't mind not having a salad," he said, "but we do have some ice cream for later if you like dessert."

I shook my head. "This is perfect. You're a great cook."

"Thanks, but one can't go far wrong with this stuff and if you're going to eat here more often I must find some vegetarian dishes." He leaned toward the plate and sniffed, nodding his head. "Mmm, not bad though I do say so myself, but wait a sec ..." He got up and went into the kitchen for some paper towels, handing me one. "Not on ceremony here and sorry no napkins. These'll have to do."

He plopped down next to me on the sofa again and I was again aware of just how big he was, almost filling the space of what a third person would do had they been there. Kay was sitting expectantly next to him by the arm of the couch, her tail softly thumping the floor. "Generally I sit in the middle and she squeezes next to me," he said. "She's not used to dinner guests—me neither." He twirled some of the pasta on a fork and held it out to her and she leaned forward and very gently eased it off the fork without dropping anything. "Good girl," he said.

"She takes that very well," I said, "I'm impressed. Most dogs would've lunged and grabbed it, fork and all."

"Yes and I love her." He picked another piece from his plate and Kay took that from his fingers.

"I can see that. You two are quite a pair. Can I give her some?"

"Of course although we mustn't give her too much otherwise she'll get the runs. Go to Maggie, Kay, she has some for you."

She cocked her head, this wasn't something she completely understood.

"Here, Kay," I said. "Come here, baby!"

Seeing the pasta held out at the other end of the coffee table, she backed out and trotted around to me, taking the food as gently as she had from Alex. "What a great dog," I said, "I don't think I've ever seen one so well behaved—in church or out of it."

"Shepherds are really smart. She's my third." Alex paused and stared at Kay. "Lost the others when they were about nine or ten and it still rips me apart but I go out immediately and adopt another pup. They never replace the last one or the ones before that but become a part of me just like the others were a part of my life. Wish they could live forever."

I nodded. I understood from his voice that heartache was involved and decided not to say more. I had lost animals I'd loved too. We continued in a comfortable silence, listening to the music, Kay trotting back and forth around the coffee table between us, her claws a soft click on the wood floor.

"Hope you don't mind but she likes to finish what's left," Alex said putting his plate down without waiting for me to respond. "It freaks John out, though." He laughed as Kay began licking the remains of the pasta, pushing the plate in circles as her nose pressed against the surface.

"Not me. My friend, Shelly, has a lab called Buddy, and he does the same thing. If I had a dog I'd probably do it too. I just have Mewfus, my cat, but he'd be quite put off by garlic pasta." It hadn't been an easy decision leaving him to go see my mother. I loved him more than her and in that moment I missed him being there too.

"How come not a dog? You seem to enjoy being around them."

"I do and did but when Mellow, my beautiful Golden Retriever, died of old age last year, it was a huge loss. She was a rescue dog but had a few happy years with me before she went. I decided not to get another dog until I had a house instead of a condo."

He pursed his lips and said, "I'm sorry, then you know what it's like." He was quiet for a few minutes then said, "But a condo?

How come? Can't imagine being in one of those or seeing you in one either."

"Me too, but after my divorce and we sold the house that was what I got and planned it as a temporary place. It was still my own until I could decide where I wanted to go and what I wanted to do. Somehow time slipped by and I never really made any final decision."

I wondered how my life would be different if I had my own house instead of a glorified apartment. Perhaps on some level I knew it would be easier to transition to something else although what that was I had no idea. Thoughts of moving to Oregon was a part of that and yet another area of my life that required closer inspection. Perhaps my present state of uncertainty was because I had permitted myself to settle into a rut and now life was shaking me into recognizing that; forcing me into making decisions.

Alex poured more wine into my glass. I leaned back into the sofa and realized that with the brandy and the glass of wine I was becoming too relaxed and slightly light headed. I wondered how I would drive back to Norma's place and looked at the digital clock above Alex's hi-fi. It was already close to ten. Where had the time gone? I decided not to think about it.

He stood and picked up the plates and silverware and carried them into the kitchen. I curled my legs under me into the corner of the sofa and Alex's phone rang. I wondered who would be calling him at that time. From what he had told me he didn't seem to be that social although his manner was friendly. It was a strange combination, a social recluse, I thought. Then I recognized an element of myself in that description.

"Do you mind if I get this?" He had the phone in his hand and looked around the doorway to the kitchen. "It's John. He generally doesn't call this late."

I nodded my head. "Course not. Say hi for me."

Alex nodded and said, "Hey John, what's up?" Then silence. "Yes, yes she's here." More silence. "Yes, she seemed upset so I asked her to come over and we just finished dinner." There was another pause, then, "No, I don't know if she's going back to the house but she seems fine. Do you want to talk to her? Okay. Hold on I'll give her the phone." He was walking toward me extending it toward me. "John wants to speak to you."

"Hi John. Anything wrong?"

"Not with me, Maggie, but I was more concerned about you. Cheryl stopped by this evening and we had a long talk. She was very upset about the earrings and said you were too and had refused to talk to her at the hospital. She wanted to explain they were a gift. She didn't steal them, Maggie, thank God for that."

The events that had transpired earlier seemed as though they had happened in another lifetime to another person. I had separated myself from what had occurred between Cheryl and Norma. I was now in another quite different world; a safe Alex and Kay world. I knew I still had to deal with what had occurred earlier and even more so on what to do about my father, but was unwilling to let it invade the haven I was in and to confront it then.

"Thanks, John. Yes I know that now and happy to think she's innocent but it still doesn't explain why Norma gave away something so precious, so important, that was ultimately mine."

John knew about the jewelry but he didn't know that they had become almost analogous to losing and finding my father. They were something else Norma had taken from me. I didn't want to discuss the details, though, I needed to gather enough strength and courage to know what I was going to do and how to handle both situations but not now. "Can we discuss this tomorrow? I really appreciate your concern and your help. Perhaps later I'll be in a better state of mind and can deal with it then."

I waited for a response with Alex hovering between the kitchen and the living room, seemingly unsure of what he should do as John agreed. "Okay," I said, "let's meet at the church then, perhaps lunch around one. I'll call tomorrow morning to confirm, and John," I paused, "please don't invite Cheryl. You and I need to discuss this very carefully. It's not her though. It's Norma. It's my mother who's at fault and I want to make sure that her actions don't continue to poison anything more than has already occurred."

I suddenly felt sorry for Cheryl who was caught between us, "And thanks for your concern, John," I said. "You're such a love and between you and Alex I'm in good hands. Bye." The phone clicked and the disconnect tone hummed in my ear. I stood up and went into the kitchen to give the phone to Alex. He took it gently, placed it in the receiver and, just as gently, took me in his arms.

He didn't question me, but lightly pressed his cheek against my head. Neither of us said a word, the quiet filled by the music. It wasn't an uncomfortable silence needing to be broken, it was the silence I felt when I was alone and content and was the first time I had experienced a similar feeling with someone else.

"I don't know what I would have done this evening if it hadn't been for you," I said eventually. I didn't want to add 'thank you' it would have formalized and made less of the moment as something special.

He stared down at me and smiled. "Good. Kay, too? She's seems to understand when something isn't right even before I do."

I nodded. I didn't want to leave them both and wondered how I could go back to the cold and empty house with the unresolved thoughts that preoccupied my mind, even though the emotional desolation I had experienced earlier was gone. Just by being there for me, Alex and Kay had erased that. But he seemed to sense my unwillingness to go.

"I have to take her for a little walk, soon," he said moving one arm from me and cupping Kay's jaw who stood looking up at him expectantly, her butt and tail wagging. He laughed. "She knows the word w-a-l-k."

"Perhaps I should leave. It's getting late." I saw the clock over the stove was almost past eleven o'clock.

"Kay gets to go out around this time and she's a creature of habit and although it's a bit late, we haven't had dessert or coffee." He hesitated, "Do you even *want* that?"

I didn't want the ice cream but did want the coffee. I knew it would keep me awake although figured a jolt of caffeine would clear my head from the brandy and wine although still preferred the state I was in to a more alert one. "Coffee sounds good but maybe not a lot. So let's take Kay for a little wa ... w-a-l-k then. That would be nice. I'd enjoy that."

Alex moved to the living room and Kay bounded toward the door, "I think she wants to go," he said.

"I think she knows how to spell!"

The air outside was cool and I shivered. "Oh I forgot, you get cold don't you," Alex said. "Hang on a minute and I'll grab something for you to wear." He disappeared back into the house and I could hear his footsteps go back beyond the kitchen then he returned holding a sweater. "Here," he said draping a huge, soft blue turtleneck across my shoulders, "bit big but it'll keep you warm."

"Can I put it on?" I said, unwrapping it from around my neck.

"Don't blame me if you get lost in it."

I was already pulling it over my head and felt engulfed in the smell of Alex. I paused, wanting it to remain close to my face then giggled and pushed my head through the opening, struggling to find the end of the sleeves. "If I do, you'll have to come in and find me."

218

Kay bounded back to us and started to sniff the sweater that came almost to my knees. "Now she's puzzled," Alex said, "she's got two favorite scents all wrapped up in one person." He took my hand and as we moved out of the gate and along the narrow pavement, wrapped his arm around my shoulder. I slid mine around his waist although it reached just a little further than the middle of his back. I'd never been with a guy that big and wondered what it would be like to sleep with him.

"You know you don't have to leave if you don't want to." It was as though he'd read my thoughts. "You can stay here tonight if you like." He seemed hesitant and I didn't answer. I wanted to stay but only to curl up in his arms. I wasn't ready for any intimacy beyond that.

Alex stopped and turned me to him, looking down into my face. I couldn't see his eye but sensed his sudden concern that I might have misunderstood what he was asking. He hesitated, "Maggie, that's not what I meant, I mean you're welcome to stay here tonight. Kay and I can sleep on the couch, we've done it before when we've conked out and had a long nap. I hope you weren't thinking I was suggesting ... suggesting that ..." he seemed uncomfortable and looked away.

I was surprised but not totally. Surprised he had clarified himself and was suddenly self-conscious but not, because it was another example of what I had come to expect of this giant of a man. His sensitivity and awareness was something so new to me I had difficulty believing it was true. I reached up and touched his beard and drew his face towards mine, kissing him gently.

"I would like nothing better than to stay," I said, "but I wouldn't want to turn you out of your bed to sleep on the couch. But ..." I hesitated, "... I just want to curl up in your arms, I don't think I'm quite ready for anything more than that."

He nodded. "It's been a while, a long while, since I slept with anybody," he chuckled, although it was more of an amused exhalation of breath, "and I'm not sure I would know what to do if we did."

"Me neither, although I suspect between the two of us we could figure things out." I thought it silly that we were two adults and so self-conscious, reluctant to trust ourselves to make love, but it was a careful testing of our emotions and an unwillingness to have them be wounded.

"So that's arranged then. You'll stay here and I'll make you breakfast in the morning. Oh," he said, "damn, I have a music lesson student at nine-thirty. I forgot about that."

"Breakfast sounds great and not a problem, I have things I must do too." I had to return to the house and change. I wasn't going to see John until later in the day and decided not to visit Norma in the morning. Since I wouldn't have time to see my father and already knew where the earrings were there was no real need to go through her stuff although I was curious about the rest of the things my grandmother had left me. I still wanted to understand what had prompted Norma to give them away although recognized I might never know the reason but I still had to go through her files and bank accounts. I wanted to know how Daddy was being supported.

I wondered, and not for the first time, what went on in Norma's head that she could be the way she was. Then I realized I had something my mother could never give away. I had Alex or at least I had him now although what the future held I had no idea. At some point I would have to return to California and for the first time since I had arrived, I didn't want to go back. I already knew that Mewfus was nervous around dogs because of Buddy but he was more rambunctious than Kay and then I wondered if she liked cats.

Back in the house, Alex ground the coffee and poured in the water for it to percolate. He started to gather the dishes together and ran the hot water over the plates and silverware. I stood wondering what I could do. "If you have to leave early, why don't you leave the dishes, and I'll do them tomorrow," I said.

"Good idea, but I'm just cleaning them off and will put them in the dishwasher. I kinda need a clear space to make breakfast but you can put this Brie in the refrigerator and while you're there get the cream. I think I remember you like cream in your coffee? I don't care for it black or," he added, "without sugar." He glanced down at his body, "Guess that's pretty obvious though, huh?"

"Cream and sugar for me too. But I have to take a w.a.l.k. too. May I use your bathroom?"

"Of course," he indicated another door that led off the kitchen, "the bedroom and bathroom's back there."

I found myself in his bedroom with large windows that looked out onto what was probably the back garden. The blinds were up and I wondered if he had neighbors close by that could see in. I saw no lights and figured that perhaps he had more privacy than Norma did at her house.

There was an unmade king size bed and, like the sofa had been when I first arrived, cluttered with more books. One bedside lamp was on and the overhead fan and light were off. The place smelled of Alex combined with the peppery scent of Kay—so distinctly theirs and those I had grown to love. One wall was filled with paintings and I wondered whether they had been done by Alex although they didn't look like something he would do. I wondered why I would think that as he called to me from the kitchen. "Sorry about the mess in there, I wasn't expecting company."

"I was admiring your artwork. Did you do it?"

"Wish I did," he had followed me into the bedroom. "No. These were done by my brother. I couldn't draw a straight line if you paid me to."

"I really like them." I moved closer to get a better look in the dim light. "I'm not crazy about all modern art, but these are beautiful. I love the energy they emit and they make me feel good. I didn't know you have a brother."

"Had. He was older than me but died in a motorbike accident about three years ago. Not his fault, some drunk cut him off and that was that. Great guy. I miss him." He leaned down and rubbed Kay's head keeping his face away from me.

"I'm so sorry." I was at a loss for what to say. Expressing my condolence seemed too inadequate and remaining silent unsympathetic.

He stood up, "Yeah, but I keep his spirit with me with these. He still lives in his art and in here." He tapped at his heart then changed the subject. "If you want to take a shower feel free. I'll give you a clean towel. Think I have one somewhere," he joked.

I wondered at his ability to seemingly dismiss his brother's death and switch so quickly to the mundane although felt a relief that the subject had been changed so smoothly. I was curious but knew he'd tell me when he was ready. He'd already made me feel comfortable without asking questions. I got the feeling that despite his light humor, he missed nothing and that it was perhaps a shield he'd created to protect his own sensitivity. He seemed to possess the ability to remain vulnerable but instead of rejecting it, reflected on what most people dismissed or failed to recognize as significant to the human condition. I wanted to learn more about who he was and the way he thought; wanted to immerse myself in what I discovered. I got the feeling that whatever he shared should be valued as something precious and given in trust, then I wondered if I was the right person to do that.

It seemed Alex had already invited me into his life and I questioned whether I had the capacity to meet his expectations although wondered what they could be. Then I changed my mind on that, too. I knew. Of course I knew. I hadn't gone through life without meeting a guy like him and then failing to recognize all the signs of someone unique when he did eventually show up. I had known him before we ever met. He was someone I had visualized as a partner. I had been prepared to remain alone because I had concluded he didn't exist. Now that Alex had seemingly materialized out of nowhere I had to adjust my thinking. I'd spent too long viewing myself as remaining single and the concept of that changing and being the other half of a pair was overwhelming. It was like meeting me as another person.

I switched on the light to the bathroom and closed the door. The area was smaller than I'd expected and his toothbrush and paste was left lying on the counter next to the sink. I smiled—he squeezed from the top that was already flattened, the bottom half filled. I did the same thing and then had difficulty getting that to the top, resolving that the next new tube I'd start from the bottom and work my way up. I never did.

I caught sight of myself in the mirror above the sink. It reflected back a face with still puffy, red ringed eyes and hair disheveled from removing the sweater. Dear god, I thought, I look terrible and laughed. It was the universe's reminder not to take myself so seriously.

Lowering the toilet seat I then looked around and glanced behind a plastic curtain that partially hid an old clawfoot tub with a wall mounted shower—his shampoo and soap lying in a pool of water on a tiny ledge. I wondered how he fit in such a confined area and one definitely too small for both of us. But yes, I decided, this was charming and I would like to take a shower and one of his big towels would be just perfect.

CHAPTER SEVENTEEN

The following morning on my way back to Norma's place, I was unable to stop thinking of the evening before. After walking Kay we had sat on the sofa with our coffee and despite the caffeine I felt exhausted. I hoped that Alex was as good as his word because I didn't want the evening spoiled by sex. Then I thought that was funny. There had been a time in my life when I would've thought the evening would be spoiled without it.

I had taken a shower then pulled on his terrycloth robe and, much like the sweater only bigger, it had engulfed me. I padded into the living room trying to push up the sleeves, the pockets somewhere around my knees and the hem dragging on the floor behind me. "Ta dah!" I said and struck a pose with my arms above my head.

"Perhaps that's one of the best fashion statements I've seen," he laughed, "not that I've paid much attention to fashion ever. The color suits you, though." It was light blue and I was pleased he didn't have a red one. It would have been a disastrous color with my eyes still pink rimmed although I had taken time to run cold water over my face to lessen the swelling. I was grateful that he'd not once mentioned or asked about what had upset me until we were in bed later and I had initiated the subject.

Prior to that there had been a slight awkwardness about going to bed despite him holding and kissing me on the couch. I felt myself nodding off and he gently nudged me and suggested I go to bed and asking again if I preferred he sleep on the couch.

"No," I said. I wanted him with me although was apprehensive about saying so. I knew at least a dozen men who would've taken that as an invitation to do more. I wondered what I would wear and asked to borrow a t-shirt.

He went into the bedroom and I heard him rummaging around in a drawer until he eventually returned with a large, gray shirt that had VIVALDI written across the chest. "Here, wear this," he said. "It should fit."

I held it up to me over the robe and the bottom of the shirt reached my knees. "Perfect," I said. "What a great nightshirt. Be careful when I leave tomorrow that I don't take it with me."

"I won't let you do that because then you won't have anything to wear when you sleep over the next time, although ..." he hesitated, "perhaps you *should* take it with you and the next time I won't have anything that's clean for you to put on. That's an old shirt and pretty soft from wear and not as scratchy as my others."

I decided the man thought of everything as he left to take Kay for a final walk outside. "I won't be long," he said. "This will be just for a quick pee. You get into bed and I'll join you." I wondered what he would wear when he did.

Having walked Kay and undressing in the bathroom, Alex climbed into bed and pulled me to him. He was wearing pajama bottoms and a tank top. "I generally just wear shorts," he said, "and wondered if I would find these. They're my winter pajamas and too warm for me to put on in the summer but you're here and, hmm, it could get even warmer, but definitely worth it."

As he said that, the Shepherd put her front paws on the bed and startled me but I laughed, "She wants to come up too."

"You're in her spot," Alex said. "She jumps up after I've fallen asleep. She's not really permitted on the bed only because she likes to make a nest of the covers. That said she still manages to find her way on here but doesn't disturb me then because I sleep like a log," then added, "and probably snore."

He sat up and pointed to the floor. "Kay. Down. Stay." She trotted round the bed to his side and looked up expectantly.

"So which side should I be on then?" I asked.

"Tell you what," Alex said, "you're on her side of the bed so if we switch she might be more willing to stay on the floor. Er, no hang on, let me get something for her to lie on and I'll climb in the other side once you've scooched over."

I laughed, now fully awake again. "Musical beds and poor Kay's out."

Alex went to the closet and pulled out a pair of sweatpants. He tossed them on the floor and Kay pawed them and then turned round and round in circles for a few seconds before thumping herself in a ball on top of them.

"I hope she doesn't jump on us when we're asleep," I said. "I'm used to a sedate cat that uses a more subtle approach to taking up space."

"If she does then she'll jump on me. That's why I wanted to change sides and I'm used to her. But," he said, "I'm not used to you either but this is rather nice having you here."

He pulled me to him and I snuggled under his arm, against his body. Beneath his tank top a thick mat of hair covered his chest. Generally I disliked hairy men but on Alex it seemed right and fit the image of a great bear.

He nuzzled my ear, "Do you always wear earrings to bed?"

"Actually, yes. They're pierced so I don't trouble removing them unless they're particularly dangly ones. Does it bother you? I can take them out if you like."

"No. That's okay. The earrings will help keep me true to my word and honest."

"Honest?" I was puzzled, "How come?"

He laughed. "I won't get carried away by nuzzling your soft little ears."

Although I knew him to be joking, his comment about the earring and using the word honest reminded me of what had transpired earlier between Cheryl and my mother. It seemed like eons ago, but I was painfully aware of what had made me so unhappy and how, coincidentally, it had brought me into his bed instead of the one at the house or, equally unpleasant, a motel. I didn't realize I had become quiet and that the memory had caused me to stiffen slightly.

"Maggie," he said. "I'm sorry—didn't mean to sound like I was coming on to you." He started to remove his arm from around me.

"Alex, no it's not you, it's … well it was what you said that reminded me of what happened earlier. You said earring and honest in the same breath."

I could sense his confusion but he waited for me to finish. I was silent for a few minutes and decided that if I didn't at least explain it would actually create a distance between us. "Do you want to know what happened?"

"If you want to tell me, yes."

"It may seem like nothing but it was something to which I attached a great deal of importance and underscored a lifetime of living with Norma. She's not a nice person, you know."

"I've already come to that conclusion. John's told me a bit about her."

"John? When? Recently? Did he tell you about the earrings?"

"Earrings? No. But he had to deal with your mother when she wanted to talk about her burial arrangements. Poor guy would quake when she made an appointment with him."

"Poor John. He doesn't need that."

"Nobody does. But what's this about the earrings and your mother?"

So I told him. While I was telling him I cried a bit more but managed to explain coherently what it was that was so painful.

"I know she dislikes me although I've never known why. She can be quite hateful and I resent Cheryl having the earrings. It may seem like a small thing, but they belonged to me from my grandmother and her mother before that. Norma never wore them because she was afraid to get her ears pierced. They meant nothing to her and she gave them away because they meant everything to me. It was just the final twist of the knife to tell me how little she cares without actually saying the words." I was silent.

"Why on earth did you come all this way to be with her then? Although," he added, "I'm glad you did. The universe works in mysterious ways. But why?" he repeated.

"It wasn't easy. I'd been in touch with her by phone for the past four or five years but I called primarily to speak to my father until he died—or thought he had." I hesitated, not wanting him to see my less generous side, "I wasn't overly keen on helping her after the fall but decided I should. I hoped I could understand why she rejected me but it was mainly to take care of my father's ashes and get my grandmother's jewelry and with Daddy dead, I also wondered about my inheritance since she never mentioned his will." I was quiet. I hadn't even told Shelly about that and this was the first time I'd admitted it to anyone.

Alex let the silence continue then said, "What do you mean you thought your father had died?"

"Norma said he had but it was a stroke. She lied."

"Nice woman! But wouldn't you have eventually found out?"

"Not really. She was vague about where his remains were and if not for Cheryl telling me he was alive I might never have known."

"Have you seen him?" He was propped up on his elbow and looking down at me.

"Yes. I located the nursing home and went there immediately. He's frail and can't speak but he knew who I was and we chatted via a small laptop."

"My god, I can see why you're conflicted. Why would you care about a woman like her?"

"I don't although still hope that she'll relent and accept me. Whether she does or not I still want to know why she hates me."

"She doesn't seem like the kind of person to give you that satisfaction, either by accepting you or providing an explanation."

"I still hope."

"But you shouldn't let that consume you."

I felt with that one last comment he had summed up what I had been struggling with for so long. It had consumed me and I had compromised myself because of it.

"Yes, you're right, it has." I thought of the hours I'd spent with Anne in therapy and countless hours during my life where I had questioned and doubted myself because of it. "No. It's not worth it … she's not worth it. That's it. That's really it." I took a deep breath and exhaled as though expelling Norma from my whole being.

"So I guess you had a miserable childhood?"

"Pretty much."

"But you eventually left."

"Yes."

"And you got on with your life and made something of it without her but keeping the door slightly open to stay in contact."

"Yes, although that makes me seem awful. It would've been more honest to just cut her out of my life altogether."

"Not really. Have you heard the expression, 'What's bred in the bone?'"

"The book? Robertson Davies?"

"The proverb precedes his writing. Norma is part of your heritage. She is very much a part of you ..."

"... dear god, are you suggesting I'm like her."

"Not at all although it's still possible and her fire might be yours only better directed. What I'm trying to say is that I think you held on despite the invective and all the criticism you experience because you are ... you seem to be a thinking, sensitive individual and I suspect you believe that if you continue to hold her in your life—no matter at what distance—you will eventually understand what makes her tick and how that affects you. Whether you do or not, she is still part of you and part of that Shadow you refer to. But one lurks in every soul and our job is to try and confront it, accept it being there, and recognize it for what it is. Not always an easy thing to do and there are too many people who are totally clueless of its existence."

He stroked my hair and leaned his mouth onto my forehead to kiss me. "Am I right?"

I wondered how I had found myself in his bed, in his t-shirt, not engaged in any passionate lovemaking but having a conversation that clarified and explained what I had been unable to completely define my whole life. "So you don't think I'm a completely unmitigated loss of a human being for taking her crap?"

"Put that way you might want to reevaluate the situation and determine what it is you want out of this relationship and go for it—limited and constrained though it might be."

His words were the catalyst to establishing a different kind of relationship with Norma that I had been unable to vocalize. I felt a sense of freedom from her tyranny and one that even I had contributed to, without fully understanding why. It took two and I was no longer willing to play and whatever grief that had caused me I was in a better place to understand and hopefully deal with it. Perhaps grow from it.

Alex kissed me gently and lay down again, pulling me closer into his arms. "You know, Maggie sweetheart, if I don't get some sleep tonight I'm going to be playing all the wrong keys tomorrow. There's obviously more to this but I think we've made a good start on something significant with respect to your life ... and, anything significant is of major importance to me. Now I'm going to sleep and I hope you like to cuddle because that's another significant thing about you that I consider important."

Of course we overslept and it was Kay who eventually woke us wanting to go out. Alex had prepared the coffee the night before and threw some bread into the toaster. "Not what I had in mind for breakfast, but this will have to do," he said. "I hope you take rain checks." He kissed me and said he would call later during the afternoon.

I told him I was meeting John around one and unsure of how long it would be and said, "But I think I'll go see Norma before I go see him."

Despite my decision to confront Norma, once in the car and away from Alex, my resolve weakened and instead of heading for the hospital decided to go back to the house to take a shower and change. I felt rumpled and could still detect the lingering smells of both him and Kay on my body and clothes. I felt possessive of them and wanted to deal with Norma from a neutral space where there would be nothing other than the determination, and hopefully the opportunity, to learn why she was so hostile and another day when I would present myself with wet hair.

The answering machine light was blinking when I arrived and I hesitated before deciding to press the button and listen. It was Norma, no longer strident but still demanding. "I suppose you think it's perfectly fine to leave me, your mother, here with no attempt to see how I am. Well, I'm very, very sick. Not that you care!" There was the sound of a telephone being scraped as though the receiver was being dragged across the machine in search of being replaced then a click and silence.

Damn, I thought, she sounds worse than she did yesterday. She'd managed to make me feel guilty though and I wondered if I should dispense with the shower and head straight for the hospital but nixed that idea and to continue with my original plan. Clean shirt, clean jeans no wonderful Alex smells to share intentionally or otherwise. Norma would probably never know but if she did detect something I didn't want to be in a position of having to explain. No, I thought, this is going to be Norma's time for an explanation for all the years of unhappiness she's caused both me and Daddy. Of course no explanation might be forthcoming but I was open to any kind of dialogue, including rejection.

While the hot water ran over my shoulders and my fingers were laced with soap in my hair the thought of what might follow the encounter came as a surprise. I hadn't considered what might happen afterwards. If it caused a complete end of communication would I continue to remain at the house until Norma was well or return to the States and disconnect from her entirely? Well that's presupposing there's no resolution to this impossible hostility, I decided, and besides which I now had my father and Alex to consider. I wasn't prepared to leave just yet; to leave them and John and even Kay made me feel the loss before it had ever occurred. The realization that I was now connected in a way I had never considered came as a shock. It was all becoming much more complicated and making the right decisions more difficult.

The telephone rang again and I grabbed a towel and answered knowing that Norma was probably on the other end.

"Hello."

"Why didn't you answer the first time I called? You should be here and I shouldn't have to be the one calling you ..." Norma's voice cracked and she started to cough and gag.

"I know, I'm sorry but ..." I hesitated as I thought of an excuse. "I was in the shower and I was just about to call you back, but I'm leaving now and should be there in a short while. You don't sound very good, how ..." There was a click as Norma hung up on me. That woman makes it so difficult to be sympathetic, I thought, as I ran back into the bedroom and dragged out a clean pair of jeans and a shirt.

The sound of rain against the window caused me to look up. This was a downpour. Weather wise this country was the pits, I thought, remembering California and Mewfus sitting in the sun on my balcony surrounded by my container plants, and felt a wave of homesickness unlike anything I had previously experienced since arriving. Then I thought of Alex and his little house and his green, cottage garden with the roses that grew in profusion round the walls and windows. I loved my patio but preferred his garden.

I grabbed a sweater, pulling it over my head, my wet hair stuck to my shoulders as I did so. It felt cold and clammy. I seem to be turning into a mermaid I thought. Back home it would air dry. I smiled at the stupid pun, "Oh well," I mumbled, "things could be worse."

I remembered waking next to Alex, his arms around me, my back pressed against his chest and groin. I felt his erection and flushed with anticipation but he rolled away from me, kissing my shoulder. "C'mon Kay," he said. "You need to go outside and I need to exercise restraint here." He chuckled, "But I'm not sure for how much longer."

"Me neither," I said, "and I'm beginning to hope for sooner rather than later." I found it amazing how convinced I had been that my libido was dormant, but could be so quickly aroused. After the failed efforts and discouraging attempts with other relationships after Richard, it was reassuring. I had wondered if I might spend the remainder of my life alone without lovemaking. That someone to be with had seemed unattainable—until Alex. Yes, I hoped it would be very soon when I could find out.

The rain beat down on my windshield and the gutters were awash with leaves, carried down by the rushing water towards the drains. Enjoy this while you can, I thought, it's still gonna be a few months before you'll see this kind of downpour in Southern California, if at all.

I pulled into the hospital parking lot and reached back for the umbrella, pressing against its spring while thrusting it up outside the car door that I held open with my foot. Grabbing my purse I leaned out and under it, stood and slammed the door closed. I could hear a thunder roll in the distance and as I ran toward the building, saw a zigzag flash of lightening. I wondered if Alex would still go to practice or whether he might stay in and wished I could be there with him, wherever he decided to be. Kay too. I wondered what the Shepherd did when it pelted down like this.

Shaking the umbrella before entering the swing doors I felt self conscious about the puddles I was making. A large mat had been placed inside for traction although there was no place for the umbrella. Perhaps they have a stand at the desk on Norma's floor, I decided. The thought of my mother stopped me momentarily. The rain and thinking of Alex had been a temporary block from the confrontation I knew might lie ahead of me. I hadn't wanted to dwell on what would be said or how it would progress. I just knew it would be an uncomfortable situation and didn't want to cry or lose my temper both of which I knew could happen. I'd cried enough already and it was time to control the temper that had most recently shown itself.

I saw an umbrella stand next to the front desk that already contained three other umbrellas. My mother's light gray one, conservative next to the two black ones, appeared very British compared to the gaudy purple and green one that had taken its own place there and I wondered who the colorful visitor was who owned it. It added a cheerful note to a dowdy container. "Ah, so you do have one. Good," I said to the nurse, a middle aged woman with dyed black hair. "Wondered what I would do with this thing in the room and didn't want it dripping over everything."

"Neither do we," she said. "Yes, leave it there in our brollie bin, luv, it ain't going to run off by itself. Bit of a deluge out there ain't it? Heavier than usual."

"It is and thanks," I said, and hoped it wouldn't be me who would be doing the running off before I was ready.

Norma's door was closed as usual and I hesitated before turning the handle but knocked gently before pushing it open. I wasn't sure what to expect, I never am, although I thought I'd see her sitting up, facing the door, perhaps watching television but was surprised to see my mother lying down and sleeping. Small guttural snores escaped her open mouth and a silver thread of saliva hung from the corner of her lips. Now if I were a loving daughter, I thought, I would gently wipe that away but since I'm not I'll just sit down and wait for her to wake up. I was pleased I would have time to adjust my mind to being there. I felt it gave me an advantage to see Norma asleep and poised for whatever tirade might be her waking response.

I wished I had brought a cup of coffee and wondered if I could leave and grab some hot water for tea. As I stood and gently pushed back the chair, lifting it slightly so that it didn't scrape against the floor, the telephone rang. Norma gasped and her eyes flew open, she clutched the top of the sheet and attempted to pull herself up, dislodging the pillows behind her. Without her glasses she peered toward me, squinting as she did so.

"Here, I'll get it for you," I said, and while lifting the receiver and saying, "Hold on," to the caller, helped raise Norma to a sitting position. It was an impulsive and quick gesture and just as quickly I regretted my action, expecting my mother to yell, but she didn't, instead breathing heavily in her attempt to sit upright. She felt warm and I suspected that although pale she was still running a fever.

"Give me the phone," Norma said and grabbed it from my hand. "Yes, who is it?" I hoped it wouldn't be John because her tone was rough and without the pretense of being polite it would make him nervous. "Who? Just a minute." She covered the mouthpiece with her hand and stared at me. "This is private. Go outside. Leave."

"Go as in leave completely or just wait outside go?"

"Outside and stay there until I call."

"What if I don't hear you?"

"For goodness sake, Margaret, don't be an imbecile!"

"Fine. I'll go get a cup of tea." I grabbed my purse and stormed out. I wished I could've slammed the door but heavily weighted to close firmly but quietly it resisted my efforts. I wondered who had called her as I realized my resolve to stay calm was shot. "Practice makes perfect," I mumbled, "and around her I'm likely to get a lot of that."

I decided to get some hot chocolate instead from the machine while I was outside and held the extra cream and sugar buttons hoping it would make it more palatable. It looked almost purple instead of dark brown although smelled like chocolate. I carefully sipped it, blowing gently into the cup and walked slowly back to the door and knocked. No answer. I turned the handle and opened the door a crack and saw that Norma was lying against the pillows holding the phone against the blanket. "You through now?" I asked.

"Yes. Put this back. I can't reach. Why didn't you come back in when I called?"

"I was getting this. Did you have a nice chat?"

"It's none of your business."

"John?"

"I said it's none of your business but no, and there'd be no point in having a private conversation with him now. The two of you are in cahoots together and he'd probably tell you everything anyway." Norma started coughing again, waving her hand toward the box of tissues. I slid the box toward her and settled it on her bed, deciding to ignore the comment about John.

"Do you know what your temperature was the last time it was taken?"

"Almost a hundred and two."

"Mmm. High. When was that?"

"I don't remember but obviously when you weren't here. You don't care and have no respect for your mother."

"Perhaps that's because it's never been earned." Whoa, Maggie, I thought, didn't expect to get into the fray quite as fast as this and she *is* sick so go easy on her.

"How dare you speak to me that way. You obviously don't want to be here so you might as well leave now for all I care."

I drew a quick breath and decided to try and be neutral but honest. "You certainly don't make it easy to be any other way, Norma, and perhaps I will but before I do I have one question I need answered." I stood staring down at her. She continued to stare at me without answering so I continued. "Why do you hate me the way you do?"

My question reminded me of John asking more or less the same thing. Life had a funny way of coming back on itself but like John I wanted to know; and even though I felt I had changed because of my talk with Alex, I still wanted to clarify something I felt to be wrong with me even though it might be an erroneous judgment.

The room was silent except for the soft hum that came from the monitors beside the bed. Norma closed her eyes and her mouth tightened. She suddenly looked frail and vulnerable and I wondered if I had been correct in addressing her so bluntly. She was still an old woman and sick. I decided it didn't matter and waited for a response and took a sip of the hot chocolate. The heat felt reassuring in my hand and I was pleased I had that as a distraction. I could always hold it up to my mouth if I needed to stall.

"Hate you." It was a reiteration and not a question of one surprised as I had been with John's.

"Yes. For at far back as I can remember," I said. "Frankly you've been a bitch toward me and Father too, for that matter. Why? What did I ... what did either one of us do to deserve that?"

Norma's eyes opened and the watery pale blue fixed on me. I felt chilled by their gaze as they reminded me of icy glaciers remote and distant but without their beauty. I was repelled by the absence of any hint of love or affection, devoid of any warmth or feeling.

"Yes I suppose so. And rightfully, too. It was because of you that I lost my chance of real happiness. You were a nuisance and do you think I was happy with your father?" She almost spat the rejection and coughed slightly. "I didn't love him. He was a wimp. Not a manly bone in his body."

I wanted to interrupt her and protect him. "You were the one who married him and he certainly managed to keep us supported. I haven't seen you reject that."

"He was in love with me and I knew that we would have nice vacations and thought that would be enough but then I had the opportunity to have more. I could've left him but it was you who stood in my way."

"Me? A child?" I suddenly remembered the old letter and wondered if Norma was referring to that relationship. "How come?"

"I never wanted children but accidents happen and I got pregnant. Your father prevented me from getting rid of you. Yes. There were ways back then, but it was risky, so I went ahead and had you. Big mistake."

"A mistake in having me. Thanks a lot." Although not unexpected, hearing the truth hit me hard. Being rejected was bad enough but hearing the words cemented the reality and made it final. I wondered if perhaps I had clung too hard to the chance of hearing something else instead; some indication of acceptance that would have validated my need to be loved as a daughter.

I held my breath. I still didn't want Norma to stop. Not now. Not when the truth was coming out. I wondered if it was because she was feverish and perhaps a little delusional. Maybe the knock on her head was affecting her. Certainly my mother had never opened up about anything, ever, but her voice was agitated and seemed now to be directed at some inner demon that was influencing her thoughts. Her eyes no longer pierced the distance between us, but were closed and her brows, under the dressing were furrowed. To my surprise she started to cry. I put the cup down on the table and placed a tissue in her hand. It lay there as though she was oblivious to it under her fingers.

"No I didn't want you, squalling needy little brat that you were. And as you grew and became a pretty child—and yes you were pretty, you took after me—everyone paid more attention to you than they did me."

"But ..." I stopped and shook my head. This was making her cry? It wasn't what I was expecting to hear and the perversity of her words shocked me; I wanted to race back in time and protect the little girl I once was.

"No buts about it. There was one person who noticed me, though, and not you."

"I was a little kid. How could you compete?" I felt overwhelmed with the realization that my mother's problem was deeper and of longer duration than I'd ever suspected. She had such a need to be wanted but managed to alienate those closest to her that could have fulfilled that need.

"Yes, he noticed me. He wasn't afraid to be a real man. He did something about it. And so did I." Norma clenched her mouth and although her eyes were still closed, looked triumphant. "I fell in love with your father's business partner and that kept me sane. I felt as though I was treated as a woman separate from anyone or anything else. You, your father, anyone else."

I thought that she had still maintained that separation which divorced her from any warmth or communication. "What about Father?"

"What about him?"

"Did he know or suspect?"

Norma seemed to collect herself and become more aware that she was disclosing personal information about herself. She opened her eyes and stared in my direction. "Why are you asking me all these questions? It's none of your business."

"So you've said but while we're on the subject and I feel I have a right to know since I seem to be so involved, you might as well tell me everything. Then," I added, "I'll leave as you so obviously want me to."

"You owe me."

"Owe you what?"

"The years I sacrificed for you."

"Sacrificed, Norma? You sacrificed nothing."

"It was because of you he left me."

"I was a child. A little girl that depended on you."

"It was because you were small you got in the way. He didn't want children and didn't want a married woman either. He said it was too complicated so ended it between us. I've never forgotten him or what my life could've been like with him. He was a wonderful man."

"From the little you've said, he sounds like a prick."

"A what?"

"A prick. A self-centered loser, a guy who's worth nothing."

"How would you know?"

"I was married to one. Remember?"

"Yours left you because of you. Mine left me because of you. Not the same thing at all. You see, you're trouble."

I felt the heat rise to my face, furious. I realized that within two days I had experienced a rage that went beyond any previous anger I had experienced; abused and under attack. But I also felt a strength that went deeper and that regardless of what Norma did or said, she couldn't hurt me again. I no longer cared. That part of my Shadow, at least, was under control.

"And yes, your father knew."

"How? You told him?"

"I didn't have to. It was obvious."

"So you didn't have the decency to be discreet."

"Men found me attractive—still do when I'm not like this." Norma fluttered her hand over the sheet and turned her face into the pillow and started to cough. The hacking sound alarmed me and I reached for tissue box and handed her one. She expelled some mucus into the tissue and it was flecked with blood.

"This isn't good, Norma, I'm going to get the nurse. I'll be right back."

"No! I don't want anyone pulling and pushing me around. I'll be fine once I get out of this place."

I hesitated and decided to report the incident when I left. I wondered if Norma would continue to speak about the past and felt conflicted that I was taking advantage of the woman's situation to resolve my own.

"So, er … Father didn't want a divorce then?"

"No! Because of you."

"Me? It's all about me again."

"He couldn't care for you and there was nobody else. He ended the partnership with Bob who went to Canada. Said he couldn't bear to be living in the same country and not have me."

"And you've resented me ever since."

"You and your father."

"But he supported you despite all that."

"Perhaps, and so he should have because I gave up something more precious."

"Something more precious than a child and a husband who loved you?"

"The child I could've done without and it was good riddance when you left and when he died for that matter."

I remembered how my father would sit outside in the garden or potter in the greenhouse or read when he didn't bring work home and escape to the small room he used as an office. I thought of him now confined to his wheelchair. "He's not dead and you know it." I was watching Norma carefully, intent on her response and I wasn't disappointed. She started to raise herself from the pillow but slumped back down again.

"Well he should be."

"Dead? Oh my god, Norma, have you no feelings whatsoever?"

"He had a stroke, a small one and didn't want anyone to know but I did. His voice was strange and he seemed weak. Then he had the second one and couldn't speak or move his arm. That's when he went into the nursing home."

I remembered the last phone call I'd had with my father and asked if there was something wrong. His voice seemed odd but he said he had a slight cold and, unable to see him, I assumed that was what it was. "You never thought to tell me." I was furious. "Did he see a doctor?"

"Yes and then to his solicitor."

"Why on earth … ?"

"He wanted to set up an annuity so that he would be cared for in a nursing home if it happened again. I couldn't take care of him, and wouldn't want an invalid around the house even if we did have help."

"And you chose to dismiss him when he had the second stroke and tell me he was dead."

"Like I said, he should be instead of being half paralyzed in a nursing home. I didn't know what I was signing away when he brought me the insurance papers. All that money going to waste. It was our savings and ruined any chance for us—for me—to go on holiday. Not that I could now even if I wanted to and when we did go he sat and read or went on walks by himself so I might as well have been alone."

Poor Daddy, how ironic that their savings and Norma's vacation money was keeping him in a beautiful environment and cared for in peace even though he was incapacitated. I wished I remembered more of him when I was a child. "Was Father always a quiet man?" I was beginning to think that perhaps living with Norma after the affair caused him to withdraw.

"No fun to be around you mean?"

"I'm not sure what your idea of fun is unless it's dress up and party."

"Exactly. No he was no fun."

I drew in my breath and looked down at my mother. How on earth had I inherited such a woman to produce and raise me? Then I felt relieved that I resembled my father more and that concerns of being like Norma were simply my fears of inheriting such miserable characteristics. I knew I wasn't selfishly motivated. That was Norma's personality and she seemed never to have recognized them and if she did, to not work and change them. Instead she had become worse. Then I wondered how I could discuss the earrings.

"Neither were you exactly. You made our lives miserable … and still do."

"Misery loves company."

"Don't be so vengeful. I suppose you gave Cheryl the earrings to be spiteful."

"They were mine to give."

"So you said, but Grandmother promised them to me and assumed they would be passed down. They were an heirloom and precious—to me at least if not for you."

I paced the small room and stared out of the window as the rain lashed against the glass, watching abstractedly at the streams of water pouring onto the sill and falling to the street below. I wanted to leave, get out of there and go see John. I knew that when I had lunch with him I would be a different person than the one who had cried earlier.

I turned toward the bed and gazed at Norma who lay so helplessly in it. She looked old and haggard and ill and her breath seemed more labored than it had been earlier. I wondered if she might be dying but then decided she was ill and would recover.

"Well I'm sorry I made your life so miserable. But we have to make a decision now. Do you want me to stay and help you when you get out of hospital or leave?" I suspected that Norma would be hospitalized for at least several more days if not longer so her immediate departure probably wasn't imminent. I also suspected that I would be with Alex. The thought of going back to California and leaving him stopped my thoughts. Why the hell couldn't I have met him back home instead of here? I would even miss John.

"You're my daughter and should take care of me until I'm well and forever if necessary but I'm going to be out of here and walking around so you won't be needed and can go back where you came from. Cheryl will help me around the house. I prefer her company to yours, anyway."

The woman's delusional, I thought, then realized that she always had been. She was convinced that people found her charming and it never occurred to her that anyone thought her rude and self-centered. She had no friends and the one sister from whom she had been estranged was dead. She had nobody. I wondered if my father had provided for her in any way. Knowing him and despite her attitude, he probably had. I was curious if the house had been mortgaged

246

because of the retirement facility or even what their financial situation was.

"And I suppose if you could you're going to leave her the house, too."

"Her and the Church but not that now you and John are so lovey-dovey."

I was dumbfounded. "You'd really do that wouldn't you? Grandmother's earrings and the house Father worked for. Thank heaven he's still alive and his will still holds." I thought of the document he had given me.

"Well, I can't do anything yet. Your father made it so that I didn't inherit the house. I could live in it until I went then it went to you. That's what I'm working on now."

"What do you mean?"

"I'm speaking with my solicitor to see if I can inherit the whole thing. I deserve it and can leave it to whoever I want."

"Was that who you were speaking to when you wanted me to leave just now?"

"Yes."

"Only now you're pursuing it? Why not earlier?"

"I tried to after your father had the stroke and I found out what he'd done. But then I had the fall. He cheated me. But he's incompetent now and I'll win yet."

"Like you cheated on him."

"Not the same thing at all. It's wrong that you should get the place after I stayed there all these years. And suffered."

"Suffered? How?" I thought of the place that had provided her with security and although not to my taste, it was to Norma's. I had never thought my mother lacked for any physical comfort, but her mind over the years had continued to fester over imagined wrongs.

"I don't want to talk anymore. I've said enough," she said and moved further down into the pillow. "You don't need to hear what isn't your business."

"Yes, I'll be going but I'll come back later unless you prefer I didn't."

Norma dismissively waved her hand at me. "Please yourself, although you make me tired with all this talking you should show up as a sign of respect for me. The staff would expect my daughter to come—John too, since he's my minister even though he's two-faced."

I decided not to pursue that comment. Norma's voice cracked and she coughed again, struggling to relieve her congested lungs.

"I'm going to send in a nurse to check on you. I want to speak with Dr. Suffolk for an update. You could be developing pneumonia again."

"It's just bronchitis. Pneumonia would keep me in here longer than I intend to stay. I need to be out of here and home, getting stronger so that I can live my life again."

The woman really was indomitable. I might not want to be like her but would love to have had some of her spirit. "Let's hope you're right." She didn't need to feel worse than necessary. I opened the door and stood gazing at Norma and had the thought that she might not make it out of there. I bit my lower lip, shaking my head. She was an old harridan, though, and I wished it wasn't so. She was, after all, my mother and I wondered what my life would've been like had she been different. Something I would never know.

CHAPTER EIGHTEEN

After I retrieved my umbrella and asked the nurse to check on Norma, I splashed through the rain and puddles and settled myself in the car. I checked my cell phone and saw two messages; one from John and the other from Alex. It was twelve forty and I had planned to see John at one so called him back first.

"Hey John, it's Maggie. We still on for lunch?"

"Of course but dearie me, what a storm you have to contend with."

"Bit damp, yes, but I'm starting to get used to the weather. D'you still want to meet?" I didn't like the idea of him having to go out in it if he didn't have to.

"I thought perhaps you could come see me here at the vicarage since ..." he hesitated, "... since you might feel more comfortable instead of the café. But you do sound so much better than you did. Your voice is much stronger. Dearie me yes, and that's a good thing. How are you feeling?"

"Good, actually, although I'm sitting in the hospital parking lot and I've just left Norma. She's not doing so well and I want to speak to the doctor when I can get hold of him." I reminded myself to call when I was through with him and Alex.

"Poor dear lady, although hmm, perhaps not quite as dear as one might suppose, huh?"

"No, although, the caustic tone is not as strong as it was, and an indication she's not feeling her usual feisty self. I feel rather sorry for her."

"Me too, me too but I plan to stop by and see her later. Hopefully the rain will have abated somewhat by then … not that I would let that interfere with my decision. Dear me, no."

"Knowing you, John, you'd probably haul yourself out regardless of weather."

"It's my job but I really don't mind, you know. Not if it brought comfort. Do you like egg salad?"

I smiled. I was pleased I was going to have lunch with him. I was also curious to see the inside of his house.

"Egg salad is perfect."

"Brown or white bread? I have both you know."

"If by brown you mean whole wheat then I'd like that and I hope you didn't go to any special trouble to get two kinds of bread."

"It's whole meal which I suppose is the same thing and actually, I keep that for Alex who stops by. The white is for me. So yes, I'm fully stocked and the eggs are fresh from the farm down the street and provided by a lovely lady who has chickens and insists on giving me what I need. But why don't you come on over instead of chatting in the car?"

"Good idea, the windows are starting to get all steamed up. Is there anything I can bring?"

"Thanks. No. How nice of you to ask. Hmm, yes very nice since you'd have to get out in all this rain."

"Not a problem and for you John, anything. See you in a bit then."

I pressed the doctor's number but got a recording that it was his lunch hour. Making sure I left a message for him to call, I rang Alex but it was his message too that picked up. I wondered if he would be playing when I went over to John's and my heart performed a small flutter as I remembered him holding me. You're in trouble, lady, I thought, and you'd better start giving some thought as to how you're going to feel when you eventually have to leave.

I shook my head at the thought and turned the key in the ignition, watching the blades swipe the outside as I cracked the window to dispel some of the fogged that had collected. I leaned forward and wiped the inside glass with a tissue, waited until I could see more clearly, then pulled out of the lot.

The driveway to the church had large pools of water and little rivulets swirled around the stones. The rain beat down on the roof of the car and I reached for the umbrella that was still already sodden from the race from the hospital. "I'm gonna be drenched," I said aloud. "Oh well, here goes."

I ran up the path to John's house and saw him open his door. "I was watching for you," he said. "Come in, come in, and what a wet welcome to be sure. Here, let me take that for you."

I eased out of the saturated California raincoat that was seeping through to my shirt as John took the umbrella and pumped it open and shut outside before closing the door. He stood it in a large bucket that sat beside it and I wondered why he didn't place it in the umbrella and coat rack stand that was laden with jackets and raingear nearby. "How come …"

"… I don't put it there?" John finished indicating the stand. "Well, it's because it's rather ancient you know, quite on its last legs although still a handsome old thing and probably an antique but the bottom is rather rusty and leaks." He laughed nervously as though he was at fault for failing to provide the correct container. "But do come in."

I was surprised when I looked around me. I'd rather expected a simple, orderly little place but was amazed to find it filled with open and closed cardboard boxes loaded with a miscellaneous collection of stuff stacked on top or falling out and all rather messy. I stepped around an old, upright cane chair that had a small, needlepoint pillow sitting over what I could see was a worn hole because of all the spiky raffia that poked beneath the cloth and followed John through a tiny hallway past his office. That too was filled with paperwork and books piled high, around an equally untidy desk, his computer and keyboard almost submerged by files and a large Dracaena plant that leaned against the window behind it.

"Follow me, follow me, careful of these boxes. I really should get them out of here. Old clothes, you know, for those in need but I've not gone through and separated them yet. Dear me, I'm sorry the place is a bit of a tip."

"Tip?"

"Rubbish dump. Although not quite rubbish otherwise I'd have tossed it out. Usable. All quite usable, you know and useful to someone I'm sure. I thought we'd eat in the kitchen because ..."

"... your dining room is full?" I laughed. I felt immediately comfortable in all John's clutter.

"Yes. Mmm, but you're quite, quite wet. Can I give you a dry shirt or a towel or something? You're soaked." He stood staring at me while clasping and unclasping his hands that I now knew was a self-conscious habit.

"A towel would be nice actually, John. My hair is dripping down my collar and cold. Do you have a shirt I could wear?" I wondered what I would look like in a black dog collar shirt. There's a first time for everything, I thought. I seem to be wearing guy's clothing as a matter of course now and thought of Alex's large t-shirt and wondered if a shirt of John's would fit me.

"Hold on a sec, I have just the thing."

I hoped he wouldn't rummage in one of the boxes of donated clothes for something although even something dry would be more comfortable than what I had on but he came back into the kitchen holding a towel and a green and black tartan flannel shirt that looked larger than I would have expected. "Didn't think you would wear something like that, John," I said. "But it's perfect. Where can I change? This'll be much more comfortable while we eat."

"It's the McLean tartan and I rather love the colors." He smiled and nodded to another open doorway.

The bathroom he indicated was off the little hallway. I pushed open the door and was surprised that, compared to the rest of the house, it was spotless and without the clutter. Guess Cheryl does something here after all, I thought, then felt my mind close against the woman and the unhappiness I felt even though I knew it wasn't her fault.

I removed my sweater and pulled on the shirt before wrapping my hair in the towel then laughed at my image in the mirror before I went back to the kitchen.

"Where shall I put this?" I asked. "Do you have a dryer I can throw it into?"

"Here, let me take it from you. I suppose it would go on medium heat. Yes? I really don't do my own, you know. Cheryl … er yes Cheryl takes care of my laundry." He looked uncomfortable mentioning her name but then continued, "And speaking of whom, I have some rather good news for you there. But let's eat first. Tea? Coffee?"

I pulled out a blond pine chair from the table and sat down. "Coffee, please. That would be great."

"It's instant, I'm afraid. Is that okay?"

"Fine, as long as you have some cream or something. Do you?"

"Yes, keep it for Alex when he comes over. And he did say he would stop by after his practice later."

"So he is in church then? I was in such a rush to get inside and with the rain I didn't hear the music." I was thrilled that I might see him.

He nodded. "And these are the sandwiches, I wasn't sure if you like tomato or cucumber so I cut up both separately and you can slip them under the bread. I have some biscuits for later, although dear Mrs. Engleby gave me some of her homemade pie." He glanced to the pie I saw on his counter. "Do you know her? Hmmm, perhaps not. She's a parishioner of mine who really *is* a *dear* lady and keeps me supplied with baked goods. She runs the Bingo night with me. You'll have to come one evening." He hovered over the table, pouring hot water into the cups and sat down, then jumped up again for the cream, placing it on the table.

"Sit down John, you keep hopping up and down and this is lovely. Pleased you chop the egg up separately," I said. "Norma insists the tomato is mashed into the egg and it gets rather sloppy and wet." I lifted the sandwich to my mouth and part of the salad still squished out. "Oops, guess I must learn how to eat egg salad without a fork. Do you have a napkin, John ... er serviette, by any chance? A paper towel will do."

He jumped up again and pulled some sheets off a roll by the sink, "I think I have some cloth ones somewhere but ..."

"Don't go looking for them. This is fine," I interrupted him, wiping my mouth. "So what did you want to tell me about Cheryl?"

"It's rather good news, actually, really good and I was so very happy when she came over to talk to me about the situation. But before I do I'd just like to give thanks for our food."

I swallowed the egg and bread I had just put in my mouth and nodded. I felt embarrassed that I hadn't waited for him to sit down to his or that I'd not anticipated a short prayer. I would have to remember in the future. Guess he must've given thanks while I was in the bathroom at the café.

John seemed oblivious to my discomfort and closed his eyes, his hands resting lighting together in his lap. "Thank you, Lord, for everything you provide for our sustenance both physical and spiritual. Amen."

He had incorporated his acknowledgment to a higher power as something he did without question and continued where he had left off, before saying grace. "Poor woman was most upset by it all. Dear me, what a lot of tears have been shed over the earrings. She was quite as unhappy as you were, although," he added, "of course you were probably more unhappy because they were yours. But then, dear me, she thought they were hers too, so understandably distressed."

He seemed to be caught up in the memory of the encounter and oblivious to my sitting there in his shirt. "So what did she say, John? What happened?" I felt the memory of seeing them on her yesterday and my own response beginning to reoccur and I focused on stirring cream and sugar into my coffee to maintain control. I refused to lose it again and distress John in the process.

"Why she wants to return them to you. Of course. That would be the right thing to do, wouldn't it?" He glanced up at me and poked some cucumber into his salad, then took a slice and nibbled it carefully. "She wasn't happy to think that your mother could do such a terrible thing. Cheryl is really a very kind, nice person, you know. That's why I was surprised initially."

I nodded. I remembered our earlier conversation in the hall where I had felt warmly for her kindness toward Norma. My ill feeling was partly because of what I considered a betrayal of that and perhaps having stolen them. "Well, I was pleased that they were given as a gift and not stolen, although I was obviously unhappy they were gone. But she really wants to return them?"

"Yes indeed. She said as much although wants to give them to you herself. I thought that you both could meet here to do it. That is if you don't mind. I could always get them from her and give you them myself. She suggested that as an alternative."

Tears sprang to my eyes as I considered the kindness being offered by both of them. "Of course, John. Of course. And you know what?" I rushed the words as the thought occurred to me, "I want her to have something lovely to make up for their loss. She didn't have to give them back but she plans to. Perhaps we could go shopping to a jewelry store somewhere and she can pick out another pair to replace mine."

"Excellent. Excellent." He clapped his hands together and held them as though in prayer, "That's a brilliant idea and I think she would like that. Indeed she would." He beamed at me then his smile faded and his face sobered, "But goodness me, I think you should hang onto them and not return them to er … to your mother."

"Never!"

"I dislike subterfuge at any time," he said, "but it might be wise to keep it as a little secret, a deception if you will, and not let Norma know. Why risk a possible scene unnecessarily." He glanced at me out of the corner of his eye to see if I approved.

"Yep. I agree. I'm so happy this has worked out so well. Poor Cheryl having to be part of all this. And John, I could hug you."

"I'm a bit egg salady right now, although thank you for the thought. Can't say I've been hugged in a while. Pity that."

"Then you shall have one. You have become such a dear person to me and I really appreciate your friendship. I'll miss you when I've gone."

"And I you. In fact I have been thinking the same thing. I really don't know much about you and your life in California. Do you have to return? But I suppose it has to happen sooner or later and will undoubtedly depend on your mother. Yes?"

"Yes, and something I must think about. My last conversation with her earlier, was rather revealing in how she feels about me and if not as sick as she was or is, I'd probably return home immediately. Certainly if she was at the house it would be unbearable but hospitalized the situation is very different. But there is something else I must consider. Were you aware that my father is in a nursing home?"

He stared at me. "I believed him to be dead. I only met your mother quite recently when she was hospitalized the first time despite this being such a small parish with a number of other churches. I knew he wasn't buried in my little church and rather surprised she didn't want to be buried next to him when she came to discuss her own funeral arrangements. I thought perhaps that might be impossible or inconvenient and didn't want to impose on what I thought might be painful memories. I suppose this explains a number of unanswered questions in my mind."

When he forgot about himself, John spoke with more conviction and depth that helped convey the image he so wanted for himself. I thought of my own growing sense of self with respect to Norma and how, ironically, she was indirectly responsible for the positive changes in so many lives. Perhaps on some psychic level she was well-intentioned and it was that having an effect but it had no chance of being fully enacted while she focused on her own happiness. It occurred to me it was her own Shadow that had taken over. Poor Norma. How miserable that must be.

John continued, "Perhaps you can tell me where the poor man is so that I can go visit him. Yes, yes, splendid idea. Now what else were we saying? Something about you returning home. Not a happy thought though, not a happy one for me at all to think you won't be around."

I thought of Alex and his little house and glanced at the cozy clutter of John's. "Life is certainly presenting me with options I had never ever visualized and making things a lot more complicated."

"Complicated? Really? How so?"

I hesitated. I wasn't sure if speaking of Alex and our growing affection was appropriate but neither did I want to withhold that from John. God knows he had shared his most guarded secret with me and taken me into his confidence.

"I'm falling in love with Alex."

"Why how perfectly delightful. That's wonderful news!"

"Yes, but please don't mention anything to him just yet. We had dinner last night and he helped calm me down after all that crying and I stayed over ..."

"Really? That's rather splendid."

"John, you're such a romantic you know, but we didn't do anything ..."

"... you don't have to tell me even if you did." He was becoming flustered and filled the kettle with more water. "Tea? Oh that's right, coffee but I want some more tea. Well, well, you and Alex. What a great couple you would make. Dear me, who would've thought. Alex seemed like he was all set for bachelorhood, like me, although different you understand."

"Yes, different," I laughed, "but perhaps there's someone in your future too! Wouldn't that be nice?"

"Difficult though and would raise some eyebrows around here and perhaps generate some controversy. But any relationship such as the one I would like is a big topic of discussion and perhaps one day will be accepted. But first I have to make the effort and find someone or at least open my heart so that someone finds me. I feel that God would approve even though the Diocese might not."

He was interrupted by the phone ringing in my purse. I pulled it out and stared at the dial. It was the doctor. John nodded toward it for me to answer.

"Hello. Yes this is Margaret Resnick. Thank you for calling me back doctor. You did, and she's what? Running a high fever? Worse? You think pneumonia? Really? I wondered about that this morning, although hoped not. Yes, I can see you this afternoon, certainly, what time?"

I glanced at the clock above John's sideboard. "It's almost two thirty now and I could be at the hospital in half an hour. Around three thirty? Yes I can be there then. Thank you and I will speak with you then." I clicked off the phone and stared at John.

"You probably gathered from the conversation that Norma is worse. Much worse. Her temperature has soared to a hundred and four and her lungs are congested. She's got blood in the fluid and Dr. Suffolk has put her on oxygen and a stronger antibiotic. Poor woman. Now I'm really worried."

"Can I do anything to help? Shall I come with you to the hospital?"

I thought of Norma's reaction to my friendship with John and realized that the two of us walking in together wouldn't make for a good reception. "Thanks John, but Norma's convinced that you and I are more than friends and that I've made off with you."

"But ...?"

"Yes, obviously not true but the woman's delusional and has probably been so for years, but under the circumstances why exacerbate the problem by showing up together."

I rose from the table and set the plate down in the sink. "I should probably get my sweater if it's dry although your shirt is very comfy and quite warm."

"It's the one I use for camping although I really don't like to camp. But occasionally when I know it's not going to rain I go with the boy scouts." He laughed. "I was an awful boy scout when I was a boy, but why don't you wear it, it'll be warmer and you can return it later. Do you want some biscuits to take with you?"

I still had to translate the English word biscuit into cookie, the American one for it. "Actually, that would be a lovely idea," I said. "If I have to hang around there, something to occupy my attention would be a good thing if she's sleeping. I can read and have a hot chocolate or something from the machine until I see Dr. Suffolk."

"Perhaps we can get together soon and after I've spoken with Cheryl. I'll call you when ..."

We were both startled as the front door opened and a gust of cold, wet rain blew in and the hallway was filled with the sound of a shaking dog and a booming "Hello" from Alex.

My heart beat faster and I walked toward him as he came into the kitchen and said, "Did I miss lunch? Egg salad I see and better yet, a Maggie! I'm wet but let me take off this jacket and can hug you. Kay, you're making John's kitchen all wet." He beamed at us both and set his cane down against the table and took me in his arms. "So good, we're all together. It's okay John, I can just eat the egg salad separate with the bread. No need to go to the trouble of making a sandwich. So how's Norma? I got your message."

"I just heard from the doctor and am about to leave for the hospital again. Norma has pneumonia and doing worse."

"Sorry to hear that. Do you want me to come with you? I can leave Kay here with John or in the car although she doesn't care for that much."

"John just asked the same thing and thank you but I think this is one visit where I must go alone. I doubt she will be in any shape for visitors and besides which she prefers to look well and in control around other people."

"Will you call me from the hospital and we ..."

John coughed slightly. "Excuse me, I'll leave you both alone for a few minutes. Have to do something in my office." He trotted out and we heard him close the door.

"He did that intentionally," Alex said. "Probably knew I wanted to kiss you. You look so cute in his shirt, although you looked much cuter in mine and I prefer my bed to his kitchen."

I reached up and put my arms around his neck, bringing his face down to mine, lightly brushing my lips to his mouth. His beard was wet and smelled of rain and I wondered if my breath smelled of egg salad. Didn't matter, wrapped in his arms and feeling him close was unexpected.

"So d'you think you want to come for dinner and perhaps stay over again and I'll cook a decent breakfast for you tomorrow morning instead of oversleeping?"

"Sounds wonderful. Can I borrow your shirt again?"

"Can I take it off if you do?"

"Thought you'd never ask."

"Then it's settled. Big question is what to feed you. How do you feel about pizza? I could get one from Gino's and make a salad."

"Perfect!"

"I'll get a side of chicken and may even eat some of Kay's. Perhaps Janet will top it off with extra cheese. Anything you don't like on pizza?"

"Artichokes and black olives."

"You don't like olives? But didn't you have those at Ginos?"

"Green ones in salad yes and I like those but not black ones on pizza for some reason."

"Pleased I asked although I don't care for artichokes on pizza but like them separate. Hah! I learn something more about you every day." He kissed me more firmly, our tongues exploring together, warm and inviting. He pulled back slightly, rubbing his nose against mine. "Didn't think that anything could improve on John's egg salad," he laughed. "I was wrong and thank heaven I'm wearing something that makes me appear respectable in a vicarage even though my thoughts may not be, but I'll reserve my love making until tonight. John just opened his study door."

"I have to go, anyway. Thanks for lunch, John, and for handling things with Cheryl. Alex, I'll see you this evening but I'll call as I know how things go at the hospital."

"Drive carefully," John said. "It's still raining heavily out there."

Alex was holding my still wet raincoat. "Maybe John can lend you one of his macs instead of this lightweight thing of yours. He must have something here that will fit."

"Of course," John said, "there is and are and that's what they're there for and will certainly keep you dryer than when you first came in. What color? You chose!"

I laughed. "How about the big blue one there and I'll return it next I see you."

"It's really a riding rain coat," he apologized, "but dear me even though you don't have a horse it's very adequate in this rain and no rush, no rush at all and why don't you take one of these extra large brollies. I've got extras of those too."

I laughed as I pulled on the oversized raincoat and slipped the hood over my head. Clutching my purse I held the umbrella above me as I ran for the car and opened the door. I enjoyed being pampered and cared for and I paused to reflect that in California, the only male to pay me any attention was Mewfus. It was just as well it didn't rain there very often.

CHAPTER NINETEEN

The lunchtime trolleys and trays were being removed from the rooms as I arrived and I paused at Norma's door, wondering what I would find when I opened it. I visualized Norma sitting and staring at the door as she usually did with perhaps her own tray pushed aside and the food barely touched. I was pleased that I had not only been well egg sandwiched but that I had some of the biscuits—as John called them—in my bag and they were home baked. I was feeling prepared to meet whatever Norma had to offer and hoped her temperature had gone down and was responding to the medications.

I pushed against the door and stopped as it opened, astounded to see my mother with tubes in her nostrils and attached to an oxygen tank. Over the gurgled hum it emitted, I was aware of her labored breathing, so much more pronounced than when I saw her before lunch. Her skin had a slightly bluish tinge and the intravenous needle that had irritated her by catching in the coverlet was now attached to an IV. She appeared more listless and her eyes were dull and seemed not to register my presence. How had she declined so fast?

"My god, Norma, what happened to you?"

"Did you tell Margaret I'm dying?"

Confused, I stepped closer to the bed thinking that Norma's eyesight was even more reduced because of the circumstances.

"I'm Magg … Margaret. It's me, Norma, I'm here." I was unsure what to do or say and lightly patted her shoulder although expecting my hand to be brushed away. "And you're not going to die although you might feel very sick."

"I'm cold, Cheryl dear. Can't you see me shivering?"

I wondered why she had called me that but decided to ignore it. I felt the heat being generated from her skin beneath the hospital gown and knew she was running a high fever.

"You have chills from the fever. I'm sure Dr. Suffolk must've prescribed something for that. Norma, I so wish I could do something to help you feel better."

"You can get that worthless daughter of mine. She should be here. I'm her mother and she owes me that at least. Show me some consideration for all ..." She broke off in a fit of coughing that shook her body. "Oh it hurts," she gasped and brought her hands to her chest, leaning forward as she did so before collapsing again onto the pillow. "Call Dr. Sutton. I need the doctor."

I stared at her. She doesn't recognize me, I thought. What's happening to her mind? I remembered the conversation that morning, how Norma had seemed different then and I'd attributed her revelations as simply those of a woman who had held onto her secrets too long and wanted to express what she had kept hidden. This was different. Now she was delusional.

"I'll go find him," I said, "if I can." Then under my breath said, "I hope I can."

I hurried to the reception desk where the nurse who had occupied the chair sat as she had that morning. "I'm sorry, I don't know your name."

"Gloria."

"Yes Gloria, Mrs. Resnick in room twenty-three seems much worse than she did only a few hours ago. Much worse. She doesn't recognize me."

"Pneumonia can affect the mind, especially in the elderly," she said, "and they often become easily confused."

"I spoke to Dr. Suffolk earlier and he said he wanted to discuss her situation with me. Is he here?"

"He's doing his rounds somewhere, I can page him for you but it might take a while before he can get here. Depending, you know, on what he's doing." She looked over the top of her glasses as though to convey that patience was expected and for me not to anticipate a quick response.

"Of course. I understand. He's busy but yes, please do that and I'll go back and wait in my mother's room."

I wasn't sure if I wanted to go back again but thought that perhaps my presence, known or not, might provide some measure of comfort to the woman. I reflected that even now, I had no reservoir of warmth or love to give. It was an intellectual evaluation of providing support for someone who was in pain. I flinched and thought that Norma had even deprived me of experiencing my own heartache as a daughter for her mother. But regardless of that, I thought, as I pushed open the door, stop thinking of yourself, lady, that's too much like Norma.

I heard the intercom calling for Dr. Suffolk and wondered how long he would be and what I could do to help alleviate some of Norma's discomfort, then wondered if I would even be recognized by her. That could be a good thing or bad.

Norma's white sheet and cover was speckled with brown flecks that she had obviously coughed up while I was gone. Her eyes were closed and her breath rasped as she drew in air. I moved the visitor's chair and set it down softly by the bed then sat waiting expectantly for some signal of recognition or awareness.

I had removed John's oversize mac and hung it on the hook behind the bathroom door and pleased I was still wearing his shirt. It was warmer than mine. Perhaps, I thought, that was the reason Norma didn't recognize me. I'd removed the raincoat before stepping through the door, then remembering how wet it had been, hoped it didn't drip and form a pool—not that it would have been a problem for Norma. She had been confined to the bed since I'd arrived. I wondered how her ankle was healing and what it would take for her to start walking again when she was released. I bit my lip and paused, now with the pneumonia in addition to the concussion, I wondered how long that release would be. Not anytime soon I guessed.

With almost three more weeks before having to return back to school, that prospect seemed to loom before me as a problem I hadn't really considered. I'd assumed I would go back and pick up where I'd left off then wondered where that was exactly. I would have some new and returning students and hoped that the summer instructor who was teaching while I was absent had maintained the vegetable garden and kept it watered. At least the perennials and trees were on an automatic system and even though that wasn't always reliable and required frequent adjustments worked well enough to keep things alive.

School and the four acres I had so lovingly tended seemed very far away. Even my condo seemed like a dream and only Mewfus was still real. Dear cat that he was, he'd been a little feral stray I had discovered crying pitifully among the roots of a glorious large shrub of red Pineapple sage.

At first I thought the little mewing was further away and glanced up from my pruning, before I continued to deadhead the roses. Then I heard it again and looked around unsure where it was. I walked slowly back and forth, peering into the shrubbery that grew along the path opposite the roses. A wall of rock boulders leaned against the slope that kept the soil from spilling down onto the path during the winter and it was behind it that the salvia sprang, alive with bees and the occasional hummingbird.

Standing very still I listened, then called, "Here, kitty," and pursed my lips, making little sucking sounds. Wonder how animals came to respond to such noises? I'd thought. I had seen feral cats around the garden and had set kibble by the classroom door after I left for the day. I never saw them eat although it was gone when I returned. Occasionally, when I walked quietly up to the building before the students arrived with their noise and chatter, I would see a black and white cat and another little calico before they sped away when they saw me.

I knew that this was something much smaller from the sound it made. I leaned against the wall parting the shrubbery and a pair of eyes peered back from the base of the plant. The kitten opened a tiny pink mouth, revealing little white teeth as it hissed.

"Yeah, right," I said, "you're so fierce. I'm quaking in my boots." I reached carefully into the brush, pleased I was still wearing my work gloves, moving cautiously so not to scare it and wondered if the mother had abandoned it or if it had wandered away alone. I looked around hoping that she would come and rescue the baby after I had gone.

I let the branches fall back into place but decided to work close enough to the shrub to observe. I knelt and began weeding, pulling out the Oxalis that was competing with a bed of Aquilegia. If the kitten was lost in anyway, I didn't want it straying off and perhaps dying somewhere or worse be caught by a coyote that strayed onto the property from the surrounding hills. I decided that if the mother failed to show I would try and rescue it but also knew that a feral kitten could administer just as painful a bite or scratch as something larger.

Except for the sound of distant traffic beyond the school and garden, there was silence until it cried again. I lay down my trowel and said, "Okay. Ready or not, here I come."

I parted the leaves again and the kitten watched me from its nest of brown and green branches and didn't move. "Here, kitty little mewing face that you are," I said, drawing my teeth to my lower lip and making little tsk tsk sounds. I laughed. "Here," I whispered, "mew, mew," taking my voice softly to an octave higher.

It stared without moving and I stood motionless, "Mew," I said again, more hopefully thinking that something in my voice would communicate. I pulled off the glove and reached down, caressing its head with my index finger before extending my reach down its back. It mewed again and I smiled and said, "Hey we're bonding," as I pulled it out.

It barely filled my palm and holding it more firmly I could feel little bones underneath the long hair. I stared at the tiny ball of gray and white fluff and couldn't believe its mother would leave it intentionally. Perhaps she had fallen prey to a coyote. I then made a decision. "Guess you're coming home with me," I said. "And I suppose that means stopping and getting you some food and a litter box."

I carried it to the classroom and upended a carton of papers and decided to put the kitten in that with a towel for the drive home. "What am I going to call you?" I said. "And bigger question yet, what on earth am I going to do with a cat?"

Later, when it scraped the litter box and proceeded to squat I was delighted it hadn't gone elsewhere. "Who would've believed I'd enjoy seeing a cat shit," I said, then watched as it proceeded to investigate the rest of my condo. At first slowly, sniffing and cautious, then with more confidence, its tail moved and held high above its back I decided to keep it overnight with food and water in the bathroom and close the door.

As I climbed into bed, the mewling started. I put down my book and listened, then tried to read again. I admitted defeat and opened the door and the kitten sped out and tried to climb my pajama leg. "Ow," I cried as it dug in its claws. I lifted it off, tugging at the fabric and carried it onto the bed hoping it wouldn't pee on my comforter. I lay against the pillow and watched it carefully and wondered if I had been in my right mind to bring it home. I decided if it didn't work out I would take it to the animal shelter the following day. Putting it back in the bush wasn't an option.

I scrunched further down into the pillow and watched it paw my duvet, purring before curling into a tiny ball. "Well, maybe we can work things out," I said at last. "You'll be easier to get used to than a husband. And I can still keep my books on the bed." I turned off the lamp and in the dark gently stroked the kitten's head and added, "Even if you are a little mew face."

Oblivious to Norma and thinking about Mewfus I was startled when the door opened and Dr. Suffolk strode into the room.

"Bit late. Sorry. But that's okay, hmm? Other things to do. Your mother not doing as well as I thought." He paced to the bed and lifted Norma's limp hand and felt her pulse, looking at his watch. She remained with her eyes closed.

Dr. Suffolk continued, "Unexpected but not unusual for an elderly patient. Developed pneumonia. Unfortunate thing, that. Prescribed a stronger antibiotic and placed her on oxygen." He peered down at Norma as though hoping she would recover under his gaze.

"Just how bad is she, doctor?"

"Too early to tell. Not good though. Will know more by tomorrow. Receiving best care. Best care possible." He stared down at me over his glasses, hesitant and clutching Norma's clipboard against his white jacket.

"Should I stay? Go? Will she die?" I felt at a loss and overwhelmed with the possibilities. Suddenly Norma's health and survival were in the balance and any ambivalence I felt toward her was expelled as her fight became mine.

"Not much you can do. Probably unaware you're here. Recommend a good night's sleep." Dr. Suffolk set the clipboard down and held Norma's wrist again, checking her pulse against his watch. "Do what you feel best. Stay. Go. Sorry. Call if necessary and I'll try to provide updates."

I decided his bedside manner was in need of serious attention but respected and appreciated his honesty. "Will she remain asleep throughout the night?"

He stopped by the open door while he held it open. "Probably. May be delusional if she wakes. Not know who you are."

"She already did that. When will you know she's out of danger?"

"Depends on response to medication. Other patients. Bit of a hurry. Must leave. Sorry."

"Of course," I said, "and thank you doctor for your honest advice. Please don't let me keep you."

"Yes, yes. Very well," he said in his abbreviated communication, "call me tomorrow when I know more." He opened the door and was gone.

I felt weak. I wanted to stay, not necessarily for Norma who probably wouldn't appreciate it anyway, but to know that I had done all I could to provide support. But then I also wanted to leave to gain some separation and objectivity from the situation. If I left and Norma woke or even died would that change anything had I stayed? I thought not. The negative dynamics between us were too firmly entrenched and unlikely to resolve within hours. "Damn it, Norma," I said, "you certainly managed to create a bitch of a situation and whether I decide to leave or stay, it'll be the wrong thing to do." I began to weep, silently. My mother generated conflict and confusion even in what might be her final hours. I walked to the bedside table and withdrew a tissue, wiping my eyes.

I stared down at the woman who lay against the pillow, her breath uneven, eyes closed. "Norma, can you hear me?" I asked softly. There was no response. "Norma, do you want me to stay?" I waited wondering whether to continue to sit by her side even if she answered or not.

"No, you definitely don't make it easy and never have," I said. I didn't want to leave her alone nor did I want to stay. I felt sorrier for myself than for the prostrate woman before me although the thought of walking out of the door and leaving for the arms of Alex made me feel guilty of insensitivity. So what if I do leave? I thought. What difference will it make to anyone and especially now? Yet still I remained glued to my uncomfortable chair by Norma's bed.

I continued to sit as the minutes passed into hours. I was numb and immobile, unable to make a decision one way or another while my mother seemed unconscious to everything that was going on around her, periodically mumbling and coughing and occasionally crying while I remained by her bed.

I was aware of nurses who came into the room and who adjusted the monitors. One gentle female asked me to excuse her while she drew the curtains to change and clean Norma. Nodding I waited, listening to the sounds of a my mother's being moved and sounds of husky but feeble protests, letting both the nurse and me know she was still, if not kicking, alive despite appearing listless.

The nurse reopened the drapes, still wearing her surgical gloves and moving her trolley of supplies from the room. There was an unpleasant pungent odor that wafted past me as I sat there and I had the thought that no way could I devote my life so generously as she and others did. I hoped that I would be more gracious and giving if the need arose for someone I loved.

I gazed at Norma, who suddenly opened her eyes, as though receiving a silent communication from me. We stared at each other for what seemed an age, then just as suddenly, she closed her eyes again and said, "So you're still here. I'm not going anywhere. Not yet. Go home. Go home."

This time she had recognized me. That was a good thing. I stood, my legs stiff from sitting and realized I was cold inside John's shirt. I wondered why I had remained so long, whether I had expected any change in attitude, some softening and expression of affection while she was affected by her illness.

There was no warmth in my mother's tone of voice or facial appearance. I experienced a wave of sadness and loss. "You know, Norma," I said quietly, "I'm very sorry that you can be so distanced from love and those closest to you. Yes, I will go, I'm tired but I'll be back again tomorrow. There's still time for you to have a change of heart. This is all so uncomfortable for you, all this," I indicated the bed and machines that surrounded her although my mother's eyes opened briefly before closing again, "but perhaps you can take this time to reflect on what it is you've missed."

I patted her hand and thought of leaning down to kiss her cheek but was unable to follow through. I sighed. "Okay, I'm going. I hope you feel better by tomorrow." I also hoped that on some level she could understand and that the medications would work their magic and do something while I was gone, even if it meant having Norma be spiteful. At least that would show more life than what was happening now.

I went into the bathroom and retrieved my raincoat. It was still wet and made John's shirt damp and uncomfortable when I placed it over my arm. I hesitated by the door, opened it and went out closing it again behind me. There was a hush of inactivity in the hallway and I realized that it was probably late. I stopped by the desk and picked up my umbrella, John's umbrella, and said goodnight to the nurse. "Will you or somebody call me if anything changes?" I asked, "You have my number I believe?"

"Yes, we do and now go home and get some rest. Your mother is stabilized for now otherwise she would be in ICU. I'm sorry she's so sick."

"Me too, me too." I wondered which of the mixed emotions I felt about Norma might be the correct one for feeling as sad as I did.

CHAPTER TWENTY

The rain had become a light drizzle as I walked across the car park and the hospital lights glanced off the puddles with multi colored oil streaks swirling across the asphalt. My sneakers were still soaked from when I had walked in the downpour earlier and it wasn't until I trod carefully across the rain soaked ground I realized that I'd sat in the hospital unaware my feet were so wet and cold.

My immediate thoughts were to go home and take a hot shower and change. I was emotionally exhausted and wondered why my reaction had been so strong. Was I hoping that Norma, in her reduced and vulnerable state would suddenly show a softer, more loving side of her personality to, if not embrace me physically, then to indicate some sign of affection no matter how small? If that was so then I didn't know how it would reveal itself—I had nothing to compare it to. So why had I sat there so long? It was a puzzle and I was tired, cold and irritated.

As I unlocked and opened the car door I flung the umbrella in the back and eased out of John's mac, tossing it onto the floor then moved my purse over to the passenger seat and wondered if Alex had called. I switched on the ignition and turned the heater to high. Cold air blasted me and I quickly turned it off again. "Bloody engine needs to warm first," I muttered, kicking the accelerator as I pounded the wheel in frustration, hitting the horn so that the sound echoed loudly across the wet parked cars, oblivious to my irritation.

I was pissed and knew why. It was clear. I'd spent hours—uncomfortable hours—waiting for Norma to respond to me and she failed to do so. I could've spent that time with Alex who would have provided the affection and warmth I so desperately wanted and I had ignored him for Norma. And for what?

I wondered if the engine had warmed up so I gingerly turned the heater on again and could feel the heat creeping into the icy air that drifted from the grill. So did I go back to the house or arrive like a drowned rat at Alex's place? I looked at my watch. It was almost eight thirty and not too late for supper and certainly not too late for brandy. I picked up my cell phone and wondered if he had called and saw two messages from him and one from John.

John's was brief. He wanted to know how Norma was and when he thought he could go visit. "Any time of the night or day," he said. Then added, "I still have lots of brollies and macs left."

"Sweet guy," I murmured as I clicked onto the first message from Alex.

"Hey Maggie, Maggie," he said. "Don't worry about dinner or calling but when you get chance let me know." Then as though he had listened and heard John's message added, "Doesn't matter what time of the night or day, I'll be here."

The second message was short. "I already said call when you get chance, but just want you to know that I really meant that it didn't matter what time."

The heat was beginning to blow out of the vent and I leaned toward the hot air. What would I have at the house? Silence, nothing to eat, a hot shower perhaps and climbing into bed with the lingering smells of Norma that still infiltrated my room and the rest of the place helped me decide. A no brainer, I thought, but I was reluctant and didn't want to arrive wet and bedraggled to someone I was just getting to know. I'd done that last night and was tired of myself. "Oh well," I said to the windows that were beginning to fog, "just do it anyway, Lady. Just do it!"

I pressed the number for Alex and he picked up immediately. "Hey, Maggie," he said, "if this doesn't test the mettle of our relationship, not much will. I suppose you're cold and hungry, huh?"

"You guessed."

"Kay told me. Where are you?"

"Hospital parking lot."

"Is your mother okay? I'm sorry I should've asked that first but it was you I was thinking of."

"Alex, you make me feel so … so ..."

"Good? Wanted? Then hope so. When can you get here? Or do you plan to stay there?"

"No, she's stabilized and sleeping and frankly I'm exhausted and don't want to shove myself on you in this state."

"No shoving. Let's say easing because you're having a hard time and I can help make that easier. Are you hungry?"

I realized I was starving. "Yes."

"I got the pizza and keeping it warm in a low oven. Will that work for you?"

"Do you still have any brandy?"

"Always! I actually picked up another bottle just in case we needed it."

I visualized the liquid slipping down my throat, warming my inside as I waited for Alex to get the pizza ready.

"Mind if I take a shower before we eat?"

"If I wasn't still on my best behavior and it was large enough I'd suggest I take one with you but we both wouldn't fit."

I pictured my own bathroom and shower in California and imagined Alex in there with me. Big as he was we would both fit. I wondered if we would ever be together at my place then thought of making him dinner in my kitchen with Mewfus sliding around our legs instead of Kay.

Alex misinterpreted my silence, "Maybe I shouldn't have said that, but," he added, "it still seems like a good idea."

"It would be," I said, "but I was just thinking of a larger space where it would work."

He laughed, and I could imagine Kay starting to thump her tail as he did so.

"Let me call John first, and I'll be right there," I said as I drew a heart inside the fogged window and wrote 'M luvs A' in the middle. "See you soon."

It took John a little longer to answer and I wondered if he was at home, relieved when he picked up. "John?"

"Yes Maggie, I was just getting ready to leave for the hospital."

"I think Norma's going to be sleeping through the night. She's worse but the doctor says she's stable."

"Yes, yes I was thinking I'd stop by, but there are actually two other parishioners of mine who are there."

"I'm sorry, I didn't mean to presume ..."

"Not at all, not at all. Your poor mother has been on my mind and I will pop in to see how she's doing. Dear me, one of the patients is an old man on life support while the other is a young woman who has just given birth. The link between life and death never ceases to amaze me." He tut tutted slightly under his breath then continued. "I hope you're okay. Are you?"

"Thanks John, yes. I'm going over to Alex's for supper and a glass of brandy. Thanks for lunch, by the way, it seems like so long ago." Norma, I thought, could make all good things seem like a dream.

"If you have time tomorrow, let's touch base. I'd like you to chat with Cheryl and I know she's anxious to speak with you."

I had forgotten about Cheryl and the earrings suddenly seemed unimportant although not so minor that I didn't want them back. "I'll call in the morning, John, and we can schedule something then." I added, "If Norma happens to wake and speaks to you, could you tell her I was there and will be back again tomorrow?"

"Yes, yes. Of course. Now I have to go. I think the rain has almost stopped. Has it?"

I unwound the window and looked out, shivering slightly as the cool air changed the warmth from the heater. "Yes, a drizzle but as you know, it can change in an instant, so stay warm and dry." I liked that I could project caring and concern back for a change and have him know it was meant and genuine.

He detected that in my voice and his quavered slightly, "Maggie, what would I do without you? I really hope you can find it in your heart to stay here."

I paused. "Whether I stay or leave John, I think my heart will always be here."

Rolling up the window as I said goodbye to him, I tossed the phone into my bag before easing the car into drive, unlocking the hand brake as I did so. I wished I had a change of clothing but that would mean stopping by the house which would not only take longer but the thought of going back to my mother's place caused me to feel the emotional slump and sense of caution I had learned to expect. Even clean clothes, I thought, now seemed grubby just from the association and the smell that percolated into everything. I just wanted to throw everything into the washer and experience what it felt like to be really clean.

I turned the windshield wipers down and the blades swiped lazily against the light drizzle falling against the window. The rain clouds made the early evening darker that it might have been otherwise and wet and shiny shadows of passing cars splashed against the puddles that had pooled in the road.

Think I've had about enough of this weather to last me for a while, I thought, and missed the warmth of the dry California air. But what is worth more—being wet in this damp English countryside and being happy with Alex or staying dry and warm at home and except for Mewfus, lonely? A no brainer, I murmured under my breath then wondered if it was because I had been lonely that made Alex so attractive. Was he just an excuse to escape that? Uh-uh, I decided, it's him. It's who he is and I could love him anywhere.

I leaned forward to peer ahead. There was a turn I had to make and in the mist I wasn't quite sure. Unlike Norma's house, Alex lived in an area that was more isolated and the small cottages were further apart. In the daylight the landmarks were unmistakable but in the light fog with wet windows dripping on the outside and the inside still a little steamed from my breath, I didn't want to miss the turn. Ah, I thought, there's that long old farm gate to the field just about half a mile from his street—if you could call it a street. It was hardly a lane.

As I slowed down my cell buzzed. Maybe it's Alex again, I thought. Well I'm almost there and if I pick it up I might miss the turn. But why would he be calling again? Maybe it's John and he has news of Norma. Well, that can wait too, I'm not about to go back to the hospital right now. Well, *would* I though? I wondered. What if she's taken a turn for the worse? Would I go and sit with her for more hours?

I remembered my earlier conversation with Norma and the unmistakable rejection of who I was and what I meant in her life. No, I decided. No. I owe her nothing but why do I still feel so bad that I'm not there despite who she is, even if her heart is cold as ice and doubtful it will ever thaw. I wondered what would have to happen for that to occur. But nope, she doesn't love me and doesn't care what happens. She's stuck in the past, which poisons her present and everyone and everything in it. How do people manage to sink into such a negative state, I wondered.

Then I remembered how she had mistaken me for Cheryl and called her 'dear.' Obviously she was fond of the woman and certainly had been in love with Bob. Although she might reject me she was capable of affection and warmth. That it was so heavily buried caused me to pity her. How lonely she must be.

I shook my head to dispel more thoughts of her. The cell stopped vibrating and went silent as I found the turn I was looking for and pulled up to Alex's house. He'd left the porch light on and it left sparkling lights reflected on the door and the rose that scrambled in an untidy climb of buds and blooms against the wall. It had a wonderful spicy fragrance, and I realized I'd been only slightly aware of how lovely it was because my attention had usually been focused on him and Kay. I smiled and parked, happy to have arrived then turned off the engine, reaching for my purse and cell and saw there was a message but decided to listen when I was inside as the front door open and Alex appeared with Kay who bounded past him toward the car.

"Hey, you made it! Kay, let her get out of the car." He grabbed hold of her collar and pulled her away from the door as I stepped out. He embraced me with his free arm moving me toward the house. "You have no idea how pleased I am that you decided to come here," he said. "I was thinking that with everything going on you might want to trot off somewhere and be alone with your thoughts. It's probably what I would do."

He pushed open the front door and the warmth of the inside reached out and I sighed. "I'm pleased too because yes, I do have the tendency to creep off somewhere and it's not really a good thing." I remembered the message. "Did you just call me?" I asked, "because I didn't answer since I was just down the road and almost here. I wondered if you thought I was lost."

He looked momentarily puzzled. "No. You would've had to be later than I figured it takes to get here. Maybe it was John. Why don't you listen while I get you a brandy." He gave me a quick hug and kissed the top of my head before moving toward the kitchen. I didn't recognize the number then keyed in my code to listen, surprised when I heard Shelly's voice.

"Maggie. Maggie. Can you call me as soon as you get this? Oh, I hate to leave a message but it's Mewfus. He's had an accident and it's all my fault. Shit, I'm so sorry, Sweetie, but I need you to call me right back. He's in bad shape but the vet said he will make it. Call me."

I gasped and cried out, bringing Alex from the kitchen with two brandy snifters. Kay whined as she sat and pushed against my legs. "Are you okay?" Alex asked. "Is it bad news about your mother?"

"No. It's Mewfus. Shelly said he's had an accident and hurt. I have to call back right now."

I scrolled down the menu and pressed the number for Shelly. There were some clicks before the familiar American call tone was heard and I waited, holding my breath and dreading the worst.

"Hello?" she said.

"What happened? What happened Shelly? Is he alive?" The thought of losing Mewfus and so far away from being able to do something was too much after so many other blows to my psyche. I felt myself being led to the couch by Alex as he sat me down.

"Yes. Alive," Shelly said. "But let me explain. He got out and entirely my fault. I hadn't secured the front door properly and when I went to find him realized he had bolted. Of course I went after him but he ran into the road and …"

"… and was hit by a car?"

"Yes but it was backing up to park and the rear wheels caught him as he ran. The driver didn't even know he had hit him and Mewfus was under the car and I thought for sure he was dead. But he wasn't and I crawled under and got him then wrapped him in a towel and raced off to the emergency vet."

Shelly's voice was almost indistinct from crying and I was listening in disbelief. How could this be happening to me? I was lost for words but he was alive. Alex raised his eyebrows and glanced at the brandy he was holding out to me. I nodded and took the glass.

"Hello? Are you still there?" I heard her say as though it was coming from another planet.

"Yes. Here. So what happened? When was this?"

"Early today about two hours ago. The vet gave him a sedative pain killer and surprisingly there were no visible wounds other than lots of oil in his fur, but they took x-rays and an ultrasound and he broke his back leg."

"Oh my god! Are there internal injuries?"

"No. That's the good news. Bad news is that he must be kept under observation for about two more days then sent home and will require focused care for the next four to six weeks. Maggie, I'm so sorry and feel so bad that this has happened." We were both silent and Shelly added, "I can't take him home with me since you know that will cause him more stress to be in an unfamiliar environment … and there's Buddy …"

I knew that Shelly's dog was not a cat lover. "No. I have to come home."

"What about Norma? I forgot to ask about her."

I shrugged although she was obviously unaware of the dismissive rise to my shoulders. "At this point I don't see it as a problem and frankly Mewfus means more to me than she does." I wondered if

Norma felt the same way, caring more for Cheryl than me and what her reaction would be if I were sick. I took a sip of the brandy and felt it coursing down my throat, feeling its sweet burn down my esophagus to my stomach. I needed that jolt to kick start my thinking and I still felt chilled.

"Can the vet care for him longer than a couple of days until I get there?"

"I would imagine so."

"Listen. This is long distance on my cell. I really need to email you so we can discuss it in detail when I know more. I can probably get a flight back within the next two days —and it's still gonna take a day of travel. Before you go though, Shelly, give me the vet's number and I'll call from a landline." I glanced up at Alex who nodded.

How quickly life could change one's plans, I thought, and yet another thing I hadn't bargained on. I had known Shelly would stop by daily to feed and clean up after Mewfus and I had agonized over whether to put him in a boarding facility for the duration I was gone but decided that although lonely, he would be happier in his own place. Now this.

"Don't worry," I said with less confidence than I felt, "he's alive and that's what important. Thank god, he's alive." I wiped my eyes. "Guess I'll see you sooner than I thought. Thanks for everything and I'll be in touch when I have my schedule. Will you be able to pick me up from the airport?"

"No problem. Just tell me when."

"You're a love. Better hang up now. Bye." The line went dead and I felt myself slump down into cushions of the couch. My legs felt as though they wouldn't support me.

"It's my cat. Mewfus. He was hit by a car."

Alex sat down next to me and put his arm around my shoulder. "I figured something like that had happened. You're going back of course."

"Yes. I must get flight times and see what's available. Poor old guy. A broken leg." I shook my head. "But he's obviously in good hands and there's nothing I can do right now." I thought of my cat isolated and alone in a strange place in a sterile cage with no reassuring familiar hand or voice. "Maybe Shelly can take one of my sweaters to put in his cage."

Alex stroked Kay's ears as she sat pressed next to him. "But you still have to eat and the pizza's warm and ready. Are you hungry?"

I nodded. I had forgotten just how hungry I was and needed the food in addition to the brandy that was making me a bit light headed. "Pizza a good thing. Comfort food in all kinds of ways." I smiled and nodded again.

"You stay right there and I'll bring it in here." He glanced over to the wood stove then rose to open the metal door and throw in a log before going into the kitchen. I heard the oven door open and the clink of metal as he picked up some silverware and the rustle of paper as he pulled off some sheets from the paper towel. "It's a large and mostly mushroom and double cheese," he said, as he returned to the couch, "so even with me there's plenty for all of us. Even some crusts for Kay. She likes the cheese but not the mushrooms." He grinned. "When we're through if you want you can use my computer and get flight times." He paused before adding, "I hope you plan to come back here."

I hadn't thought that far ahead. When I had originally purchased my ticket I had left the return flight open. A return back to the UK again was a whole new concept. Certainly I didn't care about Norma although she was an issue and if she died then I would come back to make funeral arrangements. But there was my father to con-sider and Alex was a whole new complex of issues—perhaps with new beginnings. The thought scared me. I was used to the regularity of my life in the States with only me to worry about although always knew that it wasn't a perfect situation. But then I had never known what any solution to that would be. Life was presenting me with op-tions. Somehow Mewfus had escalated the decision-making.

I picked up a slice of the pizza from the box and set it on my plate after taking a bite. Hot and delicious it helped me feel more sol-id and less like I was about to float away. "Good! Thanks." I looked at Alex. "Maybe I should pack you and Kay and take you with me."

"Actually I was thinking along very similar lines. Not the suit-case or even Kay but going back with you for a brief visit. Haven't seen California in years and being there with you and seeing your place would be great! If you'll have me, that is."

I stared at him. "You'd really do that? What about Kay?"

"That would be the difficult part and of course my music but I could always lean on the goodwill of a church somewhere and offer to play for them. Kay ..." he paused and gave her a piece of the crust coated with melted cheese, "... she could stay with John for a bit. He's cared for her before when I had to ... had to go and attend my brother's funeral. Of course you don't have to decide now and it might be better to sleep on it. Or you." He chuckled and the deep hu-mor that helped make him so unique seemed to roll from his throat. Then he stopped as though a more sobering thought had occurred to him. "But what of Norma? What's happening with her?"

"Today was not a good one although earlier this morning be-fore she got worse, clarified that I was never wanted or loved. Her heart lies elsewhere and always has. She blames me for having it bro-ken."

"*You*? You broke her heart?"

"Nope. She was in love with my father's business partner and he left her because she was married and had a kid. Me. He wanted no ties. So she maintains that her life would've been different otherwise." I leaned back against the pillows. "It would've been nice to have had a reconciliation of some sort but she essentially dismissed me. It seems my visits distress her as much as they do me." I moved my plate to the coffee table and lay back again. "I'm not sure what will happen when she gets out of hospital and she may eventually have to go into a nursing home, too." I considered if that occurred then it wouldn't be Aidenscroft. "There's no one to help her here. She tends to alienate everyone who tries and I don't know if her financial situation would stretch to home care." I wondered if Cheryl would take on those duties.

"Maybe she could refinance the house or remortgage as they say here although either way that would affect you in the long run wouldn't it?"

"My father's still alive and I have him to think about." I paused as I thought of the call Norma had received earlier. "I believe she thought she could find some loophole to wrest control from him but apparently not and my father, gentle soul that he still is, was tough enough and certainly smart enough to see that it didn't happen."

"If anything happened to him and the place was yours, would you refinance it so she could remain there?"

I thought a few moments. "Probably not. I'd still have to make the house payments and if she was a different kind of mother I'd have her move out and live with me." I shook my head and raised my eyes to the ceiling. "God knows that's not a solution. No, I think that with all the government support for the elderly here she could go to a facility too although not Aidenscroft and heaven help the nursing staff wherever she went to."

I thought of Norma, infirm and in a nursing home and felt momentarily sad for her. Then I thought of Mewfus in a strange veterinary clinic somewhere in L.A. and experienced a quite different concern. I had to return and nurse him back to health. That cat had provided me with more love and company than ever Norma had given me over a lifetime. "Guess it seems unsympathetic to abandon one's mother for a cat, huh?"

"Not at all, and from one animal lover to another, I know exactly where you're coming from—and your mother is Norma which makes the decision much easier. Did you want to use the computer tonight or in the morning?"

"Perhaps in the morning, if that's okay, since I left mine at home. Mewfus will be in the vets for the next few days and I'll call tomorrow when I have a better idea of flight schedules. I'm in no shape to start staring at a screen right at this moment."

"How about staring at me from a pillow." He laughed. "Did you want to take a shower first?" His arm had been across the back of the couch behind me and he moved his hand to my shoulder and gently rubbed along the side of my neck into my hair. It gave me tingles down my spine and I shifted my weight toward him and nodded. "Okay then," he said, "I'll take Kay outside while you go do that. I don't have to show you your way around anymore. Is there anything else you need?"

I shook my head then realized that I'd been wearing the same clothes and John's shirt and would have to put them back on the next day. "Actually, yes. Can I throw these things in the wash? These jeans are mud spattered and could do with a clean."

"Of course but take your shower first otherwise the washer will compete for hot water and you'll find yourself taking a chilly cascade. And don't worry about leaving enough hot water for me, I took mine about an hour before you arrived. C'mon Kay, let's go," he said, "and Maggie, you can leave the pizza box where it is. I'll put all that stuff away while you're in there."

"I can still take these plates to the kitchen on my way." I smiled up at him as I rose and gathered the dishes, realizing how comfortable I felt, as though he had been a part of my life forever.

I undressed and threw my clothes in a heap on the bed as I wondered what I would put on afterwards since my things were to be washed and I didn't see the t-shirt I'd worn last night. I decided I'd wrap his robe around me then hop into bed between the covers. But lying there naked didn't feel right either. I decided there had to be a transition between being clothed with him and undressed. Instant naked woman I'm not but then neither am I overly modest.

I heard Alex come into the bathroom and saw his shape behind the plastic curtain. "It's okay, I'm not going to get in there with you but can I take your things and throw them in the washer when you're through?"

"That would be great."

"And I've put my big sweatshirt on the hook behind the door here." I heard him chuckle, "No panties though you'll have to do without because I'm tossing those in too although from the looks of them I wonder that they can be called that. More like ribbon with lace attached—not that I'm complaining. Just never thought I'd see something like that in my bedroom."

I laughed. I didn't think anyone but I would get to see my bikini panties either. The guy thinks of everything, I decided as I turned off the shower and stepped out to dry myself. I was feeling more alert but still tired and worried about Mewfus and wished I could be instantly transported six thousand miles away to reassure him. It never occurred to me to think the same way about Norma less than six miles away and in what could be a more life-threatening situation.

I pulled on the sweatshirt and somewhere off the kitchen I heard the washer start pumping water. As I walked barefoot toward the sound, Alex came from behind a door I had seen earlier and had wondered what was behind it. Obviously there was a little laundry room because he said, "I threw in a few things of my own. Hope you don't mind. You don't do you?"

"No, I think you're wonderful," I said shaking my head. "How did you ever get to be so thoughtful?"

"Someday I'll have to tell you about *my* parents. Sweet people who made sharing and doing things for others seem like a given and they're sorely missed. I loved them both."

"You were fortunate to have had them and I'm sorry they're gone." I rubbed my hand down the front of his shirt as he came up to me. He took it and raised my arm placing it around his neck before holding me next to him. He moved his face down my neck into my shoulder and gently nibbled my skin. I felt a shiver run through me and trembled as he slid his hand under the shirt against my thigh, before slowly moving it between my legs.

"If we stand here like this," I whispered, "you're going to have to hold me up because I feel like I'm going to crumple any second."

Without a word, he leaned me into his arm and placed his other beneath my knees and lifted me as though I weighed nothing at all. Holding me next to him, he eased me through the kitchen and into the bedroom before placing me on the bed while pulling back the covers.

I watched him unzip his jeans and pull them down before sitting next to me. Kicking them off and leaving them on the floor he unbuttoned his shirt and slid out his arms, before pulling off his t-shirt underneath. A long jagged scar ran down his shoulder and across his chest showing white, separating the dark hair that grew there.

I gently drew my finger down the line, "This too?" I said, and glanced along his leg where the scar tissue had healed in deep pits, digging into the bone. "You were so lucky to ..."

"... to have you here with me? Yep!" He lifted the covers and shifted his weight alongside me, taking me in his arms and kissing my brow, then cheek and gently nibbling my lips. "Now though, it's your turn," and he lifted his sweatshirt above my breasts and I was buried in the folds as I raised my arms and he pulled it off over my head.

"You're lovely," he said, gazing at my brown body and legs. "Guess you have a small tan line though," he said running his finger along the top of my pubic bone, "but none here." He lightly touched below that and then moved his hand up and over my belly to my breasts before he circled each nipple and taking one gently in his mouth where it pulled erect against his tongue.

The tremor that ran down my body must've been obvious to him and if I had wondered whether I would be in any state of mind to make love after leaving Norma those thoughts were quickly dispelled as I held his head, digging my fingers in his hair as he proceeded down, lingering a moment as I eased apart my thighs and shuddered as I felt his lips and tongue moving over me. I began to pulsate as my hips and thighs rose against his head and hands. I wanted him in me, aching to move together. "Come here," I whispered, tugging on his hair. He slid his face against my belly and breasts and I was aware of my own musky odor damp in his beard and his erection against my thighs.

He lay on his side and pulled me up against him before drawing me on top where I straddled and wrapped my legs around him, easing him deep inside me. He groaned slightly and pulled me against him, urging me closer as I pushed down. I began to spasm and moved harder, pressing him into me as he grasped me from behind. Small moans caught my breath, holding, releasing until I cried out and felt him shudder and say, "Maggie, darling Maggie."

I lay next to him, nestling my face against his chest feeling tired and released in a way that was wholly new to me. Nothing else seemed to exist except both of us together in that moment and that place. I fell asleep but not before I heard Alex whisper, "Come back to me, Maggie."

I was startled awake by the sound of a phone. It wasn't mine and momentarily I felt confused as to where I was until I heard Alex say, "Who's calling this time of night," before reaching out for the phone next to the lamp. "Should've turned the bloody thing off. Hello? John? It's you—wasn't expecting you to call. Thought someone had a wrong number or something. What? Yes, she's here. Hold on." He leaned against me, "It's for you sweetheart. John."

I took the phone and held it to my ear. "Hi John, is it Norma?"

"Yes. I didn't want to call so late and since your phone didn't respond I thought you'd be with Alex. I'm at the hospital and your mother's been transferred to the ICU. So, so sorry to wake you with this information and I wasn't sure if I should or not. But oh dear, I thought you should know."

"Yes, John, and don't worry about it. Is she cognizant?"

"I don't really think so, but she keeps asking for Bob. Is that your father?"

"No, John. And if she's asking for Bob then she's delirious. Bob was her lover who deserted her years ago." I felt a rush of sympathy for the woman who had shown me none. I felt Alex lean against me, wrapping his arms around my waist. I thought of his warmth and then of organizing my flight home. Going to the hospital now was the last thing I wanted to do. "I'll be there in about an hour. Not sure if

it'll do any good but if she understands you can say I'm on my way."
Although that could be a bad thing, I thought, knowing her.

"Yes, I think that might be a good idea for you to come. I'll stay here until you do and if you want me to remain with you, then I will."

"You're such a love, John, but I'm going to hang up and get ready."

Then I thought of my clothes, probably still wet in the washer. Now what? I turned to Alex, "I've got to go to the hospital. Norma's in ICU and hallucinating, but I've nothing to w…."

"… wear? Yes you do. After you fell asleep I had to get up for Kay—think all the excitement threw her off a bit and she was whining. So I also tossed your stuff in the dryer while I was up."

"Come here," I said, "I want to hold you for a bit longer. But although Norma can wait, I don't want to keep John there by himself." The musky odor of our sex was still strong and it turned me on. I hoped it wouldn't be evident to anyone else.

CHAPTER TWENTY-ONE

Norma resembled a small-wizened old lady. I thought I had been shown into the wrong room and turned back to the nurse who had taken me there. "But ..." I hesitated, "... this isn't Norma."

"Yes, dear, it is," the nurse said. "She's very sick and a person can look quite different when they're seriously ill. I'm so sorry." She patted my arm. "You can stay here as long as you want and just press the buzzer if you need me although," she nodded toward Norma, "I'll be coming in quite often to check on her progress."

I moved closer to the bed. It seemed as though Norma had dwindled in size, smaller than she had been the night before and her skin was stretched tightly across her face. Her breath was uneven and raspy and her eyelids closed. She was muttering and I leaned over her to hear what she was saying.

"Norma," I said, "it's me, Margaret." It felt foreign to refer to myself by the name she called me but I wanted to make contact. Calling myself Maggie, I knew, wouldn't get through to her. I wished I could understand what was being said among the inaudible words that were lost in her labored breathing.

I heard the door open behind me and figuring it was the nurse, didn't turn around until a gentle hand was placed on my shoulder. "Maggie, would you like me to stay with you?"

"John. It's you. Yes that would be lovely although," I looked into his face, "you don't have to. You look exhausted."

"Dear me, yes. Yes I suppose I am. It's been a long night and I've already lost one dear soul and it looks like I may be in the process of losing another." He gazed down at Norma and shook his head. "Poor dear lady, she struggled and for what? She could so easily have been surrounded by happier thoughts and love but resisted those until the end. Well ..." he corrected himself, "... perhaps this isn't quite the end and things could change." He took out a large handkerchief and blew his nose then replaced the cloth in his black jacket. "So sorry to be emotional Maggie, but this sort of thing always tends to upset me no matter who it is. The good or the bad, although your poor dear mother wasn't really bad, just a little misguided." He smiled and I saw that his eyes were glistening behind the tears.

"John, it's okay and it's probably me that should be crying but I can't. I wish I could." I stopped and turned back to Norma for although her breathing seemed to catch and hold, I heard her say, "Bob."

I turned to him, "Now what? Do you think she understands on some level? What do I say? Anything to reassure her? What?"

John shook his head. "We can't lie to her and say he's coming but perhaps we can say he's with her in her thoughts and perhaps who knows, she might well still be in his." He stroked Norma's cheek and momentarily she held her breath before resuming the gasps that were becoming deeper and more alarming.

Her hand felt thin and lifeless as I took it in mine. This was the hand, I thought, that had slapped and pushed me away so often when I was a kid, it wasn't only the words that thrust me away and caused me to stop loving her. Then I leaned closer, I thought I had heard my name. "Margaret," Norma said. "Where's Margaret?"

Startled, I looked at John then back to my mother, "I'm here Norma. I'm here."

Norma's eyelids fluttered without opening. They looked blue and transparent and I was unsure if I wanted them to remain closed, hiding the cold eyes, or whether I wanted them to open to indicate some life, even if it was the spiteful gaze I remembered. I decided I wanted them open and began to weep softly. John handed me a tissue and patted my shoulder nodding his head as though to convey his concern in an attempt to comfort me.

Then quite clearly Norma said, "Where can that child be? Are you hiding again?" She coughed and blood flecked across her lips and I gently wiped it away with a tissue.

"John, can you go get the nurse?" I asked him. "This isn't looking good."

He nodded and left me with Norma.

"Norma, I'm here. I'm not hiding," I said, then remembered how as a child I would hide from her; the closet or down in the green house, anywhere to find silence. I wondered if my tendency to be alone and silent had followed me into adulthood. That would explain so much about myself but I didn't need to hide any more.

She coughed again and I stood up and back as more blood splashed across the sheets. Her face looked as white as the sheets that were stained. She was trying to speak and her head moved restlessly back and forth. "That child will be the death of me," she said, "and where's Bob? Bob are you there?" Her voice whispered into another cough as the nurse returned with John.

Taking one look at Norma she said, "I'll go call the doctor and be right back."

"Norma still thinks of me as a kid," I said. I felt useless standing there by her bed. "I might just as well be hiding for all she knows. She certainly doesn't recognize who I am now."

"That's her cross to bear, Maggie, not yours," John said. You're here and with her and that's important. Remember that. Dear me, yes. Remember that." He patted Norma's hand. "Would you mind, Maggie, if I said a little prayer for your mother? I think she might need a few words of strength even if she doesn't hear or understand what I'm saying."

"That would be lovely of you, John. I'll listen. It'll probably be of some strength to me too although I probably wouldn't have thought of doing it myself."

I thought that Norma might soon be gone and with no chance of reconciliation although now I had hoped that the reconciliation would be for Norma. Alex and John were right in what they had said. I would move on but without the regret that failing to try would have caused. I had tried and although I hadn't failed it was a different form of success. I could let go.

John finished his prayer of gentle words and I thought how loving and reassuring he was. He smiled and said, "I'll step outside for a few minutes. Perhaps you might want to add something to that."

I was surprised. I knew no prayers and certainly didn't feel I was in a position to ask any favors of a higher power to save her life although did consider we were subject to something much greater than us all. The inevitability of what was occurring seemed like a given and a transition into a different state of being. I nodded though, and watched him leave before looking back down at Norma.

What did you say to someone who's dying and who never wanted you to be there when they were alive? I wondered. I took her hand, expecting it to be withdrawn but she was still and it gave me more confidence to proceed. "I'm sorry you couldn't let me have a mother," I said, "and so sorry I was prevented from being a loving daughter. Perhaps," I said, surprising myself with the thought, "perhaps one day I'll have my own daughter and this whole dismal relationship with you will become a thing of the past and something to remember not to do. Not that I could ever be like you with anyone," I added, "and especially not with my own child."

I had never seen anyone die and didn't want it to happen to Norma although knew it might not be long. I wondered if she had heard or even understood. "You know this isn't easy to say but whether you like it or not, I do care for you although not as much as I would've wanted, but it's true otherwise I wouldn't be here now."

I leaned towards Norma's face and stopped. Kissing her felt inappropriate and not something she would've appreciated when alive and feisty, so I kissed the tips of my fingers and placed them lightly on her cheek.

Norma's breath ceased for a moment and I glanced up at the monitor that showed her heart was still beating. My god but this is grueling, I thought, then as she resumed the rasping sound, I suddenly wondered how long she could last and how it would impact my intention to return home. I didn't like having the thought. It seemed ungenerous and uncaring. I looked up as John walked back into the room.

"John," I said, "I have a problem. I have to return to the States for Mewfus, my cat."

"Cat? Now?"

"He was badly injured and I must get back to care for him."

John paused carefully squinting at me as I said that. "There would be many who might disagree with that decision, Maggie, in light of all this," he pointed to Norma, "despite the nature of the relationship."

I didn't have the sense I was being reprimanded. "That's the problem."

He paused as he thought more about it. "Love comes in many different guises and you have to follow your heart there."

"Would you stay?"

"I'd be troubled and have to ask God for guidance but the answer would have to be mine. Between me and my conscience."

"So you think it would be wrong to go?"

"I doubt God draws the line between all his life creations. Each one is important to Him." His voice had lost the nervous stutter and awkward pauses as though he was more confident of his communication with that higher power I seemed not to understand. "Alex would probably choose to go for Kay if in your position so perhaps Mewfus means the same to you."

We both stared toward the bed as a deep, rattling gurgle emanated from Norma's lungs. John moved past me as I drew back surprised by the sound. "Maggie, she's going. That is the sound of the final breaths. If you are going to say your last words perhaps now is the time to do it."

I felt numb. Norma would never know what they were but I would and the thought of saying nothing or the wrong thing might haunt me. I shook my head and stared at my mother. What do you say to someone who has locked you from their heart and mind? What last words can be uttered that are correct and right ones? I didn't know. I felt my own breath held tight within my own healthy lungs and let it escape with a gasp as another rattle escaped Norma's lips. It was as though it was being drawn to another dimension where the living could not go.

I considered the loss of my mother's wasted life and wondered if Norma too was aware of all that might have been. I took her hand again. "Norma, I wish I could call you Mother, but I can't. I wish I could bring you the love that you felt you deserved and lost. I wish I could bring you peace and make your journey easier." I wondered if Norma would be making any kind of journey or transition and something I had wondered about in the past. I decided I would talk to John about that. Later.

Then I leaned over the bed and gently kissed the brow that was still covered in the strip of adhesive cloth and drew back. "Goodbye, Norma. I'm so sorry you couldn't love me as I would have liked but it's too late now. I wish I could say goodbye to you for Bob—if he's still alive—but Daddy is and I know he loved you in his own quiet way." I hesitated then continued, "You were a huge influence on my life and I wouldn't be who I am if not for you and my responses to you. But it was worth it. Without you I might never have met Alex and John, so thank you for making the space for them to come into my life even if it was unintentional."

Norma remained still and then her eyelids fluttered and opened but the eyes that stared at me were unrecognizing and dull as though she saw something or someone else. I would never know whether my final words got through to Norma as I had intended or whether it was the tone in which the words were delivered but as another gasping rattle escaped her lips she said, "Bob," then closed her eyes. .

The door opened and another doctor walked into the room. "I'm Dr. Clayton," she said, "on duty for Dr. Suffolk tonight." She moved to the bed and took Norma's wrist and listened to her heart, glancing at the monitor by the bed as she did so. Her attitude was less abridged and more sympathetic. She turned to me, "I'm sorry but your mother won't be here much longer and there's nothing else we can do. We also discovered earlier that she developed septicemia that's shutting down her system already compromised by the pneumonia."

"Is she is pain?"

"She was given morphine earlier so I think not. Any more and it will be the contributing factor to her final breath. I'm so sorry," she repeated. "I'll leave you alone now."

I nodded. "Thank you for everything," I said.

John and I stood quietly watching Norma. We heard her breathing stop before it began again as though the air from her lungs were making a final escape. We were silent as the departing breaths came less frequently and with the final gasp, the monitor let out a long drawn peep that surprised us both. I wished that modern technology hadn't pierced the natural sounds of Norma's last breaths, no matter how painful.

The nurse came running into the room and turned off the machine and leaned over Norma. I was stunned. She was gone and yesterday she had been giving me grief. Life can be taken in a second and how important that one makes those valuable seconds count.

John placed her hands over her heart with one still attached to the equipment that had been sustaining her. "Goodbye, dear lady," he said, "I'll take care of your final resting place as you requested," then looking at me continued, "and thank you for bringing your daughter into my life. I will be forever grateful."

His words brought the tears that my mother's never could. I saw that the early morning light was beginning to show through the window blinds and under my breath said, "Yes, to that Norma, and now this is the beginning of a new day." I turned to John and said, "So what happens next?"

"Would you like to sit with her some more?"

I stared at her lifeless body, not believing that the thin eyelids wouldn't suddenly flick open and stare back at me the way I remembered. I felt relieved to think that the icy gaze would never return although it was inscribed in my mind and knew I would never forget. I wanted to leave but felt compelled to stay, wondering if there were any memories I had of Norma that were pleasant and could balance the distance I was experiencing.

My mind seemed to react to what I was expecting from it and thrust image after image of an unhappy woman who throughout my life was unpleasant. Then I remembered her laugh, which although not often expressed always delighted me because that meant Norma was happy and would be ignoring me. It was a deep laugh and to the unaware, filled with humor, but I knew that it could often imply that she was finding fault with someone or something and covering that with laughter to make it seem more acceptable.

My mind went deeper as I thought of Norma's funeral and who would be there. John, obviously, and me too. Perhaps Cheryl would bring some flowers, Norma's sister obviously would not and I wondered about Daddy. I would let him know what had happened and let him make that decision.

The thought of placing flowers on Norma's gravesite brought a quick image of her years ago unaware she was being watched by me when I was a child. She was wandering around the garden and stopping to smell the flowers that were in full bloom. It was a riot of color from the annuals she had planted; petunias and pansies and geraniums. Intense colors that seemed to reflect her personality; I remembered wishing my mother showed me the same attention then realized I was more like a dependable perennial, not as flashy as the colorful splash of annuals that only lasted one season. But that was enough; I saw my mother who might at some time in her life have been truly happy, if only for a moment.

"I think not, John, thank you. Do you want to stay?"

"If it's alright with you, yes I'd like to say a few prayers and then I can call the mortuary as your mother wished. These are such sad times, sad times indeed."

"You were wonderful to her John, and she was fortunate to have you in her life."

"Do you think so? I do hope that is right. I always feel I should be doing more. The funeral should be in a couple of days."

I felt uncomfortable and suddenly guilty that I was thinking of my flight home. There was so much to do at the house and I still hadn't spoken to Cheryl and got back the earrings. "I'm not sure,

John, although it's possible. I have to get back to California rather quickly and I still haven't spoken to Cheryl."

"Dear me, yes, I had quite forgotten that. Would you like to meet her at the rectory later? I think she would appreciate it and wants to return your earrings."

I hesitated, "You know if you could tell her I understand and I'm not angry with her, perhaps you could tell her to meet me at Norma's house. I would like to suggest that she gives the place a thorough cleaning and open up all the doors and windows." I stared at John, "And I still want to replace mine with another gold pair. It was a birthday present after all."

"Lovely, lovely idea and yes I will do that. That's splendid. Where will you be going after you leave here?"

I wasn't sure. I wondered what Alex had found regarding the flights back. "Perhaps I should go to Norma's first and then to Alex."

I felt a quick fluttering of my heart as I remembered his arms around me only a few hours prior. So much had happened it was almost overwhelming and there was so much to do. I decided to call Shelly and then the vet to determine exactly how badly injured Mewfus was. Again I felt the quickening of my heart at the thought of losing him and smiled as I thought that the heart responds to so many different kinds of love and concerns.

CHAPTER TWENTY-TWO

I called Alex from the parking lot and wondered if he would be home. He picked up by the second ring, his voice concerned. "So what now, Maggie?"

"She's gone."

"I'm sorry, really sorry, but it's probably for the best although perhaps I shouldn't be so quick to think that. How are you doing with the news?"

"Okay, actually, and yes for the best although I was wishing her life had been happier." I paused, "Did you find out what flights are available?"

"Yes, and they made me wish that I was going back with you. Can we talk about that when you get here?" I nodded. It seemed unreal to think of Alex in California with me. "Maggie, are you still there?" he said.

"Yes. Sorry. I was thinking of you coming back with me. I'll be going to your place later but right now I have to go to Norma's to speak with Cheryl and I must also speak with my father's nursing home." I began to experience the pressure of having to make too many decisions in too short a time and expelled the deep breath I had been holding. "What about Kay if you went?"

"John would probably watch her for a while."

The early morning sun was beginning to shine between the scudding clouds. It reminded me of a spring day in L.A. after a rare shower. I thought of Alex, big Alex, loving Alex in my condo and cooking in my kitchen. Then just as quickly I realized that I needed space to be alone in my own environment and to think about the past several weeks. I needed to recover and establish how those events had affected and changed me. I wanted to see if I still fit into the old patterns of my life and teaching in California and if that was something I still wanted to do. It would be like trying on an old comfortable dress that I loved that might no longer fit as I remembered. But I had a new one to change into and it was looking more attractive all the time.

"Wish I didn't live so far away," I said.

"Me too, but it doesn't have to be that way. Come live with me, Maggie."

"It crossed my mind."

"Then that's a start we can work on." He changed the subject, "So, you're going back to Norma's first? Hmmm, I guess the place is yours now."

"Actually still Daddy's." I thought of the house I hated and of going back to get my things. At some point I would have to decide whether to sell the place or rent it. Decisions, decisions but first it had to be cleaned and aired and painted and the furniture donated or tossed. Again I felt the sense of overwhelm. One step at a time, I thought, no hurry to decide now; not this minute. "I think I'm going back to the house and pack and meet Cheryl there then if it's okay I'll drive back to your place and if you don't mind, take a shower there." Somehow I felt cleaner at Alex's place.

"Will you have eaten?"

"Probably not but I'm not hungry right now."

"How about an early supper here and I'll make sure there's brandy and wine and some nice cheese and French bread." He chuckled. "Kay just nodded her head, too."

"You spoil me. I'll call before I lock up over there."

I called Cheryl after I hung up from Alex and she said she'd just heard from John, too. She seemed genuinely upset about Norma and I could hear the catch in her voice as she said how sorry she was but agreed to meet at the house.

I stopped off at the ATM for four hundred pounds. My earrings were priceless but more because of their connection although I still wondered about their value. Was I giving Cheryl a fair exchange? She could certainly purchase a very pretty pair of gold earrings for the equivalent amount in the currency exchange—almost six hundred dollars. I wanted to have cash to make the exchange more real, since their actual replacement wouldn't be there. Somehow a check for the same amount seemed insubstantial although I decided to write another check for the housekeeping.

Then I thought of Norma's banking and finances. I hadn't a clue where that was or what was involved. Again that sense of dismay and overwhelm caused me to feel weak. "Well, lady," I said, "you haven't eaten and it might be a good idea to get some food in your stomach." I remembered leaving some cheese and grapes in the refrigerator and decided to nibble on that to hold me over until dinner. Maybe I'd have an early glass of wine and wondered if Cheryl would join me.

Her car was already at the curb and she was waiting at the wheel and waved as I pulled into the driveway and got out. She was smiling although I thought she had the same cautious expression that she had when we first met.

"Hi Cheryl," I said. "You could've waited inside. You still have the key. Right?"

"Yes but you know it gives me the creeps to think I would be in the house now that Mrs. Resnick has ... you know, passed. Besides it's much fresher out here." She smiled and gave me a look that invited support and agreement, "And I know that things weren't happy between you and your mum but again, I'm really sorry for your loss."

"Thank you and yes, I totally understand. Maybe we can sit in the garden and chat." As I unlocked the door I turned and said, "Would you like a glass of wine?"

Cheryl looked surprised then glanced at her watch as though to determine if that would give her the answer. "I don't usually drink this early, although ..." she paused, "it would be like an early lunch on a Sunday or a holiday."

"My thoughts, too. Come on in." I walked into the living room where Norma's chair sat as a reminder of the woman who had occupied it. The pillows had her indentations as though expecting her return. I leaned into the windows that Norma had always kept closed and flung them open, letting the lace curtain blow. I was determined that they would be among the first to go. I felt momentarily guilty that I was already mentally discarding and dismantling Norma's home.

Cheryl hovered behind me nodding, "Would you like me to go open some of the other windows, too? Seems like a lovely idea to me. This place could do with some really fresh air."

"Probably needs a gale force wind to do that, but yes, if you don't mind and I'll go and pour us some wine. White or red?"

"Actually, I like the white Mrs. Resnick used to drink. It's sweet not dry. Although it was her own special wine she used to give me a bottle of that for Christmas. She could be thoughtful that way."

"Really?" I said. "I knew she ordered it by the case and have no idea how much is left. Why don't you take what's in the house. Consider it Christmas."

I was looking in the drawer for the bottle opener. I had hated cleaning everything when I first arrived but now it was an almost tolerable grubbiness that reflected the home of an aging woman with poor eyesight.

"You sure?" she said. "Ooh, thank you. Don't mind if I do and my hubby will be tickled pink."

I looked around the kitchen and out into the hall. Filled with Norma's possessions, there was only one thing I wanted and that was my grandmother's jewelry but it could wait. "Cheese and crackers?" I called out.

"Lovely. That way I won't get so lightheaded. Here, let me hold the door for you," she said as I loaded a small tray with the wine and cheese.

The sun warmed through the apple tree as we sat on the bench beneath it. Because of the rain the grass was now green and made the place, despite the weeds, a quiet little oasis. I drew in a deep breath. "Cheers," I said, raising my glass, "in memory of Norma. An unhappy woman if ever there was one, but may she ..."

"... rest in peace," said Cheryl as we lightly touched glasses.

We were silent as we took our first sips then Cheryl began to open and dig into her big leather bag. "I've brought you these," she said. "I can imagine why you were so unhappy with me when you saw them. Makes me a bit mad too that I was placed in the position of you thinking I'd stolen them."

"I did at first and apologize for the way I treated you. And I'm so sorry for that. John suspected that it wasn't true although I never realized just how spiteful Norma could be until this." I nodded toward the little tissue package that Cheryl handed me. "Thank you, and thank you again. These belonged to my grandmother and mean a great deal to me."

"Yes, they're beautiful."

"Wait, I have something for you, too." I jumped up from the chair and went back into the kitchen for my own purse, returning with the cash I had got earlier. I handed it to Cheryl, "Despite the intent to hurt me, I think Norma really liked you and wanted you to have a gift.

I don't know that you could ever find anything quite like these but there are some very pretty antique jewelers or even new ones that could replace them."

Cheryl held her palm out in front of her, "Really, Maggie, this isn't necessary."

"I think it is and I want you to find something you like. You deserve it." Cheryl was gazing at the little pile of twenty pound notes that I had put on her lap then quickly placed her hand over them as the wind shifted and threatened to blow them away. I continued, "And if you're okay with the idea, I'd like you to do a thorough cleaning of the house from top to bottom. I have to return to the States unexpectedly but will come back in about a month or even earlier if I can." I wondered how long it took a cat's broken leg to heal, "And I'll have to take care of all this." I waved my hand toward the house. "There's a lot of work to do. A lot of cleaning. Would you be willing to work on some of it?" I wondered what I would do if Cheryl refused. Perhaps John knew of another cleaner.

"I don't mind at all and I'd really like to do that without any interruptions." Cheryl glanced quickly at me to see if I understood. "It always bothered me that I couldn't do my job as I liked to do it."

I was curious. I had wondered the same thing. "Why not?"

"Well you know until you arrived, Mrs. Resnick wanted me to do her grocery shopping and to take her to the doctors, and all, and then she didn't like the vacuum going while she was napping or looking at the television which was pretty much on all the time." She nibbled on a piece of cheese and took another sip of wine. "Then she would want me to sit and talk with her."

"Really? About what?" I was surprised.

Cheryl hesitated, "You know … this and that."

"No, actually, I don't. Tell me or if you prefer not then I'll understand."

"She liked to tell me of the places she'd been to with your dad—you know, the cruises she loved. Used to describe getting photographed after winning the fancy dress costume."

"Fancy dress?"

"Yes, she liked that and showed me photographs of her all dressed up and winning a prize. Think she'd rather have me sit there listening to her than cleaning although that didn't feel right." Cheryl shifted uncomfortably in her chair.

"What else did she talk about?" I felt I was beginning to get a glimpse into the mother I never knew.

"Not much else other than the television but she wanted me to sit and watch it with her so's I never got my work done."

"How boring that must've been for you."

"More sad than boring. I think Mrs. Resnick was very lonely. Least that's what I told my husband." She carefully folded the money and put it in her purse. "But I'd love to work for you, Maggie, and is there anything else you'd like me to do until you get back?"

"No, thanks, Cheryl. You have a key and I'll leave my telephone number and I'll give you a check before you leave here. Do you use the internet?"

She giggled. "Not really but my son is trying to teach me. What these youngsters know today is amazing." She stood and picked up the tray and empty glasses. "I'll just rinse these and have to leave but you have my number at home. Yes? When do you think you'll be back here?"

"I won't know for sure until I get there but I know this place will be in good hands. I really appreciate all your help, Cheryl."

"You're welcome I'm sure and Maggie ...?" She paused.

"Yes?"

"Do you think I could go to your mum's funeral? She wasn't always mean and nasty and I think she had a good streak though sometimes one wondered why it didn't get out more often." She smiled. "Poor old lady. Pity she was so alone like she was."

I wasn't sure if this last comment was directed at me but decided it was a simple observation from someone who probably spent more recent time with Norma than anyone else. I felt an unexpected sympathy for the mother I never really knew and who would never permit me knowing.

It didn't take long to pack and a quick look around was enough not to care if something had been left behind. Cheryl would hold it for me until I returned. The place looked brighter with all the drapes pulled back and the windows opened as though the house was inhaling fresh air. What the place really needed, though, was stripping everything down; painting and removing the carpets and I wondered if even that could get rid of the stale atmosphere. Perhaps I was projecting my own images on the place and someone else would see it for its potential. Well, it won't be my problem, I thought, and certainly Daddy can't live here alone any more.

I didn't like the idea of what would be involved in selling the place and wondered if John knew a good solicitor to handle the transactions. Perhaps Daddy would be well enough to participate with providing suggestions. It wasn't something I anticipated when I first walked through the door, nor had I anticipated that Norma would die although I was pleased I had made the decision to come. I'd got a lot accomplished although with more to go.

Even though I knew Norma could no longer rage at me for going through her things, I still felt guilty when I did, as though still spying on her personal belongings. It was a hasty look though and a quick glance at some of the paperwork she had left lying on her desk. I discovered a few overdue bills and was pissed that it meant more to think about. I gathered up what I thought was urgent and decided to deal with that in California.

It was Norma's jewelry box that interested me and I found what I was looking for. The rest of my grandmother's jewelry was where I was hoping it would be. I touched my ears and felt reassurance that the earrings that had caused so much grief were now returned and safely a part of me.

At the hospital I had wondered whether to leave Norma's wedding ring but slid it off her finger. It was something my father had given her and since my mother viewed her marriage as an inconvenience I decided to take it as representative of her fickle and vain behavior.

I remembered the gold band as always being on that rough hand and although meaningless to her it was symbolic of everything I considered important. Maybe I would throw it into the ocean and let it sink somewhere deep below, I thought, but I didn't want that ring to rest on my, or any other, finger.

Norma loved gold though and that was apparent when I opened the box. I didn't know she had so much or if I should take it with me or what the regulations were for carrying gold into the States. I wondered if they were her purchases or gifts from my father. I wanted to go through the pieces carefully and ask him. Perhaps I could find something else for Cheryl or maybe donate stuff to John's church and then wondered what I could do with it while I was gone. I didn't want to wear any of it. Perhaps Alex would hold onto it for me until I got back to take care of everything. I paused. Doing that would impose some sort of hold that I didn't want to create. I decided I would ask John.

After Cheryl left I called the vet from the house and he said that Mewfus was doing okay, he was eating and mewing, although the sooner I got him home the better he would feel. "Me too," I said, and told him that it could still be a few days. I felt a pang of guilt that I was more concerned about traveling six thousand miles to tend to my cat although I had decided to stay for the funeral. Mewfus would survive a few extra days at the vet.

There were still three weeks left of my school vacation and I could be with him then. I had even thought I should take a leave of absence for the next school semester. A family emergency leave. It would certainly free up my time to take care of everything and to carefully think of what needed to be done next.

My cell phone began to vibrate and I looked at the dial. John. Perfect and I could ask him if he'd mind holding onto the jewelry. "Hey John," I said, "I was just thinking of you. Where are you?"

"Home. Did you talk to Cheryl?"

"Yes and thank you for all that you did. I'm wearing the earrings now."

"Excellent. Excellent. I heard from Alex that he's found some flights leaving tomorrow. Will I get to see you before you go? I do hope so. I'm really going to miss you, Maggie."

"And I you, John, but I've decided to stay for the funeral if we can arrange that soon and when I do leave I should be back in about a month. Could I ask a favor and have you hold onto Norma's jewelry for me. I need time to sort through it."

"Of course. When will you drop it off?"

"I thought on my way to Alex's place if I could. I'm about ready to leave now."

"He's playing right now. Should I tell him to wait?"

"Please and I'll be there in about fifteen minutes." Suddenly the time left with Alex was becoming more important as each minute passed.

CHAPTER TWENTY-THREE

I turned my head to look at Alex who lay next to me. "I can't believe that in eight hours I'll be on the plane headed for home."

I had made a last visit to see Daddy and told him about Norma. He had nodded and pursed his lips but wrote that he wanted to attend the funeral, which was this morning, after which Alex and I drove him back to Aidenscroft. Daddy loved Kay and I thought how her presence could help him recover and Alex said he would take her and go visit while I was gone. I said I would send him emails and would return as soon as I could.

Tonight, my last evening in the UK, I had dinner at Gino's with Alex and John with Kay happily on our feet under the table. When I mentioned going to the airport, both guys immediately insisted that a taxi was out of the question when I said that would be my transportation. It was easy to agree. I nodded, "It'll be so different from the way I arrived and I think I'll probably cry." My eyes had filled with tears as I visualized the moment of saying goodbye to them both.

"I'm not really happy with the thought of you gone," Alex said, "but at least you agreed to let John and me drive you to the airport. You'll call me the minute you land. Yes?"

I nodded. "And when I get home and walk into my own place, too. It's going to be so strange not to be here." I looked around his bedroom and wondered if taking pictures would be appropriate. "Can I take some photographs before I leave?"

"If they include Kay and me."

"The place wouldn't be worth taking without you both. Just wish I could capture some of the scents and smells and take those too."

"Wanna take one of my shirts?" Alex laughed. "You can bunch it up and make a bed of it like Kay does when she gets hold of my stuff."

"Good idea. You want me to leave something of mine?"

"It's okay. I already took something of yours."

I sat up and looked at him grinning at me. "If you say a pair of my panties I'm going to smack you."

"Go ahead. Smack."

"You didn't."

"Well I did and I'm going to keep them under my pillow."

"Just don't put them on the couch where John will see if he comes over."

"I'm going to really miss you when you're gone, Maggie. D'you still want me to come over in a few weeks when Mewfus is better and ready to travel?"

"Of course. I'd be heartbroken if you decided this was all a mistake."

"How could this be a mistake?" Alex pulled me down next to him and rubbed his cheek against my shoulder before moving his mouth along my breast. "Is your bed big enough for us both?"

"It's a queen but it'll have to do."

"All the better to hold you in my dear," he laughed. "And when I'm not in bed with you I have work to do."

"Work?"

"Yep. Thought it might be a good idea to start locating that ex of mine."

"Ex? But aren't you still married?"

"Actually, I didn't think of her at all prior to you and you're the reason for me thinking in terms of ex. Maybe when it's legal John can marry us."

I felt my stomach churn and my heart beat faster. "Are you proposing to me?"

"Without flowers or fanfare or bended knee which would be difficult for me to accomplish gracefully and make the moment romantic ... yes."

I thought of how quickly I had married Richard and rushed off to California and what a mistake that had been. I loved Alex that I knew, but marriage was something I had pushed from my mind as being something in the future. It meant a forever decision. I didn't want to rush into a second marriage although Alex was not Richard.

"You're very quiet. Is that a no?" He pulled away slightly and I could feel him tense.

"Not a no, and much more a yes, but it took me by surprise. I love you, I know that and ..." I moved against him and drew his face toward mine, "... and I can't imagine you not being in my life." I thought of him being free to get married. "How much can you do to find out her whereabouts before coming to the States? It might speed the process." I laughed, "Maybe Daddy can give me away."

"Then I take it that's a yes. Hold on." Alex pushed back the covers and stepped out of bed while Kay stood up and watched him expectantly. A walk, perhaps? At two in the morning? She followed him out of the bedroom and I heard Alex in the kitchen and the sound of utensils being shifted in one of the drawers before hearing the front door open. I sat up in bed and waited, wondering what he was doing then laughed. If any neighbor happened to be passing by at that time they'd be surprised to see a naked man on his doorstep.

I heard the front door close and the soft click of Kay's paws on the hardwood floor as she followed Alex back into the bedroom. "For you." Alex said, "with love. And nothing fancy from a florist. And careful of the thorns although I think I managed to pull them all off." He handed me two roses he'd clipped from the scented vine over his door. "From me and Kay. Take them back to California as a reminder until you get back here and then you can have the whole vine at your disposal."

I held them to my nose. "I'm not sure how I'll get them into California through customs. Maybe I'll hide them in your shirt and if anyone checks I'll act surprised."

Alex climbed into bed next to me again. "Would you like me to do anything over at Norma's place until you get back here?"

I had told him and John over dinner that I'd left Cheryl in charge to thoroughly clean the house and to get rid of Norma's recliner and have the carpets cleaned. I planned to remove the drapes myself and contact a charity to take the clothes and other pieces of furniture later. The recliner, though, I never wanted to see again and wanted that gone.

"I don't think so, although ..."

"... although what?"

"If you could find someone to work on the garden that would be lovely. The roses need trimming and if you got a gardener to do the weeding it would be a start to looking nice again. When Daddy was well he used to mow the lawn which is growing wild because of the rain and Norma's vibrant annuals made it better than it is now."

"Would you live with me here or there?"

Another question that had crossed my mind and one I had avoided. "Probably both places although I prefer yours and would

317

stay here. I'd thought that when Mewfus was better and well enough to travel he could stay at the other house and he'd love the garden."

"I could bring Kay over to get introduced. She's pretty good with cats and tends to ignore those she sees wandering around the garden here."

"I know but Mewfus hasn't been used to dogs. It might take a while."

"Have you thought what you'll do with the house eventually?"

"Eventually sell it I suppose when Daddy's gone or before if that's what he wants. He still needs the nursing care but he can come visit and sit in the garden although Aidenscroft is far more beautiful and I think he'd be happier there." I shook my head and remembered my grief when Norma had told me he was dead. Not dead but not as alive as he once was either. "But that may be a long way in the future yet."

"You could bring him here. He might enjoy that more. What about your condo?"

"Probably sell it," I pulled him closer to me, "and maybe I can be looking for an agent to list it while you're looking to officially end it with your ex." I realized I would have to quit my job. That would be hard to leave but perhaps Laurie Hargreaves would employ me for the Manor and that would be even better.

I could smell the roses along with the musky male scent of Alex combined with the doggie smell of Kay and wished I could bottle them and carry them with me. I was concerned how Mewfus would travel but knew it could be done and pets were transported all the time. I thought of what I would do with all my things in the condo. Probably have a giant garage sale and ship what I loved and make Alex's place feel even more like home.

Then I wondered if Shelly would like to have my plants. I knew I would miss her. Perhaps she would come over for the wedding. She could be my maid of honor and Brian could be the ring bearer. The picture it created in my mind made me smile. That, I thought, in John's beautiful old church, would be perfect.

Made in the USA
San Bernardino, CA
27 March 2015